Ben Elton's career as both performer and as writer encompasses some of the most memorable and incisive comedy of the last twenty years. In addition to his hugely influential work as a stand-up comic, he is the writer of such TV hits as *The Young Ones*, *Blackadder* and *The Thin Blue Line*. He has written seven internationally bestselling novels, including *Popcorn*, *Inconceivable* and *Dead Famous*, and three hit West End plays. Ben Elton wrote and directed the feature film *Maybe Baby* and recently the books for two West End musicals, *The Beautiful Game* with Andrew Lloyd Webber and *We Will Rock You* with Queen.

His personal recreational drugs of choice are alcohol, which he hopes never to give up, and tobacco, which he intends to give up tomorrow.

Ben lives in London with his wife Sophie and their three children.

Dead Famous

'One of Ben Elton's many triumphs with *Dead Famous* is
that he is superbly persuasive about the stage of the story:
the characterisation is a joy, the jokes are great, the
structuring is very clever and the thriller parts are
ingenious and full of suspense. And not only that – the satire
(of Big Brother, of the television industry, of the arrogant
ignorance and rabid inarticulacy of yoof culture) is
scathing, intelligent and cherishable. As House Arrest's
twerpy contestants would put it, wicked. Double wicked.
Big up to Ben Elton and respect, big time. Top, top book'
Mail on Sunday

'Brilliant . . . Ben has captured the verbal paucity of this
world perfectly . . . devastatingly accurate in its portrayal
. . . read Elton's book'
Janet Street-Porter, *Independent on Sunday*

'Elton has produced a book with pace and wit, real tension,
a dark background theme, and a big on-screen climax'
Independent

'Very acute about television and the Warhol-inspired
fame for fame's sake that it offers . . . certainly delivers a
readable whodunnit'
The Spectator

'One of the best whodunnits I have ever read . . . This is a
cracking read – a funny, gripping, hugely entertaining
thriller, but also a persuasive, dyspeptic account of the way
we live now, with our insane, inane cult of the celebrity'
Sunday Telegraph

Inconceivable

'Extremely funny, clever, well-written, sharp and unexpectedly moving . . . This brilliant, chaotic satire merits rereading several times'
Mail on Sunday

'Extremely funny without ever being tasteless or cruel . . . this is Elton at his best – mature, humane, and still a laugh a minute. At least'
Daily Telegraph

'A very funny book about a sensitive subject. The characters are well-developed, the action is page-turning and it's beginning to seem as if Ben Elton the writer might be even funnier than Ben Elton the comic'
Daily Mail

'This is Elton doing what he does best, taking comedy to places most people wouldn't dream of visiting and asking some serious questions while he's about it. It's a brave and personal novel'
The Mirror

'A tender, beautifully balanced romantic comedy'
Spectator

'Moving and thoroughly entertaining'
Daily Express

'Somehow Ben Elton has managed to write a funny, positive love story about one of the most painful and damaging experiences a couple can go through'
The Weekend Australian

'Anyone who has had trouble starting a family will recognize the fertility roller-coaster Elton perceptively and wittily describes'
The Age, Melbourne

'With his trademark wit and barbed humour, Ben Elton tells a poignant and heart-rending story . . . a novel that is both entertaining and emotionally rich . . . This book is a marvel'
Pretoria News, South Africa

Blast from the Past

'The action is tight and well-plotted, the dialogue is punchy and the whole thing runs along so nicely that you never have to feel you're reading a book at all'
Guardian

'A strong beginning, and the reminder that it is fear itself that makes you jump wouldn't be out of place in a psychological thriller. *Blast from the Past* is a comedy, but an edgy comedy . . . a slick moral satire that works as a hairy cliff-hanger'
Sunday Times

'Elton at his most outrageously entertaining . . . Elton is a master of the snappy one-liner, and here the witty repartee hides a surprisingly romantic core'
Cosmopolitan

'Elton again underlines his mastery of plot, struture and dialogue. In stand-up comedy, his other forte, it's all about timing. In writing it's all about moving the narrative forward with exciting leaps of imagination and, as before, he seems to have the explosive take-off formula just about right. This literary rocket burns bright'
Sunday Times (Perth)

'*Blast from the Past* is a wicked, rip-roaring ride which charts the fine lines separating hilarity from horror; the oily gut of fear from the delicious shiver of anticipation'
West Australian

'Only Ben Elton could combine uncomfortable questions about gender politics with a gripping, page-turning narrative and jokes that make you laugh out loud'
Tony Parsons

'As always, Ben Elton is topical to the point of clairvoyancy . . . Fast, funny and thought-provoking'
The List

Also by Ben Elton

STARK
GRIDLOCK
THIS OTHER EDEN
POPCORN
BLAST FROM THE PAST
INCONCEIVABLE
DEAD FAMOUS

HIGH SOCIETY

Ben Elton

BLACK SWAN

HIGH SOCIETY
A BLACK SWAN BOOK : 0 552 99995 4

Originally published in Great Britain by Bantam Press,
a division of Transworld Publishers

PRINTING HISTORY
Bantam Press edition published 2002
Black Swan edition published 2003

1 3 5 7 9 10 8 6 4 2

Set in 11/12pt Melior by
Falcon Oast Graphic Art Ltd.

Black Swan Books are published by Transworld Publishers,
61–63 Uxbridge Road, London W5 5SA,
a division of The Random House Group Ltd,
in Australia by Random House Australia (Pty) Ltd,
20 Alfred Street, Milsons Point, Sydney, NSW 2061, Australia,
in New Zealand by Random House New Zealand Ltd,
18 Poland Road, Glenfield, Auckland 10, New Zealand
and in South Africa by Random House (Pty) Ltd,
Endulini, 5a Jubilee Road, Parktown 2193, South Africa.

Printed and bound in Great Britain by
Clays Ltd, St Ives plc.

For Sophie

St Hilda's Church Hall, Soho

'My name's Tommy Hanson and I'm an alcoholic.'

The young man had risen from his place in the circle of grey plastic chairs and now, having thus announced himself, surveyed the ring of expectant faces. The atmosphere in the little church hall, which until then had been quietly respectful, was suddenly electric.

'But of course you know that.'

That famous smile. Those puppy-dog eyes. That jolly, wise, endearing Accrington accent, still only slightly Americanized.

'We're all alcoholics, us. That's why we're here. AA – Arseholes Anonymous as I like to call it.

'Why state the fookin' obvious? But we have to go through the motions, don't we? Do it right. That's the rules, in't it? Make your confession, pray for serenity, chip in for the biccies and wash up your teacup.'

There wasn't a woman in the circle who wouldn't have washed Tommy's teacup for him and more besides – some of the men, too, but everyone tried to concentrate. This was after all supposed to be anonymous.

'So, like I say, my name's Tommy Hanson and I'm an alcoholic. Plus I'm also a cokehead, but that's me narcotics meeting. Eh, I've got a full day 'aven't I? All day talking about being a stupid, screwed-up,

11

self-indulgent twat. I'll be knackered by teatime. I'll need a drink and a nice line or two of charlie.

'Don't get me wrong. I love my meetings, I do. Live for 'em. We all do, us arseholes. Testifying, emoting, talking about ourselves. That's all we've got left, in't it?

'So I'm going to tell you about that night – the famous night of the Brit Awards – because I don't think it would be possible for a person to be any more drunk than I ended up that night. Well, you've seen it all in the papers, anyway, so I'm not telling you anything you don't know, except that this is what really happened, not what them bastards put in the stories they wrote. As it happens, I'd fallen off the wagon that day, see, so I was a disaster waiting to happen, weren't I? You know the score, all you repeat offenders. That's the problem with laying off the beer for a while. You lose your tolerance, so when you do give it a shake, you're monged on three halves of shandy. I'd been dry for a whole month, which had been a huge effort for me 'cos I love me pint, I do, but Elton John had said that if he ever saw me with another drink in me 'and he'd whack me with his tiara. So I was making a special effort. Well, he is rock royalty, so you have to do it, don't you?

'God, though, I were sick of being sober and there was just no way I was going to keep it up. You know the rules, you have to *want* to get clean, don't you, and I didn't. Well, *come on*. It was the Brits! What is the point of being sober at the fookin' Brit Awards? Believe me, I've won a toilet full of them things in my time and that is one crap night if you're straight. One crap boring night. But if you're buzzing, if you're pissed up and mad for it, if you're Champagne Charlie on a spree, then it's *brilliant*. And when I say charlie I think you know what I mean. Because I wasn't off the charlie, don't forget. No *way*! One wagon at a time, I say, so I was wired even before I started drinking, strung out tighter than a duck's arse. But I wanted to be *drunk,* see. Some nights you want to do drugs, but some nights you want to get lathered, and the Brits is a booze night for sure, or at least that's how you want to kick off. If you're pissed up at the Brits the night's your oyster. You can fight all the other pop-star lads. You can chuck ice and bread rolls at the pathetic politicians who are sat there pretending to be hip and leering at all the birds. You can pull a couple of the dancers and you can make a speech so dazzlingly shite that it actually sounds ironic and a bit John Lennon-ish. Basically, you can do what you fookin' well like. You can have it as large as you fancy. But you can't if you're sober. Like, if you're kidding yourself you're on the wagon.

'So as I live and breathe, God save me from ever being sober at the Brits. Which is why, as of this moment, seeing as how I've definitely gone straight and I'm here talking to you lot at this meeting, I have sworn I will never go to another one. Mind you, I said the same thing last year, didn't I?'

The Paget household, Dalston

Peter Paget stared at his wife. She stared back at him. In all their years of marriage never had they felt such a bond. Never had they been so alive together, locked in union as a single force. They knew that the decision they had just made would change their lives for ever. Their lives and their daughters' lives. It would certainly bring down untold anger and contempt upon Peter's head. It would cost him the party whip and almost inevitably his job come the next election. The path that he had chosen led directly to professional ruin.

'You have to do it, Pete. I'm proud of you. Really, really proud. The girls will be, too, when we tell them.'

'Oh sure. Hey, girls, your dad's going to make himself

unemployed and unemployable on a point of hopeless principle.'

'They won't see things that way and you know it.'

'No, I suppose not. They're good girls. Smartarse little cows, of course, but good deep down.'

'Smartarse is in the genes, Peter. Your side, of course. It's why most of the party hates you so much.'

This was true. Peter was too clever to succeed within the party, or at least too clever but without the essential ability to disguise the fact. Clever is fine in politics as long as you know how to act stupid. Peter never had. He believed passionately in his political ideals and argued them with a strength and intelligence that were bound to alienate less gifted and less principled colleagues in the lacklustre world of parliamentary politics. He had entered parliament as a twenty-six-year-old bright spark, a spark that had grown steadily duller over the years until he had become what he was now: a forty-something 'didn't quite'. Despite his skills and his firm belief in the principles for which he stood (or perhaps because of them), he had failed to circumnavigate the Labour Party machine. The greasy pole had proved too slippery and his irritatingly well-cut trousers had remained firmly glued to the back benches.

Angela crossed the room and sat beside Peter on the couch. She put her arm around him and he rested his head on her shoulder. 'To be honest,' she said, 'I think they'll withdraw the whip simply for what you've done already. I heard there's a book in the tea-room on how many days you've got left in the party.'

'Well, for God's sake! If ever there was a wrong-headed, half-arsed, bound-to-fail, pointless bit of bad law-making it's this drugs initiative. Decriminalizing pot is never going to work, it just makes the police look like headless chickens and gives the gangsters more room to manoeuvre. The Home Secretary is being pathetic. So is the PM.'

'Yes, so you've said. Astonishing that they don't like you, isn't it?'

'Yes, well, they don't represent the people of Dalston, do they? The whole bloody borough of Hackney is collapsing under the strain of the drug culture, a drug culture the law has created!'

'I know, darling, I know.'

Like many a person of principle, Peter was as happy to preach to the converted as to the sceptical. He had been making the same point all evening and Angela agreed with him absolutely. She shared his anger at the utter failure of drug policy to protect communities from becoming criminalized ghettoes. She supported him in his lone voice objections to the decriminaliz-ation of cannabis, not because it went too far but because it did not go far enough, and she supported him completely in the decision that they had made together regarding the opportunity that fate had placed in their hands.

Each year Parliament allows a single backbench MP to introduce a Private Member's Bill on a subject of their own choosing. A small sop to those who believe the two-and-a-half-party machine is designed to strangle initiative and crush the spirit of the creative individual. The lucky recipient of this honour is chosen by lottery, and normally the spotlight falls upon a nonentity who makes an idiot of himself and little or no career glory follows. This year, however, Lady Luck had chosen well. Or at least so Peter and Angela Paget felt, for she had chosen Peter and they were certain that he had the talent to use this once-in-a-lifetime opportunity to propel the greatest issue of the age to the very forefront of public consciousness.

Peter and Angela Paget had that evening decided that Peter's Private Member's Bill would propose that Parliament immediately legalize all recreational drug use. Not just decriminalizing pot, not just downgrading

E. But legalizing everything. Cocaine. Heroin. Even crack. The lot.

Peter jumped up from the couch, too excited to sit still.

'Yes, even crack. I'll call for the legalization of crack cocaine!'

'You do realize they'll crucify you, don't you?'

'I know, I know. But by then I'll have made the point that crack is just *too dangerous* to be left in the hands of criminals. Nobody *likes* the fact that some people choose to smoke such horrifying poisons, but they do it nonetheless, and we have to bring it under proper control. License it, make it available only through a doctor, tax it and put all the profits into rehabilitation. *We have to do something* other than bury our heads in the sand until the whole country goes to hell in a basket!'

Angela smiled. It was good to see her husband filled once more with such passion and conviction. This was the man she had married, a man fired with a burning desire to do good. To make a difference. He looked young again, as if this one idea had washed away the frustrations and disappointments of all the dreary years of constituency infighting and parliamentary compromise. It would be worth the pain that she knew must inevitably follow such a radical and unpopular stance. Not just because of the undoubted importance of the debate it would provoke, but also for what it would mean for Peter as a man. He was a politician born to fight, and now he had his chance. He would lose, of course, and no doubt be cast out, but for a man like Peter it was better to have fought and lost than never to have fought at all.

It had been ten days since Peter and Angela Paget had made love, a fact of which she was uncomfortably aware. She wanted to make love to him now. Would he want to too? She hoped so. Turning him towards her,

16

she took him in her arms and pressed her lips upon his.

Within moments they had tumbled together to the floor. They had not had sex on the carpet for years.

An amusement arcade, Piccadilly, London

He had been watching the skinny girl with the full breasts and the big dark eyes for nearly an hour, following her from one tawdry arcade to another. In all that hour she had bought nothing, nor had she fed any machine. Destitution was written large upon her as surely as the tattooed dove that flew upon her shoulder. But she was pretty, very pretty. The greasy hair and grimy skin could not disguise that.

'Hullo, baby, what's your name?'

She told him, but she did not look up from the dancing ninja on the screen in front of her, endlessly repeating its single violent kick, inviting her to pay and play.

'Jessie? That's nice. Cute. You look real messed up, Jessie baby. Want a coffee? A drink, maybe? We could play the video games for a while. I got plenty of cash, that's for sure. Where you been sleeping?'

Still she did not look up at him, but none the less the conversation had begun.

'Oh, man, that's bad. Baby, you don't wanna be hanging out that place. No wonder you messed up. That ain't safe for no young girls, no way. Not pretty ones like you. You gotta get your ass right out of that area. Girls like you get bad stuff done to them if they ain't got no one to look after them and see them right, OK? What's that accent, girl? You weirding me out, you sound like you got a knot in your tongue or something.'

The skinny girl was Scottish.

'Oh, baby, you're a long way from home now. Me too,

OK? We both foreigners, outsiders, right? I'm from Marseilles, but I ain't like you, I got connections in this town, I got it all sorted out, right, that's for sure. Down and dirty, oh yeah, that's me. I'm connected. No smartass boy messes with this bad guy less they wanna get cut up bad. You better come with me, Jessie baby. I reckon you lucky I found you, that's for sure. You coulda been talking to any bad guy 'stead of me. They gonna cut you up bad and use you real tough. But I'm François, I'm cool, I respect ladies, that's for sure. I'll protect you. You come with me, sweet baby. We get you some clothes and maybe something to eat. You gonna stay at François' place. Warm you up good, baby, make you smile. You're real lucky, girl, 'cos now you got a connection. This city ain't no safe place for no pretty runaways. You gotta get a connection and now you got one, baby.'

As they left the arcade together the Frenchman took her hand.

St Hilda's Church Hall, Soho

'Right from the start I were in a crap mood. They were holding the show at the Docklands Arena, which really ought to be called the Docklands Big Crappy Concrete Box. Having the Brits there is like deciding to have a party in a multistorey car park. What's more, a multistorey that's been located at the furthest point in London from anywhere even remotely happening. I mean, *come on*. You can't have every pop star in the country sat for three hours in a limo crawling through the sadlands of London. Particularly not Tommy Hanson – number-one UK recording artist and *uber*lad. The man who finally took Robbie's crown.

'No, if you want Tommy Hanson to turn up at your gig sober, don't ask him to get to the Docklands Arena in the rush hour. Particularly seeing as for some reason that has slipped my memory I was coming up from Brighton, so I had it even worse. M23, Croydon, Brixton, I mean, *come on*.

'Anyway, I started drinking in the car. *You'd have been the same*, I swear. There I was, sat in a big, stupid limo. Opposite me there was three twats from the record company who were all trying to impress me with stories about going off shagging with Motley Crue, as if I give a toss about who they've been off shagging with. And next to me there was my triple L. I call 'em triple Ls because that's what the press call 'em. '. . . and Tommy arrived with his Latest Leggy Lovely . . .' Triple L, see. Even if they're short, that's what they get called, and as it happens I quite like short birds. I mean, Kylie's got to be your benchmark, in't she?

'Actually, it were this fookin' triple L that drove me back to the booze, as it happens, or at least I reckon if she hadn't been there I would have lasted till we got to the Arena.

'She was just such a *right pain in the arse*. Emily, her name was. Well, you all know who she is. She's that posh bird, in't she? The one who became a celeb because she's a lord's daughter, or duke or whatever, and she got her tits out in *GQ*. Fookin' 'ell, we British are pathetic, aren't we? Who'd have thought in the twenty-first century the premiere magazine for the British bloke would be getting itself all in a tizzy because a *lord*'s daughter was letting us see her tits? We're still serfs, us Brits, the lot of us, always will be. I mean, don't get me wrong, I'm not saying Emily's bad looking, she's all right, but there's at least twenty birds as tasty in any club in any town in the country on a Friday night, even Doncaster or Skeggy. But they're not *posh*, see, and what we British lads want is to get a look at the knockers of our *betters*. We want to feast our eyes on the forbidden cookies normally only laid out before some arrogant rich twat who's running the country because he went to the same school as the Prince of Wales.

'I'm as bad as anyone. I *love* shagging posh birds, besides which, you know me, if every lad in the country is slapping his monkey over Emily's knockers in *GQ* magazine then I have to have them wrapped round me ear'oles. Just *have* to. It's my job, I'm Tommy Hanson. I'm the top lad. I shag the birds all the other blokes dream about.

'So I pulled her. The minute I saw her oiled-up, airbrushed, cheeky little fun bags staring up at me with a staple between them, I knew I had to pull her.

'Not exactly a difficult assignment, I have to say. I just sent a car round with a note saying, "Congratulations, my sweet Lady Em, you've been pulled. Get in the car, signed Tommy H."

'I knew she'd come. Any bird who gets her jollies out for *GQ* wants to be in the papers so bad it in't funny, and the best way to get in the papers *bar none* as of this point in time is by shagging me. Honest, the euro could collapse, the ozone layer evaporate, the Pope get run over by a plane while kissing a fookin' airport, but if I'm shagging a new triple L, me and her get the front page. I am a bird like Emily's idea of a dream come true. For her, it simply does not get any better than me. All right, maybe Prince William, but that's it; after him, I'm next. So of course she got straight into the car and came round to my place.

'She walked in, asked for some charlie, did about a suitcaseful of it, and by way of payment climbed aboard.

'I can't deny it were top sex. Superb. Most exhilarating. Loved it. Posh bird, see, can't resist 'em. I'm banging away, looking at those tight little cup cakes jiggling about and I'm thinking, "I am shagging a *lord*'s daughter. Me! *How fookin' good is this?*" Like I say, it's absolutely pathetic, but I've told you, I'm English – to me shagging a posh bird is an act of conquest because secretly I don't think it's my place. Like the way them black pimps always used to make sure they had white girlfriends, it's stealing the enemy's most prized possession, in't it?

'Anyway, me and Emily became an instant item, as they say, and pretty soon we had that many press camped outside my house we invited them all in for vintage Cristal and we were that pissed up and wired we told them we were engaged.

'It was a lovely night that. Emily had had "Tommy the Tank" tattooed round her belly button because she reckoned I shagged with all the awesome power of a Challenger Tactical Assault Vehicle (her uncle was a general), and she showed this tattoo off to all the snappers. Well, the next day her taut, muscled little tummy was on the front page of *every* single paper in the country, not just the *Sun* and the *Mirror* and the *Star* but *The Times* and the *Telegraph* and the *Guardian*, an' all. Course, the *Guardian* tried to play it all ironic and amused like they weren't so much doing the story as the *story* of the story, but they still fookin' showed the photo, didn't they? So what a bunch of twatty little hypocrites they are, eh?

'Emily *loved* it. It was like she'd won an Olympic gold medal or got a Nobel Prize or whatever. She just spread them front pages on the floor and knelt among them sort of squeaking with happiness, drooling at all them photos of her belly button with *my* name round it looking up at her from *every single* one of 'em.

'Well, what was I to do? Not a difficult decision. I got behind her, hoiked up her Versace pink suede miniskirt, thumbed the G-string from between her tanned, golden arse cheeks and gave her one from behind. Well, it were a celebration, weren't it? We were the business. Britain's number-one story. Two coked-up

21

fookwits, me banging away and her giggling and moaning and preening over all them front pages of herself, which she'd got just through being posh and shagging me.

'Top morning. Does it for me, I can tell you.'

The circle of recovering alcoholics sat in stunned silence like so many open-mouthed wax dummies, tea half finished, biscuits perched on the saucers on which they had lain un-nibbled since Tommy had begun to testify.

'Afterwards we rolled around on the floor for a bit and had croissants and champagne and another shedful of my charlie, and Emily sent out for more copies of the papers to give to all her mates. Then I turned her over, ripped five grand's worth of designer daywear off her rock-hard, worked-out, emaciated little bod and banged her till she went off and puked . . .'

For the first time the circle stirred.

'Don't get me wrong – she would've gone off and puked whether I'd been banging her or not. There was no way she was going to let herself digest those croissants, mate. Believe me, the closest a girl like that gets to having a square meal is agreeing to swallow.'

Only Tommy could get away with that one. Somehow with Tommy it sounded cheeky.

'Lovely morning. Lovely, lovely morning. Me and Emily were so happy together. But the funny thing was, even though it was obvious who the real star was between us, even though she'd jumped from third-billed spread in *GQ* to front-page saturation media coverage solely on the strength of letting me up her on a regular basis, she was that well bred and posh that she still acted like *she* was the top dog in the relationship and I was *just* some jolly bit of rough. She had so much *confidence*. They all do, those posh birds. Loud voices, officers' accents, loads of deafening mates and a couple of great big cunty brothers in jumpers who are the only people they will defer to because they're just "sarch a farking larf, right? So-o-o droll". Let me tell you, after a month or two of having her baying in me ear'ole, love was well and truly dead. I was sick of the sight of her, and by the time the Brits rolled around I was looking for a way to dump her. That was partly why I'd given up the booze, as it happens, in order to dump Emily. I'm better at reality when I'm sober.

'"Oh, farking Christ, I hate the farking Brit Awards," she was shouting at me and the record company twats like we were in the next county. "They always give best newcomer to some little farking Scotsman nobody's ever heard of and the big Americans *never* turn up, so they don't usually have any really proper stars at all." Can you believe it? There she was, sat in a stretch with a bloke who'd sold *fifteen million* albums in the previous twelve months, and she's moaning about the absence of proper stars! I mean *fookin' 'ell*. Well, that was it. You remember that old Paul Simon song, "Fifty Ways To Leave Your Lover"? I love Paul Simon, me. Anyway, he says don't agonize about it, just get out, make a plan, don't be embarrassed, just fookin' do it. Well, he never mentioned anything about waiting till your limo stops at traffic lights, opening the door on the bird's side and sliding her out onto the street with your boot, but I think he would have done if it had scanned because it's a top way of dropping a bird. Makes the point, let me tell you.

'I even remembered to grab my bag of charlie off her as she went. Bang, into the street, right on her arse. There she was, sitting amongst the McDonald's wrappers in a *fifteen thousand quid* Gucci number, which basically consisted of three small handkerchiefs connected by bootlaces. Me and the twats were pissing ourselves as the limo pulled away, let me tell you.

'I looked back at her and waved. Brixton High Street,

five in the afternoon, almost naked. The only white face I could see. I don't think I've ever seen anyone looking so scared. That's what charlie does to you, empowers you to be an arsehole, makes you think kicking girls out of cars because you don't like their accents is funny... I wish I could pinpoint the moment in my life when I turned into such a complete *cont.*'

Suddenly there were tears in Tommy's eyes. The circle of faces were amazed. They were used to raw emotion in their meetings, but this had come so suddenly.

'Don't worry, it's just the booze seeping out through me tearducts ... Anyway, that's when I had my first drink. Like I say, I'd still been doing the coke, so it wasn't as if I was properly dry. I'd just started me detox programme with booze because booze makes you fat whereas coke helps you slim. But, bollocks, I wanted a drink. I *needed* a drink. The record company blokes were all cacking themselves about what a great bloke I was for kicking a coked-up, half-naked girl out of a car in the middle of south London, and not for the first time in my life I realized that if I didn't get drunk quite quickly I might notice that I was a sad, arrogant, bullying bastard.

'I stopped the car at the next off licence and got a crate of Special Brew and six Kangaroo's Arse *Method Champenois*, which was all they had. Well, you're not going to get vintage Cristal in the Brixton Londis, are you?

'Then I went and sat in the front with the driver. I didn't even give the three twats from the record company any of my booze. I just left them behind the glass and went and sat up front, just me, the driver and of course my old mate charlie. By the time we got to the Arena I was well and truly on one and I'd also decided that what I did to Emily was a top move and she'd deserved it and she'd be all right anyway.

'I like Australian wines.'

A house in Chorlton-cum-Hardy

Billy was ten, Kylie was nine. By rights, they should never have been left alone, but Billy's mum was a single parent and she had to go to work. The children were in the care of Billy's seventeen-year-old sister Michelle, and she had gone out for milk and coffee. Besides which, Michelle was sick to death of Billy and Kylie and she felt that the five-minute walk to the shops might restore her sanity and thus prevent her from throwing one or both of them out of the window.

Billy and Kylie went upstairs to Michelle's bedroom, which they knew was strictly out of bounds, and lay on the bed together beneath the Eminem posters. They practised kissing until fits of the giggles made further experiment impossible and then Billy showed Kylie Michelle's condoms, which he earnestly explained were a 'contradiction device'.

'So Mish doesn't get up the duff,' he added, 'although she says fat chance of that anyway, which means she hasn't got a boyfriend at the moment.'

Kylie had recently agreed to be Billy's girlfriend, and Billy had been hoping on the strength of this that Kylie might take her knickers off and show him her bits. Disappointingly, Kylie demurred, but offered instead to show him her knickers. This she did and Billy stared for quite a while, which he enjoyed, although he didn't know why. Kylie declined the offer to see Billy's pants and the conversation moved on. Billy said that he knew where Michelle hid her special things – her cigarettes and sometimes some money. Billy suggested that they look to see what they could find. Kylie, who was harbouring a major craving for a Honeycomb

Wispa, agreed. Besides, if there was no money they could at least have a smoke.

Billy pulled out the drawer of Michelle's bedside table to reveal the space behind. They found no money but they did find a small decorative box in which were six tablets, each embossed with a bird. They both knew that it was dangerous to put pills in their mouths, but they were bored and these little pills didn't look like medicine. It seemed more than likely that they were sweets.

Billy and Kylie ate three pills each.

When Michelle found them writhing on the floor of her bedroom she saw the empty pill-box and knew exactly what had happened. Grabbing the children in turn, she forced her fingers into their mouths in an effort to make them sick. Then she rushed to the fridge and brought milk, thinking in her panic that it might help. As the children began to lose consciousness she called her mother at work, who told her to call for an ambulance.

Later Michelle was to admit that as much as fifteen minutes might have passed between the discovery of the stricken children and her calling the emergency services.

The Paget household, Dalston

When Peter came out of the bathroom he could see from his wife's expression that it was bad news.

'Peter, we couldn't have picked a worse day if we'd spent our lives planning it.' Angela handed him the sheaf of newspapers brought by her daughter Cathy from her paper round. Cathy was aware of what her father was intending to do that day and her heart had sunk when she'd seen the front pages. Two small children – a ten-year-old and a nine-year-old – had died after taking ecstasy tablets.

Peter glanced from headline to headline. Angela had already read them all. 'It's clear that it was a terrible accident. These kids found big sister's little party stash and ate it. They might have necked a bottle of cream sherry or rat bait, but it's being spun as if the poor girl forced the bloody things down their throats. The mother, too. It's like she'd left the children in the care of a Yardie gang.'

Cathy Paget called from the living room. 'The police van the sister and mum were taken away in was stoned by an angry mob. It's on Sky every five minutes.'

The newspapers were almost unanimous in their interpretation of the tragedy. This was no accident. E killed these children. The people who took E killed them, and the people who dealt E killed them. Ecstasy was an instrument of child murder and those who apologized for it were apologists for infanticide.

Peter bit his lip. Not a good day to raise the subject of drug legalization in Parliament. The achingly cute photographs of the dead children stared at him from the front page of every paper. Innocent victims of evil drug-takers.

Cathy emerged from the living room. 'They're going to kill you, Dad. Every report, and I mean every *single* report on your speech is going to be accompanied by the photos of those kids. They're going to say that you're proposing a Private Member's Bill to kill children.'

'Thanks, darling. That makes me feel a whole lot better.'

'She's right, Pete,' said Angela. 'You don't have to do this thing if you don't want to.'

They went into the sitting room and watched *Sky News* for a while. The footage of the mob trying to get at Michelle and her mother while they were taken in for questioning was horrible to watch.

'She's just lost her son,' Angela said, with tears in her eyes. 'Oh my God, people are terrible, aren't they?'

Every now and then the footage was punctuated with shots of Peter, the commentator reminding the viewer that the MP for Dalston North West intended *that day* to introduce a bill proposing the legalization of drugs.

'Pretty poor timing,' one anchor remarked.

'Tasteless and insensitive would be better descriptions, I think,' her colleague replied.

It was much the same spin on all the channels. The general feeling was that this new and terrible tragedy must surely now bring the legalizers to their senses.

'Do you want me to drop it?' Peter asked his wife.

'No, of course not,' she replied.

'Thought not,' said Peter. 'Sod them. This tragedy has got nothing whatsoever to do with my bill. Nothing. Like you say, Angela, it could have been booze or cleaning fluids. How many kids have died through alcohol this week? Beaten by drunk parents, run down by drink-drivers, poisoned on fucking Alcopops? Where are their pictures? Why aren't they on the front page?'

'Dad. They're going to kill you.'

The Hilton Hotel, Bangkok

Sonia had finally found a television station that met with her satisfaction. There were plenty in English but they were mainly American and she had soon got bored with the unfamiliar cartoons and sitcoms and the weather reports from Arkansas. BBC News 24 had been worse: some dreary report about an English MP who wanted to legalize drugs. Sonia had smiled at that at least. Lucky for her he hadn't managed it yet. There'd have been no free holiday in Thailand for her if he had. She'd still be stuck in Birmingham.

She had finally found a pop channel with a

half-hour special on the lead-up to the Brit Awards. Tommy Hanson, the people's pop star, was of course expected to clean up as he had done the year before. Could it really be only four years since he had emerged victorious from *Pop Hero* with the biggest popular majority in the show's history? Sonia had voted for him eight times.

It was as Tommy sang to Sonia via the Asian Star Cable Network that her employers came to transact their business. Sonia was nervous but pleased to see them.

Excited.

One big, bad, mad-for-it Brummie bird.

'I've never been in a Hilton Hotel before. Noice, in't it? Didn't know they 'ad them in Bangkok, it's just loik England, in't it? Top tune, this. Tommy 'anson, I love 'im I do, 'e's dead lush. *Let me be the tattoo on your thigh*. Brilliant. I've bought loads of CDs while I've been here, they only cost about three American dollars each, which is two quid. Two quid for a CD! I mean, that's mental that is, that is just stupid. I got three copies of everything so that's Christmas sorted. Eminem, Dido, Slipknot for mates, U2 for me mum and of course loads of Tommy. I'm going to see 'im in concert at the NEC in Birbingham next month. Have yow ever been to Birbingham, or is it just your mate in England?'

The Brummie babble stopped for a moment. The man's briefcase was open on the coffee table. It contained only one item.

'Jesus Chroist! I can't swallow that! It's loik a bag of sodding flour!'

The man explained that they would lubricate the condom with vegetable oil. Sonia wondered if it might be possible to divide the load into two lots, but the man had made his preparations and wanted

29

to stick to them. He was anxious to be about his business.

'Oh, screw it, all roight, that's what I'm 'ere for. You're sure this thing won't burst? I mean it'd kill me, wouldn't it? I read that if the condom bursts yow wroithe around in agony for about foive minutes then youm dead, bang, just loik that . . .'

Suddenly the reality of why she was in Bangkok at all was lying on the coffee table in front of her. A sinister shiny white sausage, a pale, evil-looking slug. Swallowing it was a terrifying prospect, but Sonia reminded herself that she was no crybaby, she was a tough, up-for-anything, Brummie bird and she wasn't going to let some drug-pushing foreigner see that she was scared.

'Come on, then, let's get it swallowed. Down't blame moi if I puke. Give us one of them Courvoisiers out of the mini-bar to wash it down.'

The House of Commons, Westminster

'No, Madam Speaker, I will not withdraw! Nor will I apologize. The terrible, terrible tragedy reported in this morning's papers is entirely irrelevant to the issues that I have come today to put before the house. Except in this one point! It has been established that the poor older sister Michelle, whose drugs were taken by her younger sibling and friend, waited twenty minutes before calling for an ambulance. Were those twenty minutes crucial? They might have been. I don't know but I can certainly imagine why the girl hesitated. She hesitated because she was terrified. She knew that calling an ambulance must inevitably mean her arrest and her disgrace. So this seventeen-year-old girl, faced with the appalling circumstance that her little brother and his friend were dying because of her, panicked,

Madam Speaker. She panicked and in order to avoid the consequences of what had happened she attempted to remedy the situation herself, with tragic results. I suggest to you, madam, that had this girl's pills been legal she would have called for help twenty minutes sooner than she did. What's more, the pills would most probably not have been hidden away; they'd have been on display but out of reach, in much the way that alcohol is arranged in most homes.'

Peter Paget was sweating visibly, but he was in control, nervous certainly, but in control. And hugely exhilarated. This was his moment, the moment for which he had been waiting all of his life. Fifteen years of rejection and petty frustration might just be about to blossom into glorious and celebrated political maturity. Peter Paget had gone into politics in order to improve people's lives, and he had of course very quickly discovered that this was not generally considered to be the business of government. But today, on this one day, on *his* day, he was going to make a difference.

'And in answer to my Right Honourable colleague's question, no, I do not consider drug use a trivial thing. I can assure you that I have better things to do than waste this house's time with trivia. But I feel bound to add that nor do I think it a trivial thing that the vast majority of police time in my constituency is consumed in either pursuing drug users or dealing with the consequences of drug use – theft, prostitution and gun law! It is a matter of simple fact that a vast proportion of the young people in this country take drugs. That does not make them all drug addicts, but it does make them all criminals! Yes, Madam Speaker, criminals! Along with the numerous prosperous, law-abiding people who smoked marijuana at university and still take it occasionally at dinner parties! Class B? Class C? Class X, Y and Z! It doesn't matter: they are still all outside the law! As are the young professionals who snort cocaine as a weekend treat. And prominent celebrities . . . pop stars such as Tommy Hanson . . .' Peter waved a newspaper above his head. '. . . who only last week was once more on the front pages of the tabloids openly discussing his thousand-pound-a-day habits and his efforts to kick them! Along with the members of this house . . . Yes, Madam Speaker, the members of this house! Those who took drugs in their youth and who *continue to take them now*!'

The pandemonium that had been ringing around the debating chamber redoubled. Peter faced them down. It was David and Goliath, a great throng of baying, screeching school bullies against one small brave voice of honest reason. Peter knew that never again in his life would he do anything as significant as what he was doing at this moment. His hour had come.

'No, Madam Speaker, I will not withdraw! There are over six hundred and fifty members of this house, all adults, mostly born in the fifties and the sixties, educated in the seventies, the eighties and the nineties, educated at British universities which, like the rest of the country, are awash with drugs. It is absurd to pretend that none of us here today has experienced illegal drugs, impossible to imagine that there is no member of this ancient body who might not still indulge in such a thing. I will not withdraw!'

The stern-looking woman in the Chair enquired whether the Right Honourable Member for Dalston North West had anything to confess himself. Peter was, of course, ready for this. He had rehearsed it with Angela playing the role of speaker. He rose up to take the challenge between his teeth like a lion bringing down an antelope.

'Yes, Madam Speaker, I am perfectly happy to inform this house under parliamentary privilege that as a student I occasionally smoked a marijuana cigarette, or "joint". I no longer indulge in the habit, but I most certainly did at one time and I have many friends who continue to do so, and who do so on occasion *at my house!*'

Peter's confession took his audience by surprise, quietening them momentarily. Allowing one's premises to be used for the purpose of drug-taking was, after all, illegal. Peter was admitting to a criminal offence.

'I would, however, be loath to make such a confession outside of *this* house, for I should not wish to inconvenience the police by putting them to the trouble of interviewing me, which would certainly be their duty under the current law. Although, as we all know, the police have scarcely the energy or the resources to carry out such a duty . . . No, madam, I am not trying to be funny. You will know when I am trying to be funny by the simple fact that people will be laughing . . .'

This was cheek indeed from a lowly backbencher, but Peter was on fire. What was more, the joke actually played rather well and would later be much reported. Could it be that he was making progress?

'I am attempting to point out that, under British law, pretty much the entire population of this country has been criminalized. We are all either criminals ourselves or associates of criminals or relatives of criminals. We buy CDs produced by criminals, we see films that star criminals, watch award shows compered by criminals! Our stocks and shares are brokered by criminals, our roads are swept by criminals, our children are taught by criminals. Can we not admit it? Are we not a mature enough society to face the clear and obvious truth? We *must* admit it. Our future way of life depends on it. For this vast nation of – how shall I put it? – *social* criminals is linked arterially to a corrosive, cancerous core of *real* criminals. Murderers. Pimps. Gangsters. Gunmen. Lethally unscrupulous backroom chemists! We are all connected to these people because there is no legal way for an otherwise law-abiding population to get high, which it is *clearly intent upon doing*. The law is effectively the number-one sponsor of organized crime!'

Once more there was pandemonium in the house. The opposition waved their order papers and the government front bench sat stony-faced. It was, after all, one of their own backbenchers who was delivering this inflammatory heresy. They hated Peter Paget, had hated him for years. But now he had become dangerous; not happy with merely opposing their mild decriminalization policy, he was now calling for legalized anarchy. They feared he would bring discredit upon the whole party, perhaps cost them the next election. The Prime Minister turned and glared at Peter with a silent steely gaze while the house descended into uproar.

'You may try to shout me down, but I will be heard, and I will tell you this. An officer in my constituency was killed in a Yardie gang shooting last week. I attended his funeral. I watched as the dead man's coffin, bearing the union flag, passed by his weeping family. That same flag, Madam Speaker, flies above this house! And above every government building. It is the symbol of our law. And yet it was this law that *killed* the brave officer I saw buried last week!'

Now the front bench were no longer stony-faced. The Prime Minister's visage was a mask of grim fury; the Home Secretary waved his arms like a new boy. The Speaker felt moved to warn Peter that it was no part of his duty as an MP to insult the flag to which he had sworn allegiance, but Peter would not be warned: he felt inspired. What was more, he knew he was right. And he knew that *they knew* he was right. That was what was making them so angry. The only thing that stood between the government of Great

Britain and the stone-cold logical truth of his argument was that his was a truth that so far nobody in any position of responsibility had been allowed to acknowledge. Well, Peter Paget would do that for them, and he would make them listen.

'No, madam, I am not trying to score cheap points! If you think that I would invoke the memory of a recently dead hero merely in order to decorate my argument, then I am afraid that it is I who must protest to you. I am stating the simple fact that an officer in my constituency was shot dead while pursuing a criminal whose income is derived solely from supplying cocaine to otherwise entirely law-abiding people. If those people were able to get their cocaine at the off licence, properly licensed, taxed and restricted to adults, then the man who killed that officer would have to find some other means of making a living and there would be one less police widow! And it is not only the police who walk in fear in our increasingly violent society! We all do! In some communities people count each day a lucky one if their homes are not broken into and their persons not assaulted by depraved junkies desperate to finance their terrible craving. We all know that the vast majority of muggings and burglaries are drug-fuelled! Why should we have to suffer for other people's addictions? Let me ask you this, let me put the unashamedly selfish argument for legalization: would you honestly care if the number of addicts in this country doubled, even trebled, if it meant that your home was no longer in danger of being broken into and your children were free from the fear of being mugged for their pocket money and mobile phones?'

For a moment the uproar died. This was an interesting point.

'As a matter of fact, I'm not at all convinced that the number of addicts would rise dramatically anyway.

35

Experiments in Holland suggest that they would not, but I put it to you again, even if they did *would you really care* as long as they were properly housed, properly looked after and above all *not stealing your VCR?*'

The House of Commons lobby, Westminster

Peter Paget's parliamentary assistant felt her heart pounding with excitement. She could hear the roars from inside the debating chamber and knew that her employer was truly in the lion's den. Samantha had been with Peter for almost four months and had shared with him the build-up to this moment. She felt that it was almost as much her day as his. Unable to stand the tension any longer, she phoned her mother on her mobile phone.

'He's in there now, Mum. It sounds like they're tearing him apart.'

Forewarned by her daughter, Samantha's mother had been watching the debate on the Parliament Channel and assured Samantha that Peter was acquitting himself splendidly.

'Oh, he's so wonderful, Mum. He went through the speech with me this morning, sitting on a bench in Parliament Square. It's incredible, his passion, his commitment, the things he believes. He's the only real man in that bloody place. The Prime Minister's just a moron compared to him. Oh, Mum, I wish you'd seen us out there working together, right in the shadow of Parliament. I felt so proud that he chose me to try out his lines on. He even took a couple of my suggestions! I know! He's got this bit about the Union Jack draped on a police coffin and as he was talking I looked up and saw the flag that flies above the house and it seemed like providence, so I said that he should draw a comparison between the two flags. He said it was a brilliant idea and promised to use it! He did? Oh, that's amazing! But it's all him, of course, I mean it's him that makes it work. He's just brilliant, that's all. He claims his wife helps him with his stuff, but I doubt it, I mean, come on, *as if.* What would she know? She's just a boring little mouse. Although I do think it's sweet of him to be so supportive of her. Honestly, Mum, it was just *so exciting* going through it all with him ... with Big Ben looking down on us and the sunshine on the roof of Westminster Abbey, *so* romantic ... And then when he got up to go in he said "Wish me luck" and I did and then he kissed me! In public! He's never done that before ... I'm not being silly. I just think it's a sign, that's all.'

The House of Commons, Westminster

Inside the debating chamber the object of this girlish affection was hot. Peter wanted to remove his jacket, but he knew that there would be dark rings of sweat at his armpits. He wished that he had worn a lighter-coloured shirt. He was experienced enough a politician to know that sweaty armpits were just the sort of thing that could blow an entire speech by securing more coverage than the issues under discussion. Although on this occasion such was the force of Peter's performance that he could probably have stripped naked and still have the content of his speech properly reported. He had galvanized the emotions of the house in a manner not seen since the heady days of Mrs Thatcher.

'I am not alone in my thinking, Madam Speaker. I can see that there are Honourable Members here today sitting on all sides of the house who see things as I do, although they're scared to admit it. And let me tell you this: no less a figure than the senior policeman in my

37

constituency, Commander Barry Leman, agrees with every word I've said. He has been my trusted adviser during the preparation of my bill and would be happy to appear before a parliamentary committee to offer a police perspective.'

Madam Speaker observed that it was not for police officers, senior or otherwise, to invite themselves to address parliamentary committees. Madam Speaker wondered if Mr Paget was suggesting that Commander Leman represented the official view of the Metropolitan Police.

'No, Madam Speaker, I suspect that he does not, just as my views do not represent the official line of my own party. Nonetheless, Commander Leman and I both believe passionately that it is the *law* that is killing officers in the drugs war! For the law refuses to acknowledge the patently obvious fact that the drugs war is lost! Yes, it is *lost*, Madam Speaker! Will this house persist for ever in its self-deception? Sufficient people take drugs to make life in this country and indeed the entire world an ever worsening misery. But *only*, Madam Speaker, *only* because they must buy them from criminals! *We have lost the war!* We are currently living under the yoke of a victorious army of occupation! An army of drug barons, gangsters, pushers, traffickers, murderers, petty thieves, prostitutes, muggers, corrupted officials and all the low lifes of a criminal economy, a vast world trade existing outside all law. Can not we, who sit in this house, this house, which is the mother of all parliaments, the proud cradle of democracy in the modern world, can we not once more give that world a lead? Have the courage to do the unthinkable! To do that which would in a single instant pull the rug from beneath ninety per cent of the criminals on this planet? Can we not move to legalize, *legalize*, mind, not decriminalize, *all drugs*?'

Afterwards, in the lobby of the house, Peter Paget stood blinking in the light of his instant fame. His had been one of the great parliamentary débuts, for, despite his seventeen years of service, to all intents and purposes début it had been. The kind of bravura, fire-cracker performance that weary lobby correspondents had thought had long since been consigned to the romance of history. By the end of his speech, as he himself had noted, Peter had without doubt begun to make a favourable impression on many of his colleagues, and his back had been slapped and his face snarled at in equal proportions. This is not to say that half of the Members of Parliament were going to vote for full legalization, but many were grateful to Peter for having the courage to raise the issues. Particularly since they all viewed his bill as career suicide. Nobody in recent years had sparked such instant and furious debate. Peter Paget was blinking in the limelight and as he smiled at the starstruck face of his parliamentary assistant he knew that he was finally above the radar.

The Leman household, Dalston

Ten minutes after Commander Barry Leman left the house the phone rang.

'Hello, Leman residence.'

'Mrs Leman?'

'Yes. Who is this speaking?'

'I'd like to speak to your husband.'

'Who shall I say is calling?'

'A friend.'

'I know all his friends. I presume you have a name.'

'Just put me on to your husband, please, Mrs Leman. It's in his interests.'

Christine Leman pressed the record button on the

answerphone connected to the Snoopy phone's plinth. She wondered if the caller heard the click. 'I'm sorry, but we don't speak to people who refuse to identify themselves.'

'Then will you give him a message?'

'Of course.'

'Tell him to drop his support for Paget's Private Member's Bill.'

'Ah, I see—'

'And tell him to drop his inquiries into Drug Squad corruption.'

'If you have views on either of those subjects you can address them in writing to Dalston Police Station, or alternatively my husband's email address at the Met is—'

'Tell him to drop what he's doing or we'll drop him. Did you hear that, Mrs Leman? Do you understand?'

'I'm recording this conversation.'

'You can record what you like, Mrs Leman. And once you've recorded it, why not play it to your daughter? The one who attends Kingswood School for Girls. The one who walks unaccompanied to drama classes every Saturday morning. The one who attends netball practice Monday evenings six till eight and then gets a lift to the corner of Jackson Road and cuts home through the allotments. *Do you understand, Mrs Leman?*'

The House of Commons, Westminster

The Shadow Home Secretary glared furiously at the Speaker, to Peter Paget, and then back again.

'Madam Speaker, in all my years as a member of this house, and they span no less than five parliaments, I have never been so revolted as I am by the comments made by my honourable colleague the Member for

Dalston North West. That such an irresponsible man with such dangerous, anarchic opinions feels able to remain a member of Her Majesty's Parliament simply beggars belief. Just as it is astonishing to me that the high-ranking police officer whose support he claims to have secured, Commander Barry Leman, openly advocates drug use and yet feels able to remain a member of the Metropolitan Police. If there is one thing on which I think all sane and right-thinking people in this country can agree it is that people, particularly young people, particularly *children*, must be protected from the evils of drugs! Surely that single principle is one which must cross all party boundaries? And yet we have been forced to sit listening to a member of this house, a government backbencher, suggesting that we legalize these lethal substances. That we make them readily available to any bored teenager who might imagine that he or she wants them. I am sickened by the whole idea. Will the Prime Minister not immediately condemn his errant colleague? Will he not withdraw the whip? Banish him from his party, a party which, for all its many faults, has never thus far harboured apologists for criminals and advocates of anarchy!'

The Prime Minister did not need this. He had an extensive legislative programme to push through and already too much parlia-mentary time and no doubt every headline in the next morning's papers had been hijacked by the MP for Dalston North West.

He rose to reply.

'Madam Speaker, as my honourable colleague the Shadow Home Secretary is well aware, the Member for Dalston North West has introduced a Private Member's Bill, which is his privilege. His opinions form no part of the government's policy and, like my honourable colleague, I reject them utterly. We shall continue with our cautious approach to the decriminalization of

41

cannabis while committing ourselves with ever more energy to the rigorous enforcement of the law on Class A drugs.'

He sat down to respectful applause, but nonetheless there were doubtful faces on the benches. Paget had lit a touch paper; he had said the unsayable and the genie was out of the bottle. Everybody knew that the war on drugs was if not lost at least unwinnable, and if Paget continued to pursue his crusade with the vigour with which he had started it, the ostrich politics that had informed the drug debate for so many decades would no longer be an option.

St Hilda's Church Hall, Soho

The early-morning meeting of Soho Alcoholics Anonymous was normally finished by eight o'clock. Many of the people who attended it were busy professionals who had work to get to. The current session was already overrunning, but nobody seemed minded to leave.

'Backstage at the Brits was the usual bollocks. They'd given me the second biggest dressing room after Elton John, so I knew immediately that Emily had been right about the Yanks – they hadn't turned up again. Bastards. I don't know what's more pathetic, that they care so little about pissing us off or that we care so much when they do . . . Actually, I reckon the saddest thing is that they don't even care that we care that they don't care. They just don't give a toss about what we think either way. We might as well be Bela-shaggin'-rus or Iceland or whatever. And we invented the Beatles! But that's all just ancient history now, in't it? The Yanks are back in charge and that's the way it's going to stay. Everybody wants to crack the States. That's the one, in't it, the only one.

'I've got seven Brit Awards and I'd swap the lot for one Grammy. I've headlined the MTV Europe Music Awards for three years in a row now, but I'd happily go bottom of the bill if they'd just knock off that one little bastard word "Europe". The proper MTV Awards aren't called MTV USA, are they? No, because everybody knows where they're at. It's like with American email addresses. We have to put "dot uk" at the end of ours, but not them, everyone knows where they live. Bastards.

'I might get there. I keep trying. I really thought I'd scored when I went on Jay Leno a few months ago. Leno hugged me in hospitality and said I was a star. But then Pammy Anderson walked in and I realized I was only a star to Jay Leno until a real one came along.

'I couldn't believe Pammy Anderson, incidentally. I mean, those knockers are just stupid, aren't they? She's deeper than she is long, that bird. I reckon her nipples were at the bar before the back of her arse was through the door. Doesn't do it for me at all, that. I couldn't raise a smile.'

Tommy basked in the laughter of the assembled recovering addicts. An audience was an audience to him. It didn't matter whether it was ten thousand kids at the Birmingham NEC or a tight ring of screw-ups in a church hall in Soho. Tommy always rose to the bait.

'Anyway, the good thing was that with no Yanks or U2 turnin' up, I was unquestionably the second biggest star in the house after Elton. I mean, I had outsold him about fifty to one on our last albums, but it's about longevity, in't it? So respect and all that. He's queen of England is Elton. Everybody knows that. They'd put a little astroturf garden with a picket fence an' all outside his dressing room, which in my coked-up state I thought was the funniest thing I'd ever seen, particularly when I pissed on one of his trees. I could see that the Manics were dead annoyed that they hadn't thought of that first. Good thing, I reckon. If they'd pissed on Elton's tree it would have been some sort of political protest. With me it was just a laugh.

'Backstage it were the usual set-up: concrete hangar, Portakabin dressing rooms, a Hard Rock Café in the middle and a sponsored bar, which meant of course that the beer was shite. Decent beers never sponsor poxy backstage bars, because they don't have to. You never see Stella giving their nectar away, or Boddingtons, do you? And what beer was it? What else but the ever-present, ever-shite Budweiser! The beer with the best ads and the worst taste in the world. Fook American beer! No, really, I mean it. *Fook* American beer. Why does it have to be so *sweet*? Because everything Americans consume has to be sweet, that's why. I've been to Disneyworld, mate. They have M&Ms on their fookin' Coco Pops!

'Anyway, there I was in me Portakabin screaming for someone to find me a decent beer and feeling dead bored, and the thing is that when I get bored I get randy. Well, you do, don't you? What's more, as of the incident at the traffic lights on Brixton High Street, I was officially single again. On top of which, I'd just got on an E that the A and R people had given me. They thought that was terribly funny, by the way: an E from A and R. I said, "Yeah, and an F, U, C and a K from me.

'Anyway, like I say, suddenly I was feeling totally randy and although there was plenty of birds around I decided that I fancied having a crack at Lulu. I've always fancied Lulu and I reckon she still looks top even if she's fifty or whatever and also she looks like she likes a laugh. I mean, she's always on *Ab Fab*, in't she? She'd come to the ceremony with Elton, I think, or else she had a single out or was getting an award for having such a great arse for a granny . . . I don't know. The point was she was wearing fantastic tight leather trousers, so I went straight up to her and told her she was pulled.'

Samantha's flat, Islington

'Hello, darling? Can you hear me? I'm on my mobile.'

Peter Paget felt a great sickness in his stomach. What was he doing? What was he *doing*?

This was madness. Sheer lunacy. And yet . . . yet . . . He could not deny himself. Peter hated lying to his wife more than anything, almost. It burdened him with such guilt that sometimes he felt that he would be unable to get out of bed in the morning and he knew that the sickness in his stomach would prevent him from eating all day. Yes, he hated deceiving Angela *almost* more than anything . . . But not more than he would hate to have to give up the reason for his lies.

'Yes, there's been an adjournment. It was pretty rough, couldn't believe the hostility. Did you watch it on the Parliament Channel? Well, yes, of course I knew you would . . . So you thought I was good? . . . Well, I can't deny I was pleased with it too . . . With any luck there'll be a good chunk on the news. It was absolute bedlam outside the house. The newspaper people just sort of swamped me. It was incredible. I've never felt like a star before, strange but . . . well, exciting : . . But the questions they asked were so ignorant they beggared belief, made it sound like Barry Leman and I want to distribute heroin in school playgrounds. People are so *scared*. They can just about stomach talking about legalizing dope, but the minute you start using words like crack and heroin they run for cover.'

Basking in the happy memory of that invigorating media scrum, Peter almost forgot the sickness in his stomach. He was proud of himself, he had done well. He loved using words like 'crack' and 'heroin'. They sounded so uncompromisingly realistic. He wondered whether he could risk calling heroin 'smack', but held back. Angela Paget's bullshit detector was very finely tuned and she would instantly detect his posturing. Peter had once been part of a select committee visiting an army base and had accepted the offer of a combat jacket and beret to wear for the duration of his visit. Angela had never let him forget the resulting photograph that appeared in the local newspaper. He smiled at the memory.

He should be at home. He ought to go home. This was their day. Angela had practically written half of his speech. This was the first day in years when they could genuinely celebrate Peter's career together. As they had done on that wonderful first night he had been elected to Parliament. This should be their night. *He should go home.*

'The PM has summoned me to his rooms tomorrow morning to explain myself, as if I didn't make myself quite clear in my speech . . . I'm quite sure that the Chief Whip will be pushing the boss to chuck me out, but so what? The bloody party's never going to promote me anyway. I've got as much chance of making a difference outside it as I have in. More, in fact. What they don't understand is that I actually *care*, I mean *really* care, about what I'm trying to do. Principle, you see, they just can't get their heads round it . . . I almost think I might do better outside Parliament anyway.'

Across the room Peter Paget's parliamentary assistant removed her jumper to reveal the pale blue brassière beneath. Paget was momentarily distracted.

'I'm sorry, darling, I didn't catch that, it's this stupid mobile . . . Threatening phone calls? What do you mean? To you? To the Lemans? Well, I don't see why you need me to come home because of that . . .'

Again that pain. His wife was worried. She needed

46

him. She was always there when he needed her. He should go to her. Now . . .

But what good would he do? It had only been a phonecall. In fact, it had only been a phonecall to someone else. They were not even the ones being threatened. She didn't need him. If she *really* needed him, he told himself, he would go.

His parliamentary assistant's hips wiggled as she pulled the smart little pinstripe skirt down over her thighs, gathering her tights along with it. How smooth and flawless her skin was.

How young.

It had been nearly two months now, seven weeks of tortured deception and frantic passion. Peter knew that while he might possibly continue to deceive his wife, he could no longer deceive himself. This was no moment of madness, no potentially forgivable stupid sex thing. This was a relationship. An affair. A proper, drawn-out, *cliché* of an affair.

'Well, of course it's upsetting if Laura Leman has had a threatening call, but I'm sure it was just a hoax, Angela. These things almost always are. Some crank doesn't like Barry and wants to make his life unpleasant . . . I mean, he is investigating police corruption, for God's sake. Those people are proper hardmen . . . I really don't think there's any reason to be scared . . . You haven't had a call, have you? Well, then . . . Look, I can't just drop everything. I'll come home as soon as is humanly possible, all right? I promise . . .'

The tiny triangle of Samantha's G-string looked exquisite against her beautifully waxed groin. What there was of the flimsy garment was of the same colour and expensive material as her bra. She smiled at Peter as she ran her thumbs around the frilled waistband. No one had ever bought her such nice underwear before. In fact no one had ever bought her underwear before at all. She was only twenty-three. Her boyfriends at university had spent their money on beer. Their idea of erotic bedroom attire was seeing her in their rugby shirts.

Peter reminded himself that he must dispose of that receipt. It had been some time since he had bought Mrs Paget any underwear. He would, though, he really would. Soon.

'. . . It's just there's so much work to do on this bill. I'll get through it as fast as I can. Samantha has agreed to stay back and help, which is amazing of her because there'll be no extra money, but she believes in this thing as much as I do. As much as we do. This is the defining moment, darling, I've lit the blue touch paper. I have to be here on the ground to see it through. Yes, yes, I knew you'd understand. Thank you, darling.'

Peter Paget turned off his phone.

Samantha joined him on the bed. 'You were like a lion today, my darling. You thrilled me. You made me hot inside.'

He closed his eyes as she kissed him. Angela need never know. The kisses made him giddy. Or perhaps it was the speed with which his life was changing. Only a few months before he had been so very depressed, with a career that was going nowhere and a happy but increasingly unexciting marriage. All his promise wasted, all his hope behind him, facing the featureless prospect of an extended middle-age watching his daughters grow away from him and his wife grow old.

Now suddenly everything had changed. He had ached after Samantha from the moment she had come to work with him. Simply ached. She had clouded his thoughts utterly, his desire for her finding some place to intrude on every single waking moment of his life.

It was not that he did not love Angela. He did love her, truly. But he *wanted* Samantha. He was obsessed.

Nonetheless, Peter Paget had never dreamt that he

would end up putting his marriage at risk. He knew that his marriage was safe. Of course it was safe. Why would a beautiful twenty-three-year-old woman like Samantha, a woman who turned heads in every corridor that she walked along, be remotely interested in him, a tired, slightly balding man of almost twice her age? It was nonsense. His peace of mind might be utterly ruined, but his marriage at least was safe.

But Peter Paget had been wrong. Nothing was safe. It turned out that Samantha wanted him just as much as he wanted her. Why, he did not know, but she did, and one day she had told him so.

'The way you're looking at me, Peter,' she had said when they were alone together in his office. 'I think you're imagining me naked.'

Peter had been too stunned to reply. He had not needed to.

'You don't have to imagine, you know . . .'

And so had begun this insane affair, which he hated and loved in almost equal proportions. Almost.

And alongside this extraordinary and unexpected madness had come his great chance. His opportunity to break free from the confines of his unfulfilled career and make the world a better place. He had given a stunning parliamentary performance, he was on the front page of the *Evening Standard* and no doubt would be on all the other papers in the morning. His ideas were being debated on every radio chat show, his name damned and deified in the space of two callers, and he was having an affair with a beautiful, intelligent young woman who thought him a god and proudly undressed in front of him.

Peter felt himself reinvented, a man reborn. He returned Samantha's kisses. Enjoy it. You deserve it.

The Dog and Duck, Soho

Detective Sergeant Archer collected the pints of lager from the bar. He had not paid for them – policemen tend not to pay for things when going about their manors, not in Soho, at least. A perk of the job. And why not? What small business owner is going to charge his protector for a sandwich or a pint? Of course the girls in the doorways of Dean and Wardour Street knew that for some policemen *gratis* entitlement went beyond a lunchtime snack. Some policemen expected sex and money too. The girls in the doorways knew that some policemen ought to be locked up.

Detective Sergeants Archer and Sharp were two such policemen, but of late their cosy world of casual corruption had felt a chill wind blowing through its dirty streets. A commander from Dalston, an ex-Drug Squad detective, had been tasked with investigating his old colleagues. He had been very public in his assertion that corruption existed. He seemed to be getting close to naming names.

'The bloke's dangerous because he's stupid. And he's stupid because he thinks it fucking matters that we cream a few bob off here and there. Better we have it than the bastards who push the stuff, eh?'

'He's got an agenda. This is political. He wants to use us as an example to push his poxy legalization theories that him and his fucking MP have cooked up. He wants to say that if the drug laws are turning the cops bent then they have to change.'

'But that's just bollocks. There's always been bent cops. It's a tradition.'

'Tell me something I don't know.'

'There's no way he's going to pull it off, surely?'

'Not in a million years.'

'Well, I don't know. Even the Home Office are talking about decriminalizing skunk.'

'Toe in the water, window dressing, a sop to the liberals. It'll pass.'

'I just can't believe it. A copper, *one of our own*, trying to legalize drugs. That's betrayal, that is. That's turkeys voting for Christmas, that is. Commander Barry fucking Leman deserves what he gets.'

'Yes, and he needs to get it soon.'

'Exactly. Did you see that article he posted on the internet? "The only coppers who are making progress in the drugs war are the bent ones." '

'That's going to fill the public with confidence, I must say.'

'Problem is, he can prove it. He's been digging very deep. He knows what goes on. It's like Countryman all over again. And he's feeding everything to that MP mate of his. Our fucking business is getting discussed in Parliament!'

'Paget? He's a nonentity, a backbencher. Who'll listen to him?'

'Well, it was always going to be a nobody, wasn't it? No one with a snowball's chance of getting into power is ever going to say what Peter Paget's been saying, but anyway, Paget ain't the issue. Nobody is going to get drugs legalized in a million years. Our pensions are assured in that area, no sweat. Leman is the issue, because he's putting the spotlight on us. He needs to be told in no uncertain terms to mind his own fucking business.'

St Hilda's Church Hall, Soho

'I can't remember the last time I were knocked back when I tried to pull a bird, but Lulu was ever so nice about it. She said she was very flattered and all that but she'd just had her hair done, besides which she reckoned that once she got them leather trousers off

51

she'd never get 'em on again. So we had a laugh about it and I told her she was a top bird and she told me I was a right naughty young man so everyone was 'appy.

'Still, it *was* a knockback and I must say I did feel a bit of a twat when she turned round and buggered off as fast as she could back behind Elton's picket fence. I suppose it should have been a wake-up call, but when you've had a shedful of booze, about twenty noses full of charlie and a whole tab of E and all you've eaten is three Hard Rock chips nicked off a passing plate, you ain't very receptive to reality checks.

'So there I am, staggering around the backstage hospitality area trying to chill and looking for someone to pull, when suddenly the paps are all over me because they've realized that I'm looking pissed-up and lairy, and Emily, my betrothed, is nowhere to be seen. The press is supposed to be controlled backstage at the Brits, you know, stick to the music and no snapping the bird stars in their knickers (although most of them bird stars only *wear* knickers these days). There's supposed to be rules and journalistic integrity and all that. However, if the UK's number-one record-ing artist who is supposed to be happily engaged to a lord's daughter tries to pull Lulu in full public view, word gets around sharpish, so I was fookin' inundated. "What's happened to Emily, Tommy?" they were all shouting. So I says, "I dropped her, the engagement's off!" Well, that was it. Bang! They went crazy. Guaranteed Brits front page and I hadn't even been try-ing. Whatever poor sod won best newcomer that year was not going to make it into the papers, because once more I *was* the story of the Brits. "Why'd you do it, Tommy?" they shouted. "Because I didn't like her voice," I said. "It were grating on me nerves, and any-way I've gone off tattooed birds."

'Eventually my people managed to drag me back to me dressing room, but I still hadn't pulled and, like I say, coke and E just give me the horn like I don't know what. It doesn't strike everyone that way, but at the end of the day that's how it is for me. It's all about metabolism or whatever. I was gagging for it, I can tell you, shouting, "I need a bird! Get me a bird!" but we were trapped in my dressing room with hacks six deep outside.

'Well, you won't believe this, but it's true, I swear it's *fookin' true*. One of the A and R blokes has his girl-friend with him and he says that I can shag *her* if I like! I'm *not* lying!

'He sort of grinned knowingly and said, "Corkie's happy to do her duty by the record company." Corkie, that was her name. She's stood there, all blond hair and jewels in her belly-button and her *boyfriend* is offering her up for my delectation like a fookin' canape. Is it any wonder that I'm all screwed up in me 'ead?

'Well, that was it. I do have some fookin' sense of decorum, you know. I had a jug of vodka and orange in me 'and and I just whacked the bastard round the head with it. Crack! Bosh. Thank you very much and good night. It didn't break properly, as it goes, just at the handle, in fact, but it made a hell of a clunk and he went down like the sad immoral pimping bastard that he was.

'Want to know what the other A and R people said?'

The assembled recoverers most certainly did. This was one story worth missing work for.

'They said, "It's OK, it's OK. We can sort this out . . ." Not to him, mind, not to the bloke laid out on the floor in a puddle of vodka and orange, but to *me*! "We'll get him out and get him a doctor. It was an accident. It's OK, it'll be OK." That was what they said. I'd just assaulted their colleague but it's me that they're worrying about. It's me they're trying to protect. And why wouldn't they? I've got a twenty-seven-arena tour plus six stadiums, *six stadiums*, starting in a fortnight and there was no way I was going to make those dates if I was remanded without bail for GBH.'

House of Commons terrace

'Surely, Barry, you're not suggesting that the person who threatened your wife was a police officer?' Peter Paget put the drinks down on the table. He had decided on a large gin and tonic, while as usual the Commander drank only water.

'Yes, I think it was. I've been expecting some form of retaliation and it's beginning.'

'But why? We're trying to make the police's life easier, free up their time, let them get on with their proper job.'

'Peter, please don't be so naïve. We both know that there are plenty of bent coppers around. Bent coppers get paid in bent money and most of the bent money in this country is generated by the drugs trade and associated industries.'

'But phoning up and making threats—'

'I don't *know* it was a policeman. I merely suspect it was. But quite frankly it could be anyone. There are literally tens, possibly hundreds of thousands of people in London alone, *violent people*, who'll be ruined if we manage to get even a few drugs legalized, from the thugs at the school gates to the mega coke importer sitting on his yacht at Cannes. The fact that I received the threats even though you are by far the more prominent one in our little crusade makes me think that they have a specific agenda.'

'Police corruption?'

'Exactly. The caller mentioned corruption specifically, and there's no doubt that the effect of the failure of drug policy on the police morale is a powerful part of our argument. I want to show that the law is actually a corrupting influence on the force. Officers are helpless to enforce it and some end up breaking it instead. We're rocking a lot of boats here.'

'Yes, but it's absolutely bloody obvious that we aren't going to get what we want anyway. They'll never legalize drugs in this country. Just look at the editorials; they're calling me a crack-pusher and you PC Pothead.'

'The fact that you've even managed to get the issue *discussed* is bad enough for these people. We're pissing into their tent, Peter.'

The MP smiled ruefully. 'I should've gone for fox hunting.'

'Look, it was probably a hoax, and even if it wasn't it was directed at me, not you. I'm just saying you should be careful, that's all. Think about your life a bit, take stock. Is there anything that makes you personally vulnerable?'

'Of course there isn't.'

Across the table Samantha toyed with a glass of Chardonnay, thrilled to be attending such an important meeting.

The Groucho Club, Soho

For some members of the Groucho the great bore about the gentlemen's toilet is the number of other members who insist on using it for the purpose of urination.

Milton perched his large backside on the edge of the basin. 'You know what they should have done? Instead of putting in a bloody snooker room and that crappy little upstairs bar they should have put in an extra bog just for coke-sniffing. I mean it's bloody outrageous, isn't it? We have to sneak into a *toilet* to get our jollies like we're bloody criminals. What's more we come in here to *sniff*. I mean, under normal circumstances you wouldn't walk into a bloody toilet with the specific intention of taking a series of ruddy great sniffs, would you? But that's what we're forced to do. The one bloody activity that cannot be indulged in without deep inhalation and it has to take place in the bloody bog! It's disgusting and bloody unhygienic. *Particularly* this bog, which is heated and ventilated like the black hole of Calcutta and full of pissed-up, over-fed, fat, flabby-arsed flatulents like me. It's a bloody disgrace. Everybody knows that a percentage of the members of this club who use the toilet use it to snort coke. We pay our fees, don't we? We should have our own bog! They wouldn't even have to plumb it in, better not to, in fact, so that the farters wouldn't use it . . .'

Milton's companion, a showbiz manager who specialized in providing quite famous comedians to appear on blokey game shows, had chopped out a line of cocaine on the cistern. Milton lowered his big red nose towards it, and the folds of his sweaty neck bulged over his collar as he did so. He inhaled greedily.

'There we go . . . beautiful . . . aaaaaaaahhhh. Ooh! Yes! Oh yes. Very nice indeed. Brings tears to your eyes. Very, very nice indeed, thank you. Bloody should be, the price we're paying for it. Still, got to have the best tonight, I think. I'm onto something. Got a tip-off on the news desk, anonymous unfortunately, but I think it's genuine. Well, we shall see, shan't we? Peter Paget's daughter has been taking ecstasy. Yes, of course Paget the drug nutter, the bloke who wants to legalize everything. Not surprised he wants to legalize everything if his own daughter's a bloody space cadet, eh? Unbelievable. The double standards of these politcians is just gobsmacking! Remember the Home Secretary's son! Not to mention Prince sodding Harry. Mind you, at least HRH looked suitably horrified. This Paget bloke's just a hypocrite. Talk about corrupt.

Trying to change the law of the bloody land just to keep his kid out of trouble. I mean, if that isn't an abuse of his position as an MP I don't know what is. Well, that's how we'll spin it, anyway. We'll show these poxy politicians and their stuck-up little celebrity kids that nobody is above the law in this country and the British press will hound down any overprivileged little shit who thinks otherwise. I'm going to set one of my Rottweilers onto that Paget girl, you see if I don't. Aaaaahhhhh! Very nice. Very, very nice indeed. Chop us out another, will you? I'm going to have a slash.'

St Hilda's Church Hall, Soho

Tommy had paused briefly to get another cup of tea. Some of his audience seized the opportunity to make calls on their mobiles to inform colleagues that they would be late for work.

'Well, after they'd got the unconscious A and R man out of my dressing room (saying he'd slipped over while helping me with me yoga), I shagged his bird anyway, and it was top. She was as coked up as me and mad for it, so I gave her an E (not her first of the night, I reckon, by the way she were stroking all the furniture and everything) and gave her a right seeing-to. I do love a dirty girl with ideas of her own. It was the first time I've touched a dressing room fruit basket in years. The fruit in those things is always shite, like in hotels. It looks great and tastes of fook all. But I do recommend eating it off an E'd-up naked bird. It looks even better and who gives a fook what it tastes like?'

A council flat, Lambeth

François looked up at Jessie and smiled as the brown

57

melted slowly in the dirty spoon. 'OK, Jessie, I got a present for you. Make you feel good, real good. You like to feel good? Sure, everybody wanna feel good and this is the best stuff, baby. No bullshit, this is pure . . . What do you *think* it is, little girl? It's heroin, that's for sure, golden brown, like in the song. A little silver twist of magic to make the world OK. I just gotta warm it up a little, make it smooth and easy, like honey, OK? Don't worry, baby, I just give you a little taste, gotta brand new needle, too, see, straight outa the plastic wrapping. You ain't gonna get no Aids or hepatitis or nothing offa this. I told you, I'm looking after you now. You're my little girl. For sure are you lucky you met me.'

The skin on Jessie's unblemished arm was so white it almost glowed. So white it was translucent. François had no trouble finding one of the veins that ran pale blue beneath their gossamer cloak.

A female detention centre, Bangkok

'Please. Yow have to get me out. I'm desperate. I'll doy if they put me back in there.'

The girl from Birmingham who had been so excited to be buying cheap CDs in Bangkok wore a blue smock. Her hair was pulled back and gathered with an elastic band and her canvas shoes had no laces. The man sitting opposite her was the first English person she had spoken to in ages.

'Sonia, it's taken us two weeks to even get access to you. You have to understand that there is no possibility of our getting you out at present.'

'But . . . but . . .' Sonia stared in shock and bewilderment. 'I . . . want . . . to . . . go . . . howm.'

'Sonia, we only have an hour to talk. Pull yourself together and talk to us.'

The girl had fallen from her chair and was now writhing and weeping at the consular official's feet. She thrashed her bare, bruised legs about like the helpless trapped animal that she was.

'Sonia, please, get up! Pull yourself together. If you scream like that they'll certainly suspend our visit. Stop screaming, Sonia, calm down, please try to calm down . . . Stop it, Sonia! Stop hitting your face . . . If you hurt yourself they won't let us see you any more . . . There, sit on the chair, Sonia, stop hitting yourself! . . . That's better, OK now, breathe slowly. Focus on the moment. Here, wipe your eyes . . . Good . . . good . . . well done.'

A council flat, Lambeth

'Jessie! Come on, Jessie! You been out long enough. I didn't give you no big hit. Come on, baby, we got things to do . . .'

Slowly the ebony eyes opened. Dark ebony and blood red.

'OK, good. You hear me now? Sit up, little girl, get up offa that couch. I got stuff to say. OK, so we got some nice clothes here. Little skirt, booby tubey, all nice stuff, the best, make you look beautiful like I promised. First you gotta take off all that shit you wearing now. What you want jumpers and jeans and that stupid coat for? Make you look like a fucking tramp, girl, 'stead of a sexy baby which is what you gotta be. Come on, take all that stuff off now . . .'

Jessie was slowly coming to her senses. Was he asking her to strip off in front of him?

'Sure, in front of me, of course in front of me, that's for sure. What? You shy? That's a laugh, come on, baby, ain't no shy girls round here, 'cos they pretty soon starve to death, OK? So get those fucking filthy rags off and let me see what I got here! You hear me, bitch! I wanna see how clean you are. You don't wanna take your clothes off? Who cares what you want, girl, you think I'm interested in what you want?'

She pulled her big coat closer about her. Trying to remember where she was. Who she was.

'OK, baby, I'm gonna tell you this right now and I'm only gonna tell it once. If you're a good girl and do like I say I'm gonna give you another little taste right now. Sure, baby, more honey in your arm and you can have it any time you want. But if you keep sniffling and moaning and standing in that corner crying like some little kid who don't know the score, then I'm gonna have to mess you up good, you hear? I'm gonna whack you till your own mother wouldn't recognize you . . .'

The skinny girl with no home began to cry. It would make no difference whether her mother recognized her or not. Her mother had betrayed her. In fact, she had no mother.

'OK, bitch, you makin' me do this! There!' It took very little effort to knock her off her feet.

'Now, you listening to me, right? Get up off the floor, I don't want no blood on my floor, you dirty bitch! You want I should punch you again? You gonna get up and take your clothes off, or do I tear them offa you then cut you up good?'

Jessie raised herself to her feet and undressed.

'That's better . . . That's nice. Very nice. Cute, that's for sure. OK, Jessie . . . Now you letting me see what you got I reckon you're a sweet-looking baby and that's lucky for you, Jessie, because I'm telling you now that food don't come for free around here, no way, and shelter gotta be rented, oh yeah, that's for sure too, baby. What's more that arm candy you liked so much is gotta get paid for too and that costs plenty. In fact you already owe me for what you had, you gotta give me money for the hit you been on . . .'

One of Jessie's arms stretched across her naked breasts, the other reached down below her waist. It had been into this arm that François had made his puncture mark; a congealed trickle of blood lay dark upon the whiteness. Jessie's eyes widened in fear . . . Surely that had been a gift?

'What, you thought that good golden smack was *free*? You think I can afford to *give* it away? You dumb or something? You give me some money right now or you don't get these nice new clothes I bought you, which incidentally you gotta pay for too. Hey, baby, if you got no money then you're in big trouble, real big trouble . . . It ain't me, little girl, but some of the guys I work with. I'm scared for you, real scared. They really bad people, especially when selfish ungrateful little Scottish bitches think they get to eat, sleep and get high for free while François pays!'

Jessie could not wipe away the tears without further revealing her nakedness and so they just rolled down her cheeks and fell.

'Listen, baby, I'll tell you what. We can sort this out, OK? It can be cool. You don't have to get cut up none if you don't want to. If you don't got no money then all you gotta do is go to work, OK? Like I said, that's one cute little body you got there. Lotta guys like skinny, scared, fucked-up little girls. They gonna pay a lotta money for a piece of what you got. In fact, you know what? Since you owe me for that last jack I put in your veins, I can be your first client, baby. Oh yeah, you come over here right now.'

New Scotland Yard

It was the first time that Commander Leman had been in the office of London's Chief Constable, the most senior policeman in the country. This was the pinnacle, the highest point to which a police officer might aspire, and the most Olympian height from which to be crapped on.

Commander Leman had not been offered a chair.

'I don't like publicity hunters, Leman.' The Chief Constable had not even greeted him, nor had he deigned to look up from the papers on which he was working. He barked his comments directly at the set of annotated minutes that lay before him.

'I believe that a policeman, whatever his rank, is no more than a part of a team. Of course he must show initiative and think independently within the force, but from the outside he should be entirely anonymous. Particularly to the media. My father used to say that a gentleman's name should appear in the newspapers only thrice in his lifetime. When he is born, when he is married and when he dies.'

'I agree, sir.'

'Do you? Do you indeed? Then how is it, I wonder, that half the nation seems to know your name, Commander? How is it that I have received fifty press inquiries on the subject of no one but yourself this morning alone?'

'I've been investigating corruption in the Drug Squad, sir.'

'You have been washing the Met's dirty linen in public, Commander.'

'No, sir. I've named no names and I've made no specific allegations and won't do so until I have proof, something which I'm aware I may never get. All I have done is state the self-evident fact that a small minority of police officers have been corrupted by the enormous profits to be made in the drug trade . . .'

'You say you have no proof. How can anything be self-evident without proof?'

'I have no proof that an invisible force anchors me to the ground, sir. Nonetheless I consider the existence of gravity self-evident or else I'd float away.' Leman knew that it was madness to offer up such cheek, but he had never in his life been able to stomach those in authority using their position to be pompous.

'You are blackening the name of the Metropolitan Police. What is more, you are giving your personal opinions on matters of politics to anyone who will listen.'

'I'm responding to the inquiries of my constituency MP on a subject of national urgency. How should I reply other than with the truth?'

'Your opinions are not necessarily the truth, Commander.'

'Do you deny that there is corruption within the Drug Squad, sir?'

The Chief Constable did not reply. He fixed his gaze as if absorbed by some matter or other in the minutes that lay before him.

Leman pursued his advantage. 'Sir! The current situation is insane. The police must speak out on the subject. If we don't, who will? We're on the front line. If the government decided tomorrow to declare war on the whole world I'm sure that professional soldiers would feel it within their right to speak up on the utter impracticality of the policy. Well, we are being asked to pursue the whole population, and I consider this to be no less ridiculous. Britain is an outlaw society! A criminal nation! Every country is.'

'You don't need to employ your sensationalist rhetoric with me, Commander. I have read your internet site.'

'Then surely you must agree, sir, that we in the police are entirely impotent in the face of our sworn duty to uphold the law. *We can't do it!* The *only* police officers who are winning in the drugs war are the bent ones.'

'You have no proof of that!'

'I have the proof of common sense and human nature, sir! All power corrupts. If history teaches us nothing else it teaches us that—'

'I will not be lectured to in my own office, Commander!'

'I'm sorry, sir, but all power corrupts and absolute power corrupts absolutely. Well, there's no greater power than to live beyond the law. The rule of law is at the heart of a civilized society and yet on every street in the country the law is in disrepute! The illegal economy is awash with trillions of pounds of easy money and it's madness to suppose that this does not have a cancerous effect on the police. We have to sit and watch evil people who we are powerless to touch grow richer and richer and richer. We have to sit and watch as guns flood the streets and gangs take control of estates. Is it any wonder that some officers are corrupted? In the long run if your side has lost the war a practical man considers joining the victors.'

There was a silence. The Chief Constable did not like being harangued. On the other hand, he was a reasonable man. 'I will protect you for as long as I can, Commander, but whatever your private convictions I would advise you to temper your rhetoric in public. Being right does not usually make a man popular and it certainly hasn't done so in your case. You're not popular, Leman. Not with the media and not within the police. Both are powerful enemies.'

The Leman household, Dalston

As Commander Leman got out of his car a figure emerged from the darkness. Leman sensed a second man behind him. He knew that it was possible that they had come to kill him. If they had, these would be his final thoughts. The faces of his wife and daughter sprang almost unbidden to the forefront of his mind.

'Commander Leman?'

He knew the voice. 'Detective Sergeant Archer?'

There was a pause. The shadowy figure had not expected to be so readily identified. 'Why would you think that?'

'Because I've listened to your voice on a number of occasions.'

'Phone-tapping. Very naughty. Very inadmissable.'

'Perhaps soon I shall have sufficient cause to apply for a warrant.'

The second figure spoke from behind him. 'And perhaps soon your missus will have sufficient cause to put on black.'

Commander Leman did not turn round. 'You may kill me if you wish. It isn't a difficult thing to do. But know this. All that I've unearthed is contained within a file kept secretly with a colleague and addressed to the Chief Constable.'

'If there was any proof in it you'd have already sent it.'

'Certainly, that's true. But if I were to be killed, then it seems likely that the Chief Constable would take a greater interest in my suspicions and the circumstantial evidence I've amassed. I've written a letter detailing those I think might want me dead. Your name is on it, DS Archer . . . And yours, DS Sharp.' For the first time Leman turned round.

'We ain't thinking of killing you, Leman. Snitches and grasses like you ain't worth the price of a bullet. But there's another reason your wife might want to put on mourning. Same goes for you.'

'Don't your missus tell you about the phonecalls she gets? Calls concerning your daughter. Pretty little Anna. Sweet fifteen.'

Commander Leman tried with all his might to make his reply sound as convincing as any sentence he had ever uttered. 'If any harm comes to any member of my family I shall kill you both.'

'Oh no!' Archer sneered. 'I'm shittin' myself. Nighty-night, Commander Leman, and don't forget: little Anna's safety is in your hands.'

Samantha's flat, Islington

Peter Paget had never felt so wonderful in his entire life. Astonishingly, and without warning, even the ever-present feelings of guilt that lay heavily in his stomach had disappeared. He had not a care in the world. Everything was beautiful. He had also developed a deep fascination with the tactile properties of water.

'I can't believe that I've lived for forty-three years on this planet and I've never understood the texture of water before . . . I mean really *felt* it. Do you understand what I mean, Sammy?'

'It's beautiful.'

'That is so perfect, Sammy, the perfect word for the perfect thing. Water is beautiful.'

Sammy's feet rested on Peter Paget's shoulders; his were under her arms. The bath was not really built for two and yet for them it was just right; it seemed to mould itself so naturally to their bodies that it might have been designed around them.

'I love you, Sammy, you're the most perfectly wonderful human being in existence. No, I really mean that. You are truly, deeply and completely wonderful.'

'You are too, Peter. It's kind of awe inspiring how beautiful you are, it's like you've been reborn into perfection.'

Eventually they got out of the bath and dried each other by the light of many candles. The towels felt like cotton wool. The lino on which they stood was exquisite to their feet, firm and delightfully smooth. They towelled each other gently for what seemed like a lifetime, a lifetime spent in heaven.

'We have all night, beautiful Sammy, beautiful, beautiful, beautiful Sam-an-the-e-e-r-r.' He pronounced the syllables separately and luxuriously, tasting them on his tongue, feeling their weight, their shape. Experiencing the loveliness of her name. 'There's a late sitting at the house. Angela knows not to call.'

'Your wife is lovely. She's very, very beautiful.'

'Yes she is, she's very, very, very beautiful.'

'I think that if she was feeling as we do now, she'd understand.'

'Yes, I believe she would.'

And he did believe it. Angela was lovely and she loved him and everything was all right.

Naked, they walked from the bathroom into Samantha's living room, a room lit only by the rich, crimson, velvety light of a two-bar electric fire. They drank deep from jugs of the purest glittering tap water. The hint of citrus imparted by the lemon slices was delicious in a way that Peter Paget had not previously experienced.

On the table Samantha's little pill-box lay open. Inside, two tablets of E remained, the symbol of the dove embossed on their centres.

'This stuff is amazing. Quite utterly wonderful. Why did I wait so long?'

'No regrets, my love.'

She took up the pill-box. Beside the ecstasy lay a collection of small blue diamond-shaped pills. She placed one on her tongue and offered another to Peter Paget. 'It's Viagra.'

'Viagra?'

'Sure, everybody's doing it. I like to make love on E but sometimes it's not easy, it's too intense, too much, so we'll just take these, eat some fruit, put on some sounds, chill a little, and in an hour you can fuck me to heaven.'

St Hilda's Church Hall, Soho

'Look, I know this is a long story, but I've got the conch, 'aven't I? I have to tell this story my way or it ain't therapy, is it? Anyway, it's a good story, the papers would pay a mint for it and you lot are getting it just because you're alcoholics. How good is that? So where was I? Oh yeah, at the Brits. Well, you'll never guess what happens next, you will never guess who comes knocking on me dressing-room door just as the A and R bloke's bird was trying to wipe kiwifruit out of her arse . . .

'Only a *fookin' copper*! Only a Commander of Her Majesty's Constabulary! Can you believe it? Backstage at the Brits! That's like Islamic fookin' Jihad turning up at a Barbra Streisand concert! A copper at the Brits! Fook me, if he'd had a sniffer dog with 'im I reckon they'd have had to close down *Top of the Pops* for ten years till we all got out of prison. I were *shitting* meself. At first I thought the bastard had turned up to do me for kicking Emily out of the limo. I thought her dad, his Lordship, must have got me sentenced to be beheaded or whatever, but it turns out he had an *appointment*! My tosser of a tour manager comes in and tells me that I'd agreed to meet some cop and a poxy MP who wanted to talk about drug abuse. Well, *fook me!* There I am, coked and E'd up to me eyeballs, I've got a fruit-covered, half-naked bird who's on one too, a bagful of the charlie on the table, and my tour manager wants me to talk to a copper and an MP.'

The Brit Awards, Docklands Arena

Peter Paget MP beamed proprietorially at Tommy. He felt that artists and singers were his type of people. He was an important person himself, after all, the politician of the hour, the man everybody was talking about. He had a right to be in Tommy Hanson's dressing room. The only shame had been that he had been unable to persuade Hanson's management to issue Samantha with a backstage pass. Still, he'd got her a seat for the ceremony, which had thrilled her no end. She was only twenty-three, after all. It was her culture that was being celebrated.

'I am so grateful that you've agreed to see me, Mr Hanson – or perhaps I might call you Tommy? I'm Pete.'

'Um . . . OK. Yeah. Whatever.'

'I feel certain that you and I share the same agenda on drugs, Tommy.'

'Yeah, def', big time.'

'Which is to protect children and young people from the consequences of drug use.'

With enforced casualness Tommy Hanson perched himself on the edge of the table, positioning himself between his two visitors and the open bag of cocaine. 'Well yeah, for sure. Yeah, big up to that. I mean, like, we've got to get the kids off drugs, that's like really really important. I mean, just say no, that's my message . . .'

Behind him Corkie finished adjusting her top and gathered up her little bag, a bag just big enough to hold a set of keys, a packet of Marlboro Lights, a wrap of cocaine and two Es. Tommy did his best to play the host, but of course he could not rise from his defensive position on the table. 'This is . . . I'm sorry, I've forgotten your name, love.'

'Corkie.'

'Corkie, right, yeah, well, um. See you, then, Corkie.'

'See you, Tommy, it's been mental.'

'Yeah right . . . You've got a bit of star fruit in your hair.'

'And half a kiwi in my knickers. Good luck tonight. I'll be cheering.'

'Thanks. See ya . . .'

Corkie left. Tommy turned once more to his unexpected guests.

'Lovely girl. Known her all me life. So um . . . What were we talking about again?'

'Young people and drugs.'

'Yeah, right, we've really really got to get them off all that stuff. I really really believe that big time. That stuff is evil and it does your 'ead in.'

Peter Paget smiled indulgently. Had this guy really managed to remain unaware of the media frenzy that his Private Member's Bill had been causing? 'Tommy, mate, I'm not talking about trying to get the kids *off* drugs.'

'You're not?'

'No way. I mean that's just not ever going to happen, is it?'

'Um, in't it? I thought that was the whole point of . . . I mean, in't that what we're all trying to . . . Look, what are we talking about?'

For the first time the policeman spoke up. 'Mr Hanson, we believe it is time to accept the fact that young people take drugs and recognize that the most serious consequence of this is their involvement with criminals. We all know what the real side-effects of drug use are.'

Tommy was swaying now, his hands gripping the side of the table on which he sat, his face a picture of hopeless, helpless concentration. 'Yeah, right, 'course we do . . . The munchies, right?'

'I mean the social consequences.'

'Well, that's what I'm saying, in't I? You try finding something to eat at five in the morning in this fookin' country. Sometimes you have to drive miles and then all there is is kebabs or fookin' petrol stations. In the States you can buy a car twenty-four hours a day. A fookin' house if you want.'

'I'm talking about associating with criminals, Mr Hanson. Even for weekend recreational users every night out means maintaining a direct financial relationship with dealers and pushers of deeply dubious character. These people are often violent, they charge extortionate prices for on the whole highly suspect products. Surely any sane person would agree that it is this aspect of drug use from which young people must be protected.'

'Well, you've got that right. I can't tell you how many times I've . . . I mean people I know have been ripped off.'

'That's the least of it. The unlucky minority who become full-time users are forced into lives of crime themselves in order to maintain their criminal habit.'

Peter Paget was fidgeting, clearly anxious to re-enter the conversation. 'Some become crack whores.'

'Crack whore' was a term he had only recently come across. Samantha had heard it in an American film and Peter had found that it packed a terrific punch.

'Well, yeah, absolutely. Right. Look . . . Sorry an' all that, but where you going with all this? I mean, am I being thick or what?'

'What we are advocating, Mr Hanson,' continued the policeman, 'is the legalization of drugs.'

'Fook me, I thought you were a copper.'

'I am. A copper who would like to wipe out the vast majority of the crime in this country by the changing of a single law.'

'That's brilliant. Fair play to you.'

'But most people prefer to ignore the problem,

pretend it doesn't exist. We want to make people aware of the extent of drug use in this country. What we're saying is that the law is making criminals of an entire generation and that we all have to suffer the consequences of their crimes. We need somebody, somebody young, very high profile, a hero, an icon, to associate with our cause, to come forward and admit to their own regular drug use and to that of their friends. Someone who will be completely upfront and cut through the bullshit, someone who will explain that he moves in a circle where drug use is an integral part of the recreational lifestyle. We need someone to talk about what their experiences of drugs were at school, at raves and at rock concerts. Someone to spark a national debate.'

St Hilda's Church Hall, Soho

'Yeah, just like Noel Gallagher did when he said getting on an E was like having a cup of tea. The only fookin' debate he sparked was the entire press and politicians and cops and whatever crapping on his head from a very great height. They made him out to be some kind of irresponsible moron for saying what everyone knows anyways, which is that as far as the lads and lasses down my way are concerned, E is the new lager. But as it happens I wasn't even thinking of the shit I'd be getting into if I agreed to be this daft twat's stooge, because – get this – *I didn't believe a word he was saying*. I was that strung out on charlie that I had that well-known "side effect", as the cop would have put it, of suddenly being completely and utterly paranoid.

'Honest, if you do enough coke – and any user will tell you there ain't never *ever* enough – you can believe your own mum hates your guts and thinks your music's crap. So obviously being a nose-bleeder from way back I was convinced that this was a sting, right? An entrapment or whatever. I reckoned that all I had to do was say, "Yeah, sure, I've been a coke'ead for years and all my old mates would be coke'eads too if they had the dosh but instead they're all fookin' up their 'eads with dodgy speed," and about fifty Drug Squad goons would leap out of the beer fridge and stick me away for ever.

'So, let me tell you, I ignored the MP bastard and gave my answer straight to the copper. Bein' very careful to enunciate every word.'

The Brit Awards, Docklands Arena

'I don't know what you're talking about, pal. I never take drugs of any sort and my message to young people out there is "Just say no."'

Peter Paget was about to attempt to argue the point, but Leman was a shrewd judge of character and knew not to waste his breath. 'Well, in that case I can only thank you for your time, Mr Hanson, and wish you good luck at tonight's ceremony . . . One piece of advice: I'd wipe your top lip before you go on if I were you.'

St Hilda's Church Hall, Soho

'He got up and buggered off and I went and looked in the mirror and nearly crapped meself. I had so much marching powder on my face I looked like Father fookin' Christmas. Except Father Christmas don't usually have little trickles of blood running out of both nostrils.'

A female detention centre, Bangkok

The man from the Consulate was relieved to find Sonia much calmer this time.

'Tell me how the prison authorities are treating you.'

'There are eighteen of us in our room . . . I'm the ownly English girl . . . All the others are Thai. I never understand anythink so I'm always in trouble. I'm sick, I down't loik the food, we never wash. Sometimes I dream that I'm back in Brum, gowing shopping in the Bull Ring or 'aving KFC with moi mates and then I wake up and I want to kill myself so badly that I throw up and then the other girls get really angry. I've tried to do it twoice, but they down't let you have nothink dangerous, not even shoelaces. I drank the stuff we scrub the floor with but I just puked up a bit of blood and the doctor made me drink a loud of milk and then I was in even more trouble with the other girls . . . Please, yow've got to make them understand, I don't belong 'ere, I made one mistake, I'm not a killer or a rapist or anythink. I just met this blowk at a rave . . . He promised me an 'oliday in Thailand and a thousand quid and . . . He said nowbody ever got caught. I can't believe it's happened, it ain't real, it can't be . . . I've got a loif in England . . . moi mates, moi bedroom, moi mum, they're all still there but I'm not . . . I just met a bloke at a rave . . .'

The Brit Awards, Docklands Arena

'Hey, Tony, what's going on? I mean, what the *fook* is going on? That were a copper, man! A policeman! I'm carrying about a ton of charlie and you bring a copper into my space! I mean, what was all that about, man?'

'Tom, Tom, calm down, man, it's cool, it's cool.'

'It's *not* fookin' cool! It in't remotely cool. That were a copper!'

'He's a cool copper. Very hip. Besides, you said you wanted to see him, Tom, you said to set it up. It's all on your schedule, look . . .'

'You know I don't read the fookin' schedule. Why d'ya think I have a fookin' entourage? Why d'ya think I have people? They in't there just to drink my booze, you know! I have people to read my schedule!'

'I swear, Tom, you told me to bring the bastards to the Brits! It was Emily who put you on to him.'

'Fookin' Emily. What's she got to do with it? I dropped her.'

'Don't you remember her telling you about that bill in Parliament? Peter Paget the MP and that batty copper who wants to legalize drugs! He's been in all the papers, you know: PC Pothead! She's mad for all that is Emily, it's her crusade.'

'Course she is, she's a coke'ead, she's worse than me. 'Course she wants to legalize it, silly cow, like it's difficult to get anyway.'

'Yeah, well, she got you all wound up that night we were at Soho House. You must remember, you said you wanted to meet PC Pothead.'

St Hilda's Church Hall, Soho

'Well, then I did remember. Emily had got all evangelical about it, told me I had to get involved, help this campaign and all that, give it a public profile. Yeah, right. Great idea, that. Why don't I completely destroy my career in about ten seconds by getting on some nutter's bandwagon what he's probably only doing for his own career anyway? Hey, listen, we all do drugs, you know that. Fookin' 'ell, Prince Harry's a pot-head by all accounts. Everyone knows I do 'em and I don't mind, to be quite frank. Publicity-wise, drugs have not done me any harm at all, quite the opposite in fact. All my "drug hell"s and trips to rehab have been very colourfully reported as I'm sure you're aware, and incidentally made me look right fookin' hard when I was still trying to shake the pretty boy thing after I done *Pop Hero*. People expect a bit of drug hell from their celebs, don't they? But whereas nobody minds you *doing* drugs, you can do as many as you like, and you can *talk* about it as much as you like, you have to remember one thing: drugs are *evil* and whenever anybody asks, you say so, that they're evil and you've kicked 'em, or you're trying to kick 'em, because you only took refuge in 'em because of your demons anyway. And any kid that does 'em is mad and needs help and counselling and the whole thing's a wicked shame which you deeply regret. As long as you remember to say all that, you can stick the gross national product of Bolivia up your nose every night of the fookin' week and people will see it for what it is, right? A laugh. Having it large. No 'arm done.'

The Brit Awards, Docklands Arena

'Listen, Tommy, forget about the copper, he's gone. I made it sweet, I gave him some merchandise and all that, but look, something's happened. I wouldn't tell you till after the ceremony, but there's that many press around they might get onto it and I don't want you to hear it from them.'

'What? What's happened?'

'It's bad.'

'Robbie Williams ain't cracked America, has he?'

'Tom, it's your auntie. Someone done her flat in. She was there, she got worked over.'

St Hilda's Church Hall, Soho

'You see, this is where Peter Paget and PC Pothead have got it all wrong. I mean, it's all very well for them to be going on about legalizing all drugs an' that, but there's a lot of evil drug addicts out there that *should* be locked up. Like the bastard that did over my auntie's house in Salford, for instance. I expect you saw it in the papers. That was all going on while I was on me way to the Brits, except the press didn't make the connection until after 'cos it's my mum's sister, so it's a different name. I love my auntie, we're a very close family us Hansons, and this fooked-up smackhead whacked her. That's the evil side of drugs, mate, I can tell you, an' as far as I'm concerned they should cut the bastard's bollocks off.'

A squat, Salford

Everything in the room was at floor level – the mattress, the mould-filled coffee mugs, the rotting takeaway food cartons, the cigarette butts, and the people. There was virtually no furniture.

'I was nearly out of there, man, but she come back from the shops. I was nearly out of there, two more minutes, but she come back, didn't she? Come back and started screaming an' all.'

'Was there any money? Did you score yet, Jay?'

The girl wasn't listening to the boy; she was lost in her desperate craving.

The boy wasn't listening to the girl; he was back in the flat, beating the old woman.

'I whacked her. What could I do? She was screaming, Natalie. I was stood standing in her living room with her video recorder under me arm and she was screaming. I fucking whacked her. But she was still screaming

77

and I freaked out, Nat. I just freaked out. I punched her in the face and then grabbed this thing off the top of the telly and bashed her head with it. Then I just fucking ran.'

'But you got the video, right? You stole some stuff? Have you got any smack, Jay? We need to score some smack.'

'She was screaming, man.'

'Jay . . . I'm totally strung out here. Have you got any—'

'Oh yeah, yeah, me too, yeah, sorry, I got it. Yeah, no worries. I'll cook it up, yeah . . .'

The crystals dissolved in the dirty spoon.

'It's just she was screaming, Nat, freaked me out . . . Get me works, will you? There was cash for sure. In a fucking biscuit tin. I got a video and it was weird, Nat, because she had these fucking . . . awards! Yeah, it was one of them that I whacked her with. I didn't notice what it was at first but then I saw it all shiny with blood on it and there was all pictures of Tommy fucking Hanson on the wall. What's all that about, eh?'

'Maybe she's a fan. He plays granny music now, anyway.'

'I didn't want to beat her up, Nat, but she came back and she was screaming an' all . . .'

'You had to do it, Jay, you had to . . . Come on, in't it ready yet? Hit me up, for fuck's sake.'

'Yeah, yeah, beautiful . . . Give us your arm, then . . . She just wouldn't shut up, Nat.'

But Natalie's arm had long since become a ruination. Jason had forgotten that for a moment. She pulled down her tracksuit bottoms and, raising a knee, presented her bruised and prick-marked groin to Jason. She wore no knickers.

'There's some good ones up by me cunt . . . You had to do it, Jay. I were getting desperate, really strung out. Besides, we got to get some food . . . and nappies and stuff for Ricky. He's had that one on all day.'

'Yeah.'

'Did you get any while you was out?'

'Nat! For fuck's sake! I just done over a fuckin' old lady's flat and then I whacked her with an award! I ain't been down fuckin' Tesco's for nappies! I just done the job, went round Zani's, scored the smack and then come straight home.'

'Yeah, yeah, 'course . . . Well, we'll go out later, soon as you've hit me up. Oh yes, that is fucking fantasti . . .'

St Hilda's Church Hall, Soho

'Look, I'm not proud of this, but after my new manager Tony told me about my auntie I decided that I really needed some brown. That was my way of dealing with it. I was just so angry. Some evil bastard had beaten up my aunt. That was all I knew at the time – that she'd been done over and was in hospital. He was robbing her flat, see, some poxy smack'ead for sure, it's always fookin' smack'eads round our way. Every other kid seems to be strung out these days. All the cops could see had been nicked was the video and that's a sure sign of a smack'ead. All those pathetic fooks ever nick is the video or whatever, just grab enough to flog for another hit and fook off. I was so angry I would 'a killed the bastard if I could. Beating up a woman in her own home . . . Cowardly, pathetic bastard. I'll tell you what: if PC Pothead, who wants to help drug addicts, had come back in right then and there I'd have told him to string 'em up, every one of 'em, the bastards. Cut their hands off! Beating up my auntie for a poxy VCR which he'd sell for a quarter of its value and then doing the whole thing again the next day. Fookin' bastard.

'Look, I can see what you're thinking, but I never beat anyone up to get a hit even before I had money. Well, I didn't do that stuff then, just a few pills. Anyway, I were really upset and what with all the stuff I had swilling round my system I knew that I needed to chill. After all, I did have to do a number later, climax o' the show, and "Let me be the tattoo on your thigh" is a bloody long sentence if you're totally out of your head. So I had to find a way to mellow out, and I'm here to tell you that there ain't no better way to mellow out than H. So in a way it were medicinal. I were being professional, weren't I?

'Look, I don't bother with heroin at all as a rule. Well, it's all a bit heavy, in't it? Like coke is just a laugh, I reckon, but smack is proper drugtaking. Serious big-boy stuff. You can't be messin' about wi' it. I've only ever smoked it, anyway, so it's not like taking it properly or anything, is it? But at the end o' the day, I needed to chill out very badly. What with the coke paranoia and coppers barging into my dressing room and, if I'm honest, feeling a bit bad about kicking Emily out on her arse like that. And trying to shag Lulu, and whacking that A and R man in the face, then eating fruit off his bird and banging her on the coffee table, and then hearing about my auntie . . . I were feeling really, really not together at all. So I gave me man a bell and told him to get his arse in a car and bring some stuff over pronto and I'd have someone leave a security pass for him at the artists' entrance.

'Well, you'll never believe it. Well, actually you will believe it, but I didn't, not at the time. The bloke said, "Sorry, Tommy, I can't get you any."

'Now that to me was unbe-fookin'-lievable. Because nobody and I mean *nobody* ever tells me I can't have something when I say I want it. It just *does not* happen. I have people. I have a posse, a crew and every member of that posse knows I get what I want, when I want it.

Like Oasis said, "All my people, right here, right now." That's the rule: if you're in my gang you jump when you're told. Because let's be honest, if you've sold fifteen million records in under two years then you *deserve* to get everything you want, and also never to be contradicted. Fifteen million albums means you get the lot, no questions asked, and I wanted some smack. "Listen, you dozy hippy!" I said. "Get me some horse or you can forget hanging around with me and pullin' the birds I don't want."

'Well, he started telling me all about how it weren't his fault, that the Thai police had been cracking down at Bangkok Airport. He said Thailand wanted the next Olympics or the next tour of Riverdance or whatever, and so they were papering over their druggy reputation. That don't mean having a go at Mr Big or anything, no, just nicking a few of the donkeys who bring the heroin over stuffed up their arses or whatever.

'Well, frankly, as far as I was concerned, *who gave a fook*?

'When you want some smack there's only one short conversation to have, and that is have you got any or haven't you? Everything else is an irrelevance. I was so angry. I bunged the mobile in the bog pan and tried to flush it, but it wouldn't go, so I kicked the bog with my steel-capped Wannabes and cracked the bowl, then I pulled the cistern off the wall of the Portakabin and with a couple of gallons of water pouring over me I raised it up above me 'ead. Then I bunged it through me dressing room mirror, cutting me 'and on the glass and knocking the pisspoor little cardboard wall over right into the next dressing room, which contained some three-bird girl group stood there in their bras. Not sure who they were – they were white, so it might have been Atomic Kitten but maybe not.

'Well, you'd 'a thought they might have got arsey

about a pissed-up wally crashing through their wall with half a bog in his 'ands, but don't forget I'm Tommy fookin' Hanson, so for these birds Christmas had arrived early.

'They shrieked and giggled and said stuff like, "Wild, Tommy. Mental. Top entrance. Big up!" and for a split second I were that monged I thought, "I know what I'll do, I'll shag all three of 'em. That'll calm me down." So I gets up off the floor and says, "All right, girls, sorry to burst in on you in your shreddies," and they said, "These ain't our shreddies, Tommy, we're in costume," and it's true, them bras and knickers was their *stage costumes*. Birds, eh? What must their mums think. So I said, "Well, how about getting out of costume, then, eh? Tits out for Tommy or what? I'll show you me knob," and they all shrieked again and laughed and said I was "dead mental", but I don't know if they would have come across because then I just sort of collapsed. Literally. My legs gave way and when Tony came in with Christophe, my gofer, I was curled up on the sofa fookin' sobbing me eyes out like some kid with these three stupid Scouser birds stood there wondering if it was a wind-up or what.

'Basically, if you do as much shit as I do it's about getting the mix right. The right amount of booze, the perfect proportion of charlie, maybe only half an E, or whatever. Quite frankly, in my experience the difference between a half and three-quarters can be the difference between a nice mellow chill and smashing up your dressing room and then bursting into tears on a girl-group's sofa.'

The Leman household, Dalston

'What, may I ask, are you doing up?'
    'Dad. I'm fifteen.'

'Yes, I know that, Anna. Now, returning to my question, what are you doing up? It's past midnight on a school day.'

'Did you meet him?'

'And again we return to the core of the issue, what are you do—'

'Dad! Shut up! Did you meet him?'

'Meet who?'

'Don't be sad. It's so sad the way you think you're funny when you're not.'

'Yes, I met him.'

'Unreal! Absolutely, totally unreal! You met him! I cannot believe you met him!'

'Well, I did.'

'What's he like?'

'He's a stupid, arrogant, spoilt brat.'

'No way! That is *so* not true.'

'It so is true. I've met him.'

'You were probably being a pain. Trying to be funny or something.'

'I did not try to be funny.'

'Well then, you're just jealous because he's the most fantastic person on earth and you're a boring policeman.'

'Well, put like that, who wouldn't be jealous?'

'Did you get his autograph and loads of stuff?'

'Stuff?'

'You know – hats, tour jackets, fleeces, T-shirts. *Stuff*, Dad. They give all that to people who meet them.'

'Well, nobody gave me anything, I'm afraid.'

Suddenly Anna was fighting back the tears. 'You're pathetic, Dad! Pathetic! I hate you! You were probably being all know-it-all and pig-like! You probably put him off! I can't believe it! My dad does one decent thing in his whole life by meeting Tommy Hanson and he doesn't even get any stuff!'

'I'm sorry. I didn't think.'

'But I *told* you to get his autograph.'

'And I said I would if it was appropriate and it wasn't.'

'It's always appropriate to get Tommy's autograph. He loves his fans, he says so. He loves us. He'll never be too big to chill with his fans.'

'That's very commendable, but it really wasn't the time for me to ask for an autograph . . . But I did get myself a nice new baseball cap, look, and a mug and a fleece, and a scarf and a programme. Sadly no tour jacket but everything has been pre-signed by Tommy. Mr Hanson's tour manager assured me so.'

'Dad, that's *fantastic*! Give me!'

'You want my stuff? Can't I keep any of it?'

'Dad!'

'Oh, all right.'

'Look, he's signed everything!'

'As I say, I didn't see him do it.'

'Yeah, right, like Tommy's going to lie to his fans about a thing like that.'

'No, absolutely. Of course not . . . Anna, do you think Tommy Hanson takes drugs?'

'He did, everybody knows that, but he's kicked it. It's in his autobiography. He struggles with an addictive personality. He's got demons. It's very hard being Tommy.'

'He hasn't given up.'

'He has. He said.'

'When I met him he had cocaine all over his top lip.'

'No! That is so *cool*!'

Anna was halfway up the stairs when Commander Leman called her back.

'Anna. You do think about what I told you, don't you? Every day?'

'Yes, Dad. God, how many more times?'

'Every day, Anna. Every single day you have to remind yourself that I've made you a potential target. I couldn't bear it if I thought you took the threat made against you lightly.'

'I don't, Dad, and you haven't made me anything. You have to do your job. I'm proud of you.'

'How many rape alarms do you have? Where are they as of this instant?'

'Five. Schoolbag. Jacket pocket. Handbag. Under pillow. Gaffered to handlebars of bike.'

'Under what circumstances would you set one off?'

'At the slightest hint of suspicion. Bugger embarrassment.'

'Good. Most important that. At the *slightest* hint. Bugger embarrassment.'

'Don't worry.'

'And where is your pepper spray at this moment?'

In one quick and decisive movement Anna Leman reached into the breast pocket of her pyjamas and the Commander suddenly found himself facing the tiny nozzle of the illegal little can that he had procured for her. If ever it were discovered that he had removed one from the station he would almost certainly lose his job, but that was not an issue. He smiled at the girl standing on the stairs, legs apart, both arms outstretched, the can held in her hands like a movie cop's Magnum. He half expected her to say 'Freeze!' Strange how young she seemed when discussing the subject of Tommy Hanson and how mature she seemed now. He knew that he was a very lucky man to have such a daughter.

'Very good, darling.'

'Aikido training, Dad. I'm a cat. In fact I'm a minx.'

'D'you sleep with it in that pocket?'

'Hardly, Dad, bit uncomfortable. Under the pillow with the rape alarm, but I move it into whatever I'm wearing, just like you said.'

'Good girl. Oh, you're such a good girl, and I'm so sorry, darling.'

'Shut *up*, Dad.'

'Good night.' Commander Leman stepped up the stairs to embrace his daughter. As he reached out to her he suddenly found two fingers hovering inches from his face, a vicious polished fingernail pointing straight into each eyeball.

Anna smiled. 'Do you know, Dad, I can push them all the way through an orange in a single thrust? If I decided to take a guy's eyes out, by the time the bridge of his nose had stopped my thrust I'd be at least an inch and a half into his brain. Who needs a pepper spray? 'Night.'

Anna Leman put her pepper spray back into her pocket, kissed her father and, hugging her Tommy Hanson merchandise, went to bed.

Central Criminal Court, Bangkok (Translation)

'For too long the moral and cultural strength of this country has been drained and corrupted by the insatiable Western appetite for hard drugs. We will no longer tolerate the pernicious influence of the drug gangs who feed this market. I am aware, miss, that you are a tiny part of the problem, a small fish in a big pond. Nonetheless, the role you chose to play in this crime was a central one. Whether it was your first and only excursion as a drug courier is neither here nor there. You are nineteen years old, a grown woman. It is absurd to imagine that you did not know that what you were doing was wicked and criminal and wrong, and that the consequences should you be caught would be severe. As I am sure that the counsel whom this court has appointed to speak in your defence has explained, it is within my power to pronounce the death penalty upon you. However, in view of your age and apparent inexperience, I am minded to be lenient. You will serve thirty years in prison.'

'What did he say? What did he say? Am I gowing home?'

The Brit Awards, Docklands Arena

'Well, ever so slightly weird, actually. He wanted to play around with the fruit a lot, so I had to be really careful about my dress. Christ, though, he had some excellent cocaine, like diamonds up the nose, I'm not kidding, the best . . . Unlike this champagne – can you believe it? It might as well be fizzy bleach. Probably is, actually, takes the back off your neck. But anyway, as I was saying, Tommy's totally losing it. I mean, what about him biffing you like that, Harry? Incredible. I think it's because you said I was your girlfriend. He had a moral moment. But it was so obvious you were joking. Reality is no longer Tommy's strong point, I think . . . but so incredibly good looking, though, you can see why he's such a star. God, but I still can't believe it. I've done it. *Yes!* I've shagged Tommy Hanson. I said I was going to and I bloody have . . . Oh my God, he's won another one!'

'This is for the fans! Because the fans are . . . Well, they're the fans, in't they? An' at the end of the day, this award's for them. The fans . . . So this is for you . . . The fans, because the fans are what this industry is all about, the fans are, and this is for them. Yeah! The fans! Yeah!'

A drop-in centre, King's Cross

'Ma name's Jessica. They call me Jessie. Yes Ah'm a prostitute, yes Ah'm a heroin addict. How did ye ever guess? Glasgow. Well, a little village near Glasgow, actually. Dumgoyne, it's called, very nice, lots of hills, if you like hills, which Ah don't, well, Ah didnae then, anyway. Ah miss 'em now . . . No, Ah can't give it up, not the smack or the game. Christ, you ought to know better than to ask that. How long have ye worked here? Ah've told you Ah'm an addict, Ah need the junk, Ah like it and whoring's the only way Ah can get it. Besides, the fellah Ah work fur's no very pleasant, if you get ma meaning. Ah imagine you meet a lot of girls in ma position . . . Don't feel you have to talk to me, hen, Ah'm no' after counselling and Ah'm no' looking for a methadone programme, Ah've only come here for the free coffee and a bit of a warm, it's effing freezing out if you hadn't noticed and there's me standing about in hotpants and a boob tube. No no, don't get me wrong, Ah'm nae trying to get rid of yez. Ah don't mind chatting if you don't mind – Ah'm just saying Ah don't need help, that's all, or at least there's nothing ye can do for me, which isn't the same thing, Ah suppose . . . But Ah don't mind chatting, telling you how badly Ah've screwed up ma life, confessing, Ah suppose . . . Ah used to go to confession when Ah was a wee girl – Ah was a good Catholic then – every week: forgive me, Father, Ah stole some sweeties, forgive me, Father, Ah put glue on my teacher's chair, forgive me, Father, but Ah must be bad because ma stepfather says it's ma fault what we dae together . . . Sorry, I'm rambling, Ah didnae mean to say that. Ah hate other people's hard luck stories, it just came out. To tell you the truth, Ah'm still a bit wasted . . .'

Jessie's eyes were far away, the pupils almost invisible. The volunteer worker offered her more coffee, but she seemed not to hear.

'As long as Ah live nothin' will ever feel as good as the first time that Ah took heroin. On the other hand, back then when Ah took it nothing had ever felt worse than bein' me. When François stuck that needle in ma arm Ah stopped hurting. Instantly years and years of pain and fear disappeared. Everything that had happened to me at home and on the streets went away. The months I spent freezing to death around Charing Cross, the fear, the cold, the hunger, the never-ending loneliness of living like a rat among rats was all ancient history. Ah laid back and truly believed Ah was in heaven. Then of course Ah woke up in hell. Ah can't believe it was only three months ago. Ah think Ah've used up most of the rest of my life since then.'

The Paget household, Dalston

When Peter arrived home shortly after 2 a.m. he brought the early editions of the morning papers with him. Angela was in bed but still awake and they devoured the coverage of the Brits together.

'It's amazing,' Angela said. 'You're in every single one.'

Inevitably most of the reportage concerned Tommy and his antics, but Peter was definitely prominent amongst the lesser figures.

'Well, it's not every humble backbencher who gets hugged by an ex-Spice Girl.'

'What's she like?'

'Emma Bunton?'

'Of course.'

'Gorgeous, absolutely gorgeous.'

'I can see that, Peter. What's she like?'

'*So* sweet. I mean genuinely nice, not remotely starry. I must write and thank her. Let's face it, it's her that's got me all these photos.'

'Well, she does look lovely.'

'But the great thing is all the articles mention my bill and my having seen Tommy Hanson to talk about it. I was worried that they'd spin the Brits against me. If there's one thing the press hate it's politicians trying to look cool.'

'Yes, but drugs is such a youth issue.'

'Exactly, and I'm making the PM uncomfortable, which the press always like. I really do seem to have caught the public mood or at least the mood of the younger generation. Oh, and I forgot to tell you, they've asked me to go on *Newsnight* as well as *Question Time*.'

'Well, so you damn well should. It's so obvious you're right. You're the only politician talking any sense on the issue at all. I mean, look at Prohibition in the States: total failure. All it did was invent Al Capone. There's no point banning things people want, because they'll get them anyway.'

'Exactly, an absolute no-brainer.'

'You're not going to use that phrase in public, are you?'

'I certainly am. I got it from Samantha. It's useful having somebody vaguely hip around.'

'I thought you said she was a serious sort of a girl.'

'She is, but you can be hip and serious as well, can't you? Look at Dido.'

'She's very beautiful.'

'Who? Dido?'

'Samantha.'

'Not my type.' He wondered how well he'd played it. Probably a little too quickly. 'Anyway, youth is always attractive. She'll be a grim-faced, twenty-stone junior minister in fifteen years' time.' Too much, way too much. First rule of politics: when you are in a hole, stop digging.

'I'll have to be up early tomorrow. I'm going to King's Cross. They're showing me round a drop-in centre they have there, then I'm having lunch with the Party Chairman. I think they're beginning to realize that I'm not going to back off and that I may be on to something.'

'D'you still think there's any danger of their withdrawing the whip? Chucking you out, even?'

'I doubt it, but it's possible. My line is that this has to be a conscience issue and that the government and the party should allow a free vote. The Chairman's line, of course, is that I'm a dangerous, crazy drug-pusher, which actually I don't mind at all. Churchill was a maverick. You have to be a stirrer if you want to get on.'

'Oh, so suddenly you're Churchill already?'

Peter Paget got into bed beside his wife. It was two thirty. Knowing that Angela would be awake, he had taken the Viagra while driving home. One hour. Perfect, better get a move on. Even before Peter had begun his affair with Samantha he had been finding it increasingly difficult to maintain an acceptable level of sexual activity with his wife. Since Samantha had begun to satisfy him so regularly it had become nearly impossible. Viagra had saved him. He still found Angela attractive in a sort of a way, and the little blue pills gave him just enough edge to muster a performance. Once a week was quite enough, though, and, Brits or no Brits, tonight was the night.

The Priory clinic

'My name is Emily and I am a cocaine addict . . .'

Emily reviewed the circle of faces, a mixed group of screw-ups. Druggies, alkies, eating disorders and even a sex addict – a compulsive masturbator to be precise. Emily knew one or two of them slightly – the super-model and the American actress. Not, she was glad to note, the masturbator.

'. . . So I'd got to where Tommy kicked me out of the

cab, hadn't I? I suppose I should be grateful to him. In fact I am grateful to him, because it wasn't until I found myself sitting in the gutter on Brixton High Street that I realized how mightily I was ruining my life. Well, if I'm honest, the realization was not immediate. Brixton High Street wasn't quite the road to Damascus, but it would eventually turn out to be the road to recovery of sorts. The road to here. Of course, as the lights turned green and Tommy's limo pulled away I was absolutely transfixed with terror. I'm not going to lie to you and say it wasn't about colour, because it was. I've met very few black people in my life, and when I have it's been mainly abroad – servants and hotel staff in Africa and the Caribbean, you know the sort of thing. There were two black girls at my school. One was royalty and the other a president's daughter. They seemed like nice enough girls, but I never really spoke to them, and I'm ashamed to confess that we called them the Coco Pops. They said they didn't mind, that they thought it was funny, but I doubt they did. Anyway, there I was in the gutter, and suddenly almost every face I could see was either black or brown and there were plenty of them because, let's face it, when a girl in a tiny little Gucci number falls out of a stretch limo and rolls into the gutter, flashing her G-string and shrieking obscenities, you're going to stare, aren't you? I had no money, no cards and no phone and that alone would be enough to make me feel utterly naked (which I practically was anyway), but on top of that I felt like I had been parachuted into an entirely alien land. I was suddenly in my own private chapter of *Bonfire of the Vanities*. I was terrified, absolutely shitting myself. Of course, the fact that my system was saturated with cocaine was not helping my state of mind. It makes you paranoid, you know. Well, I expect most of you know that.

Anyway, a few people, kids mainly, were sniggering and laughing, but mostly people seemed surprised. I don't blame them. After all, I was the alien, not them. Anyway, I must have sat there for as long as a minute before a big man with dreadlocks leant down and reached out his hand to me, but instead of taking it I shouted at him not to touch me. He didn't care, he just shrugged and walked away. Then there was a screech and a shout and a little bell ringing behind me, and I turned to see a bicycle courier, the chunky front wheel of his machine barely inches from my nose. He was one of those superb specimens that these guys always are, just a great streak of muscle in a Nike bodysuit, plus, blessed relief, he was white. Yes, I'm being honest. That was the thing that mattered to me most at that moment. Pathetic and terrible, I know.'

The supermodel nodded. She was generally considered to be one of the most spectacularly beautiful women on earth, but she had lost count of the magazine covers that had gone to white girls when by rights they should have been hers. Emily avoided her eye.

'I looked at this young man all sheathed in shiny purple as if he had been sent to me by the League of Superheroes. "Please can you help me? I've lost my phone. I need a phone," I said, fluttering and pouting and generally turning it all on. "Get out of the fahkin' way, you stupid fahkin' cow," he replied. "This is a fahkin' cycle lane, not a fahkin' chill-out room." With that he stuck out a hand to stop the white van that was about to pass us and to the accompaniment of much hooting and shouting he rode around me.

'Tears were coming now and then I heard this deep friendly voice. "You'd better get up, girl." It was the big man who'd first reached out his hand. He'd heard the commotion and turned back. "You're blocking the road."

'I let him help me up and the little crowd that had begun to gather started to disperse. A few boys continued to gawp, but, let's face it, I'd worn that tiny

93

dress with the express purpose of making boys gawp, so I was hardly in a position to complain when they did. I asked the man if he knew where I could get a taxi and he smiled and pointed to three different minicab places within fifty metres, the ones with the orange flashing lights, the sort you go to at three in the morning in Soho, feeling rather brave, because there are no proper taxis.

' "Take your pick, girl, but make them tell you the price before you start."

'He laughed and then I laughed too. This wasn't an alien nation at all, it was just five thirty in the afternoon on just another London high street. I wasn't going to be raped or killed and there were three separate cab companies within a minute's walk, any one of which would have been delighted to take me back over the river to where my money and my life lay waiting, any time I wanted.

'But, you see, suddenly I didn't want to, because just as quickly as the paranoia had engulfed me so did the euphoria. I'm sure some of you know the feeling.'

Emily avoided the masturbator's eye.

'I was still drunk. I was still coked up and E'd up and I was still a wild wild naughty little miss who got what she wanted, because boys love good-time girls. I'd even got Tommy Hanson, briefly, which is gold medal stuff amongst us wild wild naughty little girls, you know.

'No, I wasn't going home just yet. I'd set out for a big night and I intended to have one. I was in Brixton, after all, and even though it was still only the afternoon various dub beats could be heard emanating from upstairs windows. This was real life. Tough, street, a little bit scary, but I was a wild naughty girl. Nothing fazed me.

' "Actually, I was wondering if I could trouble you for some ganja," I said.

'He smiled again. "Where you keep your money, girl? Up your arse?"

'It was a fair point. If I'd had any money, up my arse would have been just about the only place I *could* have concealed it.

' "Well, actually, I'm afraid I don't have any money. I wasn't trying to score, I just fancied a puff. Is that terribly rude of me?"

'He just laughed and took my arm. As we walked together up the high street, many heads turned. It was obvious what people thought of this big rasta and the white tart who had put her arm through his, whore and pimp, had to be, and I loved it. Bad old Emily being bad again, with her long golden shiny legs the focus of a thousand eyes. Fuck Tommy, fuck the Brits. I was where the real people were, not all those rock industry fuckwits. Let's face it, black people invented rock music, didn't they?At least I think they did, and Elvis stole it, is that right? I know I've been told that. And here I was, hijacked on my way to some honkey lovey fest by a proper bro', a homeboy. The house he lived in was pretty much like my brother's rooms at Cambridge in as much as the curtains were drawn and there were lots of people lounging around on couches, cushions, the floor, etc. Very loud *duf-duf* music which could have come straight out of my bro's collection was playing, and a thick fog of pot smoke stretched from the floor to the ceiling. In fact, now I come to think of it, the whole thing was an exact negative image of my bro's place in that the set-ups were identical except that in his rooms everyone was white except for one black girl who was doing law and whom *all* the boys wanted to sleep with, and at my new friend's place everybody was black except me and from the whistles and shouts I got when I walked in I would not have had any problem getting laid myself.

'God, that spliff was strong. I don't use pot at all as a

rule. Charlie is my darling, as every *News of the World* reporter knows, but when I do have it, it's just a bit of hash rolled up with tobacco. This was different. This was a huge trumpet-like thing filled with pure grass. I took one toke and nearly passed out.

' "Actually, I think I might have to lie down for a bit," I told my new friend, whose name I don't think I ever knew, and like the gentleman he was he showed me upstairs and offered me his futon.

' "If you're going to throw up, girl, the toilet's through there. My sheets is silk, OK?"

'Do you know, I think I was a little offended. Not about the throwing-up thing – I must have been bright green – but there I was in this bloke's bedroom, a famously hot bit of totty, stoned out of her box, dressed in stunning minimalism, and yet he wasn't hitting on me at all. I mean, he'd brought me back to his place, we were standing by his bed, for God's sake, and the fellow was simply not making a move.

' "Aren't you going to try and screw me, then?" I said. I say things like that quite a lot. I'm known for it. Good old Emily, she'll say *anything*.

'He looked at me for a long time, clearly rather torn. "I would love to, girl, but my old lady will be home in half an hour, you know what I'm saying? She's a meter maid and she knocks off at six. Those meter ladies are tough. She'd kill me, girl, stone dead. She'd kill you too, then she'd eat you."

'I looked at my watch. "We could be quick."

'Well, he was only flesh and blood, after all, and he had *tried* to knock me back. But I'm a difficult girl to refuse when I'm being a complete twat, so I hoiked off the silky G and we had a quickie on his crimson sheets and I felt tremendously real and brave and adventurous, and I suppose he must have felt rotten because afterwards he said, "I wish I'd let you find another black man to fuck."

'The shag at least seemed to have cleared my head rather so we went back downstairs, but it was obvious he wanted me to go before his girlfriend came home, and since a group of his friends were going off to a party I tagged along too. Still stoned, still high, still feeling very exotic.

'The party was clearly a kind of rolling affair, because it was quite lively even so early in the evening. It was in some warehouse and I smoked people's joints and drank their Special Brew and jabbered on and bopped for what must have been hours. By this time I wasn't standing out quite so much, as there were a few other white people about the place and lots of girls had sexy dresses on. Mine must have been the sexiest, however, or certainly the most slutty, because while I was trying to catch my breath in the chill-out room I was approached by quite the most unpleasant person I have ever met in my life and I've met some horrors. A Frenchman called François.

'He was a pimp and he thought I was a hooker. Simple as that. He said he'd seen me getting kicked out of the limo and walking off arm in arm with Mr Rasta, and had drawn the conclusion that I'd been turning a high-class trick in the back of the car and having concluded my business had made an unceremonious departure before rejoining my great big black minder. What François wanted was for me to defect to him. François claimed that he would never let any of his girls get treated by their clients the way I had clearly been treated in the limo.

'And as if to demonstrate the point, he drew back the lapel of his dirty Paul Smith jacket and revealed the butt of quite a big-looking gun nestling in his armpit. Do you know, I think I was actually excited. Even without the gun I was loving the idea that this terrible, appalling man thought I was a prostitute and wanted to own me, but now that it turned out he was

97

prepared to shoot my previous owner to get me, well, it was rather flattering. Well, flattering to an idiotic, fucked-up cokehead like me.'

A warehouse party, Brixton

'Listen, foxy lady, sexy lady. You and me we're better than this. You shouldn't be getting into no cars, even if they're limos, no way, baby. You shouldn't be trading your ass on the street like some black ho'. You is high class, I can see that. I know about class, baby, because I got it too. I'm a main man, I ain't like this bullshit round here, this trash. That's why I gotta get out. I gotta get myself a ticket across the river . . . Don't make no mistake, though, don't get me wrong. Right now I'm making plenty money, fuck yes. You see this, two grand cash, no problem, any time.'

François briefly pulled back the sleeve of his jacket to reveal a thickish wad of fifties wrapped round his arm with an elastic band. Also revealed were the telltale tracks of the needle.

'Oh sure, I got plenty money, I *shit* money, but I'm sick of running screwed-up little smackheads off the streets. Those dirty little whores ain't got no class at all, they just dirt. What's more, you gotta keep them high the whole time else they won't get in the cars. What I want is to get some class, get off the streets, get in a house and run a for-real grand-a-fuck classy bitch like you could be, get out west way, work the Arabs. Man, they got so much fucking money, and they gonna like what you got, that's for sure, oh yeah. If you and me got a place maybe round Marble Arch, we'd be digging fucking gold.'

'He was even more wired than me was François. He was positively frothing at the mouth, and his pupils were like pinpricks. I'd seen the mess he'd made of his arms when he showed me his money, and even in the gloom of the party I could see fresh track marks on his neck. It won't be long before he'll be looking for veins in his cock, that boy, sure as night follows day. He was a serious junkie, and by the way he was winding himself up he did not favour a very mellow high. Suddenly I was very scared again. I know a fucked-up, strung-out loser when I see one. Well, for many a long year I've only had to look in a mirror. I'd only known the posh ones up until that night, but the desperation crosses class boundaries. The self-delusion, the bitter anger, all that malarky. Yes, it's the same story, whoever's telling it, the difference in François' case being that he was armed.

'So I said to him, "Look, François, I'm really not into that sort of thing. I mean, I'm flattered and all that, of course, but really, I'm no street walker." Which he thought was the very point he was making and he said that he intended to go and make it to the Rasta man who he presumed owned me.

'And with that, thank God, he buggered off, and not before time. I was sweating by now and in no mood to be heavied out, so the minute he turned his back I jumped into the middle of the dancing and bopped away like a madwoman, shrieking and flaunting it, rubbing my arse against every available crotch and shouting for drugs at the top of my voice. Of course nobody could hear me above the music, which was a very good thing as I was still pretty loaded . . .

' . . . and then suddenly I realized that I wasn't in the middle of the crowd any more, but right on the edge of it, and that a little gang of boys was dancing me towards an empty room at the back of the warehouse.'

A drop-in centre, King's Cross

'Ah always ask them if it's OK to have the radio on
when Ah go with them in their cars. Heart FM or
Capital Gold, that's what Ah like. Classic stuff. Before
Ah went to live in hell Ah didnae like granny music at
all, Ah was intae house and techno and rap, but now
Ah like nice tunes . . . Particularly if François' been
slightly less of a stingy bastard and Ah'm on a decent
high. When the puntas are on top o' me Ah always try
and float above masel', like astral flying if ye follow
me, an' music helps. Ah just melt through the roof of
the cars and levitate up and up until all of London lies
miles beneath me, a million twinkling lights. And
somewhere down there, some other wee girl is
crammed into the back of a Ford Mondeo being fucked
by a man who smells of beer and cigarettes. Some other
girl is leaning across the front seats, gearstick stuck in
her stomach, trying to put a condom onto some stinkin'
bastard's dick with her mouth.

'Sometimes they don't let me have my music. They
say it puts them off, distracts them. Sometimes
they say they want to hear me, but Ah've never been
much chop at doing any moaning and groaning for
them. Ma teeth are always too gritted. Besides, if ye're
paying thirty quid for a streetwalking smackhead you
cannae expect an Oscar-winning performance, can ye?
It's funny the moments that stay with ye. Most of the
time it's all just a blur tae me, but for instance I remember the other night, hearing about Tommy Hanson
getting his Brit Awards. Ah'm thinking, God, it's March
already, how long have I been daeing this? I know the
Brits are in March. Ah used to love my music, you see.
Four Brits, I think he got, didn't he? Or five? And there

he was, on the radio, thanking his fans, an' Ah was in the back of some car desperately trying tae hang on tae what was left of the smack in my veins to get through the trick that was on top of me. François' getting meaner and meaner with his drugs, see, so sometimes Ah have tae shag 'em almost straight. It's not that he gives us bad gear or anything. Nothing too badly cut. He doesn't want us dead, he just wants us dead tae the world, being screwed ten or fifteen times a night and handing over four hundred quid when the sun comes up. Anyways, so there Ah am, sitting on ma rapidly diminishing cloud over London, trying to stay aloft, looking down while Tommy Hanson's on the radio with the single of the year, "Heaven Ain't High Enough" ... That was a Christmas number one, ye know, and Ah started to think about Christmas and what it had been like before ma da' had left and the other man came, and how there had been some good times and Ah always got a load of presents, and Ah wondered where ma dolls were now. Ah had aboot twenty Barbies when Ah was a wee girl. Ah used to run a dolls' disco, all girls. Then far below me the girl in the car, who was also listening to the music, started crying, but it was OK because the fellah who was on top of her liked that. So Tommy sang about heaven and Ah hung there in the sky with hell below me, and the girl in the car cried and cried and cried.'

While Jessie had been speaking to the volunteer worker an important-looking party had entered the centre accompanied by a small group of media. The group, headed by Peter Paget, approached Jessie.

'I'm so sorry to interrupt you. My name is Peter Paget and I'm a Member of Parliament.'

'Oh, right. Ah'm Jessie.'

'And you have a drugs problem?'

'Too right, darlin'. Mah problem is Ah havenae got any at the moment. Can ye help me out?'

'Would you mind if I had my picture taken with you?'

'Ten quid.'

'I'm afraid I can't do that.'

'Oh, come on, mate, gi' us fifteen and Ah'll gi' ye a blowjob as well.'

'I'll stand you a cup of tea if you like.'

'OK.'

Peter turned to the little group of reporters who were with him and pointed out that a girl like Jessie was beyond society's ability to help because she existed on the wrong side of the law. His voice shook with emotion as once more he outlined the absurdities of a law that criminalized its victims.

'I have two teenaged daughters. Young Jessie here could easily be one of their numerous boisterous friends. But no. Instead, this young girl, utterly alone, lives outside a civilized society that is happy to forget about her. It is plainly obvious that this vulnerable girl needs protection from the law, not persecution, and yet society considers her lifestyle almost exclusively criminal. Disraeli's famous phrase Two Nations is as relevant today as in that other age when child prostitutes shamed the streets of London and every tenement contained a Fagin's den . . . Is it not . . . Is it not . . . Oh, for God's sake! Look at this poor girl. She's *our fault*. We *have* to help her!'

Suddenly Peter's eloquence deserted him. He had had his presentation all prepared. There had been plenty more Dickensian references to come, but looking at Jessie, this sad, dirty but still beautiful little junkie with whom he was sharing tea, his composure had deserted him. Supposing his own beloved daughters were so unfortunate as to fall beneath society's net? What would become of *them*? Any teenager in the country could become like Jessie if fate were first to set them on that path. Because once they fell, the law would be ranged against them.

Peter found himself struggling not to cry. This was ridiculous. He was a professional politician. He had a job to do. He was a stern and practical man. To Peter's surprise it was Jessie who decided to help him out of his embarrassment by speaking up herself.

'You're very right, Peter. As far as the police are concerned, Ah'm a criminal. They don't want tae know about me and Ah don't want tae know about them. If mah pimp gi's me a kickin' the best Ah can hope for from society is a Band Aid offa casualty.'

The assembled media nodded thoughtfully. It was an uncommon feeling for all concerned to be involved in an issue and a debate so entirely real and immediate. Public affairs had descended so deeply into trivia and gossip over recent years that it was indeed refreshing to find everyone, politicians and journalists alike, focusing on something truly meaningful and utterly urgent.

Every writer in the country was grateful to Peter Paget. By no means all of them agreed with him, but they were all grateful that he had galvanized the opinion-forming classes into finally having to form some opinions of their own.

Jessie had her tea and agreed to be photographed. Peter Paget pulled himself together and was genuine and solicitous towards her; even the assembled journalists were touched.

Samantha thought Peter had done wonderfully. Magnificent. So sincere and caring, so emotional, so beautiful. A proper man in a world of silly boys. As they left the drop-in centre she thrust some important-looking papers under his nose. Peter glanced down. Amongst them was a note that read, *I want to take you in my mouth. Now.*

Never mind two nations. Peter was two men. The one who had entered the drop-in centre and spoken to Jessie – a deeply committed conviction politician and family man. And the one who left the centre, a quivering mass of agonizing sexual desire. A man happy, indeed eager, to risk everything he loved and everything he believed if he could just get his penis into the mouth of the gorgeous, bewitching, giggling, worshipping girl/woman whose bottom swayed before him as she led the party from the room.

Bangkok Women's Prison

'Moi mum's written to the King. Yeah. She reckons once the King hears about me being a good girl underneath I'll be all roight.'

The room Sonia had been moved to held forty-five women. There was not space for everyone to lie down at the same time and some slept sitting up or draped across each other. The woman to whom Sonia was speaking did not understand her and in fact probably did not even hear her. She had to all intents and purposes lost her mind, and spent the nights swaying angrily and picking imaginary objects from her prison dress. The woman on Sonia's other side masturbated all the time she was awake, her filthy garment perpetually drawn up around her waist. Clearly she took no pleasure from this automatic activity. She rubbed herself for no other reason than that there was nothing else to do.

Not everyone in the overcrowded cell was mad. Most had come from tough backgrounds and had the mental resilience to retain some semblance of sanity in the midst of such bedlam. But some succumbed to the desperate escape route that insanity offered, and those around Sonia had certainly done so. Perhaps that was why these women did not object to Sonia's endless monologues delivered in her foreign tongue. The other women, the sane women, had soon become bored with Sonia's dull bleating and had chased her away. Increasingly, Sonia found common ground with the lunatics.

'I'm gonna get out, I am, just as soon as moi mum's talked to the King an' told 'im I'm not supposed to be 'ere. Now way. Royal pardon, that's what I'm gonna get, 'cos I'm British.'

Samantha's flat, Islington

She raised her head and looked up at him, past his unzipped fly, his untucked shirt, his skewed tie, and up at his strangely grim and unsmiling face. She'd noticed that men often looked like that when they came. They might at least try and *look* as if they were enjoying it. Peter's back was against the front door; Samantha was on her knees on the mat. She got to her feet, raising her face to his, her lips clamped closely together. Then, with great deliberation, she gulped.

Peter sighed. Angela rarely swallowed. Even in the days when they had bothered with such exotic activities as oral sex, she had never liked to swallow. Peter did not know why it felt so intensely satisfying that Samantha chose to do so, but it did, and for a moment his satiated loins spun and crackled with one final roar of sheer pleasure. And then, almost as instantly, came the guilt.

To be indulging in such intimacy . . . with a girl half his age. If Angela and his daughters knew . . . He always felt the same after Samantha and he had finished.

He had to get out of this.

And yet . . . to give it up, to give up such an entirely

105

exhilarating sexual adventure. How could he forgive himself? Man is a sexual animal, or at least that's how he started out; the social side came later. That surely was when all the trouble began. One day Peter would be old and grey and facing the imminence of death. How could he look back upon his younger self and say ... *'You gave it up?* You denied yourself the opportunity to satiate yourself utterly on a young female of the species in her prime, *for guilt*! Do lions feel guilt? Do tigers? No! And nor should you. You are a man! A male of the species. You have a right to sex.'

Peter often went through this argument with himself and it would invigorate him briefly before once more the certainty descended upon him. *He had to get out of this.*

Although Peter was due back at Parliament for his confrontation with his Party Chairman, he allowed Samantha to persuade him not to rush straight off now that the frenzied, orgasmic moment had passed.

Hers was a romantic soul and she was anxious for a moment of calm and affection. As she explained, she was not normally the type of girl to drop to her knees when scarcely inside her flat and administer oral sex to her boyfriend on the doormat. In fact, she told him, in the past her boyfriends had been fortunate if they had got any oral sex at all. This rather surprised Peter, as he had come to view Samantha as such a highly charged and vigorous sexual animal that it had not occurred to him that she might have her reserved side.

'I'm only mad for it with you,' she assured him as they lay together in each other's arms, and then, after a long, thoughtful silence, she added, 'Do you think it's because I lost my father when I was little that you're so attractive to me, Peter?'

Not, perhaps, the most flattering suggestion to make to one's older lover.

'No, I imagine it's because of my ravishing good looks and awesome sexual powers.'

106

'That too, of course. That goes without saying.'

'In politics nothing goes without saying and saying many many times.'

'This isn't politics, Peter. It's our life together.'

Once more the burning light of sexual power and professional good fortune that had lit the path of Peter's inner man since he had almost simultaneously begun his political and sexual rebirth flickered a little. Life together? Not a comfortable phrase.

'We should be beginning to think about making a move,' he said. 'I'm due in the house.'

But Samantha did not seem to wish to move. 'I was eleven when he died.'

'Ah. I can't imagine how awful it must have been.' What else could one say?

'It was cancer, but he and Mummy managed to keep it from me until nearly the end. Do you know that for five years afterwards, until I was nearly sixteen, I wrote a poem to him every single day? Every day I would wake up early, thinking about him, and I would set about my poem, eleven lines it had to be, one for each of the years he was in my life.'

Peter glanced at his watch. It was not that he wasn't interested in Samantha's life, but an appointment with the Party Chairman was not something to be taken lightly. If Samantha was aware of Peter's impatience she ignored it.

'Sometimes it made me late for school. I'm sure all the poems must have been very similar. How could they not be? But I always tried, each time, to feel his love and his passing in a new and immediate way. It didn't matter, anyway, because each morning at eleven o'clock I'd destroy my poem. I'd leave class, or what-ever I was doing, hide away and burn it and blow kisses to the face that I saw in the flames. I thought that the smoke carried my love and my sorrow up to heaven where Daddy would read what I'd written in the air.'

This was the first time that Peter had seen Samantha cry.

'Eventually my mother made me see a psychiatrist. She had no choice, I'd become an obsessive. I hadn't even begun to let go. The woman I saw was very good and really helped me. Slowly but surely we broke up my cycle of dependence on Daddy's memory. I stopped writing my poems every day and even began to talk to boys, but every now and then, ever since, once a week or perhaps once a fortnight, I still do my old thing – not necessarily eleven lines or at eleven o'clock, my shrink cured me of that – but nonetheless I still write to Daddy and send my thoughts in smoke to heaven . . .'

The tears were really rolling now and Peter felt moved to cry too.

And then Samantha's face changed. Despite the still wet tears a radiant smile lit it up. 'Except not now, Peter. Since the day I met you I haven't written him a single word.'

Samantha kissed Peter gently on the lips. Her hand stole down inside his trousers. Her warm lips were at his neck. But Peter Paget did not feel like sex any more, and it was no longer the lateness of the hour that was distracting him. It was the intensity of Samantha's emotions.

What a shock, what an extreme shock to get into bed with a happy-go-lucky young sexpot and then find oneself in the arms of a complex and damaged in- dividual. Samantha had exploded into his life naked and unencumbered. Now, it seemed, her baggage had arrived.

The Priory clinic

'Well, as I say, I had suddenly become aware of the fact that I and my little posse of young dance partners were getting further and further away from the main body of the party, but I didn't have time to get scared because at that point my whole evening was brought to an end when I was pretty much forcibly ejected by this big man called Henry. He was some sort of police community liaison officer, and suddenly he thrust himself between me and the young men. They didn't like him at all, they called him Judas because he was black and he worked with the police, but he faced them down anyway.'

A warehouse party, Brixton

'You get outta here right now, woman! You get right back where you come from. Dey's cabs outside. Get in one!'

The boys gathered round behind Henry, their hard cockney accents a contrast to his soft West Indian lilt.

''ey, chill, you Jamaican motherfukka! We jus' dancin' wiv ve bitch. Ain't nuffing to do wiv you.'

Henry kept his eyes firmly on Emily, and said, in deliberately exaggerated Caribbean tones, 'I said piss off, woman. Dis ain' no touris' 'traction. We ain' here so's we can 'muse you.'

'You have no right to talk to me like that! I'm just dancing! I was invited here. You don't like me because I'm white, do you? Admit it!'

'Dat's right, girl. Dat's for sure. Right now I don't like you 'cos you white.'

'Well, that is just totally racist. I think you're being totally racist!'

The Priory clinic

'Henry just laughed at that and then turned round to the boys. I couldn't hear a lot of what he was saying, but he was obviously taking all the fun out of the situation because after a brief altercation they just turned round and strutted off. Then Henry grabbed me by the arm and half dragged me outside. He was very angry and he didn't like me at all. He kept asking what the hell I thought I was doing there, going on about me being a tourist come to look at all the black people, which I thought was terribly unfair. After all, I had been invited to the party, sort of. But when we got outside the cold air hit me, and I saw how angry he was. Then the drug let-down began.'

Brixton High Road

'Those boys don't know who you was, honey, but I do, oh yeah. I read the papers on account of somethin' 'bout the front line gonna be in 'em most days and usually not too complimentary. You're that wild-child chick, right? Always dancing with royals and gettin' married to Tommy Hanson or whatever. For sure you're all those boys needed.'

'Why did you force me out of that party?'

'Because you're a fuckin' tourist an' you were liable to get a lot of stupid young black men into a lot of trouble.'

'What the hell do you mean? I was just dancing!'

'You were just being a pissed, stoned, half-naked little cockteaser, sister! Shaking your lil' ass at those boys and—'

'I was dancing!'

'Listen! You was gettin' herded towards a dark room by a bunch of very drunk, very horny guys! Now I don't think they would have been so stupid as to try an' do nothing to you, but *somethin'* bad coulda happened either to you or more likely to them.'

'To them?'

'Exactly, sister. I saw you, all hysterical an' full of yourself. I saw you kiss the front guy and squeeze his ass.'

'I was dancing!'

'So supposin' you got inside that room and suddenly one of them tries to push things too far and you'd got scared an' shouted rape! Or else you let him have a piece but tomorrow mornin' when you're straight you starts to think about what happened and your rich daddy finds out an' says his sweet lil' virgin flower bin defiled by a gang o' dirty black men!'

'I can look after my—'

'Look at you, woman! You are completely wired! You are totally fucked up! Anythin' coulda happened in there and who would ever know the truth? Maybe they'd 'a piled into you. Maybe you'd 'a let 'em. Either way nobody gonna be happy in the mornin'. You think we need that? You think those fuckin' boys who is already bottom of the pile ain't got enough problems in life without no tourist from the Home Counties dancing in jiggling her pooties in front of der face an' maybe blowing the whole damn community sky high? You're an important woman, a celebrity. If you get into trouble people gonna know 'bout it and the cops ain't never gonna let it go till they bust some black boys, and that's gonna start a fuckin' race war! We do not need that shit, woman! So go an' buy your drugs and get your low-life fuckin' kicks somewhere else!'

The Priory clinic

'I'll never forget the look of contempt on that man's face as he pushed me into a minicab. That was when I decided to come here. I took the cab to my place, picked up some cash and some slightly more sensible knickers and headed straight here for help. I really am

111

sick of being an idiot, and as I said I'm grateful to Tommy for helping me realize that. I'm even more grateful to Henry, even though he hated me so much. Thank God a look of contempt was the worst thing that happened that night.'

Brixton Hospital

It wasn't the worst thing that happened that night.

Two hours before Emily had finally got into a cab and had headed north of the river, Trevor, the Rastafarian who had pulled her from the gutter and taken her to his home, was shot. Now he lay in hospital, badly wounded but nonetheless anxious to make a statement.

'Listen, just 'cos I'm a Rastaman don't mean I'm a fucking Yardie. I work in a bike shop. I don't know what happened, right? We was just chillin' in my house, man. Having some music, smokin' some weed like we always do. My old lady was home from work, man, she's nearly one of you lot 'cos she's a traffic warden and she got your name on her shoulder. She's cookin' up some nice lamb for me dinner and every-t'ing is cool. I had had some friends round before . . . No, I knew them all, except for some crazy white chick. Emily, she was called, I think, but anyway, it don't matter, guy, because they had all gone off raving and it was just me and the missus. So like I say everyt'ing is cool and nice, when suddenly this white geezer just walks in off the street. We keep our door open most times because a lotta guys coming round and I don't wanna be getting up for no door when I'm sitting all comfortable. So this geezer walks in and I knew for sure that he was very badly fucked up, man. He had that look, he was crazy on drugs, too many drugs, he had tracks all over him, man, his arms, his neck, fuck knows where else, and he was staring like a fuckin' mad dog or somet'ing. So right away I'm thinking he wants to score and he's seen a black man smokin' in his house and maybe he thinks I'm chasing the dragon or wha'ever. So I starts to tell him that I don't do no horse and I don't deal not'ing anyways and I don't let no one in me house but me friends and that he should fuck off soon as is convenient, as long as that is right now, when he shouts, "I'm taking your bitch! Motherfucker! She gonna work for me!" He got some French accent or somet'ing, I don't know, European for sure, so I tells him I don't know what the fuck he's talking about and then fuckin' hell he gets out a fuckin' gun and *shoots me*, man! I couldn't believe it! I ain't never even *seen* a gun and the geezer *shoots* me, except he's so fucked up he shoots me in the leg like you see and then BAM! He gets a big pot of lamb stew round the head because my old lady she don't fuck around, you know what I'm saying? Also, you do not fuck around with her. So down he goes and that's when we called you geezers. I don't know why he shot me 'cept he definitely thought I had some woman that he wanted, which I can tell you for sure, guy, I don't. That's all I know.'

Dalston Police Station

North of the river, at Dalston Police Station, another type of interview was being conducted. Commander Leman was watching it through the glass of a two-way mirror. A woman and a teenaged girl faced each other across a table. The girl was very distressed. Her make-up was streaked with tears and her hands were shaking. The woman, a detective who specialized in sexual crimes, took the girl's hand.

'I came back from the toilet, I finished my drink and

then this man came over to our table and said he was the manager.'

'Can you describe him?'

'No, we were in a club. It was dark and noisy. He was just a man, that's all. He said that there was a phone call for me. He knew my name.'

Commander Leman knew the girl. She was a friend of Anna, his daughter. Anna to whom only a few hours before he had been handing out Tommy Hanson merchandise. The desk sergeant at the station knew that the girl was a family friend of the Lemans and so had alerted the Commander to the situation. The distressed girl's name was Joanna, but Leman knew her as Jo Jo. He watched her through the glass. She was trying to form a sentence but was having difficulty speaking.

During the previous weekend this same girl had been with Anna in the rumpus room of the Leman household, watching *Grease* for what was probably the hundredth time.

'I remember walking across the club and the lights and everything . . . and then, nothing.'

Jo Jo had been found unconscious in a doorway at around four a.m. The police had been searching for her ever since her friends had raised the alarm at around ten thirty. Commander Leman knew that Jo Jo sometimes went to adult places with older girls. That was a part of her life that he had strictly forbidden Anna to join. When she was found, Jo Jo had been difficult to rouse, and her speech was slurred. The officers who discovered her reported that her clothing was in considerable disarray.

Everything was pointing in one unimaginably terrible direction. One word pounded away in Leman's brain, one horrible, horrible word.

Rohypnol.

Victoria Coach Station

There had been an accident outside the coach station and the traffic was stationary. Jessie's coach had been waiting for over an hour and she had fallen into conversation with the old lady sitting beside her.

'All us girls who worked for François knew that he was goin' tae crash and burn. Well, we were all goin' tae, but that swine was way ahead of us. Ah suppose if you're a pimp there's no' a lot tae do most of the time except take drugs and that's what he did. All the time Ah knew him he was taking drugs and during that time he got stupider and stupider. Pretty soon he wasnae bothered what kind of shit he was taking. We used tae talk about it a lot because now that he was all fucked up he couldnae beat us up so easy, and we used to ask ourselves why don't we just leave? He had a gun, of course, but ye know, we could have just grabbed it offa him when he was crashed and put it in the bog. We could 'a run, Ah swear. Any time, we could 'a run. Why didn't we? Well, ye know the answer. Drugs. What else?'

The old lady had not known the answer, but she was learning fast.

'We're all nearly as hooked as he is, and François was our supply. We didnae know any different, we only went out to work, we had no other life. So we'd whore and gi' him the money and he'd buy shit and take most of it hi'sel' and give the rest tae us, and we'd go out and whore again. That was why Ah never went tae the police when he was beating me, or after he had basically kidnapped me in the first place. Because the thing Ah wanted most in the world was illegal, and the thing Ah did tae get it was illegal. Ah walk the streets and Ah take heroin. That's ma life. The cops wouldnae protect me. They wouldnae be remotely interested in me – they have tae earn a living catching speeding motorists.

'Anyway, Ah wouldna thought François could 'a got any more fucked up than he was, but a coupla weeks ago he really began tae surpass himself. He'd been down tae Brixton to score some gear and had stayed away all night. When he got back to the wee flat we all lived in, which he got offa the council free because he reckoned he was unemployed, he had definitely emigrated tae Planet Paranoid for good. From that moment on he only went out when he absolutely had tae, tae collect our money or score. The rest of the time he just laid about on his bed, jumpin' at every sound and peekin' out the windows. Well, we just put it down tae the drugs, of course, but this mornin' we found out that he's reason tae be nervous. We was all sittin' about after the night's work – fortunately non o' us wi' any needles stickin' out our arms – when about fifteen cops suddenly smashed down the door an' nicked the bastard. We thought it was a drugs bust, o' course, an' that we was all for it, but it turned out they just wanted François. These cops were firearms officers, ye see, which as ye know is very heavy shit indeed. They was all shoutin' and pointin' their guns at François because it turned out that when he'd gone tae Brixton that night he'd been so completely screwed up on bad shit that he'd shot some black fellah in his living room. The police didnae tell us why, they just bunged him on the floor, cuffed him and took him away. An' good riddance, say I.'

'So that was it. Suddenly François was oot o' the picture, because there was no way he was getting out on bail, and so us girls was finally free of his clutches. Four skinny, dirty teenage whore slaves had suddenly got themselves free. Got out from under one of the biggest shites that ever walked on God's earth.

'So what was our reaction?'

The old lady, who was no fool, suggested that perhaps it had something to do with drugs.

'Well, it's obvious, isn't it? Ye'd 'a been the same if ye were a junkie whore. Sheer terror, was our reaction. Where the fuck was we gonna get hit up? Where could we get a fix? We're zombies, that's what we are. Slaves tae the brown. We've lost our free will, we've no minds of our own and no life but the one François had made for us, and we was absolutely shittin' it without him.

'Get this. We wanted him back. We actually wanted the bastard back. Can ye believe it? Ah still cannae believe it. The man was an evil vicious bastard and he destroyed ma life, but if the police had offered him bail us girls would have gone out and whored for it there and then.'

St Hilda's Church Hall, Soho

'Look, this story gets worse before it gets better, all right? And then it gets worse again. I'm not proud of it, I was a disgusting bastard, end of story. It's in me for sure, I know that, and charlie brings it out.

'Charlie loves my bastard. They're best mates, charlie and my bastard are.

'Anyway, I didn't get any smack, but I did another E and forgot about me auntie. Well, there were nowt I could do about her, was there? I was stuck backstage at the Brits and she was in hospital in Salford, so, monged out as I was, I basically thought, Fook 'er.

'I won four awards that night, as I'm sure you've read, and suddenly I was largin' it again. I love winning, see. It puts me right back on top, that and the Es and the booze and the charlie. So I had a bangin' good evenin' all round. Chuckin' food, shoutin' out and whatever and by the time the show was over I wasn't bothering about any smack any more. Like I say, I don't even like it much. I'd got some more superb coke and someone had finally got me some decent beer and proper champagne and I was having it fookin' huge! Everybody wanted to get near me and I was being dead dry and witty and cool. I'm dead good at that, me.

'One of the best bits of the Brits is immediately after the show when most of the acts mill around in the backstage area for a bit, while the crowd disperses. But you don't want to hang around too long 'less you want to end up lookin' a bit sad, pukin' in a pot plant wi' a couple o' big Irish thugs who used to be in a boy band. Now let me tell you an important trick if ever you happen to find yourself backstage at the Brits. When things begin to break up, don't go to the official party. It's crap. I got caught out that way first time I was there. I were all vibed up and excited because I'd been nominated for best newcomer and hanging around with the Spice Girls when they were the biggest thing on the planet and I'd met the Bee Gees and stuff and I couldn't wait to get to the party to hang out some more.

'*Big* fookin' mistake, man. Because *nobody* goes to the official party. That party is for the *punters*, man! I don't mean the real punters, the fans in the pit, at least that would be a bit fookin' genuine. I mean all the secretaries and record-shop owners, the people from the BPI, and the only star there was me. I was fookin' swamped. Signing autographs, having me photo took. I'd only got about six foot into that party but it took me nearly an hour to get back out, by which time everybody had fooked off to the *real* parties, which happen elsewhere all over London. The real parties are paid for by the record company and basically everybody goes to their own one, so if you want to hang out with other stars you'd better be with a nice big label. But I did the Sony bash and the Virgin bash and EMI. I wasn't going to my own record company party because I was having a dispute with them, so I was fooked if I was going to let them swank and wank over my four Brits. But there

118

was nowt goin' down anywhere except cocaine, pills and vintage Dom P.

'Fookin' dull as arse.

'So I'm stood there at some bar or other laughing at Jay Kay on the dance floor. I mean the bloke can certainly move all right, but 'e *so* knows it, don't 'e? I reckon the trick with talent is to pretend you ain't got it. But fair play to old Jay, the birds love 'im. Anyway, I'm stood there with some billionaire producer I know and he says to me, "Sod it, let's get down Spearmint Rhino's." You know the place, lap dancin' an' that. Flap dancin' I call it 'cos if you're lucky they give you the full two sets of fanny lips even though they in't s'posed to, only in the private dancin' booths, of course. You can't get no bearded clam with yer oysters, *no way*!

'So we pile in the back of my car and head for the Rhino.

'He hadn't eaten so we order up a couple o' big steaks and we're sitting there drinking champagne an' eating steak an' chatting to these birds what look like *Playboy* centrefolds, except not thick, no way, all workin' their way through college, you know, really classy birds. It could 'a' been the Ivy or whatever, except that the birds all had their tits out and if I'd wanted I could have tekken 'em into a booth for a proper look. It was the best part o' the night, really, that steak, but my mate didn't last long. 'E'd only come in for 'is tea, anyway, and 'ad to fook off early 'cos 'e 'ad the school run in the morning.

'So that left me on me own, out of me 'ead and still randy as 'ell.'

Samantha's flat, Islington

Laura and Kurt were Samantha's friends from university, her best friends in the world. Like

119

Samantha, they had both done well in their two years since graduating. Laura had joined a left-leaning chambers in Middle Temple, and Kurt was a legal officer with the Transport and General Workers' Union. These people were Peter's kind of people. In a way they were younger versions of himself: clever, principled, cultured. For that evening at least Peter had tapped back into the fountain of youth and by rights he should have been feeling terrific, sitting around on cushions eating sushi and drinking wine with these hip young types, basking in their rapt attention.

How long had it been since he and Angela had sat around together on cushions chatting with smart, sexy, young friends?

This was the type of occasion of which Peter only been able to dream in the long grey days before he had been reborn. By rights he should be enjoying himself. He had a *right* to enjoy himself. But try as he might, Peter could not. The guilt was present as ever, redoubled, in fact. Since the complexities of Samantha's needs had begun to dawn on him, he had become more painfully aware that he was simultaneously deceiving both women in his life: Samantha because he knew that he did not love her, and Angela because he knew that he did, and yet he could not resist his affair with Samantha.

He glanced at his watch. Angela would be watching *Newsnight*, sitting in her dressing gown with a glass of wine. The lies had been getting more difficult, and this evening was no exception. Angela knew that there was no late-night session on, and Peter had had to pretend that he was dining with a correspondent from the *New Statesman*. He had not had a choice. Samantha had insisted on this dinner party. It was her twenty-fourth birthday and she said she felt that on at least one day a year she had the right to pretend that she had a proper boyfriend.

Proper boyfriend? This girl saw him as her *boyfriend*.

He was a married man. With two teenaged daughters.

He had to get out.

But on the other hand ... He *was* having fun. To be a part of this twenty-something dinner party, with its ill-matched crockery, cheap, thick tumblers and Ikea bookshelves.

'Mmm, not often we drink Moet. If you're going to go all posh snob on us, Sammy, you'll have to get some flutes,' Laura said, raising her glass. 'Cheers, Peter.'

Peter had splashed out on four bottles of champagne. He was not a wealthy man, but he was wealthier than they were and that was fun also, to be the cool grown-up who could afford decent booze.

Peter took the Switch receipt from his pocket and rolled it into a tight ball between his finger and thumb. He *must* remember to intercept the next bank statement when it came.

'I think what you've been saying about smack and crack and all the Class As is so right,' Kurt said. 'And the fact that you're winning people over is incredible, quite incredible. I saw a leader the other day that said you might just be the only honest politician in the country. I think it was the *Guardian*.'

'Actually it was the *Independent*.' Peter rather wished he hadn't said that. Probably cooler not to know your good reviews off by heart. But how gratifying to have so caught the mood of the younger generation. *They* understood his quest, his passion.

The champagne flowed and Peter's guilt began slowly to lift.

'So come on, then! Tell us, what did Peter get you?'

Samantha did not answer. Instead she went bright red, which was answer enough for her friends, who shrieked with knowing laughter. Peter grinned also, a silly, pleased, naughty-boy grin. Kurt punched his shoulder as one good bloke to another. Peter was one of the gang. He was among people who knew instinctively that a birthday present that caused embarrassment must inevitably be something sexual. A similar conversation at the dinner parties he and Angela held would lead the mind inevitably to a car vacuum cleaner or a useless pair of sugar tongs. But these were people for whom a vigorous and creative sex life was simply a given.

Young people.

Well, he was young, damn it. Forty-three wasn't old, especially if at that age you've managed to make it into the forefront of national life.

Laura poured more champagne. She was determined to capitalize on Samantha's embarrassment. 'Come on, Sam, tell us. What did he get you?'

'A few things. I can't tell you everything.'

'Why not?'

'Because it's none of your beeswax, Laura! Anyway, I got this.'

Samantha opened the bottom two buttons of her blouse to reveal the little diamond that hung from her belly-button ring. Peter grimaced with sheepish good humour while his new friends admired his taste. What a feeling it was to have bought one's girlfriend such a thing!

One's girlfriend? That was certainly how he'd seen it when he'd slipped into the jeweller's shop on Kensington High Street. So perhaps he was her boyfriend, after all. If that was the case *he had to get out.*

But not now, not tonight, not with that cute little jewel nestling inside his beautiful girlfriend's beautiful navel.

'Photo! Photo!' Laura demanded.

'No!' Samantha said firmly. 'I don't want to embarrass Peter.'

'No, of course not, sorry . . . Wouldn't want that getting developed at Boots, would we? Well, I'm going to photograph you anyway. Peter doesn't have to be in it. Come on, Kurt, shine that lamp on Sammy's tummy. Make the diamond sparkle.'

Samantha allowed herself to be photographed, saying that she felt like that awful posh bint whose tummy had recently been all over the papers with Tommy Hanson's name written round it.

'Come on, what else did he get you?' Kurt asked as Samantha did up her blouse.

And with a little persuasion she came clean about Peter's other presents: a sheer silk teddy and an exquisite, leather-bound antique copy of the *Kama Sutra*. Peter protested mildly at these revelations, but in truth he basked in them.

To cover her embarrassment, Samantha cleared away the dishes and emptied the swing-bin, showing that she was a practical young woman and not some bejewelled temptress.

Later on, after dinner and much laughter, the talk turned back to Peter's crusade. Samantha had brought in coffee and brandy, feeling terribly grown up, like a proper hostess, and Kurt had rolled a joint which Peter did not share for fear of coughing. All three young people were so impressed and supportive of what Peter was doing. It felt so good to wallow in their awestruck praise after the daily battering that he was taking from some parts of the house and the more reactionary columnists. He *was* right, he knew he was right, and the next generation of opinion-formers knew it too. He was their inspiration. Their champion. And he could not resist showing off to them.

'Oh yes, the Prime Minister has given me a right bollocking this last two weeks.'

Sitting at Peter's feet Samantha breathlessly bore witness to this claim. 'I was standing outside the PM's office waiting to give Peter some papers. I could hear the shouting.'

'But it wasn't all one way, was it, Sammy? I gave as good as I got.'

'You certainly did, babes.'

'The PM knows that the tide's beginning to turn my way. All right, there are still people out there who want to paint me as some dangerous maniac, but there are plenty more who can at least see that I'm right to raise the debate.'

'Of course you are. It's all so *obvious*.'

'You're the only honest one amongst them, Peter!'

And so he sipped his brandy and held his parliamentary assistant's hand and wallowed in the admiration of her friends, who smoked their joints and looked upon him as the sort of person they wanted to be.

Then Laura and Kurt gave Samantha her present. Something it turned out that they had always shared at birthdays since their second year at Cambridge. A very special treat. A gram of cocaine.

'A truly classy present,' Kurt said. 'Class A, in fact.'

'Jesus!' Peter said. 'I'm a Member of Parliament!'

'Gotta walk it the way you talk it, Peter.'

Peter was not so drunk as not to remind them that he advocated legalization, not participation. 'I don't want to see more people using drugs. I want to protect the community from those who do and protect the users from themselves.'

'I'd hardly call three birthdays a year using. We're exactly the kind of people you're talking about, Peter. Proof that drugs are not necessarily an instant route to hopeless addiction. Proof that people can be trusted to take drugs responsibly.'

Peter had never had cocaine before. Surely it was appropriate to know a little about the subject on which he was now the country's leading spokesperson?

Later, feeling elated and confident, sure of himself and his abilities and master of his destiny, Peter practised his next speech on Samantha. She listened to it from the bed, having put on her new silk teddy.

Peter was surprised to discover that while he most certainly wanted to talk to Samantha, he did not particularly wish to make love to her. He just wanted to talk and talk and talk.

When he had finally finished reciting his speech, punctuated as it was with many digressions, explanations and justifications, Samantha slipped the straps of her lingerie from her shoulders and allowed the garment to fall away, exposing the firm, full breasts that Peter had lusted after for so long.

'Well?' Samantha enquired.

'Would you like to hear my speech again?' Peter replied.

Brown's Hotel, London

'Why do you take that stuff, Tommy?' Her accent was Croatian. Exotic, eastern European – seductive, particularly combined with the elegance of her perfect English.

'Eh? What's that, love?'

'The drugs. Don't you think you've had enough?'

'Contradiction in terms, Geets. *Can't* have enough. Go on, 'ave a toot.'

'I never take drugs, Tommy, you know that.'

'Do I?'

'How many evenings have you called me up for sex?'

'Dunno, darlin', couple?'

'Six times now and you never once saw me take a drug.'

'Has it been six times? Fook. I must be in love. You're crackin' easy on the eye, love, that's for sure.'

'I shouldn't let you call me like this. The club is really coming down hard on girls going with guests. I'd lose my job if they knew I'd become your whore.'

Tommy looked up from the powdery mirror he had been leaning over. His bloodshot puppy-dog eyes seemed hurt.

'Eh, don't put it like that, love. Whore? Blimey, that's a bit strong, in't it? We're mates, you and me, aren't we? It's just that I've got shitloads of dosh, that's all, and I like givin' me money to me mates.'

'OK, Tommy, if you say so, but all the same my employers would not be happy with our "friendship". We've been told no touching in the booths, you know. No more fifty-pound handjobs. Apparently Westminster Council have given the club a warning.'

'Fookin' 'ell, you'd think they had better things to do, wouldn't you? Why don't they clean the dogshit off the pavements? Why the fook should they care about whether or not a bloke gets a quick one off the wrist before he goes home? It's pathetic, that. Come on, darlin', 'ave a toot, you'll love it.'

'I hate drugs.'

'The only people who hate drugs are people who 'aven't tried 'em.'

'Tommy, I've taken drugs, plenty of them. Before the war. I was the same as all the other little rich kids in Zagreb. I didn't know about the pain then. The damage they do.'

'Fook me, Geets, you sound like some old granny who's been reading the *News of the World*. Of course drugs can fook you up big time, but only if you're stupid. If you use 'em right there's no need to become a casualty at all—'

'Tommy, I'm not talking about the damage drugs do to the people who take them.'

'No?'

'Hey, sweetie, I come from a country that spent the last decade in the Middle Ages. Why would I give two fucks about how many little English boys and girls get strung out? And if a few of them OD and end up dead in the gutter who cares? Not me.'

'Charming.'

'I know of villages where every single young woman has been raped, not once but repeatedly. Most of the older ones, too, and the little girls.'

'Yeah, all right, hang on, fine, fair enough, that's terrible that is, totally terrible, point taken. I mean, yeah, of course, not arguing with you on that one, but what's all that Bosnia malarky got to do with drugs?'

'Let me ask you a question, Tommy. How many Croatian whores do you think there are working in London?'

'How would I know? I only know the one, but you'll do for me, girl.'

'And in Paris and Berlin, Brussels, Rome, wherever.'

'No idea. I shouldn't think there's many more of them as gorgeous as you.'

'I make a lot of money. It's easier to look good when you have a lot of money.'

'Hey, don't undersell yourself. You're different. Classy.'

'Oh, you're right about that, Tommy. I'm different, that's for sure. Different from all those other Croatian whores, because, you see, I still have my passport.'

'Eh?'

'They take their passports, Tommy, they wipe out their identities, their names even, then they lock them up inside their brothels.'

It was clear that Tommy was attempting to focus. This was not the type of conversation he had been planning to have when he had called Ghita from his car after leaving Spearmint Rhino's.

'What? Has somebody tried to do that to you or summat? 'Cos if you're in trouble or whatever, I can . . .'

'I'm not in trouble, Tommy. I'm a different kind of sexual refugee. I was educated. My family was rich once, before the wars destroyed us all. Like you say, I'm classy. When I was fifteen I'd already spent a year in Paris. I was going to be a brilliant linguist.'

'Well, you're certainly very good with your tongue, darlin', that's for sure . . .'

Tommy laughed loudly at his joke, but Ghita didn't seem to have heard it.

'But you see, most of the Croatian girls who work in the West and all the other poor white Euro-trash, the Slovaks, the Ukrainians, the Russians, the Serbs, they are peasants, or they *were* peasants. Now they are slaves. Captured, lured across borders, promised a better life, beaten, drugged, shipped in packing cases, kept in cellars . . .'

'Yeah, all right, all right! White slavery, God, we've all watched Channel Four, we know it's out there. What's it got to do with my bit of charlie?'

'The drug economy fuels it all, pays the wages, dopes the girls. The drug-trade routes are the same as the sexual slavery ones. The same people are shipping the merchandise. It's the power and wealth that drugs have brought to these people that allows them to do the things they do. The extortionate marked-up price you paid for that stuff you're sniffing, Tommy, is what finances half the misery in eastern Europe, and well beyond.'

'Here, hang on a minute. Don't give me a hard time, babes. I'm paying you.'

'I thought you said we were friends, but as I said, I'm your whore.'

'Look, d'ya want to get paid or not?'

'I don't care, Tommy, there're plenty more clients

where you came from. You British, you Americans . . .'

'Hey, don't blame us for them. There is a difference, you know.'

'French, Germans, Arabs! You have laws against drugs, you have laws against selling women, but you want the drugs and you want the women. Why don't you just take them, for Christ's sake? Take your drugs and your women! Put them in shop windows like the Dutch do, the only honest nation in Europe! Instead of hiding behind your stupid hypocritical laws that leave the rest of the world at the mercy of a bunch of gangsters.'

'Look, Geets, you've lost me. Are we gonna 'ave another fook or what?'

Ghita stopped. 'For sure, baby, right now. I'm going to make you feel so good. How do you want me?'

'Ahhh, now that's fookin' better.'

St Hilda's Church Hall, Soho

'Can you believe it? She's tryin' to tell me something important and all I'm trying to do is shag her. How pathetic can you get? That's why I've got to clean up, see? I have just *got* to fookin' clean up, because, honest, I am *not* the bloke I've been telling you about. I am not the sort of man that kicks birds outa limos and I am definitely not the sort of man that tells a girl whose family got killed and who speaks more languages than I've 'ad shits that she gives good head. I don't *do* that! That's the bastard inside me does that. Charlie's mate . . . I have *got* to clean up, I have just *got to clean* . . .'

Suddenly tears appeared in Tommy's eyes. 'Oh, fook it. I'm going to the pub.'

And Tommy walked out of the meeting. He did not stop crying until midway through his second double-vodka Bloody Mary. He told the barman he had hayfever. The barman didn't care either way. It didn't cross his mind that this red-eyed, red-nosed, sweaty, pasty-looking screw-up in the beanie hat was Tommy Hanson.

The Paget household, Dalston

Peter Paget laid a fatherly arm round the shoulders of his teenaged daughters and for a moment attempted to extend his reach to include his wife but realized halfway through the manoeuvre that the four of them were beginning to resemble a rugby scrum.

'Good morning, everybody, thank you very much for .coming. We'll be happy to pose for a family photograph for the next few minutes, but neither my wife nor my daughters will be answering any questions.'

'Cathy! Suzie! Have you ever taken drugs yourselves?'

'I *think* I just said that my daughters will not be—'

'Girls, do any of your friends take drugs?'

'Are they available in your school?'

Cathy, the elder of the two girls, laughed. 'Of course they're available at our school. Where *aren't* they?'

'Cathy, I thought we'd agreed that—'

'Oh, come on, Dad, don't you think these questions are a bit sad, like it's a big shock that you can get drugs in schools? The shock would be if you could get a decent education.'

A woman at the front of the pack was recognizable even to Cathy. Paula Wooldridge was one of those columnists who have become half-celebrities themselves, having made occasional appearances on morning television and *Have I Got News For You*. She thrust her tape recorder forward.

'So you take drugs yourself, then, Cathy?'

'Do you?'

'That's not the issue.'

'Isn't it? Why not?'

'Because my father isn't conducting a campaign to legalize dangerous drugs.'

'That's my father, not me.'

'You've chosen to associate yourself with his campaign.'

'I've chosen to stand on my own front doorstep with my family. I've chosen to allow myself to be photographed, in the forlorn hope that it might stop you following me to school like you did yesterday, Paula. These things are not illegal . . .'

Using the woman's name, Peter thought, her first name, how superbly patronizing, coldly ingratiating, a brilliant politician's tactic, and the girl was only sixteen. His daughter pressed her advantage.

'But taking drugs *is* illegal, and I'm asking you if you take them, armed with the statistical probability that you do, seeing as how your profession is notoriously riddled with drugs. If you do take them and you admit it to me then I can make a citizen's arrest and perform a public service. *That* is why it is the issue, Paula.'

Almost everybody laughed. Not Paula, of course. Cathy had made a mortal enemy there. Not Peter Paget, either. He smiled, certainly, an indulgent, fatherly smile, but through slightly clenched teeth. Paget adored his daughter, but, *bloody hell*, this was *his* press conference.

Dalston Police Station

Commander Leman had known what was in the brown card-backed envelope even before he opened it. So sure had he been that he had even donned plastic gloves in the futile hope that he might not further add to the forensic confusion which an envelope that had

131

been through the postal service might have attracted.

The photographs were large and of good quality. In some of them Jo Jo was spread on a formica table. In others she was on the floor. One by one Leman passed the photographs across the desk to Detective Sergeant Sara Hopper. After studying them for some time, the sergeant ventured an opinion.

'Four men. Three white, one black.'

'How can you tell? It looks like there could be five or six to me.'

The men in the photographs were hooded, besides which they could not be seen whole, being partly cropped out of the framing. Limbs, torsos, hands. And genitals.

'There's four of them. All unprotected.'

Leman could find no voice with which to speak. He tried, but no words came. The Detective Sergeant continued.

'We knew she'd been raped, both anally and vaginally. That was clear from the medical examination.'

'Have you told her?'

'She's no fool. She knows how she feels inside. This was not a gentle attack.'

'How is she? I mean, will she come through it? She's a strong girl, isn't she?'

'I don't know. I really don't know if one can ever recover from something like this. I can't see how she'll be the same person, if that's what you're asking.'

'Yes, I suppose that's what I meant.' Commander Leman's mind was spinning, reeling. He could scarcely comprehend the scale of the tragedy that had befallen this girl and her family. *And it was all his fault.*

The newspaper print, punk-rock-style pasted note that accompanied the pictures made that very clear: 'HOW MANY OTHER FRIENDS DOES ANNA HAVE?' They had done this to scare him. If they had hit his daughter then of course Leman would have had nothing left to lose, but this way, by using Anna's friend . . . her *friends* . . . Leman held the arms of his chair and tried to breathe.

The Paget household, Dalston

Peter Paget's press conference received blanket news coverage, though it had to be said that the majority of it focused on his daughter Cathy's now celebrated public début.

'I can't believe it. You're actually jealous of your sixteen-year-old daughter.'

'Don't be ridiculous. I'm not jealous of her. I can't afford to be jealous of her. She's clearly going to be Prime Minister by the time she's twenty and I may well be looking to her for a job next parliament. I just don't think she understands the risks she's running in taking these people on.'

'Peter, it was *you* who put us all on that doorstep in front of twenty cameramen, not Cathy. And it was you who wanted to parade us like shop dummies so that you could look steady and statesmanlike.'

'Shop dummies!' Peter protested. 'When I said that you and the girls wouldn't take questions I was trying to protect you from media intrusion.'

'How does organizing a photocall protect us from media intrusion?'

'Angela, this is just completely unfair. We agreed!'

'Yes, we agreed. You said what we should do and we agreed to do it.'

'Oh, come on!'

'I'm sorry, Peter. I'm just a bit tired, that's all.'

'*You're* tired?'

'Yes, I'm tired! I know that I don't have to carry the full burden of changing society on my shoulders, but I

133

do have a job and we do have a life, and currently I'm running it. The girls are worried about their exams. The freezer's broken and all the food thawed and now the kitchen stinks of rotten fish and ice cream. Suzie got caught smoking and I'm supposed to attend a sodding counselling meeting at school with her, for Christ's sake. I mean, even *I* fucking smoked at school. Your mother hates your dad and for some reason thinks I'm interested; what's more they want to come and stay because apparently they never see the girls, i.e. we don't make enough effort to see them. Meanwhile, incidentally, your effort to switch us over to internet banking has spectacularly collapsed, taking all our standing orders with it, and they're threatening to cut off the phone and electricity, and I'll have to find the chequebook in your bombsite of a study, which is definitely your job but you are *never* around any more, which I know you can't help, but it is a bit of a shame that on the very first full day you have at home with us in months you organize a media photocall. It's not that I *mind*, Peter. I don't. I know you have to do it, but we're a family, not a prop!'

'Angela! This is *so* unfair.'

'You sound like Kevin the Teenager.'

That made them both laugh at least.

'We agreed on this together. Royal tactics, give them a photo in exchange for their laying off.'

'Yes, and when has that ever helped the royals?'

'I'm campaigning on an issue of vital national importance.'

'You're not in the House of Commons now, Peter—'

'Well, I *am* campaigning on an issue of—'

'I *know* you are! Just give me a moment to adjust to the fact that suddenly I find myself married to a great man!'

'Angela! I can't help wondering if it's you not me who's jealous.'

Samantha did not resent his new position in life. She loved him. Why should he put up with this when he was so very loved and truly admired by a beautiful and passionate young woman? A woman who did not resent his coming greatness but embraced it. A woman whose friends (scarcely less beautiful, passionate or younger than she) hung on his every word. At that moment, Peter longed to tell Angela the truth and show her how decent he was being in sticking with a wife of forty-two whom he so clearly irritated and two daughters who so conspicuously declined to hang upon his every word.

Except, of course, he knew that he was not being decent at all. He was being dishonest and selfish, and his one hope in life was that Angela would never find out. Peter struggled to focus on the discussion that he and his wife were having rather than on the private knowledge that his marriage tottered on a precipice.

'The fact that I am a family man, a family man with two daughters who are in the direct firing line of the problem that I am trying to confront, is clearly not a circumstance I either can or should ignore. My God, when I met that poor girl at that place in King's Cross – the teenaged junkie I told you about – all I could think about was our girls. There isn't a parent in the country who won't empathize with us as the parents of teenaged children. It's essential that I show that I'm not just some tourist on this issue, that my own life and that of my family will be shaped by the decisions that are made. I thought you agreed with me on all this.'

'I agreed that if you pursued your Private Member's Bill we wouldn't be able to keep Cathy and Suzie out of it.'

'And are you saying that you would prefer me not to pursue it? Because I'll drop it if you are. I can't do this without you, and I won't do it without your honest support.'

He meant it, too. He owed Angela a great deal more than that.

To his surprise she kissed him.

'No, no, of course I don't want you to drop it, Peter, you know that ... And I'm sorry for being mean. You're under a lot of pressure at the moment. It's no wonder you've been distant. I believe in what we're doing as much as you do. You're right to say the unsayable, you're the only one who will. And of course Cathy and Suzie want to support you. This is their issue too. I'm proud of the girls. Very.'

Peter kissed Angela back. Once more the pendulum of his tortured soul swung wildly. He was so lucky to have so generous and intelligent a wife.

'I'm proud of them too, Angela, and I'm proud of you. And I was especially proud of Cathy today, honestly I was. The way she roasted that awful Wooldridge woman. All right, yes, I suppose I was a bit taken aback that it was Cathy who starred in our little media event and not me, but that's just me being a completely pathetic and contemptible old arsehole.'

'And that's one of your better points.'

'Well, even if Dad is an idiot, I am still Dad and we're a family and families stick by one another, don't they?'

'Yes, that's what they're for.'

Just then Peter's mobile rang.

'Hello, sex machine. Guess who's got no clothes on?'

Peter Paget had not spent a lifetime in politics without learning something about dealing with unexpected questions. 'Oh, hello, Samantha. No, I haven't forgotten my four thirty interview. Well done, by the way, for getting me such an instant right of reply. The Paula Wooldridge piece was the only negative copy we got.'

'I'm touching myself where I want you to put your big cock right now.'

136

'Yes, Cathy did do well, didn't she? Angela and I are very proud of her.'

'My nipples are hard just thinking about what you did to me in bed yesterday.'

'Look, Samantha, I'll have to go, I'm afraid. Family stuff. I'll be fine with the paper on my own, no need to . . . Oh, all right, good, see you there.'

The M1 motorway

The traffic jam had finally cleared and Jessie was on her way to Birmingham, still recounting her story to the old lady who sat beside her. Jessie's life did not bring her into much contact with people who wanted to listen.

'By the middle of the morning Ah was on ma own in François' flat. The three other girls had already found themselves new pimps. It's true, they went straight out and got themselves another vicious shithead slave-runnin' bastard for the price of a hit-up of smack and a mattress to pass out on.'

The old lady could not remember being so completely riveted in her entire life as Jessie's rambling monologue washed over her.

'Ah nearly did the same, Ah swear. I was that strung out and scared I nearly went out and got masel' a new pimp, but somethin' inside 'a me . . . like, a memory of the human being Ah'd bin before, stopped me doin' it. Instead I searched the whole of François' flat for money and valuables. The other girls had thought about the same thing but they'd been too frightened. The shadow of that woman-beating bastard still lay about the place heavy as one of his stinkin' blankets. Ah felt it masel' somethin' terrible as Ah checked behind the cushions of the sofa and under the sheets of that disgustin' bed where he first broke me in.'

The old lady offered Jessie a peppermint. It was the only gesture of support she could think of making.

'Honest, Ah half expected the bastard tae rear up from under the sheets and put his fist into ma stomach like he'd done many times before. He rarely hit us in the face because even in the world of kerb-crawling looks count, although of course there's a few that find black eyes attractive. Ah found about thirty pounds an' a watch, and besides that there was some cutlery and a kettle and a telly and VCR. By the time Ah'd got it all down the pawn shop in a minicab Ah had over a hundred and fifty pounds and a plan.'

'To give up drugs?'

'Don't be ridiculous.'

The Groucho Club, Soho

A wide, supercilious smile spread across Milton's pasty jowls as his colleague joined him. She was ten years younger than him, much better looking and despite the fact that he was nominally her departmental boss she was rather more successful. Therefore her humiliation at the hands of the teenage Paget girl had been most satisfying. Sweet though it was, Milton had never dared to hope that Paula would further compound her defeat so comprehensively with such a poor effort as the one he had spread out before him. As she sat down, Milton rested his beer carefully on top of her byline and photograph.

'God, your column was crap this morning, Paula. The editor's furious with me for even running it. But do you know, I just couldn't resist it.'

'What do you mean, crap?'

'Going after Paget like that, darling, and of course his fragrant daughter.'

'Why the fuck shouldn't I go after them?'

'A whole page, dear? It looks like sour grapes.'

'What do you mean, sour grapes? What on earth would I have to be sour about?'

Milton actually laughed at her. Paula was playing it all so terribly wrong. The only manner to assume under such circumstances was good-humoured acknowledgement. Put your hand up to it, admit you've cocked up and swear to get even. Toughing it out was not an option.

'What have you to be sour about? Nothing at all, except being made to look like a complete arse by a juvenile on the national news. She really was awfully good, that girl. I think we should offer her a job, voice of youth and all that. Perhaps she could have your page.'

Paula flinched.

'*Do* you take drugs, by the way? Do tell, as if we didn't know. She had you down right there, didn't she?'

'Look, Milton, I haven't given Peter Paget or his smartarse sodding daughter a second thought since we doorstepped them. I wrote my piece because Paget is a shitty little careerist and his obnoxious brat is just one more cocky little posh kid who thinks the world was put there for her own personal amusement.'

'You can't call the Pagets posh, Paula. They're not remotely posh. We're both miles posher than they are.'

'We are not the issue.'

'Yes, that's what you said to the girl, wasn't it? They played it on all the channels and it didn't sound convincing then, either.'

'Look, they're posh if I say they're posh. I can call them what I fucking like, darling, I'm a columnist.'

'They're middle-class, Paula. And first generation at that. Angela Paget's father was a miner.'

'They live in a five hundred grand house.'

'Yes, so you said in your desperate little piece.

139

Picture and all, most unethical. I expect he's already been on to the Press Council. He's an MP, you know, terrorist target, et cetera.'

'Bollocks. When did the IRA last blow up a back-bencher?'

'Oh, it's all mad Muslims these days, dear. Most unpredictable.'

'Look, this is about hypocrisy. He acts like he's one of us and yet—'

'One of *who*?'

'One of the fucking people we represent, Milton! And yet he lives in a posh snob hoity-toity house! That is something which in my opinion is a matter of legitimate public interest.'

'Paula, even the morons who read your page know that a terrace in Dalston is not posh snob hoity-toity, even a three-storey one. I saw that the picture department did their best to crop out the abandoned car and the council dustbins, but despite that it still looked like the crappy north London terrace it is. Do tell me if you find a large house anywhere in London that you can get for less than half a mil. I'll buy it.'

'Look—'

'No, you look, Paula! And while you're looking, listen too. Listen very carefully. It was a pathetic column, so far beneath you it's looking up your arse, and quite frankly it reflects badly on the whole paper. You got bagged by a kid and you went straight home and tried to get your own back and you've made yourself look like an even bigger twat than you did before.'

'We agreed to go after Paget for using his family for publicity—'

'*Not* the day after that same family scored such a whopping great point off you, dear. Not with zero ammunition beyond one perfectly reasonable photo-call and the ABC Book of Spite. I can tell you now that I think you've made yourself look an arse.'

Milton sneered at Paula. He fancied her, of course, but she had consistently denied his advances. Right back to that very first week after she had joined the paper's famous Bitch Squad of gossip columnists of whom Milton was in charge. He'd tried to muscle her into the photocopying room and shag her over the Xerox machine. She'd told him to fuck off in front of everybody and he'd hated her ever since, a fact which had not stopped him periodically repeating his efforts to pull her. Humiliating her now was an act of sexual conquest for Milton, and he was enjoying every moment of it.

'We're not happy, Paula. Not happy at all,' Milton crowed. 'Even celebrity columnists can be replaced, you know, so if you're going to go after Paget again you'd better have something worth hitting him with. Otherwise stick to slagging off Posh and Becks and Tommy Hanson.'

The Langham Hotel, W1

Peter's interview was to take place in a day room at the Langham. Normally Peter enjoyed doing these interviews very much. In his first seventeen years in Parliament scarcely any writer of any sort had sought his opinion on anything. Now his sudden notoriety meant that the world simply could not get enough of him and it was intoxicating. Peter loved the whole business: meeting in flashy hotel foyers, ordering coffee and sandwiches and bottles of mineral water at some newspaper's expense, perhaps even a drink or two if it was late in the afternoon. All in all, it was very pleasant to spend an hour or two being pampered while one's opinions were earnestly canvased. Today, however, Peter was out of sorts. He did not return Samantha's smile of greeting as he mounted the steps of the hotel and he recoiled from her efforts to embrace him.

'For God's sake, Samantha!' he hissed. 'You're my parliamentary assistant. We can't go kissing in public!'

'Of course we can, everybody hugs these days. Haven't you noticed? It's post-Diana Britain. We all show our emotions.'

'Our emotions are exactly the thing we mustn't show. Samantha, I am a married man.'

'Nobody knows that better than I do, Peter.'

'What on earth were you thinking phoning me like that? On a *mobile* of all things. Mobiles aren't secure.'

'God, you're talking like I was selling secrets to the Russians, not talking about sex.'

'Shut *up*, Sammy! Please! Now is not the time to become blasé about our . . .'

'Love?'

'Relationship. My bill is slowly working its way through the house. It would be a disaster if there was a scandal now.'

'Don't worry. I'm not going to mess up your career, Peter. I just wanted to talk to you, that's all, flirt with you.'

'Well, please don't. And particularly not on a mobile.'

'Guess what I did?'

'What?'

'I asked the paper if we could keep the room they've reserved for us for an hour or two after the interview. They said fine, it's booked for the day anyway.'

'You did *what*?'

'It's all right. I told them we had work to do and another interview later.'

'And they believed you?'

'Why wouldn't they?' And Samantha squeezed Peter's hand, only briefly, scarcely so as you'd notice.

Except that somebody did notice. Christobel, the journalist whom Peter was supposed to meet, had arrived early and had been watching Peter and Samantha's conversation from behind a teacup.

Peter put his anger with Samantha behind him and applied himself to the interview with vigour. It was an easy task, because his subject made him angry too.

'In some areas there is a drug dealer on every street corner but no corner shop! How insane is that, Christobel? There used to be shops, certainly, but now they're all boarded up. No one is interested in buying the businesses, and why? Because the surrounding area is alive with little boys selling smack and sticking knives into each other, that's why. For vast sections of the population, Christobel, buying drugs is a simple matter of taking two steps outside their front door, but if they want a teabag it's a half-hour walk to get to a Sainsbury's that's built like Fort Apache in the Bronx. Drugs are totally illegal and yet in some areas they're the only things available for sale! This is an Alice in Wonderland world, Christobel, a surreal madness. If the government had let the corner shops sell the drugs in the first place, or at least the local chemists and off licences, all those little boys who are closing down neighbourhoods would be doing paper rounds and Saturday jobs instead.'

The interview had gone extremely well. Peter's arguments had been passionate and convincing and Christobel felt confident that they would make very sexy copy indeed with all that talk of 'smack' and 'knives' and the like. It had also been clear to her that Paget was genuinely committed to his ideas. Quite obviously he believed absolutely in his cause, that there was only one way for the country and indeed the world to get out of the fix it was in, and that was to legalize all drugs. What was more, having listened to him for over an hour, Christobel was inclined to agree with him. Unfortunately for Peter, the subject of his Private Member's Bill was not what was on the journalist's mind when, after the interview, she had called her colleague Paula. Nor was it on her mind now as she and Paula hid in a service cupboard in the corridor outside the room in which Christobel had left Peter working with his parliamentary assistant.

'If I'm right about this, Paula, you'll owe me for the rest of your life.'

'If you're right I'll be happy to pay, Chrissie, till the day I die . . .'

Paula and Christobel had worked together in the early days of their careers, struggling as one against the blokey culture of the early-eighties *Sun*.

'There's certainly been no other interviewer going into that bedroom, which is what the girl said was going to happen.'

'He's shagging her in there. Got to be.'

'No proof, though. Shall we snap them when they come out?'

'No! Christ, no! We've got nothing at the moment and we'll just put them on their guard.'

'They're in a hotel room together.'

'A hotel room which you booked, for Christ's sake, Chrissie! And for which our newspaper will be picking up the bill.'

'If the bed's been used . . .'

'Oh, come on, nobody would believe we didn't ruffle it ourselves. No, we have to watch and wait. And if we're patient, and we get the proof we need, then I can get the little bastard on a family values rap and I'll kill him for ever. It would be so unutterably sweet. He's fighting the drugs war as a dedicated family man while knocking off a bird not much older than his daughters. I'd get my revenge on him, his slaggy little brat and my lovely lovely boss Milton all at once. So patience, darling, patience.'

*　*　*

'That was lovely, Peter, really lovely. It's such a beautiful thing to be making love to an older man.'

'Hmm, something of a backhanded compliment that, don't you think?'

'No, really. I had a lecturer at university and he was like you – I don't know, sort of wise . . . physically. It felt like he understood me, my body, I mean. You're like that.'

'I thought you only had young boyfriends at university. You said they were all silly boys.'

'Well, all the others were, but . . .'

'All the others? Sounds like there were great hordes of them.'

'Oh, there were. I was a terrible scrubber. I liked to break their hearts, you see. But this one broke mine. It didn't last long: two times, that was all. He ended it, position of authority and all that, he didn't want a scandal.'

'Ah yes. That I can understand.'

'He used me.'

'Just like you used all those other men, eh?'

'Different.'

'How so?'

'Level playing field. Eighteen-year-old girl, eighteen-year-old boy. All's fair.'

'Let me assure you, Sammy, eighteen-year-old boys are no match for eighteen-year-old girls. In fact, if you're talking about level playing fields, I think we've got it just about right. Twenty-four-year-old girl, forty-three-year-old man. Pretty much parity in terms of emotional development, I'd say.'

'I'm sorry I upset you by phoning your mobile, Peter. It's just I really wanted to talk to you. You see, it was eleven o'clock in the morning.'

'Meaning what?'

'Don't you remember what I told you, about my

145

father . . . when I was eleven?'

'Oh yes, of course.'

The uneasy feelings that Peter had been harbouring about his relationship with Samantha shot once more to the surface. *End it. Get out now!*

Slowly but surely the girl was revealing her emotional hand, and it was a far more complex one than Peter felt remotely comfortable with. Surely she didn't imagine herself in love with him? Puppy love, perhaps, but she couldn't be imagining that he might ever leave his wife and family for her . . .

He had made his position on that point plain, surely? Well, it was obvious, wasn't it? It had to be. Samantha was a sensible girl. Soon he would talk to her about how they must begin to think about ending their affair. He would talk to her firmly and sensibly, and secretly she would be relieved.

Soon he would talk to her. She would be expecting it . . . Of course she would be.

Peter's thoughts were interrupted by the ringing of his mobile. It was Commander Leman.

'Peter. We have to talk.'

An Oxfam shop, West Bromwich

To Jessie her flight from London was already a distant memory. So much had happened to her since then that her long coach trip, talking to the kind old lady with the peppermints, seemed like it had happened in another age. Now once more she found herself telling her story, except this time she hoped it would win her more than a Trebor Mint. What she needed was clothes.

'That plan Ah left François' flat with was the most pathetic plan Ah could 'a come up with, even if Ah'd 'a racked ma brains for a month, for the simple reason that it was no' a plan tae kick heroin.'

The old gentleman who ran the Oxfam shop nodded. Jessie could see that he was wondering whether any charity dispensed to her might not go straight back into her arm.

'Ah can see what you're thinkin', mister. But Ah'm clean, Ah swear. Ah know now that givin' up heroin is the only plan any self-respectin' smack whore should be considering if she hopes one day tae no' be a whore. But at the time, the heart of a plan, in fact the overridin' objective, was to get more heroin. The truth is that in ma entirely screwed-up state o' mind I imagined that it might be possible for a teenaged prossie wi' no home, or possessions and a hundred and fifty pounds tucked down her bra tae remain a smack-head without gettin' beaten and abused within hours. What Ah had decided was that Ah would go it alone as a whore. No more François. No more pimps. Ah would do exactly what Ah'd bin doin', but I'd keep all the money for masel'. Then Ah'd get a nice flat, plenty of good-quality junk and eventually get my life back together. Once Ah'd done that Ah'd kick the habit and go to college and become a vet like Ah'd thought about when I was a wee girl. That was ma plan, but first and foremost I needed to get fixed up, that was the important thing. Basically when ye boil it right down, ma plan was to score some smack.'

The Oxfam shop man had made Jessie a cup of tea. Jessie's story was certainly a great deal more interesting than trying to prevent teenaged girls stealing costume jewellery.

'On a whim Ah decided to get out o' town altogether. London had been shite for me from the first second Ah got off the train. With François gone Ah decided that it was time tae leave, so Ah made up ma mind tae get down Victoria Coach Station an' get the first coach out. But before that of course Ah had tae score. Oh yeah, that was for sure, Ah couldnae be sitting on no coach straight, could Ah? Suppose we got caught in traffic and Ah was trapped and strung out? Ah'd be scratchin' masel' an' fidgetin' an' trying not to puke up or shit masel', and before you knew it Ah'd be writhin' about on the floor, withdrawin' and scaring all the old ladies. The funny thing is we *did* get mightily delayed an' Ah was sat next tae a right sweet old girl, but luckily Ah was high an' Ah wasnae sick on her.

'For a minute as Ah left the flat Ah almost panicked about scoring because the funny thing was that although Ah'd been a hopeless user for months Ah'd never actually bought any gear masel'. François always fixed me up, see, that was his power. Anyways, Ah needn't 'a worried. As Ah'm sure you're aware, runnin' a business round here, it doesnae take much effort to score drugs in this country. Ah walked out of François' craphole and in the corridor outside the flat, the *corridor*, the one ye have tae walk along tae get tae the lifts before ye can even get tae the street, there's these three Somali boys hanging about, couldn't 'a been more than seventeen. Ah knew their game for sure, so Ah just goes straight up to them and asks them to fix me up with some brown an' a bit o' white, you know, just tae take the edge off. Ah couldnae even see their faces from under their hoods but Ah'd picked 'em right because this boy just grunts an' gets on his mobile phone an' two minutes later his man turns up an' spits two wraps out o' his mouth, takes ma forty-five quid and that's it, done deal. He hardly even stopped moving.

'Ah hit masel' up in the corridor there an' then. Just stuck a needle in the crook o' ma knee while the Somali boys stood round and laughed at me from under the hoods o' their big gangsta tops. Ah suppose Ah should be grateful they didnae rob me there and then. Ah were that strung out Ah never could 'a run, but Ah guess they didnae know that ma pimp was out

148

the picture and of course pimps have guns – although increasingly Ah've found so do wee boys.

'So off Ah goes tae Victoria, sitting on the tube chilling out on a substantial mellow an' for a brief moment Ahm happy, 'cos François' bin nicked, Ah've got a hundred an' five pounds in ma tits, Ah'm leavin' town. Ah'm a girl in charge of her own destiny. Like fuck, eh? Nobody who does smack is in charge of one atom o' their body, let alone their destiny.'

Starbucks, Soho

'I'm afraid I won't be able to attend the parliamentary committee session after all, Peter. Sorry, but my mind's made up.'

'But, Barry. You're my key witness. My star player. The whole thing has been set up for you to speak. A senior cop talking about drug corruption is—'

'I know, Peter, but I've decided that it's inappropriate for a serving police officer to be getting so actively involved in political debate. What's more, I've issued a statement to that effect on my internet site. I'm afraid I'm bowing out, Peter. I've made my last statement on the issue.'

'*What?!* You and I've put our necks on the line together for a cause that we believe will eventually save thousands of lives. What the hell has happened?'

'You don't want to know.'

'I *do* want to know!'

'The people I've been investigating have struck back. They drugged and raped a friend of my daughter's.'

'Oh my God.'

'I believe that as long as I continue to bring their corrupt activities to light as fuel for your legalization campaign they'll continue their attacks. They're clever. They'll probably leave my daughter alone but they'll

149

pick another of her friends. I can't proceed under those circumstances.'

'No, I can see that . . . Barry, what about my girls?'

'I don't believe you've anything to worry about. This is about police corruption. They want to stop me digging and they have done. Your campaign is a different issue and besides, it's all so public with you. Your daughters are celebrities now. If these bastards have any sense at all, which they definitely do, they'll realize that any criminal intimidation directed at you and your family would only increase the force of your argument. No. This is between me and a small group of very dangerous, very bent coppers. They want to shut me up and I'm here to tell you that they've succeeded.'

'I'm so sorry, Barry. I mean for the girl.'

'Yes. So am I.'

Fallowfield Community Hall, Manchester

Another town, another church hall, another alcoholics support group.

'My name is Tommy and I'm an alcoholic, and this is about the millionth time I've tried to straighten out. I expect I'll end up having to go to dry out in LA like all the other sad act recovering rock stars. Nobody drinks out there, see. If you order a beer they call the police. Only problem is it's so fookin' *boring*! All them stars end up worshipping their bodies, don't they? Addicted to health, or at least to some skinny, scrawny, mean-looking version of health. It's all they've got left to take an interest in, in't it? Well, fook that. I ain't spendin' the rest of my life goin' in an' out of gyms with a two-litre bottle of water in me 'and.'

Tommy was not in the peak of health. There was a small roll of flesh at his belt and he was a little puffy about the eyes, but nonetheless he was still hugely attractive. Another few kilograms, though, and the looks would begin to go. Tommy knew that very well and it compounded his drug dependency, for while he recognized that booze made him fat, he saw cigarettes and cocaine as slimming drugs.

'I went on a pretty bad bender after I fell off the wagon in Soho. Not a lot of idea what went on, really. Shaggin' and coke, I imagine. There's bits and pieces in the tabloids and celeb mags: Tommy falling out of the Met Bar, Tommy flickin' the Vs at the paps, so I know I stayed in London, but it's all a bit of a blur, to be honest. I just remember waking up in my big stupid house in Notting Hill with that bird off one of them Saturday morning kids' shows ... Not SMTV, a cable channel version, I think, you know, all pop music and chuckin' custard pies about with a couple of twenty-year-olds pretending to be eight years old and terminally hip at the same time. I've always had a penchant for the birds off kids' TV – they're always so perky, in't they? Like the first teacher you ever fancied. Cute an' perky an' mad for it in my experience, *gaggin'*. Well, it's 'avin' to be all sugar and spice all day long, in't it? 'Course it is. If your work consisted o' coaxing questions out o' shy six-year-olds what had rung in to ask S Club if they like singin' or dancin' more then you'd want it large of a night. An', like I say, in my experience kids' pop-show birds like it huge! They hang out wi' all these cool pop stars but at the end of the day they still have to get gunked for charity, so when they get off work they just can't wait to get sixteen vodkas, a gram of coke and a big celebrity dick inside them. An' who can blame 'em?

'Chloe, her name was, I think. Maybe not. Cheryl? Could 'a been. No, Mum's name is Cheryl. So Chloe, probably. Top bird, as I remember, one o' that type that tells you she in't wearing no knickers within five minutes o' starting a conversation. I love that, me, *love it.* So anyways, there's me and this bird lying in my big fook-off bed wondering whether we've got the energy for a bit o' beer breath bangin' or not and she reckons maybe with a line or two up her hooter, so she's leaning over to grab me coke when suddenly she's shriekin' and hauling the sheets up over her tits, and I looks round an' Tony my tour manager is actually standing over us lookin' at his watch an' saying it's time to go back to work.

'I never should 'a' given that bastard a key.'

Tommy's house, Notting Hill Gate

'Get out, you bloody pervert! He's been looking at my breasts, Tommy! I swear he's been standing there checking out my tits!'

'No, he ain't, love. He's a tour manager. He's immune to tits.'

Tony put a packet of cigarettes and a lighter onto Tommy's bedside table. 'Sorry, darling, didn't mean to catch you all embarrassing, but I've been ringing the doorbell for twenty minutes. You must've been out of it. Come on, Tommy, get up and get your kecks on. You're coming with me.'

'Fook off, Tone. You are takin' the piss, surely?'

'Who is this pervert, Tommy? Is it a lads' thing? Do you let your mates pop in to stare at the women you pick up? If so that's pretty sad.'

Tommy wrapped a pillow round his head. 'Sorry, love, but do you think you could modulate your voice a bit? You got one o' them piercers, great for kids' telly but it's doin' my 'ead in. This is Tony. He sorts out my stuff.'

'Does he now? Very cosy. Well, just you tell Tony to piss off so I can put some clothes on.'

Tony did not even glance at Chloe. She might as well

have been an extra pillow. 'Tommy. Get up. Put your kecks on. Come downstairs and get in the car.'

'Like I said, Tone, you are taking the piss.'

Chloe did not get to be a morning pop show presenter on cable television by allowing herself to be sidelined. 'Tommy, *you* invited *me* to spend the night with you! As I recall, there was talk of croissants in the morning, coffee also. A nice day out was mentioned – champagne lunch at Cliveden, a shag in the sauna. I did not expect to wake up in the middle of a—!'

'Look, please, Chloe . . . It is Chloe, isn't it?'

'Yes, it's fucking Chloe.'

'There's a dressing gown on the door. Tone, turn round. Chloe, put it on, go and 'ave a shower. Tone, get her a car and tell it to pick up some Starbucks on the way. Take it to Cliveden if you want, love, spend the night, treat a girlfriend, charge it to me. But I cannot handle being bollocked right now, OK?'

'You are such a prick, Tommy Hanson.'

Mustering what dignity she could, Chloe stepped naked from the bed, and, taking up the dressing gown, went through to the bathroom.

Tommy lit a cigarette. 'Go away, Tone.'

'Tommy. The tour starts in three days and it's massive.'

'They're all fookin' massive.'

'Massive even for you. Sold out arenas, half a million tickets gone instantly, Madonna and Guy rumoured to 've been knocked back when they asked for freebies.'

'Fook that. If Madge wants to see me play she can sit on the stage as far as I'm concerned. She's top, that bird, top, undisputed queen of pop.'

'She don't want to see you, Tommy, it's a bullshit rumour, that's all. I'm just saying that everybody's talking about this tour. It's the biggest of the year by miles. You're going to make more money than Bill Gates and it starts in three days.'

'Well, what're you coming round 'ere for now, then? Come back the day after tomorrow. Bring a pen and paper, we'll do the set list.'

'Set list's done, Tom. We're doing the autumn show plus "Tattoo" and "Heaven".'

'Even better. Fook off.'

'Get *up*, Tommy.'

Having had her shower, Chloe took a lipstick from her handbag and wrote 'arsehole' on Tommy's bathroom mirror.

Fallowfield Community Hall, Manchester

'Tony was right, of course. Even I have to do a bit of work, see. You can't just walk on stage and expect it to 'appen, can you? And to give Tone his due he'd left it as long as he could. The band had been rehearsing for a week – not like they needed to, they were so tight people always thought we was using tracks anyway, which is frustrating. It was really the same tour as before, just an extension and an expansion. My success came so quick and I got so big immediately after I won *Pop Hero* that it's been a constant improvisation ever since, trying to make sure we make as much money as we can with an ever-widening horizon. For two years it had seemed like my earning potential had virtually doubled every month and by rights this tour should have actually been in stadiums. Certainly up here in the north where they just fookin' love me, I reckon I could do four Maine Roads sold out. Think about it: four football stadiums here in Manchester alone.

'So Tony had given me three days to get me voice in shape, have a few shots of vitamin B up the arse and try to remember all the words to my songs. He just would not fook off until I got in the car with him and went over to Westbourne Grove where we had a rehearsal and recording studio booked for about a million quid a day. The truth of the matter is I'm pretty professional, actually, when it comes down to it. Besides, I was sick to death of myself and quite fancied the road – you know, hanging out with the boys in the band and the birds in the back line-up. We always have a laugh, us.'

Nomad Studios, Westbourne Grove

Tommy staggered into the rehearsal room doing his comedy 'I'm completely fooked, me' stagger, smiling shyly, ingratiatingly, at the familiar faces, his head bowed, his coat big, and a woolly hat pulled low, the current uniformed stance of the tortured artist hooligan. Spike and Julio, respectively the guitarist and the rhythm guitarist in the band, punched the air in greeting.

'Yo, Tommo!'

'Big up, boss!'

Then, *sotto voce*, 'What a sad bastard, eh?'

'What's he like? I mean, fuck, we've been waiting here a week and look at him.'

'It's funny, isn't it? Hard to remember him now. I mean when he wasn't a twat.'

'I suppose he isn't always a twat even these days.'

'Isn't he? When was he last not a twat, then?'

'Fair point.'

Tommy shuffled down the steps and onto the studio floor, all hunched attitude and tired puppy eyes. Big man, hard man, artiste. Top gun, back in the saddle. Chief outlaw rejoining his posse. Numero uno.

'All right? 'Ow ya doin'? Nice one. Sound. Yeah.'

Standing beneath the big 'no smoking' sign, he pinched the filter off a Silk Cut and lit up. Hey, who was going to tell Tommy not to smoke?

'I need it for me voice, don't I? It's medicinal. It's how I get enough phlegm up to lubricate the high notes.'

Tommy's assembled employees laughed. The musical director called out his orders and the band struck up. Tight, studio perfect, an awesome body of sound. Tommy took the microphone that was offered to him and, sitting on the edge of a flight case, staring directly at the floor, he pushed his voice into the first number. When the song was finished the band applauded and Spike turned once more to Julio.

'He ain't a twat when he sings.'

An Oxfam shop, West Bromwich

'Ah got off the bus in Birmingham wi' ma plan still intact. Ah asked the first homeless kid where was a good street tae whore in and got masel' down there straight away. Ah was still in the uniform François had bought me: white stilettos, little denim mini, pink boob tube. Ah'd always been a bit vain of ma tits, which are big for a wee girl. So there Ah am, on the street, ma first day in charge of ma own destiny since first ma stepdaddy felt me up. It's late afternoon and Ah'm confident o' trade. After work time's always good, lots o' men have tae work late at the office shagging a heroin addict in the back o' their cars.

'Well, Ah suppose Ah'd bin stood there for a couple of minutes when Ah look behind me an' there's these three big ugly Brummie birds all wearin' the same uniform as me, askin' who the fuck Ah think Ah am and wha' the fuck Ah think Ahm daein'. Tae be honest, Ah cannae remember whether they waited for me tae reply or not before they set about me. Bang, a big fistful of rings in the face, a hand wi' purple talons grabs ma hair, an' the stilettos are goin' in big time. They say

156

smack makes you immune tae pain, but not if your stuff was cut with a big dose o' brick dust an' glass and it's wearing off anyways, so Ah turns an' runs, realizin' what Ah should have already known, an' that is that a seventeen-year-old homeless heroin addict is in no position tae make plans.'

A brothel, Birmingham

'She got nothing, few quid, that's all, no cards, no papers. She got no ID 'cept her face.'

Once more Jessie allowed herself to be appropriated. She had no choice. Hungry, alone and suffering from the early symptoms of withdrawal, she had gone with the first group of men who approached her with an offer of work.

'What's your name, girl?'

She was sitting in the basement of the large, anonymous terraced house to which she had been driven.

'Ma name's Jessie.'

'You Scottish or what? Where d'you come from?'

'Nowhere.'

'You got family? Friends? Maybe you'd like to call someone? Tell them where you are?'

'There's no one tae call.'

The man asking the questions smiled at this. He seemed pleased with Jessie's answer. 'Where'd you sleep last night?'

'A flat in London. My pimp's flat.'

'Where's your pimp now?'

'Brixton Police Station, Ah think. He shot a man.'

'You want a hit up?'

'Oh yes, yes please. Ah'm desperate.'

'What'll you do for it?'

'Any fuckin' thing at all.'

An Oxfam shop, West Bromwich

'That was top gear. Ah mean top, top gear. Ah will say that for Goldie and his boys, they had the best stuff an' they let you have it. In fact, Ah think a grain or two more an' all o' ma troubles would o' bin over that very night, 'cos Ah was no' used to such powerful stuff. Towards the end François had bought shite and mixed it with more shite, so Ah was more accustomed tae speed than smack, an' that first dose offa Goldie nearly took me all the way tae oblivion for real. But they were careful an' kept an eye on me an' gave me some coke tae balance things out. Ah must say for a minute there, leaning back, high as heaven wi' a cup of sugary coffee in ma hand, Ah really felt like Ah'd fallen on ma feet. Ha! On ma back was more tae the point of it, because they put me tae work that very night, although Ah was bruised an' cut from the girls who'd done me over. To tell the truth, Ah was that out o' it that Ah don't think Ah realized Ah was being banged until ma second or third customer. Ah worried a lot about that afterwards, because normally, no matter how monged Ah am, Ah always remember tae slip a condom on the puntas just before they gets to it, but Ah swear that night, after Goldie's first hit up, Ah couldn'a *found* a fellah's dick, let alone discreetly bagged it up.'

Fallowfield Community Hall, Manchester

'We did one warm-up gig before hitting the road proper. Sort of obligatory these days, in't it. I mean, you 'ave ta do it, don't you, the business expects it. Any act that can do fifty thousand seats in any town they fancy has to turn up at some shithole in the Smoke and play to eight fans and two hundred and fifty celebrities plus the rock critic from the *Daily* fookin'

Telegraph. You 'ave to do it just to prove that you're still down and dirty and can still cut it live.

'So anyway, we're booked in to do this single gig at the Astoria an' I was determined it was going to be a total an' utter explanation to the entire fookin' business regarding the facts o' the matter about who was boss. I was at Madonna's when she were in the middle of the Music Tour and it were all right but it was all so *fookin' showbiz.* You know what I'm sayin'? All the birds off the soaps and half the Spices, and Guy Ritchie's fookin' 'ardmen actor mates. I mean, don't get me wrong. Madge were blindin' in a cabaret sort of a way, but I wanted my gig to rock! Now I don't know if you know the Astoria, but it's an absolute shithole between Oxford Street and Cambridge Circus. Normally it's a one hundred per cent G-A-Y gig, you know, the place where all the girly popettes and failing boy bands go to relaunch their careers by becoming gay icons. But every now and then the gig gets hired out into the mainstream for a bit of solid rock. Tonight was my night, and of course the secret had got out, not surprisingly really, since we'd deliberately told Capital Radio that afternoon. We wanted to stop the traffic, close down half the West End, cause a riot an' a public nuisance by the sheer power of my celebrity.

'It were completely irresponsible, o' course. We hadn't warned the police or nothing, but that's rock an' roll, in't it?

'Boy bands and softies warn the police. The likes o' Tommy Hanson do what they fookin' well like.'

Soho Square

Tommy's limo was stuck on the north side of Soho Square. It was about a hundred metres from its destination, but it might as well have been in China. The whole of the east of the square was a mass of kids trying to get to the Astoria. Two or three thousand more were milling about in Charing Cross Road, along Oxford Street and up Tottenham Court Road. Tommy sat in the back of the big car looking out at the bodies crushed against the darkened glass, grinning with satisfaction. Tony the tour manager was in the front, his mobile as ever clamped to his ear.

'Elton and David aren't coming, Tom.'

'You're fookin' jokin'. I belled the cont this morning. 'E said 'e was mad for it. Said he were 'avin' 'is legs waxed special. Said 'e might bring Kevin fookin' Spacey an' Gwynnie. What 'appened?'

'Tom, look out of your window. It's goin' berserk. Elton and David took one look and buggered off. So would you have done if it wasn't your gig. Nobody can get through. Jon Bon Jovi's jacked it and Ronan and Chris Evans and Billie. The PR company says there's a gang of them gathering at Teatro having a drink. Maybe you should go and do the show there.'

'Fook.'

'The Gallaghers are in, though. Apparently they just punched their way straight through to the front door. They're in the VIP bar now. You have to admire them.'

'No, I fookin' don't. They'll get arseholed on my beer an' then shout out rude Mancy witticisms during me ballads. Warrabout Robbie?'

'Still in LA, of course, but he sent flowers.'

'Flowers!'

'Yeah, and a card. Most amusing . . . "Dear Ex Pop Hero. Thanks for warming up the UK crowd for me. I'll be back next year to show them what a rock 'n' roll star really looks like." Nice, eh?'

Tommy's normally fairly indulgent sense of humour instantly and completely deserted him. He was overtaken by sudden fury, a feature of the drug cocktail that he had already consumed.

'Right, that's it. Turn round, take me to fookin' Heathrow! Get me on a fookin' plane. I'm going to give that bastard a smack in the mouth. I'll whack 'im, I'll twat 'im, I will 'it 'im wi' me knob. The sweaty little fookin' mushroom.'

'Can't turn round, Tom. Can't go forward, can't go back.'

'Well, what are we gonna do?'

'Dunno.'

Tommy did what he always did in such circumstances. On this occasion his choice of stimulant was a couple of nosefuls of amphetamines.

Behind the Astoria Theatre, Soho Square

In Sutton Row, just round the corner from where Tommy's car was stuck, a difficult social situation had developed.

Peter Paget was in the process of conducting a small group of MPs, including a Home Office minister, around the backs of various London theatres. It is an accident of architecture that these stage-door areas have become one of the prime locations of choice for the injection of heroin and the associated activities of whoring, pimping, slumping out unconscious, urinating on walls, fighting and dying. If you are a homeless and hopeless addict it is actually quite difficult to find a relative degree of privacy to satisfy your cravings. The fast-food outlets have become increasingly wise to the fact that their toilets were being adopted as shooting galleries and have made efforts to prevent the practice, in some cases installing blue lighting that prevents people from being able to see their veins. The backs of theatres, however, are no-man's-land. Nobody seems to have responsibility for them, and the mainstream of life passes them by in the glamorous streets

161

out front. Normally these dingy stage-door areas open on to alleyways, their walls indented with emergency exit crash door alcoves, while large dustbins often provide further cover. The only legitimate population of these places is the nicotine-addicted actors who are no longer allowed to smoke in their dressing rooms. This makes these areas reasonably attractive to those whose options for rest and privacy are severely limited. Not as good as a Burger King toilet, but a lot better than down by the river under some stinking, dripping bridge.

If the matinée audiences of the latest Ayckbourn revival or fascinating transfer from the Almeida had X-ray vision and could see beyond the actors and through the back wall of the theatre they were sitting in, they would very likely see the real human drama of people with their trousers round their ankles and their skirts hitched up around their waists poking dirty needles into their genitals. Were Hogarth to drop in to such a place from the gin-soaked alleys of the eighteenth century, he would find little that surprised him.

It was in order to view this unedifying offshoot of the West End's glamorous theatreland that Peter Paget had led his little cross-party group from the stage door of the Dominion Theatre across St Giles Circus and up Sutton Row to the rear of the Astoria. It had been his intention to then take his fellow MPs to the back of the Apollo on Shaftesbury Avenue, a place where the ageing brickwork is so soaked in urine that the actors inside refuse to take ground-floor dressing rooms because of the stink.

Unfortunately, Peter had reckoned without Tommy Hanson's 'secret' gig. As they stood speaking to a heroin addict named Robert, who had been seeking privacy in a crash door alcove, it was as if half the teenagers in London had descended upon them, along with every shop assistant on Oxford Street, who, having finished work, had wandered down to catch a glimpse of Tommy.

Trapped as he and his colleagues were with this dirty junkie, conversation was beginning to flag. Having established at some length that if Westminster Council were to provide a place where Robert could use clean needles and dispose of them in a socially responsible way he would go there, they had little else to discuss. Strangely, at this moment, Robert felt slightly socially responsible himself. In a way, he was the host, and now his guests were trapped with him after they clearly wished to leave. It was like an awful end-of-dinner party moment when the taxi fails to arrive despite repeated telephone calls and host and guest sit staring at each other over empty coffee cups, longing for the evening to finally end.

'Sorry about this, dude. It's normally pretty quiet at this time of day,' Robert said.

'That's all right,' Peter replied. 'It's astonishingly crowded, isn't it? Somebody's going to get hurt.'

All four Members of Parliament were being pushed closer and closer towards Robert as the ebb and flow of people seeped into every available space. It was not long before Peter was horrified to find himself actually physically forced against this filthy person. Peter was the taller and so his nose was hovering in the vicinity of Robert's lank, greasy hair. He struggled to master the heaving nausea in his stomach. The smell of piss and sweat and grease and ancient clothing that emanated from the addict was overwhelming. Peter's discomfort was increased by the fact that Robert was beginning to twitch.

'Look, man, I've got a problem now, right?'

Peter stared into the space above Robert's head. He could not answer.

'You see, that shooting gallery you want to build ain't built, is it?'

Once more Peter could only grunt.

'Which is why I came here to jack up . . .'

A pause.

'But, you see, I didn't jack up because you lot came along and started chatting . . . Well, you don't like to jack up when you're chatting, do you? So I thought to myself, I'll just sit on it, you know, man, sweat it out, control my cravings till you lot have found out enough facts, right? Then you'll go and I'll hit myself up . . .'

Peter and his colleagues were beginning to understand where this was going, although they prayed that it was not so.

'But of course you lot haven't gone, have you? Because we've got all crushed in. I mean, this has never happened before, all these girls filling up the street. It's really, really unusual. But the fact is, I'm getting really quite strung out now . . . So what I'm basically saying is I hope you won't think me, you know, rude or ignorant or anything, but I'm going to have to shoot some scag into my cock.'

And so Peter Paget's fact-finding mission got more facts than it had either bargained for or desired. Jam-packed though they were, Robert squirmed and wriggled until he was able to reach into his pocket and produce the wherewithal to prepare a needleful of heroin, the tin foil, the cigarette lighter, the twist of dirty brown powder.

'Would you mind holding the foil while I cook it up? It's just I've no room to squat down and do it on the ground.'

'I'm afraid I can't do that.'

'Why not?'

'Because I'm a Member of Parliament and it's not appropriate.'

'Oh.'

Peter's colleagues felt the same way, although the

Liberal Democrat thought about it for slightly longer before refusing.

Forced to act alone, Robert held the foil between his lips while using one hand to pour the brown powder into it and the other to hold the lighter under it. The foil soon glowed red and it clearly must have been burning Robert's lips, but a combination of necessity and the drug addict's increased pain threshold meant that he did not flinch. Peter wished that he had had the courage to offer to help. It would have been a powerful political gesture, but he did not offer now. Very carefully, Robert removed the little foil bowl of liquid from his mouth. The foil had burnt itself onto his lower lip and so he tore it, leaving a smoky scrap of tin stuck to his mouth. Then, with the concentration of a brain surgeon, he was able to produce a syringe from his pocket and using only one hand dip the needle into the liquid and draw back the plunger with his thumb. Then, having expelled the air from the body of the syringe while taking care not to expel any of its precious contents, Robert reached down and, unbuttoning the fly of his filthy combat trousers, dug out his penis from its dark recess.

Suddenly, everything went so horribly wrong that Peter's nightmares would be haunted by the moment that followed for the rest of his life. Never ever would he be free from the memory of the agonizing horror of what then occurred.

There was a scream. It came from three teenaged girls who were crushed up behind the MPs and had been watching with utter fascination as this creature from Mars surrounded by what appeared to be four bank managers prepared what they knew to be heroin. These girls had so far been privately congratulating themselves on their level of sophistication. They knew all about drugs. Heroin was no big deal to them; they knew its nicknames and called it scag or smack. Of course they knew that they would never take it themselves, but there were always rumours about bad girls at school, girls who 'jacked up'. Oh yes, these girls, like all kids their age, considered themselves entirely hip to the drug scene. They giggled when their earnest teachers tried falteringly to explain to them that which they already knew . . . But now, suddenly, innocence was lost. Seeing Robert's choice of inlet, the girls' happy air of sophistication and sangfroid evaporated completely. The appearance of Robert's dirty, veiny, bent and slightly knobbly penis, and the vicious, gleaming needle that hovered above it, quite simply horrified these not-quite-as-tough-as-they-thought-they-were girls, and together they had let out a single, involuntary, piercing scream.

Three teenaged girls screaming at once and in perfect unison is a *big* noise.

Robert jumped. Well, he did not so much jump as jerk. There was no room to jump, crammed in as he was by a four-member cross-party fact-finding committee from the House of Commons, but there was room to violently twitch, room to jerk, room for Robert's hand to fly sideways and in so doing plunge the needle he held a good inch and a half into Peter Paget's thigh.

An Oxfam shop, West Bromwich

'There were nine girls in our attic. We crashed out mornin's, mostly, when business was slow, that's where they fed us as well and where we smoked our bit of smack or crack. We rarely got given a needle. Jacking up soon ruins your skin even if it's good stuff, an' before ye know it, ye start tae look like a pizza. Goldie was aware o' that. So he worked hard tae keep us nice. Still, there was plenty tae smoke an' any amount o' pills tae pop. Well, there'll always be pills if you're working. He wanted us awake, didn't he? An' docile, o' course. Ah don't know what most brothels are like, but Goldie certainly thought it were worth the cash tae keep us out of it most o' the time. Ah was the only English-speaking girl there, or at least the only girl who had English as a first language. The others were all Eastern European. Slaves, basically. No passport, no ID and absolutely no chance. The boss, Goldie, had three houses an' he liked tae move us around, always at night, half conscious on the back seat of a Merc. It didn't make any difference to us. All three houses were the same, a gangroom in the basement and reception on the ground floor, wi' us all sittin' there in our miniskirts an' stilettos, sometimes wi' our tits out, sometimes starkers. The punter'd take his pick an' up we'd go tae the shaggin' rooms.

'It didn't take me long tae realize the sort o' hellhole Ah'd gone an sold masel' into. There was one girl, her name was Maria. Ah knew that because she was shouting it the day they took her out o' the house for ever. Always on about her name, that girl was, whenever the boys called her babe or sugar or whatever, she would say, "My name is Maria". It was her thing, the thing she wanted tae hang on tae. Everybody knew she had attitude. Even when she was completely high she'd be demanding her passport and asking for the money she'd been promised tae come tae England. So one day she just flipped, stormed out of her cubicle refusing tae service a client, downed tools, so to speak. Ah think he wanted somethin' she were no prepared to provide an' she'd just had enough. Anal, Ah imagine, that was a big problem wi' all us girls. We didnae like that at all. Believe it or not, some of the idiots we serviced reckoned it represented safer sex for them. Can ye believe the pig ignorance? Anyway, whatever it was, Maria just flipped an' started screamin' tae get out an' go home. "My name is Maria! My name is Maria!" she kept shoutin', so they took her out an' that was the last we ever heard of her. She was from Chechnya. Ah'd spoken to her once or twice because her English was no' bad. She'd got very unlucky in the war, wrong place, wrong time, et cetera. Stolen from her house by the Russian army for mobile R and R, sold on to a drug baron when they was sick o' her, shipped across Europe on the drugs mainline, an' whored all the way tae fuckin' Birmingham of all places. Can ye believe it? Chechnya tae Birmingham! I mean, how big a mindfuck would that be? Anyway, what happened tae Maria turned ma mind tae thinkin' . . . No easy thing tae do when ye're smacked out o' your head an' getting serial banged every wakin' hour, but thinkin' is what Ah did. It suddenly dawned upon me, loud as thunder, that all of us girls was goin' tae die, an' die quite soon. Either through disease, or through violence or maybe an overdose or maybe bad shite or whatever, but we were all definitely doomed. Maria was just our advance guard. She'd be there waitin' for us on the other side. Funny thought, really, knowin' you're goin' tae die.

'Did Ah tell ye about ma other self? The girl who used tae float above the cars when Ah was workin' the kerb for François? Ah hadnae seen her for a while, that other self, the one that liked music. We certainly never heard any music in Goldie's houses, except the boomin' o' drum an' bass from the passing cars. Well, Ah was lyin' on ma bunk thinkin' about Maria, an' for some reason Ah'm wonderin' how old she'd been an' suddenly Ah'm lookin' intae ma own face and ma face is sayin' tae me, "How old are *you*, Jessie? Are ye seventeen or are ye eighteen? Ye don't know, do ye?" An' Ah realize that Ah don't know how old Ah am any more. Ah don't know what the date is, what the month is, even.

'An' then one o' the boys comes in an' tells me it's ma shift an' would Ah like a nice pipe o' crack tae get me in the mood, an' Ah'm just reachin' out for it an' suddenly the girl on the ceiling that used to be me *screams*. Ah swear she screamed at me. It's ringing roun' ma brain while ma man's grinnin' at me over the pipe no' hearin' a thing. An' the old Jessie shouts . . . "No! Don't take it, ye stupid cow!"

'An' then Ah'm seeing Maria before ma eyes getting dragged off shoutin' out her name, which was all she had left, an' Ah realize that ma name is just about all Ah have left masel', because Ah don't even know how fuckin' old Ah am any more!

'So Ah grins at ma man all sheepish an' tells him thanks very much but Ah'm totally monged already an Ah'll have it later. So he shrugs and pisses off and the next thing Ah'm goin' intae one o' the cubicles with a punta an' ma other self, ma floatin' girl has come intae the cubicle wi' us, an' as I pull ma knickers down she's speakin' tae me an' she's sayin' . . . "Jessie! Get out o' there before ye forget your own name!" an' then this bloke's on top of me, trying to push his dick intae me while Ah try tae finger an' thumb a johnny ontae it, an' all the while Ah'm saying tae my girl "How? How?" but it's OK, 'cos the punta thinks Ah'm groanin' or somethin', an' my girl on the ceilin' says, "Get yoursel' fuckin' straight, Jessie! Get straight . . . Get fuckin' straight!"'

Behind the Astoria Theatre, Soho

For a moment all human life seemed suspended as Peter, his colleagues, Robert and the three teenaged onlookers absorbed the full horror of the situation. Robert recovered first. He was a decent man beneath his crust and he knew exactly what Peter Paget was thinking.

'I'm clean, man,' he said. 'No sweat. That's my personal works stuck in your leg there. Honest, geezer, I don't share my works with nobody, very rarely anyway, that's for sure, and then I'm real careful. It's clean. I use white spirit. You'll be fine.'

Peter could only stare at what had so suddenly and so catastrophically come to pass – this needle, this steely rapier of death buried deep within his flesh, a fast-track, mainline, infiltration super-highway carrying incurable infection directly to the fast-pumping veins and arteries of his defenceless adrenalin-charged system.

'Take it out.' Peter's voice was no longer his own. It came from far away.

'For God's sake, be careful with that plunger!' This was the voice of a colleague who had noted that Robert's grimy, blackened thumb still rested on the top of the poisoned pump.

'Don't worry, dude. It's my only hit.' Carefully, Robert withdrew the needle. There was a tiny shading of red about its tip.

'Eeeeuugh.' The teenaged girls were almost in shock with the horror of it all, but their object lesson in the seamy side of drug addiction was not over yet. Robert may have been concerned for the mental health of his new acquaintance, but like all addicts he was most concerned with his own mental health, which was becoming further strung out by the minute. Driven by a craving which entirely dwarfed and engulfed all other personal and social issues, he now returned to his original agenda.

' 'Scuse me, everybody, but I'm gagging for it.'

And so while the girls hovered between nauseous revulsion and rapt fascination, Robert set to the task of getting his weakened, scabby, limp and useless penis into shape to receive its delayed shot. He slapped it and squeezed it and fiddled with it until he had persuaded a vein of sufficient stature for his purposes to rise up out of the filthy, sickly skin.

Meanwhile, Peter was in a waking nightmare of such intensity that he could neither speak nor think. All he knew was that he could feel infection running through his system like a greyhound on a track, furious, straining, desperate to complete its course.

Robert was on the verge of injecting. Once more the needle hovered at his groin, but then a thought occurred to him. Even in his increasingly desperate state he was aware that the risk of infection cut both ways.

'Here. Sorry to ask this, but you ain't HIV or nothing, are you? I mean, anyone can have it, not just us users . . . You gay?'

Peter did not answer. His tongue was infected now, grown swollen and useless by the viruses he knew were destroying it.

'Oh well, whatever. To be honest, even if you said you was full-blown Aids I'd still only wipe me steel down, because there is no way this scag is staying on the outside of me one minute longer.' And with that Robert finally completed the task of injecting a massive but to him only adequate shot of corrupted, badly cut heroin into his bedevilled penis.

Soho Square

'It's all gone very pear-shaped, Tom. The bloke on the Astoria door says the cops are going ballistic. Nothing can get across St Giles Circus, not even those anarchic thugs on bicycles, and the traffic's backed up west along Oxford Street all the way to Marble Arch. East it's jammed as far as the City and south it's going all the way down Charing Cross Road nearly to the river.'

Tommy showed Tony the palm of his hand. 'Tell it to the 'and 'cos the face ain't listening.'

The speed he had taken was having its desired effect. Tommy was exhilarated. He felt powerful, confident, energetic.

Tony, on the other hand, who was entirely straight, felt anxious and nervous and no longer in charge.

'Pop some of this, Tone,' Tommy said soothingly. 'You'll feel loads better.'

'We underestimated your pulling power, Tommy. This is a mess.'

'I never underestimated anything. I reckoned this'd happen and it 'as. Brilliant, eh?'

'The police are saying we've caused a public disturbance. They say the gig's cancelled.'

'Fook that. Who do they think they are?'

'They don't think they're anything. They know who they are. They're the Metropolitan Police.'

'Fook that.'

Tommy pressed the electronic window button. The cheering and screaming spread almost instantly throughout the crowd. It was as if everybody knew at once that Tommy was amongst them. Out of view to most of them, certainly, but amongst them nonetheless.

Tommy squeezed himself out of the limo window and, with the help of many eager female hands, scrambled up onto the roof of the car, where he stood, arms stretched out like a Messiah. The amphetamine and adrenalin high were of such a scale now that he was oblivious to fear. The crowd surged around him. People cheered from every window of the square. Tommy felt as if he were flying above them all.

'I'm here! I am fookin' here! Yes! I have come to my people! I am here! I am *fookin'* here!'

The crowd kept pressing forward as those who were far away and around the corner tried to force their way into Soho Square to catch a glimpse of Tommy.

'Come to me, my people. Come! For I am fookin' here.'

Inside the car Tony could almost feel the metal of the limousine's superstructure straining and starting to buckle as all the young bodies were flattened harder and harder against it. Once more he reached for his mobile. 'Hello. Yes, police, please . . . My name is Tony Day. I'm with Tommy Hanson, I'm his tour manager . . . We're in Soho Square and Tommy's been spotted. You have to get the crowd to pull back, people are getting crushed here, little girls are getting crushed. I can see that some of them are starting to lose it . . .'

There was pain on the girls' faces now; their mouths were gaping open, but no longer to scream; now they were gasping for air.

'You have to clear this crowd . . . Yes, I know who started it, officer, I'm aware of that . . . But I'm telling you that you have to stop people pushing from the back—'

Suddenly there was a thunderous roar from the crowd.

'Oh, shit. He's gone crowd-surfing.'

Fallowfield Community Hall, Manchester

'Speed, see. Prat powder. I'm not always a tosser, honest. Mind you, what a fookin' high that was. I mean, I know we're all here tryin' to get clean, but *come on!* Everybody remembers the really good ones fondly, don't they? And that was truly amazing. I were invulnerable, a god. I got crowd-surfed out of Soho Square all the way up Sutton Row and round the front of the Astoria. Do you know, I nearly actually made it to the gig. If they'd 'a just chucked me over the crowd barrier at that point I could have been in, 'aving a drink wi' Liam and Noel. *How cool would that have been?* Crowd-surfing to your gig! Unfortunately the crowd were having too much of a laugh and to be honest so was I, so they surfed me straight past the theatre up into St Giles Circus and left along Oxford Street. Brilliant. So there I am, passing Waterstone's, borne by many hands, and I'm thinking, hang on a minute, if I can just hang a left into Soho Street and down into the square I can get back to my limo and stick a bit o' coke on top o' this speed. Top idea. Mental.

'Amazing, in't it, what drugs can do to your sense o' reality? I'm shouting, "Left! Left! You bastards! I've got some superb charlie in me motor!" when about twenty arms all in nice white cotton shirt sleeves reach up and grab me. I am well and truly fookin' nicked.'

BBC News Desk

'Peter Paget, MP for Dalston North West and prominent campaigner for the full legalization of drugs, is in fear for his life tonight, having been accidentally stabbed with a hypodermic needle while visiting homeless drug users in London's West End. The incident occurred amidst a crowd that had been gathering in anticipation of an expected appearance by pop star Tommy Hanson. Numerous teenaged girls were caught up in the crush. It has been reported that when the addict to whom Mr Paget had been talking began to brandish his needle, Mr Paget placed himself between it and the terrified young girls. Sally Ward is the BBC's medical correspondent.' Moira, the newscaster, turned to Sally in the newsroom.

'While there seems to be no question of a deliberate attack on Mr Paget or the girls, addicts in withdrawal are not entirely in control of their bodies or their emotions, and in such a tight group of people there is no doubt that an accident such as this one was very nearly inevitable. With all the attendant risks of infection, it is enormously to Mr Paget's credit that he ensured that none of the young women was harmed.' Sally turned back to Moira.

'Narinder Kumar is at the scene of the accident.'

The perky young reporter stood in the doorway that had so recently seen such drama. 'Thank you, Moira. I'm here with Fred Golightly of the drug charity Straight ... Mr Golightly, you feel strongly that this terrible accident serves only to reinforce the point that Mr Paget has been trying to make with his high-profile campaign.'

'Absolutely. Peter Paget is a very brave man and he may now pay the price for the blind stupidity of Britain's ostrich approach to our drug problems. If the man whose needle stabbed Paget had had access to a safe, clean place in which to inject himself this accident would never have happened. Thousands of people are injecting themselves with heroin on the streets of Britain every day. They would prefer to be somewhere safe with access to clean needles, but the law excludes them. With no stake in society, these people become fiercely antisocial, discarding their needles irresponsibly. It is inevitable that the wider community will come increasingly into contact with this bloodied and dangerous litter – in playgrounds, in public toilets, in council lifts and smart shop doorways. The fact that Mr Paget has become such a public victim of that which he seeks to change is a sad irony indeed.'

By the time the following morning's papers hit the streets Peter was being lauded as a genuine national hero. The protector of innocence, the stern combatant against wild maniacal junkies, the fearless voice of reason in a world of blind political fools. Sometimes the spin goes one way, sometimes another. On this occasion, it was spinning so fast Peter's way that it seemed that morning as if this one tragic incident had awoken the entire nation from a deep sleep.

Peter, of course, had given up any thought of sleep, convinced as he was that he was going to die of Aids.

University College Hospital, W1

Angela Paget had been a little surprised when Samantha had accompanied them into Dr Wellbourne's consulting room. Even in this tense and desperate time she could not help but be aware that the nature of the conversation about to take place was surely one for her and Peter alone to share with the doctor. She said nothing, but her look told its own story.

Samantha recoiled as if stung. 'Do you want me to . . . to wait outside, Angela?'

'Well, Samantha, I don't really know, it's all so terribly strange. But I suppose that, yes, I do.'

Instead of leaving immediately, Samantha turned to Peter. 'Peter, am I to wait outside?'

And in that moment Angela knew that her husband had been making love to his parliamentary assistant.

'What? Oh, well. Yes. Whatever.'

Peter was far too abstracted by his possible fate to be sensitive to the feelings of either of the two women before whom he had laid his heart. Samantha turned on her heel and left the room. Peter and Angela Paget turned to face the doctor.

'So far it's good news,' the doctor said. 'Very good news. Robert Nunn, the addict whose needle pierced you, has tested negative to HIV and hepatitis, which, considering the man's lifestyle, is an immense relief.'

Peter leapt at this nugget of hope. 'But surely if he's clean I'm clean. I'm OK?'

'Not for certain, I'm afraid, although your chances have

176

improved considerably. The current wisdom is that Aids can take anything up to three months to show on a blood test, hepatitis C the same.'

'Three months!'

'I'm afraid so. Therefore, it's entirely possible that Nunn became infected recently and that it's not yet showing on the test. Unfortunately that wouldn't stop him infecting you.'

'Three months!'

'That is to be absolutely certain, of course. In truth we'd expect the antibodies to show up more quickly, therefore for each week that Nunn shows clean your chances improve dramatically. But we can only be sure that you're out of danger when we test you in three months' time.'

'Oh, my God.'

'As I say, so far it's so good. I'd say also that the needleprick was on the low side in terms of risk.'

'How's that?' Angela asked. 'He was stabbed with an addict's needle.'

'Well, it's not great, certainly, but if you imagine a graph, with the highest risk, for instance, that of a nurse in a hospital sitting on a needle full of infected blood and its entirety being pumped into her buttock . . .'

Angela winced at this. Peter hardly seemed to hear.

'It happens, believe me,' the doctor continued. 'Then if you take the lowest needle prick risk as, say, a discarded needle on a beach, washed by the sea, bleached by the sun for weeks, then I would say that Peter's accident is closer to that. Nunn had not injected himself when the accident occurred, therefore it had been a number of hours since the needle was in contact with his blood. He had depressed the plunger to expel the air from the hypodermic, and thus any residue from a previous hit that remained in the barrel of the needle would have been partially expelled—'

Peter interrupted her. 'Basically, you won't know for three months.'

'Not for sure. No.'

Peter got up and left the surgery without a word, leaving Angela Paget to make their farewells as she left.

Outside in the waiting room Samantha simply could not restrain herself. Ignoring Angela completely, she looked straight at Peter. 'Are you going to be OK?'

'He might be,' Angela replied on Peter's behalf. 'His chances are much better than we'd feared. Thank you for your concern, Samantha.'

'Well . . . We're all concerned, Angela.'

BBC News Desk

'In a separate but connected incident the pop star Tommy Hanson was arrested today and a large part of the West End was brought to a complete standstill when the star attempted to stage a secret performance at the Astoria Theatre. News of the show had been deliberately leaked earlier in the day and huge crowds had gathered at the eastern end of Oxford Street, causing rush-hour chaos. Fearing for public safety, police cancelled the show, but claim Hanson deliberately provoked an already dangerous situation by stepping into the crowd and allowing himself to be manhandled amongst them. A number of teenage girls suffered shock and minor injuries in the crush, but fortunately no serious injuries occurred.'

The House of Commons bar

'Bloody nice for the public to see that MPs aren't all the shits they presume us to be. Peter Paget's done the whole house an enormous service.'

'God knows what he's going through now, though, poor bugger. I mean, I saw the needle go in, must have been two inches. *I'm* still in shock, so how would he be feeling?'

'He handled it incredibly, though. Just said, "Take it out." Didn't scream or anything, he was very calm about it.'

'Don't know if I would have been.'

'Well, there were all those screaming girls, weren't there? I suppose he didn't want to scare them. I mean, if they'd gone hysterical who knows who else might have been stabbed?'

'He really did save those girls' lives.'

'Yes, and don't forget that needle was still full of scag. Enough to kill an elephant.'

Suddenly the drug debate had become sexy. Everyone was using words like 'scag' as if they'd been hanging about on the front line for years.

'Christ, if that junkie's thumb had pushed down . . . It just doesn't bear thinking about.'

Shaking their heads in wonder and disbelief, the MPs made their way into the debating chamber. The Prime Minister was scheduled to make a statement on the state of Peter Paget's health. Following this, the Leader of the Opposition intended to express his own party's sincerest sympathy and best wishes to Paget and his family. The Liberal Democrat Leader had it in mind to suggest that Paget be recommended for a medal.

The Groucho Club, Soho

Milton emerged from the gentlemen's toilet just as Paula was exiting the ladies'. He was delighted to see her; the tiny crystals of cocaine that were exploding against his nasal membrane had put him in just the mood for a bit more crowing over his defeated colleague. Paula, on the other hand, was loath to waste her own cocaine buzz talking to such a loathsome toad as Milton.

'Paula! Enjoying the Paget story? Not much, I imagine. The man you've been vilifying suddenly turns up as the national hero. Must be something of a drag, eh? Going to be a bit galling when you have to change tack, isn't it? But the editor's insistent we back Paget! The only man with the guts not only to have an opinion but also to act on it. I've recommended that you do a big spread on the family. You know, talk to the wife and daughters. Editor loves the idea but he wants it really lush and glowing. You've got to make the whole world love them, just as you must love them yourself, Paula, particularly your old sparring partner, the daughter.'

Paula did not bother to reply. Instead she trotted up the stairs as quickly as she could, leaving Milton smirking behind her. And well he might smirk. It had been a terrible shock for Paula to wake up to the news that the man she wished to ruin had risen so highly in the public's esteem. To learn also that he might very well have contracted a life-threatening disease in the line of duty. There was no doubt that she would have to put the conviction she had formed while lurking in that hotel corridor aside for a time. Now was certainly not the moment to announce to the world that Peter Paget, famous family man and moral crusader, was screwing his parliamentary assistant. But the time would come. The pendulum always swung. Paula could wait.

East London Cemetery

Detective Sergeant Sara Hopper rarely cried. Her job was such that if she allowed herself the luxury of tears on anything but the rarest occasions she would find herself crying for most of her working life.

Now, however, she wept openly. Most of the congregation did. Sara had been so sure that Jo Jo would survive. She had seemed to be growing in strength, building a wall between herself and the tragedy. Perhaps that should have been a warning sign for Sara and the other counsellors who had attempted to alleviate Jo Jo's pain. How could one possibly build a wall high enough to keep out the knowledge of such a terrible abuse?

Certainly Jo Jo could not, for one day, just when it was least expected, Jo Jo took a Stanley knife from her father's toolbox, ran herself a hot bath, sat in it and opened the veins on her wrists. She left a note, expressing an emotion common to those who have been brutalized, a desperate feeling of guilt.

'*Dear Mummy and Daddy. I'm so sorry.*'

Jo Jo had not intended to increase her parents' agony with her final note, of course, but that was what she did.

With appropriate sombre melancholy, rain began to fall as the sods of wet earth fell heavily on Jo Jo's white and gold coffin. And with each dull thud the resolve that was forming like a cancer inside Commander Leman grew heavier and more solid too.

Jo Jo was dead. *And it was all his fault.*

An Oxfam shop, West Bromwich

'There's only one way tae give up scag an' that's cold turkey. Ah mean, let's face it. All a methadone programme gets you is an addiction to methadone, am I right? The only way off the junk is tae stop takin' it. Full stop. Well, as Ah'm sure ye know, it isnae easy. Kickin' heroin is no picnic, even if you're curled up under a duvet at your ma's wi' nice warm soup left at your bedroom door in case ye fancy it and a clean toilet tae puke in . . .

'But, oh ma Goad, you try doin' turkey in secret, on the inside of a brothel. Try doin' it sharing an attic wi' eight junkies, an' wi' a gang o' big bastards pushin' the stuff onta ye all the time an' acting right suspicious when ye says no tae a nice big smoke o' scag. Try doin' it when you're workin' ten tricks a night and you're supposed to shag 'em with some element of enthusiasm or at least not curled up in a shivering ball o' sweat and effluvia. Well, that's how Ah did it. Ah swear tae ye now as Ah live and breathe. An' Ah'm amazed that Ah'm still living an' breathin' tae swear anythin' at all. Ah did cold turkey the hard way, aged seventeen, Ah think, while maintaining ma occupation as the working property o' a whoremaster, an' were Ah tae try tae bicycle up Mount Everest wi' ma legs tied together, Ah will never in ma whole life do nothin' tae match it.'

The Leman household, Dalston

Commander Leman had announced to his family that he would shortly be taking some leave.

'To be quite frank, I think the Chief Constable is extremely pleased. I didn't set out to be, but I've definitely become something of a thorn in his side.'

'What are you going to do?' Anna asked.

'It's not what Daddy's going to do, it's what we're all going to do. The school holidays are coming up. We're going to have a holiday. We're going to have a month in Cornwall.'

Anna was suspicious. Her father normally had to be dragged screaming to take even a weekend off.

'This is to do with what happened to Jo Jo, isn't it?'

'Yes, Anna. This has everything to do with what happened to Jo Jo.'

'You know who did it, don't you?'

'No, Anna, I don't know who did it.'

'But you know something,' Anna persisted.

Leman did not answer.

'If I knew who did it, or who caused it,' his daughter continued, 'I'd kill them.'

An Oxfam shop, West Bromwich

'The worst time was about six days in, Ah reckon.

'Ah'd just finished ma shift and was doing as best I could tae clean masel' up in the makeshift toilet and shower cubicle that serviced the ablutory needs o' me and all ma colleagues. Ah wondered whether Ah could bear to carry on. Ah tell ye, the craving was gnawing at every cell of ma body . . . ma stomach was churning wi' it, ma skin was crawling wi' it. The nausea was almost impossible to control and the diarrhoea . . . well, I expect you're aware of the bum problems ye get with smack.' The old gentleman who ran the Oxfam shop had not been, but assured Jessie that he would take her word for it. 'It seemed tae have come tae some kind of terrible climax within me. I was in no condition tae pass the time o' day, let alone service a client. Ah knew that it had tae get better or Ah'd die. Ah knew that Ah simply couldnae face much more o' that pain.

'Ah couldnae believe what had happened to me. Me. Jessie Ross. Human being. Female. Ah went to school. Ah was the best wee gymnast in ma class, Ah could do a double somersault an' twist off the asymmetric bars like nobody else Ah knew. Ah had Barbie dolls. Ah worried about ma first kiss. Ah always liked fresh fish even when the other kids wanted McDonald's. Ah'd been a human being for some number o' relatively happy years. An' yet somehow Ah'd become . . . what? What had Ah become? No' a human bein', that's for certain . . . What? Nothing more than an agonizing collection o' limbs and organs, nae more than a shriek of pain made flesh.

'Ah have tae say that Ah've since come to the conclusion that it wasnae the heroin that brought me tae the sorry condition Ah found masel' in, although Ah make no excuses for masel' an' Ah wouldnae touch the stuff again if they gave it away at petrol stations. Nonetheless, Ah know now that it was the fuckin' law that nearly killed me. The law that not only put me outside proper society but also created a criminal society that was jus' itchin' tae scoop me up.

'The funny thing is that Ah think Ah actually served that proper community tae which Ah was denied access. Oh yes, Ah was a public servant in ma opinion. Ah mean, come on, those ten fellahs a night that Ah kept frae beatin' their wives or whatever, they all paid their taxes back in the real world, but Ah wasnae part of that world. Ah'd somehow got dumped on the outside along with Goldie and François. And poor, poor Maria, buried along with her name, somewhere on the outside, in a river or a ditch. Placed on the outside by failed laws. Hey, they say that justice is blind, well, ain't that the fuckin' truth.'

The Fifth Floor restaurant, Harvey Nichols

'Look, Em, the fact that Tommy Hanson kicked you out of a car in Brixton and you met some black man who called you a honky cockteaser doesn't give you any right to lecture me about my life. Is that why you've asked me out to lunch, to give me a lecture?' Lizzy pushed her uneaten salad aside and lit a cigarette. She was tall, beautiful and famous. One of that élite breed of clotheshorses known as supermodels. She walked up and down for a living and she did it very well indeed. Emily, having eaten the whole of her salad, now made a point of helping herself to Lizzy's. She was healthy now, after all.

'I'm not lecturing you.'

'You are. You've turned into one of those fucking NA evangelists.'

'I'm just saying that it feels good to be clean.'

'Darling, the reason it feels good for you to be clean is that you were so shit at being on drugs. You couldn't handle them. One snort and your knickers were on your head. God, it was embarrassing. Being clean for you means that you're not out at some club making a complete idiot of yourself for the delight of the tabloid-guzzling hoi-polloi. I, on the other hand, do not have a problem. I'm good at drugs. I like them.'

'Nobody's good at drugs, Lizzy. People just think they are. Drugs keep you from facing up to your problems.'

'God, if getting clean means you start talking like you're on morning telly thank God I'm a raver.'

'What have you had today?'

'As much as I fucking want. Look, I've been taking coke for years. Bit of smack, too, occasionally, pills, E, the lot, and I love it, OK? What's more, during the time I've been breaking half the laws in this country I've climbed to the top of my profession, amassed a fortune of not a few million quid, performed before royalty on numerous occasions, opened a breast cancer initiative with the PM's wife and been awarded an OBE. Not bad for a habitual criminal, eh? What's more, it's not as if what I do is a secret. I've been done over in the *Mirror* enough times. By rights the cops should have thrown me in clink years ago, but nobody cares. Drugs are fine as long as you can afford good stuff, as long as you don't screw up and start breaking proper laws, the ones that count. Even heroin is cool—'

'You are so deluded, Liz. You're in such personal denial.'

'Even bloody heroin. It isn't smack that kills you, it's bad smack and what people have to do to pay for it. All I have to do to pay for mine, and what's more pay for the very best, is walk up and down in a small piece of silk looking sulky.'

'Heroin addiction isn't a joke, Lizzy! I've seen people so screwed up that—'

'Exactly, and when you see me burgling and whoring to get high, tap me on the shoulder and give me your bloody boring ten-point lecture. Until then don't worry about it. Look at Eric Clapton: he was on the stuff for years, wrote his best music during the time, don't know why he bothered to get off it really. That author – what's his name? – Will Self, took smack on John Major's plane! Amazing, didn't even get busted, nobody gave a shit. Now he's presenting comedy quiz shows. Nobody cares about drugs any more.'

'I presume Clapton got off it because he resented his dependency.'

'Well fine. If you resent your dependency then get off it. Personally I don't.'

'All right, all right. I'm just saying that you're not as bloody healthy as you think.'

'I never said I was healthy.'

'You're too bloody thin, that's for sure.'

'What, too bloody thin to make millions a year? Do me a favour. Look, Em, I'm not saying I'm not fucked up. Of course I'm fucked up. I take a lot of coke and pills with my Rice Krispies. Most of the girls do. I'm just saying that it isn't killing me – what's more, I still look great. I'll tell you what's killing me: forty Marlboro Red a day, that's what's killing me, and they're legal . . . And I notice you've gone back onto full-strength yourself, darling, since your miracle cure.'

The House of Commons, Westminster

Peter knew, medical results aside, that his life had changed. The policemen at the door had saluted him. The cloakroom girl had seemed quite misty-eyed. Scarcely familiar colleagues and opposition members had come up and shaken his hand. Suddenly he was surrounded by friendly faces. Nothing, however, had prepared him for the reception he encountered on entering the chamber for the first time since his accident.

The entire house rose as one and applauded.

He could hardly believe it. Nor could he believe that, as he took his place behind the government front bench, the Home Secretary, the *Home Secretary* no less, turned and gave him a thumbs-up before approaching the despatch box.

'Madam Speaker. The Right Honourable Member for Dalston North West and I have had our differences in the past over policy, although I must say I've always applauded the clarity and courage of his vision.'

This was news to Peter, but you take your good fortune where you find it.

'A radical vision, a bold and challenging vision that brings into question all that which we thought was certain. Yes, Madam Speaker, of late we all in this house have had the pleasure of applauding the Right Honourable Member for Dalston North West's vocal pyrotechnics.'

Applaud? Again Peter remembered things differently, but, as his daughter Cathy was fond of saying, 'Whatever.'

'Now, however, it falls to me to salute his personal courage and offer on behalf of the house our very best wishes to him and his family. Mr Paget has fallen victim to the consequences of the very issue in our society about which he cares so passionately. We can

187

all imagine how trying a time it is for the Right Honourable Member and his family as he awaits the doctor's reports and all that we, his friends and colleagues, can do is wish him well.'

Peter Paget rose to reply. It had been some days since his accident and he was feeling a great deal better. He knew that percentage-wise his chances were very good. He also knew that if, as he had begun to hope, he was in the clear, that moment of horror cramped up against the junkie Robert Nunn might just have been the luckiest thing that had ever happened to him.

'I thank my Right Honourable Friend the Home Secretary, but I am sorry to say that he is wrong. The best wishes of this house, gratefully received though they are, are *not* all that you can do for me. Instead you can support my bill!'

A brothel, Birmingham

The Hungarian girl handed her blanket up to Jessie, who lay shaking on her bunk. 'Take it, please, you are very cold.'

'Thanks very much. Thank you very much.'

Jessie had been twitching and sniffling all night. Fortunately for her the other girls were too tired and stupefied to be irritated more than a little by it, or by her constant trips to the toilet. Jessie's nose and eyes were running and her clothes were wet with sweat, which was part of the reason why she was shivering so much. She was becoming feverish and was half hallucinating, but even in her abstracted state she knew that whenever any of her captors were near by she must not give her symptoms away. The drama of withdrawal would not be an unfamiliar sight to her abusers and they would not approve of it. Drugs played a central role in maintaining docile order in the house.

The last thing Goldie and his acolytes wanted was a girl getting straight enough to start thinking for herself. Each time her captors came to take her to work or to offer her food or drugs she struggled to appear stoned and happy. The effort was immense, as her whole body seemed bent on betraying her at every moment. Her mouth yawned even though she wasn't tired, her skin ran hot, then cold, shivering and sweating all at once. She had pains in her muscles; her bones and joints ached and she feared that they were becoming inflamed. Her arms twitched and jerked as she lay on her bunk or as clients lay on her. She suffered sudden and massive anxiety attacks followed by fits of anger that made her want to throw her fists into the face of whichever man was currently paying for her. But somehow she kept control, even remembering to put condoms on her clients.

She had two allies to help her through: allies in her mind, at least. Both girls. The girl Maria, who had been dragged out defending her name, and also the girl Jessie used to be.

Parkinson, *BBC Television Centre*

'In the past few weeks my next guest has leapt from relative backbench obscurity to being recognized as one of the foremost politicians of his time. He is a man who has almost single-handedly shaken the nation out of its apathy about what is perhaps the greatest issue that faces our society today. The issue is drugs. The man is, of course, the Right Honourable Peter Paget, MP.'

Watching him on the green-room monitor, Samantha felt an intensity of love she could hardly bear. He was not just her lover; he was her hero. A great man, who had risen to a great challenge.

189

He was her father.

Peter was cheered as he descended the famous staircase. Parky hugged him warmly, a deliberate gesture which Peter much appreciated.

'So, Peter, welcome to the show. You can hear that everybody's pleased to see you.'

'Yes, it's very nice, a lovely welcome. Thank you.'

'Yes, I wish I got a cheer like that. All I get's "Oh, it's him again . . ." But never was a welcome more deserved, because you've had the courage to tackle one of society's great taboos and you've got us all thinking, you really have.'

'I've only been speaking my mind, Michael. It's a privilege to be able to do so.'

'And you've paid a high price for that privilege. I'm referring, of course, to your terrifying accident. Has it changed your thinking at all? It must have done.'

'Yes, Michael, in so much as it has strengthened my absolute conviction that the drugs war is lost and that the only way to create a drugs peace is to give a lead to every civilized nation in the world and legalize drugs.'

'That's all drugs? No exceptions? Crack cocaine? "Ice"?'

'All drugs, Michael. Half-measures, decriminalization of dope, et cetera, will merely make matters worse.'

'You oppose partial decriminalization?'

'Of course. The criminal community sees weakness and exploits it. They go to areas where the police are taking a so-called "softly softly" approach and use the resulting shop window to pedal harder drugs. The net result is that the whole idea of legalization is fatally undermined, and then reactionary voices in the press say, "You see! We make pot easier to obtain and immediately more heroin is sold." '

'So you're saying that it's all or nothing?'

'Well, obviously, Michael! Half-measures are what

my daughters are fond of calling a "no-brainer". They're totally useless, *worse* than useless. Of *course* criminals will use areas of policy waffle and confusion to increase their grip on a defenceless community. And it's the most addictive drugs from which criminals profit most. The people who take them *have* to have more and at present they're obliged to shop from murderers and gangsters! And pay gangsters' prices! Which means the drug-takers become criminals and terrorize the wider community to feed their habit. I've said it before and I'll say it again: if you require a selfish argument for legalization look at the crime rates in your area! Drug addicts steal, that's a fact; they rob you and me to get high, Michael. When will we wake up? We're handing society over to the mob; in fact we've *already* handed it over. It's almost too late.'

There was applause at this, which Parkinson was happy to let run its full course. 'Peter, on a very personal note, and I know you won't mind my asking you about this, it's possible that, as a result of your accident with a drug addict's needle, you are HIV positive. Or perhaps that you've contracted hepatitis.'

'Yes, that's so. I'm told that it's unlikely but entirely possible. All I can do is wait the required weeks for tests to yield conclusive results.'

'All this must be terribly hard for your wife and family.'

'Yes, it is. It's very hard, but as you say, we're a family, we stick together, and my wife and daughters support me absolutely in what I'm trying to achieve. There are millions of families in Britain, families of every kind, who have a right to be protected under the law. Instead, the law as it is at the moment systematically legislates to destroy their communities.'

'And you're quite certain that if drugs were legal you wouldn't currently be in the dangerous position in which you find yourself?'

'Absolutely certain. Nor would Robert, the man whose needle I encountered, be the piece of human wreckage that he is. He might still be a heroin addict, but he'd be no threat to himself or to me.'

'But would there not be thousands more addicts? Millions, possibly?'

'Would you be one, Michael?'

'Well, no, but—'

'Your wife? Your children? I don't think mine would. President Lincoln once said that you can't permanently do more for people than they are capable of doing for themselves. He was right. Government cannot change human nature. Kids will always experiment with things they shouldn't, and they need education and protection, not police persecution. In the United States they once tried to ban alcohol. That one insane experiment tells us everything we need to know about drug control. People didn't drink less, they just drank illegally. They paid no tax, some of them went blind from wood alcohol, and they financed the birth of organized crime that has plagued American society ever since.'

'Speaking of booze, what do you think about that? Is that a dangerous drug?'

'Dangerous to anyone who has the misfortune to be out and about when the pubs chuck out. Collective consumption of alcohol is a stimulus to violence, any policeman will tell you that. This is not the case with E. Drunk young men fight, loved-up young men hug each other. It's a fact. There are clubs that once required twenty bouncers which now use only one, simply because young people have changed their drug of choice. Every week hundreds of people are injured and killed as a result of drinking. You don't see them on any front page and yet the whole nation knows the names of the handful of people who've died from taking E.'

192

'Now that's not, strictly speaking, true,' Parkinson protested. 'We all remember the tragedy of poor Leah Betts. But I'm sure you're aware, Peter, that deaths from ecstasy are doubling on a yearly basis. Forty people died in 2001 alone. Can you name them, Peter? I can't.'

'You're right, Michael, and I'm sorry, it was a foolish thing to say. But you say forty people died in a year having taken ecstasy; next year perhaps there'll be eighty. But I tell you that *six thousand people a year* die directly from alcohol misuse! Six thousand! I don't know their names either. Nearly ninety thousand NHS hospital admissions a year result from mental or behavioural problems caused by alcohol.'

'Good lord.'

'At peak times eight out of ten casualty admissions are alcohol-related. One in seven people killed on the road are killed because of alcohol.'

'Extraordinary.'

'And yet, as I said, deaths from E continue to make the headlines.'

'But nonetheless they're doubling annually. Surely that's a cause for concern?'

'Of course it is, Michael, but I put it to you that they may well be doubling *because* E is illegal.'

'Because of it?'

'Yes. If ecstasy were produced legally under licence it would be less toxic, purer. Kids could be sure of what they were taking and they would have directions for use.'

'I must say, it's a compelling argument, and there's no doubt that you've caught the imagination of the country with your views, Peter. Yet it's only weeks since you were being vilified in the press.'

'Mine is an idea whose time has come. I even have hopes that the major parties will remove the whip and allow their people a free vote when my Private Member's Bill comes before the house.'

193

'So, Peter, I have to ask you this, you know that. I know you've spoken on this issue before, but I'd like to ask you again. Do you take any drugs yourself?'

'Yes, I drink, and if it turns out that I've been unlucky in my encounter with Robert I shall be taking a cocktail of highly expensive and dangerous drugs until the day I die.'

'I mean illegal drugs.'

'No. None whatsoever. Absolutely not, and nor would I if they were legal. But you don't need to take drugs to be affected by our drug laws and drug-raddled society. We're all affected.'

'Well, you've certainly made me think. You've made us all think. Peter, you're a very good and a very brave man. Ladies and gentlemen, Peter Paget!'

The applause was loud and genuinely warm.

'And now somebody who is himself no stranger to drugs, having fought many a widely publicized battle with their insidious influence on his life. Joining us tonight before starting a massive national tour tomorrow, a tour that has already sold out, breaking all previous records . . . Tommy Hanson!'

Tommy appeared at the top of Michael's stairway striking poses that managed to be simultaneously both pure pomp-rock posturing and an indulgently amused, ironic take on pure pomp-rock posturing. Tommy always had his cake and ate it.

'You all right! OK! Sound. Yeah!' he shouted, arms outstretched.

He trotted down the stairs doing an impressive scissor-kick off the last four while swinging his arm in a superb moment of air-guitar exuberance. He answered the huge cheer that this provoked with a face and hand gesture that said, 'Yeah, I know I'm a wanker, but it's a laugh, in't it,' at which the audience laughed warmly.

Tommy crossed the studio floor, hugged Parky,

shook hands with Peter Paget, and nestled down in the chair recently vacated by Peter, who had now moved himself one seat along as instructed by the floor manager.

'All right, Parky? Thanks for 'avin' me on an' all. All right, Peter? Top chat that, big time.'

After a few moments of bonhomie Parky brought up the subject that was on everybody's mind. 'Tommy. Last night. In jail? Am I right?'

'Sadly, yeah, Parky. I were a right tosser . . . Can I say "tosser" on telly? I don't want to get into any more trouble.'

'Yes, that's fine. We're all grown-ups here.'

'What I did was dead stupid and I reckon the police handled the whole thing brilliantly, 'cos kids could 'a been hurt, so big up t'the Met. As for me, I were a twat . . . Can I say "twat"? Oh well, I 'ave now anyways. But I were. I were a right twat. I deserved to get banged up and I was. So fair play to the coppers, no complaints there at all.'

'Crowd-surfing? Down Oxford Street?'

Tommy's sheepish grin was enough to provoke laughter and cheers from the studio audience. Yes, he had been very, very naughty, but what a lad! What a boy!

'It were mental, Parky, dead mental. You should try it, man. Wind in your hair, bunch o' birds reaching up and grabbin' at you. I reckon I was moving quicker than the traffic does these days . . .' Tommy turned to Peter. 'Maybe you lot up at Parliament should think about that in terms of transport policy.'

'I'll see what I can do, Tommy.'

'Can I just say, Parky, can I just say that I think Peter here is right? He's an amazing bloke and just absolutely top 'bout the things he's sayin'. 'Cos too many kids are dyin' out there, right? And summat's got t'be done.'

Peter smiled broadly. 'Tommy and I are old pals,

Michael. We hooked up at the Brit Awards to discuss how to get young people involved in my campaign.'

'That's right, because I reckon what Peter's saying is top.'

Once more Tommy's open charm carried all before it. Peter Paget almost found himself believing that he and Tommy Hanson really had become co-campaigners at the Brits.

Samantha's flat, Islington

'You don't have to use a condom, Peter. I don't mind. I want to share everything with you. You know that. Even your fate.'

'Don't be silly, Sammy.'

She was wearing the lingerie he had bought her at the beginning. His first present. That seemed rather a long time ago to Peter now.

'What is so silly about being prepared to die with someone?'

'It's silly if it's entirely unnecessary. Besides, this is just a precaution. It's been nearly six weeks now and Robert Nunn is still testing clean, as am I. My chances improve on each day of negative testing. You know that the doctor said she has every reason to hope that I'll soon be in the clear.'

'I hardly know what the doctor says, seeing as I'm excluded from her interviews.'

'Come on, Sam. You know that there's no way I could explain to Angela why I'd think it necessary for my parliamentary assistant to attend intimate medical interviews.'

'Yes, there is. Of course there is.'

'Perhaps you could explain it to me.'

Samantha knelt up in the bed, looking as gorgeous as she had ever done, her skin taut, her breasts youthful and proud, and yet Peter could feel his passion ebbing away as she spoke.

'You could tell her that you're in love with me and I'm in love with you and that we make love every chance we get and that if you ever did love her, which I doubt, she has forfeited any claim to that love or any place in your life at all by failing to satisfy and maintain your love.'

Peter drew breath and looked Samantha in the eye with what he hoped was a look of fraternal affection tinged with a little romantic anguish. He had been waiting for this moment for weeks, the moment when he must somehow find a way gently to begin the process of disengagement. He wished that she were not nearly naked. 'Sammy, please . . . We have to talk.'

'Isn't this talking?'

'We have to talk about . . . well, we have to be practical. Our affair . . .'

'Affair? Is that what you call it?'

'Well . . . I suppose . . .'

'Is that what we're doing now? Having an affair?'

'Well . . . yes, of course . . . A love affair. A wonderful love affair. But it's only been going a few months, and you're very, very young. We don't want to rush things, do we?'

'You didn't mind rushing things that first time in your office! You just about tore my knickers off.'

As Peter remembered it they had torn them off together, but he knew better than to argue the point. Samantha was being much more confrontational than he had expected. 'I know I did, Sammy, and it was the most beautiful and passionate thing—'

'So it was all right to rush into having sex, then?'

'Well, it was, it was . . . something that happened, wasn't it? Something wonderful.'

'Fine, OK. So what is it that we mustn't rush into?'

'Um . . . I think what I mean is—'

'Mustn't rush into me being anything more to you than a convenient screw? Is that what you don't want to rush into, Peter?'

He had not expected the conversation to be easy. That at least he had got right. 'Sammy! Please. You're not letting me finish—'

'Well, go on, then. Finish. Take your time. We wouldn't want to rush anything, would we?'

'Look, Samantha, you're taking this all wrong. Of course I don't see our relationship as just convenient sex. My God, it's scarcely convenient, is it? And I'm very fond of you, as you know. Very, very fond.'

'Fond? What a small word.'

'What's small about fond? I'm fond of my children, I'm fond of my parents.'

'Fond of your wife?'

'Of course I am, Sammy. Would you respect me if I wasn't?'

'What's respect got to do with anything? I'm in love with you.'

'You think you are, Sammy, and that's so very wonderful, but you're young, you have so much love to—'

'Don't you love me, then?'

'Of course I love you, of course. But love is, well, love is lots of things, isn't it? And our love is . . . our love is, well, it's very new and—'

'This "affair" we're having, Peter. Where d'you think it's going?'

'Well, I . . . Sammy, you're in politics as much as I am. You know that we can't always have everything we want—'

'Where d'you think it's going?'

'As I'm trying to explain—'

'So you think it's going nowhere?'

Peter knew that he must tread carefully. There was to be no easy exit. However he disengaged himself, it would take time and great tact. He had not lied when he had said that he was fond of Samantha. He was, and it pained him to see her so hurt.

'Of *course* it's going somewhere, Sammy. I love you, I've told you that . . . but we have an important job to do and we can't afford to let it be derailed by silly scandal. I'm winning at the moment, Sam. We're both winning, you and I. I mean really winning.'

'You mean your career is going well.'

'That's not fair! I mean the issue we both care about. The nation's mindset is changing. Even the Cabinet is wavering. I'm not saying that the PM's going to suddenly turn round and start supporting full legalization, but at least they're finally having to talk about it. They don't know what to think any more. We've opened people's minds. You and I, together.'

Samantha's eyes were far away. Something inside her had changed. It had happened in an instant, one sudden, heartbreaking, revelatory moment. Just as Angela Paget had come to know of her husband's affair by a simple and sudden instinct, so did Samantha realize that Peter Paget was going to put his career before her.

He was never going to leave his wife. Of course she should have known from the beginning. How silly she had been.

'Fond?' she murmured.

'Oh, please, Samantha. It's a perfectly reasonable word. It means love. I love you.'

'*Fond* of you. People who are in love are not "fond" of each other.'

'Yes, they are! Or in my case they are. Look, I take the word back, I—'

' "Fond" is what he said.'

'What who said?'

' "I'm very, very fond of you," he said. We were in bed at the time, just as you and I are now. Funny, that.'

'Who? Who said that he was very fond of you?'

'The man I told you about, at Cambridge, the lecturer, Politics and Modern History, you remember.'

'Oh yes. You had a fling with him.'

'Is that what we're having, then? A fling?'

'No! For heaven's sake, Samantha. Suddenly you're picking up on my every word. Don't twist things. It's just that you said—'

'It doesn't matter what I said. I was in love with him.'

'You told me you only made love twice.'

'Is sex so central to your existence? Is that the only benchmark to measure the depth of a relationship? How many times you do it? I was in love with him before ever I let him at me, just as I was in love with you before we did it!'

' "Let him at me"? "Before we did it"? If we're dwelling on choice of language I might well ask if that's how you care to describe your sex life? You make it sound like a duty.'

'Well, isn't it?'

'What?'

'Oh, Peter, do try for a moment to think of someone other than yourself. Imagine what it's like for me. I finally meet a man I can love. A man I can look up to, who I worship, who can teach me, be my guide. And all the time all he wants to do is paw me and invade me like some horny schoolboy.'

Peter was taken aback. He had thought himself in control of the conversation. It wasn't easy, but at least he'd felt in charge, in as much as at least he felt that he understood Samantha's feelings better than she understood his. Now he was not sure at all. 'Sammy, do you mean me? Do you mean us?'

'Of course. How many men do you think I've been worshipping lately? Hundreds? I love you. You know that. I'm not fucking "fond" of you. I love you.'

Samantha very rarely swore.

'But, what's all this about horny schoolboys? You said you loved our sex. You said that I understood a woman's body.'

'Can't you recognize a line when you hear one? I thought you were a politician.'

'A line?'

'Yes, a line to flatter you. To please you.'

'Please me!'

'I don't like sex, Peter, I never have. It's better with E, but basically I don't like it. Men are pathetic the way they obsess about it. Pathetic. My father wasn't pathetic.'

'What's your bloody father got to do with it?'

'According to my therapist, everything.'

'Your therapist!'

'Yes, my therapist. He says I'm in love with my father. He says that you're just a replacement figure.'

'You've told your therapist about us!'

'Don't worry about your precious career. He's not allowed to say anything. Professional confidence.'

Peter sat naked on the bed, trying to assimilate the sudden and complete fracturing of his happy lovenest. He knew very well that unless carefully handled, the consequences of this conversation for his life and his career would be very serious indeed. Samantha was not the steady, confident girl he had imagined her to be at all. She was an emotional flake. A dangerous woman. He had suspected it since even before his accident, since first she had mentioned burning poems at specific times of the day. Now he knew for sure. She was an emotional loose cannon and he would have to disengage from her with the utmost delicacy or she would turn into what he had heard called a bunny-boiler. It was Glenn Close in *Fatal Attraction* who had first put the fear of God into adulterous men, and if Samantha really had been lying about sex all this time then she was probably mad enough to cook the odd pet.

201

'What about the orgasms?' Peter asked, and despite his general fears there was a tone of wounded male pride in the inquiry. 'You said I made you have wonderful orgasms.'

'Faked.'

'Faked!'

'Every single one.'

'But . . . Why?'

'I've told you. To please you. It was what you wanted to hear, so I let you hear it. Sex is the price I pay for everything else I have with you.'

Seldom had conversational goalposts moved so quickly. Peter was truly shocked. 'Well . . . Well, I don't know what to say. I suppose I shan't be needing this, then.' He removed the condom, which had been slipping off anyway and was scarcely an inspiring sight. Then suddenly Samantha's expression changed completely. The hard, almost spiteful look she had assumed almost from the beginning of the conversation disappeared. In an instant there were tears pouring down her cheeks.

'Oh, Peter, please . . . I didn't mean it! Really, I didn't. I was just trying to hurt you, that's all. I love you, Peter, and I love to make love to you. Screw me now, come on, please, I want it, I really do.'

And just as surely as she had been seeming to distance herself from him, Samantha fell upon Peter, pulling his face towards her, thrusting her body against his.

'You were lying? About the orgasms?' Peter asked through the rich, fat kisses that she was working into his mouth.

'Yes, yes! You make me come like a freight train! Like fireworks, bombs! I was lying. You make my whole body melt. Let me show you.'

It was all too much for Peter. He succumbed almost immediately. She was so firm, so young, so very, very sexy, and if she was faking her lust she was a very good actress . . . But then again she *was* in politics.

Afterwards Peter remembered that he had not used his condom and a sick feeling gripped his stomach. Supposing he was infected and he had infected her, then their affair really must become public . . . On the other hand, if he were infected with Aids, would he care? Peter fought down the rising fear just as he had done many times over the previous weeks. He would be all right.

He was not infected.

He could handle Samantha.

He would gently disengage from her while retaining her loyalty, and he would continue with his newly splendid career. Who knew? Perhaps they could even retain an occasional sexual side to their relationship. That would be nice.

Samantha was also in a reflective mood. 'That college professor,' she mused quietly. 'You know, the one I was telling you about? He ended up having to move from the university to the local technical college. But he didn't love me, you see, and it isn't so easy these days for deceitful old men to toy with young women's emotions.'

A brothel, Birmingham

The girl above was ten years old. Her smile shone out like a beacon of hope, her eyes flashed with such energy and promise that people felt happier about themselves merely standing in her gaze. Here was a life on the brink of splendid things, a life *force* ready to illuminate any world it chose to conquer.

The girl below was a hundred if she was a day. A century's worth of pain had dulled her sparkling eyes and sunk them in their sockets like two small graves.

The girl above had freckles on her nose, rosy cheeks

and ribbons in her shiny, red-flashed chestnut hair.

The girl below was ghostly white and sickly. Light as air. Her ribs showed through her pale skin. She had not menstruated for six months.

The girl above was ten years old.

The girl below thought that she was probably not yet eighteen.

'Think of the sunshine, Jessie, remember the sunshine. We used tae love the sun.'

'The sun never shines in Scotland, Jessie.'

'Yes it does, it shone on us. Remember, the display? Three handsprings an' a full flying somersault. Flip flip flip whoosh! And everybody cheered! We were on after the fire brigade and before the brass band, and then we were in the band too! We threw our marching uniform on over our leotard and played "Scotland the Brave" and "Ali's Tartan Army"! Remember the crowd, Jessie? Remember the sun? It shone on our coronet and on our epaulets. Hold on, Jessie! Hold on! It can shine on us again.'

An Oxfam shop, West Bromwich

'When Ah awoke after the first sleep Ah'd had in some time Ah knew that Ah was through the worst. Ah knew that Ah was clean for the first time in many months and that if Ah had any chance o' survival, that chance was now. And so Ah set about makin' ma plan o' escape. Ah knew that there was no way o' gettin' out the front door, it was locked and barred an' a madam sat there twenty-four-seven with a couple o' the boys loungin' wi' her. Some o' the rooms where we took the clients had windows, but they were screwed down tight. Ah reckoned that the only way out was through the skylight in our attic.

'Mornin' times we was often left pretty much alone

up there, an' Ah resolved tae have a go the followin' day. Ah would ha' gone there and then but Ah'd slept too long and it was time tae go tae work. As Ah trooped down those stairs tae ma wee shaggin' room Ah swore that it would be the last time Ah'd make that journey. Ah swore that Ah'd be out o' that house or else die in the attempt.

'Well, somehow Ah makes it through the next twelve hours an' once we're all back upstairs again Ah waste no time. Of course the skylight was bolted shut like all the other windows in the house. Ah'd have to break the glass. Ah turfed poor Andie out o' the bottom o' our bunk bed and dragged it tae beneath the skylight. I reckoned there'd be less noise if the glass could fall ontae the top mattress. The other girls all just watched me with a kind o' stupefied fascination as Ah gets up ontae the bunk, wraps a blanket round ma fist and waits for the next car tae come by in the street below with its windows down and its drum and bass cranked up big time. Sure enough, it wasnae long before the usual booming fills the air. *Yo motherfucker! Yo what motherfucker! Yo bad motherfucker!* And as it gets real close I smash ma fist at the glass in order tae break it, which is no' so easy as it sounds, in fact. Ma first blow cracks the glass but no' much more than that, so's Ah have tae wait for the next street disc jockey tae cruise by. It's agony, Ah can tell ye. Me thinkin' that maybe one o' the boys has heard the crack or mebbe one o' the girls will freak out and scream. But neither o' those things happened and after three more efforts Ah'd cleared out all the glass from the opening and was ready tae do ma runner. "Ah'm off out o' here," Ah says tae the girls. "Anybody comin"?' But o' course none o' them dared, because they were all too monged. Jus' like Ah could never ha' done it if not for the week Ah'd just spent detoxing. "Right then. See yeze," Ah said, and I'm up ontae the roof leaving the girls wi'

205

a hole in their ceiling wi' the rain pissing through it.

'Well, the first thing Ah does is slip on the tiles, o' course. The weather was terrible and those tiles were fifty years old. There was moss and bird shite and anyway it was just like a film, 'cos Ah'm slidin' doon the roof, heading for the precipice. Ah'm in ma best practical clothes, selected specially for ma great escape: white wetlook plastic mini and pink spandex halterneck boobtube. Ah had shoes, white stilettos, o' course, but Ah've had the sense tae tie them round ma neck wi' a couple o' rubber johnnies, so Ah'm in ma bare feet. Honest, that's the best Ah could do for an escape kit, the most practical clothes available tae me. Ah reckoned that I'd stand even less chance in a frilly G-string an' a leather bra wi' holes cut out for the nipples. Anyways, Ah'm slidin' doon this steep roof wi' a gutter an' a ledge opening out in front o' me an' Ah'm thinkin', "Fine, this is me checkin' out . . . except mebbe if Ah could just get tae that chimney-stack . . ." 'Cos even as Ah slithered an' scrambled for a hold Ah could see that if Ah were only descending about three feet along the roof to ma left Ah'd bang slap intae a big pile o' bricks. Well, what do ye know, but all in a moment Ah applies sledging rules, the same rules o' steering that Ah was such a master of when toboganning during ma real life. The trick with a sledge is tae drag your foot on the side that you want tae turn, 'cos it'll slow ye down and ye'll drift that way. A lot of kids instinctively wanted tae bung down the opposite foot, like in a boat ye turn by rowing harder on the other side. But me, Ah always had a feel for it and could guide a sledge round every bump. Well, tumbling down that roof Ah manages tae stick ma hand an' leg doon on ma right side and sure enough Ah sort of slewed across the tiles that way and came tae rest against that chimneystack, bashing ma head somethin' rotten in the process.

'So now Ah catch ma breath, and take stock for a moment. Ah'm almost naked in the pissing rain, Ah've taken all the skin offa ma right hand and knee, and I'm stuck on the roof o' a five-storey detached townhouse full o' men who will shortly be fixing tae murda me. But Ah'm free, for that moment at least Ah'm free, and as Ah look up intae the rain-swept wind and at the great grey clouds hurtling across the sky Ah want to scream for joy.'

The Thompson household, Dalston

Sylvie Thompson refused to look at the photographs of her daughter Jo Jo that Commander Leman had brought with him, but she wept just the same. Her husband Craig glanced briefly at one or two before pushing them aside and breaking down also. For some minutes Leman let them weep. There was nothing else to do. He had agonized long and hard over whether to show Jo Jo's parents the photographs sent by her attackers. Under normal circumstances he would not have dreamt of doing so, but these were not normal circumstances.

Something inside Commander Leman had changed. He had come to a decision and in order to carry out that decision he would need help. Apart from his own wife and daughter, the people most likely to be prepared to help him were the Thompson family. This was why he had shown Craig Thompson the photographs of his unconscious daughter being brutally raped by four anonymous men.

An Oxfam shop, West Bromwich

'Do ye know, for a minute there Ah was so content to be alone and feeling the wind in ma face that Ah actually considered jus' sitting up there until I died of exposure. That wouldnae 'a been such a bad way tae go, you know . . . At least Ah'd 'a been alone.

'But then the horror o' discovery occurred tae me. They wouldnae let me sit an' die. Any moment ma broken skylight could be discovered an' one o' those slavin' bastards would pop up through it tae persecute me further. Well Ah knew right then that if that were tae have happened they would no' ha' taken me back alive. As Ah crouched by the chimneypot Ah absolutely knew that if Goldie an' the boys appeared Ah'd just pitch masel' straight offa the roof there an' then. Tae be quite frank, Ah was no' unattracted tae the idea of one final glorious flight on the wind tae the ultimate freedom available tae a poor girl wi' nothin' tae lose.

'But then Ah thinks, "Come on, Jessie! Anyone who can get off drugs alone in a whorehouse can get off a fuckin' roof, right?" So Ah set masel' tae edging ma way around the perimeter in the hope that I'd encounter a sturdy drainpipe. Well, ye don't need tae be a DIY expert tae know that the advent o' plastic plumbing accessories has made the shinning up and down o' rooftops a far less common occurrence than it used tae be. The only old-fashioned metal pipe that remained on the building was sadly one that Ah knew tae run directly past the reception room window on the ground floor, then on down into the bin area at the basement, where the gang room was. If Ah went down that pipe Ah'd no' be able tae get tae the pavement and instead would descend further, straight intae a trap, 'cos the gate up from the bin area was locked an' wired big time. Goldie didnae want any o' his many rivals coming in at him through his gang room window.

'Consequently, Ah had no choice but tae take ma chances with a plastic pipe that ran down the back o' the house tae the back garden. Ah say garden, but o' course it was no more than a disgusting tip which was all tae the good as far as Ah was concerned, since Ah reckoned a pile o' rotting mattresses would make a better landing pad than any lawn. So that's it, plan made, get on wi' it, girl, no sense hanging about, get over the gutter an gi' it a go . . . Oh, ma Goad, have you ever launched yoursel' offa the roof o' a five-storey house? Jeez, but it's high, Ah mean it's really fuckin' high. I sticks one leg over, then the other, an' it feels like I'm on the edge o' the world, then Ah'm hanging on the gutter with ma fingers and ma chin, the wind roaring up ma G-stringed arse, working one hand down onto the pipe, ma bare toes searching for the first o' the brackets that attach the pipe tae the wall. And then it's time tae put ma trust in the plastic. Plastic pipe. Plastic bracket, metal bolts admittedly but intae brick which I can see is old and crumbly. Hey, one thing a heroin diet does for ye is it makes you light. Ah don't know what Ah weigh, but it was no' enough tae tear a plastic pipe off a rotten wall, an' Goad knows how but Ah managed tae work ma way right down that pipe an' end up putting ma stilettos on amongst the stinking filth that characterizes the back garden of a crack whorehouse.'

The Leman household, Dalston

Commander Leman and his family packed the last of their bags into the family car before their drive to Cornwall. There had been a long list of people to inform about their planned absence from London. The

209

milkman, of course, and the newsagent. Also the neighbours, who held a set of keys and had promised to keep an eye on the house. Anna's Aikido tutor, her netball coach and her Spanish dance class. Christine Leman's reading circle and her parents, who were regular Sunday lunch guests at the Lemans', but who would be joining them in Cornwall for the last week of the holiday.

Jo Jo's parents, Sylvie and Craig Thompson, had also been informed. The teenaged corpse that lay beneath the soil at the East London Cemetery had bonded the two families for ever with innocent blood.

'Dad,' Anna Leman said, breaking a silence which had lasted all the way to the M25. 'Jo Jo was attacked as a warning to you, wasn't she?'

There was no point even trying to deny it. 'Yes.'

'They wanted you to think that the same thing could happen to me, right?'

'Something like that, yes.'

Once more the family fell silent as the slow-grinding bumper-to-bumper miles crawled by. Finally Anna spoke again.

'There's a term they use in trauma therapy ... It means completing a cycle, getting free of something by sort of finishing it ... It's an American term; these things are always American, aren't they?'

'Closure,' said Christine Leman.

'Yes, that's right. Closure.'

'Closure,' Commander Leman repeated. 'So that's what it's called.'

An Oxfam shop, West Bromwich

'There was a hole in the fence, or more tae say there was a bit o' fence round a lot o' holes. Goldie had concentrated all his security measures on the walls and

210

the windows o' the house. The garden was anyone's who cared tae piss in it or jack up their scag. Well, the hole led intae an alley between Goldie's house an' the next one, an' round tae the front where Ah'd bin brought all those weeks or months o' hell before. Ah didnae glance back. Ah had no idea where Ah was or where Ah was goin' except that Ah was goin' tae get away from that house o' hell. Ah had no money at all, but when Ah saw a cab for hire Ah hailed it straight away.

'"Take us down town," Ah says, "an Ah'll gi' ye a blowjob." The bloke just shakes his head in disbelief and drives off. Funny, Ah'd bin down in the gutter for so long that Ah'd completely forgotten that there are people in the world who don't deal exclusively in sex and drugs. So Ah had tae walk and Ah walked quickly too. Dressed the way Ah am there was no way Ah was goin' tae dawdle on any street corners and get ma head kicked in again by territorial streetwalkers. That was the thing that had begun ma last round o' misery.

'What Ah decided Ah needed was a coat. Ah was cold and ridiculously conspicuous in ma whore's uniform, an what Ah needed more than anything else was a great big coat. Well, that's where ma story sits currently. 'Cos if ye walk long enough in any big town you're goin' tae happen upon a high street, an' if ye look about ye amongst the line o' kebab shops, sari shops and junk shops, you're goin' tae find an Oxfam shop or the like. Funny thing, it's always in the poorest streets that ye find the charity shops, in't it? Rents are low an' plenty o' people want second-hand clothes, Ah suppose. Nonetheless, it's always struck me as strange that it's the poor that have to keep the charity shops open ... Anyways, here Ah am, hen, penniless an' in desperate need o' a few bits o' clothes, in particular a coat an' some boots. Now the truth is that if ye won't gi' us anything Ah'm goin' tae have tae just

211

grab something and run, because it's gettin' on in the day now, an' I can't last a night out in a boobtube. So what do ye say?'

Not surprisingly, the man gave Jessie a coat and some socks and boots, a jumper and five pounds from his own pocket.

Newspaper Library, Colindale

The librarian stooped over the microfiche. 'All this will be crunched down and digitized pretty soon. The entire library burnt onto a small cornflake. No need for me then, I imagine. You'll be able to get what you want straight through your mobile phone.'

'Yes. Absolutely.'

The librarian studied the screen. 'You don't know the name of this lecturer, sir?'

'No, only the girl's name: Samantha Spencer.'

'Well, if it was a student–tutor scandal then I doubt that the girl would've been named. That's always the way with these things. They can hang some poor man out to dry whether he did anything or not, while his female accuser gets to hide behind a mask of anonymity.'

'Try a couple of buzzwords. Try "scandal"; "harassment"; "dismissal"; "ruin".'

'I've told you, sir, this is microfilm, not a computer database. You can't just press the search button. The *Cambridge Evening News* hadn't been digitized then. I'm afraid we'll just have to use our eyes.'

The minutes ticked slowly by as the librarian trawled through the microfilm.

'Ah, here's something. Front page, too. Well, sex always is, isn't it? ... February ninety-nine. "Promising career ruined ... Politics and Modern History". This sounds like your man.'

The librarian pointed out the relevant pages on the screen and Peter settled down to read the sad story of a forty-three-year-old lecturer who slept with a student and paid a very heavy price.

The girl (19), who has not been named, brought complaints to the University Senate of continuous and unprovoked sexual harassment. Gordon Crozier (43), Professor of Politics and Modern History, did not deny that sexual intercourse had taken place on more than one occasion but strenuously denied that there had been any abuse, claiming that the relationship was consensual.

The girl may not have been named, but the Right Honourable Peter Paget, MP, knew her name. Of that he was absolutely sure.

The accusations are of a particularly serious nature because of the girl's claims that Professor Crozier used his position of authority and trust to force his attentions upon her. She felt emotionally coerced into sex and claimed that she was allowed to feel that her success at university would be affected if she did not comply. Professor Crozier has issued a statement saying that there was no coercion and that he and the girl had simply had a brief affair, which, while inappropriate between a teacher and his student, was nonetheless legal and entirely consensual. The professor points out that he is not married and that he attempted to end the relationship shortly after it began. It was, he claims, this rejection of the girl that led her to make her accusations.

By the time Peter had finished reading the article,

the librarian had unearthed the follow-up story, which had appeared a month later. The Professor of Politics and Modern History had been dismissed in disgrace. He thanked the librarian and returned to his office, where Samantha was waiting to inform him that he had been summoned to the office of the Home Secretary.

Fallowfield Community Hall, Manchester

'I love touring. Always have. Right back to when I were a kid and I got the part of the Artful Dodger in a little regional tour of *Oliver!* Beat all the proper stage-school kids an' all, and suddenly I'm stopping in digs in different towns and seeing the backstage of all these different theatres. How exciting was that? Then when I won *Pop Hero* and we did the package tour it were just totally mental and outrageous. Ten acts on the road together, fook me, talk about clash of egos . . . amongst the other nine, of course. I were above it even then, because it was so absolutely clear who were the boss. I'd got nearly as many votes as all the others put together. But what a laugh it was. Big artics out the back, loads of fat blokes with ponytails an' arsehole cleavages humpin' gear around. Screaming girls everywhere. Mind you, they were all about ten years old so that were no good. Besides which, I were knocking off two of me co-stars anyway, so that was sorted. Do you remember Sandi – the bird who covered "Save All Your Kisses For Me" – how she come over all sweet and virginal on the telly? I'll tell you what, that girl should get an Oscar for that innocent act she done . . . First and foremost it were her who really got me into coke. She come from this village in Dorset an' from what she told me about it the local boozer sounded like South Central LA. It's always the same, I reckon.

Country kids do more drugs than city kids 'cos they're more bored, that an' the drink-driving laws, right? Like you've got all these isolated country pubs an' nobody can have more than a pint because the police are trying to earn a living entirely out o' traffic fines. Well, what's gonna happen? It's obvious, in't it, everybody starts taking drugs. Go in any olde worlde roast beef an' warm beer thatched fookin' alehouse in the country and you'll find a heroin dealer playin' darts with his mates.

'Anyway, like I say, Sandi were the dirtiest bird I ever met, and do you know how she liked her cocaine? I've surprised a few NA meetings with this one. Up her arse. True. Not a word of a lie. The first night I was with her, I'm eighteen, remember ... Mind you, I reckon she were only twenty. The first night I were with her, she says, "Oi want you to blow some charlie op moi crapper, Tom." West country accent, an' all, so uncool but very sexy, I think. "There's far more capillaries op youm arrse than op youm 'ooter, Tom, trust old Sarndi." So she gets a Bic biro an' takes the ink tube out, an' gets on her knees on the bed and suddenly I'm staring at the brown-eyed Cyclops. "Jus' youm sock a nice line op tharrt tube, Tommy, an' then stick the pointy end o' the tube in moi arrse. Only jus' 'arf an inch, loik, an' blow gentle ... Not a big puff, loik, 'cos it's dangerous t'blow in people's orifices, loik."

'She loved it, an' I'll tell you what, she were right, 'cos she done it to me and it were a very quick an' lively buzz indeed. An' sort of erotic, I suppose, particularly if you're pissed up an' mad for it. But t'be honest, I've not bothered with the method much since. I get self-conscious, see. Funny, but I do, kneeling on a bed with me buttocks spread. Bit on the intimate side, I reckon, borderin' on graphic. I like doin' it to the birds, though. Don't get me wrong, it's lovely that. An'

I've charmed a lot o' girls that way. I find they can't get enough of it.

'Anyway, like I say, I love the road. I always go on the tour bus too, no limos, even now. I like the beer and the gags and the service station food. Don't know why, but to me it's romantic. You pull into some Road Chef on the M6 an' all pile out. You've got your big fook-off minders, your drop-dead gorgeous backin' singers, your wasted, monged-out old musos . . . an' then *me*, right in the middle, the Boss, the Man. The Chairman o' the fookin' board. Everybody's lookin' an' pointin', but you're just with your posse havin' your pie an' chips like a regular dude, except for your security blokes, o' course. An' then you get in the shop and buy a load o' dirty mags to show to the backin' singers, an' water pistols an' guns with sound effects or whatever, y'know, kids' toys, and then you pile back on the coach and just 'ave it large.

'Simple pleasures, I know, but it does for me.

'An' when you get to the gig, what a buzz, man. My tours have got so out of control that it's just humungous. I get a hard-on jus' thinkin' about the size o' my operation. There's six artics parked out the back for the lights and staging. Six! Fook me, you could retake the Falkland Islands wi' my crew. A *hundred* blokes, all with my name written on 'em, all wi' laminates hangin' roun' their necks sayin' "Tommy's Crew". Tommy's Crew, eh? Cool phrase or what? Big, tough 'ard men what worked for the Who an'·Queen an' now they're Tommy's crew an' they're all working their bollocks off for *me* t'make sure I am a fookin' *rock god*.

'What a vibe the "get in" is. When I turn up for me soundcheck everythin's goin' off big time. Radios crackling, lights spinning, miles and miles of cable everywhere. Hordes o' lovely little PAs on their mobiles making sure Britney gets good seats.

'There's caterin' an' ping-pong tables an' pool an' loads o' the latest arcade games. An' I get ushered through it all by a flyin' wedge o' minders, me lookin' all serious an' intense in me big coat an' beanie hat . . . An' here's the point. Everyone knows, I mean *everyone* knows, that every single fookin' light, every nut, every bolt, every plate o' steak au poivre an' chips, every crate o' Pepsi, every case o' ozzie Chardonnay, every drum riser, guitar pick, hot dog, fork lift, scaff' rig, limo, artic an' merchandizing stand. Every single front o' house usher in their little uniforms, every grip, roadie, crew boss, fixer, publicist, site manager, health and safety fookwit bastard who reckons you've got to 'ave ten metres between each punter in case one of 'em spontaneously combusts. Every session muso, every backing singer, the entire six-tier management team, the twats from the record company, cooks, cleaners, costume girls, obliging poofs an' posh little cuties what ask me if I need anything. Every fooker in that vast arena, *every single fooker*, knows that they and everything they see and touch is down to me. I'm paying for it and I'm paying for them. They're my posse, it's all my stuff, they're all my people. It's *my* fookin' gig. An' what's more, the whole thing is surrounded, absolutely fookin' surrounded, by an impregnable ring o' security. Huge fook-off bastards wi' hands like hams, big shaven-headed black geezers wi' gold chains round their necks an' rings like house bricks on their fingers. Tough lezzos wi' skin'ead mullets an' tattoos on their knuckles – you 'ave to 'ave female security on these days in case any hysterical bird needs restraining, otherwise, bang, some fookin' mad dad'll do the tour for sexual harassment . . . Security, I love it, my own private army. I mean, how good is that?

'And there I am, being ushered into my space . . . The sanctum. The citadel at the centre of the fortified city. The castle keep from which I shall ride forth to do battle an' gross seven hundred an' fifty thousand quid a night.

'They work so hard on my sanctums, them obliging poofs an' posh little cuties what work for my record company. They do everything to give my great an' tortured artistic soul rest an' respite, because that is what I have a right to expect. Everything. Half an acre o' flowers, vast fridges full o' drinks, cushions, couches, a little gym, my special moody lighting wi' all drapes over the lamps, 'cos that's how Keith Richard 'as it. A massage bench, a cocktail bar, a cable telly the size of a wall, an' a fook-off sound system, an' I mean *fook off*. Get this, this is true, my *backstage* sound system 'as more grunt than Westlife's fookin' *show rig*. Cool or what?

'An' everyone's sayin', "What can I get you, Tommy?" "When would you like to soundcheck, Tommy?" "Is everythin' absolutely fookin' perfect for you, Tommy, 'cos if not we'll fookin' sack everybody an' start again."

'And then you sit down and, well . . . What do you do? How do you top it? How do you come to terms with being just so fookin' special that everybody in your world is there for you?

'You reach for the drugs, o' course.'

House of Commons

The Home Secretary laid a friendly hand on Peter Paget's shoulder as he led him to an easy chair.

'So, how are you feeling?'

'Not so bad, Douglas, not so bad.'

'We're all very impressed, you know, Peter. Very proud, the way you're handling this.'

'Well, you know, it's been over two months and neither I nor my new friend Robert the Junkie have shown positive for HIV or hepatitis C, so we really are

218

looking hopeful. Robert swears to me that the needle was clean and that he hasn't had sex in two years . . .'

'Do you believe him?'

'Regarding the sex? Certainly. I've seen the state of his penis, remember. About the needles? Well, I think I believe him. He really is a bright and articulate man underneath it all. What's more, he's been using for the best part of a decade and the tests prove he was clean at least until a couple of months ago, so . . . Well, look, it's idle to speculate, Douglas. It's all looking very hopeful, but I shan't get a complete all-clear until three full months have passed.'

'And Angela?'

'What can I tell you? She's worried, of course. So are the girls. We talk about it a lot. I mean, it's a strange thing to walk about with the real possibility that some alien virus has invaded your system. I manage not to think about it most of the time, but sometimes, in the night . . . Well, you know.'

'I can certainly try to imagine . . .'

The Home Secretary had seen to it that a bottle of House of Commons malt whisky and two glasses had been set out. It was early evening, a clubbable hour. Peter could not help but feel excited. This was clearly matey, man-to-man stuff. Sundowners with the Home Secretary was rising-star stuff for sure.

'Look, Peter. The number-one issue in this whole dreadful business is your health, and yours and Angela's wellbeing, but you know as well as I do that the immense publicity that has surrounded your accident has brought the issues you've been trying to raise firmly to centrestage.'

'I can assure you, Douglas, that I didn't deliberately run the risk of contracting a fatal illness in order to improve the fortunes of my Private Member's Bill.' Peter felt strong, empowered. Perhaps it was the accident that made him bold. After all, those who have

219

looked death in the face can certainly face down Home Secretaries.

'You know me better than that, Peter. You know that that's not what I meant. What I meant is that because of your campaign and the circumstances that have surrounded it the issue of full legalization is now no longer seen as the domain of hippies and lunatics—'

'Like me, you mean. I well remember your reaction to my first speech on the issue. Not sympathetic, as I recall.'

'When you introduced your bill, Peter, the drug debate stood at exactly the same point at which it had stood for twenty years. Zero tolerance, no surrender. We will fight those pushers on the beaches, et cetera, et cetera. But now the public have suddenly been forced to confront the real and present danger that traditional drug policy has brought down upon mainstream society.'

'And you have also been forced to confront it.'

'Yes, Peter, I accept that. You don't need to press your point. You've moved me on this issue. It's quite self-evident that if your acquaintance Robert had had access to a shooting gallery or at the very least a proper needle-exchange programme you would not be living under the threat that currently hangs over your head.'

'Beautifully put, Home Secretary. Are you going to use it?'

'Yes, I am as a matter of fact, at a speech to the regional conference in Birmingham this Thursday.'

'Does this mean that you intend to support my position?'

'Peter. I don't mind admitting that a few weeks ago you weren't exactly my favourite backbencher. You were talking absolute common sense but common sense that at the time I thought too dangerous ever to be even whispered. I thought you were going to drag us all into a polarized debate where you could either be

220

seen as a statesman or a drug pushing lunatic. But don't think for a moment that even then I didn't have a great deal of sympathy for your arguments. Of course you're right. In simple economic terms you're right if nothing else. The police force is buckling under the strain of drug-related crime, whole communities are becoming fiefdoms for drug gangs.'

'As I've constantly sought to point out, the savings from turning drug-dealers into honest men would run into many billions.'

'Yes, but it's not just the savings we're considering here, it's the possible *profit* of legalization. As you're aware, the government's policy on smoking tobacco is that everyone should stop immediately—'

'But if they did, the Treasury would be bankrupted.'

'Of course. Cigarettes are our biggest earner. Five quid a packet, four pounds fifty to us. People talk about tobacco-users being a burden on the National Health Service, but they *pay* for most of the damn health service.'

'And if every yuppie who had a weekend snort of cocaine was taxed for it?'

'My God. Ten quid in the kitty per line . . . we could have a decent railway network in a year!' The Home Secretary picked up his telephone.

'Joanna, could you possibly bring through the Treasury briefing I asked you to look out?'

Joanna entered the slightly dusty old room like a little ray of sunshine. Small, blond, smartly turned out in an elegant trouser suit. For a moment Peter Paget found himself speculating on whether the Home Secretary harboured a secret similar to his own. He did not speculate for long, however. The conversation he was having was simply too exciting to allow room for idle thoughts. Even this brief reminder of his affair could not subdue his spirits for long.

'I've asked the Chancellor to join us, if that's all right,

Peter, and the Prime Minister has said that he'll try to look in.'

Joanna could have been Aphrodite herself and Peter would have failed to consider her further. The Chancellor? The Prime Minister! Only months before, he had been a pariah, lucky to get a meeting with his own constituency chairman. Now this! The Home Secretary continued.

'This is a highly confidential Treasury report. A report which, I might add, we compiled some time before you began your campaign, Peter. You're not the only one who has the clear vision to see the wood despite the trees, but you were until now the only one with the balls to state the obvious conclusion. This report looks at the budgetary implications of full legalization. Of necessity it is highly speculative. We don't know what the health and social implications would be. It is of course possible that the alarmist majority are right and that we would find ourselves dealing with entire communities full of stoned, tripping vegetables, but tentative programmes abroad, particularly in the Netherlands, suggest the opposite. Our best guess is that if any increased usage did occur it would be massively offset in health and social benefits by the fact that usage would be safe and in the open.'

'Of course.'

'Well, yes, of course, Peter, but you know as well as I do the amount of protest that a policy like this, if implemented, would create. We must be aware of that.'

'If implemented? My God, Douglas, surely you're not saying that the government—'

'What I'm saying is that this secret report concludes that if we taxed drugs instead of impounding them, if we made them a simple matter of the laws of fair trade, we could destroy ninety per cent of the nation's criminal networks overnight, we could import the stuff at the cost of tea and sell it at the cost of caviar, all at an immense profit to the Treasury. If the policy became international we could liberate the producing nations in the developing world from the grip of drug warlords, and the peasant population could return to producing the food crops they so desperately need. And finally and quite frankly most importantly, we'd have so much money in the coffers we could cut income tax in half and win every election until Doomsday.'

Once more Joanna entered the room. 'Home Secretary, the Prime Minister has asked if you and Mr Paget would join him at Number Ten. The Chancellor has also been invited.'

Peter could see that the Home Secretary was not overjoyed to be so perfunctorily summoned. Clearly he felt that this was his initiative and that the PM should come to him. Peter did not care who came to whom, or if the meeting took place at the Westminster McDonald's, he was going to share conference with the three most powerful men in government. The fast track had just got a whole lot faster.

Fallowfield Community Hall, Manchester

'So the tour's been going for a while, right? Scotland were mental. I'm an honorary Scot, me. I know how to butter 'em up, see. I always open the set by saying, "I'm like Scotland. Why? Because I am also proudly inde-fookin'-pendent." Bang, five minutes o' cheering. They love all that, they do. Well, who don't? Quite frankly, I've always found that a naked appeal to petty nationalism goes down well wherever you play it. "Good evening, Doncaster, best fookin' city in the world. Hello, Southend, God's own holiday resort." The house'll go potty every time. Amazing how much people love it when you big up their town, no matter what kind o' shitehole it is. In fact, the funny thing is, the posher an' better a town gets, the less the population want to big it up. I mean, I'm not going to go, "Good evening, Royal Tunbridge Wells. You rock!" am I? It just don't have the ring. Anyway, I was talkin' about Scotland, and as it 'appens I do always feel at home in Scotland. I like the beer, I like the fried haggis an' sauce in the chippies which you'd think'd be shite but is actually not bad. I like the lamb pies an' the fact that you can see mountains most o' the time. Also I've always been partial to the birds up there. Love a strawberry blonde, me.

'The downside is the drugs, man. I mean, that is one very fooked-up scene. Well, it is everywhere, in't it, but I always seem to feel more aware of it in Scotland. Maybe it's fookin' *Trainspotting*. I bet the Scottish Tourist Board loved it when that came out. Actually, I think it's the scenery. I mean, you've got this devastatingly beautiful, healthy-looking place, what should be full o' great big fook-off hard men wi' beards an' muscles in their spit, chuckin' logs about, but instead everywhere you look there's these pale, skinny, spotty lads an' lasses monged out on God knows what shite or other.

'I mean, as I think I've made clear, I'm no stranger to mind-altering substances but fook me, some o' them Scottish estates, they *live* off 'em. Scag on their Frosties in the morning, man! *Trainspotting* looks like a whitewash, a cover-up job. Edinburgh is a city under siege. The smack'eads and dealers are massing at the gates. It's weird, that, like with most cities it's the middle bit that's the shitehole no-go area, and the outer suburbs are where you escape to when you've got a bit o' dosh. You always hear them on the news goin' on about the inner cities, don't you? Like they was talkin' 'bout Dante's In-fookin'-ferno. But wi' Edinburgh it's all inside out. The middle bit's like somethin' out of a

Disney movie. You've got this amazing castle and loads of jumper shops and little restaurants in eighteenth-century alleyways wi' twisting stairwells in the pavement that lead down to ancient basement bars wi' curling brooms on the walls and three million types o' single malt. Then a couple of miles up the road you've got downtown Sodom and Gomorrah! I'll never forget when we done the Edinburgh Playhouse on the *Pop Hero* tour. I was new to fame then an' only eighteen and bloody stupid wi' it. I didn't know much about drugs, see, I mean obviously there were Sandi the Wurzel with her coke up the arse, but most o' my vast experience, my veneer of sophistication, 'as come in the years since.

'We did the gig, which I closed o' course, and it was a total explanation, o' course, an' I was lathered on Tennents lager, o' course, and there was fookin' hundreds o' fans at the stage door, o' course, which I wasn't so used to at the time, so it was all pretty intoxicating, an' I was well up for a bit o' naughtiness. I remember leanin' out o' the dressing room window throwin' down messages to the kids, an' I saw this gang o' girls that I reckoned was a bit older than most of the fans, who were children basically for all their pierced belly buttons, so I got a couple of roadies, showed 'em which girls I meant, an' told them to go out an' pull 'em.

'Well, the next thing I knew I was in a taxi wi' four tough little Scottish birds wi' white minis an' bare goosepimpled legs, an' I never saw one o' them that didn't have a fag on the go, even when later on I were shaggin' 'em. Honest.

'So this taxi ride was about three miles, but it might as well 'ave been to another planet. We gets out at this low-rise estate, like Hulme in Manchester, you know what I'm sayin'? Three five-hundred-yard corridors on top of each other, hundreds of little front doors all graffiti'd up, piss-soaked staircases, fookin' needles crunchin' under your boots. I'll tell you, gettin' along that corridor was scary stuff, they were only a few foot wide so any old granny (or pop star wi' four birds in tow) who wants to get along 'em 'as to squeeze past every single gang o' lads that's stood about waitin' for somebody to punch. 'Orrible. I were that glad when we finally got into one of the birds' flat, crappy though it was.

'It were her mum's, but she was out so the five of us is just 'aving a party. Like I say, I were only eighteen and it was just great, the version of the night you always wanted to 'ave wi' the birds at school but never did. We was smokin' pot an' drinking Diamond White cider an' the cable's on MTV an' *there's me* on heavy rotation wi' my first single. I mean what a buzz, man, me four fans, an' I'm on the fookin' telly! They love it! So suddenly it's knickers off and 'ow's your father. All four of 'em are at me! My first genuine orgy. I was literally in heaven.

'Well, I don't know how long we was at it, but we certainly wasn't finished when the bird's mum whose flat it was came 'ome wi' 'er boyfriend. Honest, I'm 'aving it away in the livin' room wi' her daughter and her daughter's mates an' this woman walks in wi' two portions o' curry an' chips an' don't bat an eyelid! Just starts goin' on about truant officers! She's sayin' to her daughter that she's gonna have to turn up a bit more at school just for show, else the social workers will be round and where's she supposed to hide all the smack she's dealing? Yes, all the *smack* she's dealing.

'An' don't forget the truant officer bit. Truant officers do not chase sixteen-year-olds. So I'm realizing that at least one o' the birds in this orgy were underage. Fook me. I'm eighteen, remember. A year before I'd been Prince Charming at the Bradford Alhambra. I'd only done pot an' booze up until Sandi an' her biros up the arse, an' suddenly I'm beginnin' to feel a bit uneasy to say the least. The mum's gone into the other room with the boyfriend (to jack up as I soon discover), an' I'm on the sofa, trousers round me ankles, realizing that I may have fooked up somewhat. That instead o' being in a nice bar at the Edinburgh Thistle Hotel chatting up dancing girls off the tour, I'm in a drug dealer's house shaggin' schoolgirls. Not good, particularly for someone as career-minded as me.

'So I gets off the bird I'm on top of and asks them how old they are. I'd thought sixteen–seventeen when I pulled 'em. Now I'm prayin' for fifteen or sixteen. But no such luck, man. We are talkin' twelve an' thirteen! One of 'em was *twelve* years old! They're smokin' pot, drinkin' Diamond White and shaggin', an' my hostess is *twelve* years old.

' "My ma's only twenty-seven now," the bird says. Which was a shock 'cos I reckon she looked forty, but the thing was that that woman had had this girl when she were fifteen, an' by the look o' things the next generation would not be long in coming. Fook me, I ain't no social worker, but even I can see that's not a healthy situation. A grandma when you're thirty – you'd wanna take drugs, wouldn't you?

'Well, anyway, never mind all that. What about me? I'm shitting it, that's what. Just totally and utterly shitting it. I mean look, I am definitely not into givin' it Gary Glitter. That is not me, right? I'd reckoned these birds was nearly my age. Anybody would 'a done. They was faggin', drinkin', swearin' an' wandering round like they owned the bloody town. How was I supposed to know? But who's gonna believe me when I'm front-paged for shagging jailbait? So it's trousers up an' head for the door . . .

'Except the door's locked!

'Well, not just locked – locked and barred, from the *inside*, an' I'm lookin' at this door, an' suddenly I realize it's a sheet of fookin' *steel*. A steel door, right? So I take a look behind the curtains, an' every window is barred. Then I look at the stuff they've got and I'm thinking this level of security is not in order to stop people pinching their video.

' "There's a lot o' competition in our area," says this fookin' twelve-year-old, who can see what I'm thinking. "Too much scag aboot the place. Everybody wants tae put everyone else oot o' business."

'As if to illustrate the point there's a sudden bangin' at the door. An' while my little illegal harem pull their knickers back on the boyfriend emerges from the bedroom, curry sauce round his mouth, a pinprick o' blood dribbling down 'is arm an' a *fookin' machine gun* in his 'ands.

'This is Edinburgh, right? Edinburgh in Britain, fourth-richest economy on earth, right? Not Beirut, not the Gaza Strip, not fooking Croatia, an' I'm in a flat wi' a man who carries a machine gun. Not only that but the mum comes out next wi' a sawn-off! It's Bonnie an' fookin' Clyde except this couple are about as sexy as a dog's arse, sad drug-fooks the both of 'em, but heavily armed sad drug-fooks.

'Well, the knock at the door was just customers. Two women wanting to score. I didn't see them – the whole thing got transacted through a little letterbox in the door, but I do remember hearin' a baby crying.

'Anyway, obviously I was lookin' for ways to make my exit by this time, an' I asks the girls if I can call a taxi. They just laughed at that, so I'm thinking that I'd better strike out on my own, but that's no good either because the boyfriend and the ma have gone back in the bedroom and he's got the keys to the steel door an' the girls made it very clear to me he did not like to be disturbed.

' "They'll be cooking up rocks o' crack. Very profitable end o' the business," says the girl. "I'm afraid you'll have tae wait, Tommy."

'For a while after that I'm having all these paranoid suspicions that I've been set up, that I'm going to get blackmailed by these birds for having shagged 'em, but then I realize that bearin' in mind the nature of the business the mum was running they wouldn't exactly be looking to provoke press and police attention. So then I starts to relax a bit. We have another spliff an' another cider an' I'm thinkin', all right, I'll stay all night. They'll have to open up in the morning to get some milk or whatever and quite frankly I didn't fancy wandering round that estate in the dark anyway. I mean, obviously I wasn't going to get down to any more sex wi' 'em, fookin' 'ell that is *so* not me, although you won't believe it, they tried! Honest, these little girls were tryin' to get the party goin' again, but *no way*, so instead I said I fancied a bit o' smack.

'Big mistake. Obviously.

'I'd never had any before but t'be quite honest I were curious. Don't forget I had to face the prospect o' sitting up all night watching MTV wi' three thirteen-year-olds an' a twelve-year-old.

'Well, two of 'em didn't bother with H – yet – but the other two says, "Fine, let's have a wee pipe."

'An' we did. Me an' two schoolgirls sharing a smoke o' heroin. T'be honest, it makes me shiver t'think of it. But we did it, an' two of us mellowed out in a nice big easy chill, an' one of us tried to look tough and sucked down most of the whole thing before realizing that they had fooked up big time.

'That was me, of course. And as the vomit surged up and my mind and heart started to feel like they were shutting down I knew that I had overdone it a bit. Uncool or what?

'I came round in casualty. The first thing I saw were a flash o' light that turned out to be a camera. I'd been recognized an' my first drug-related front page was already being written. They'd dumped me by some

229

dustbins in the car park of their estate. I suppose I should think myself lucky they didn't just shove me down the rubbish chute. Clearly having found themselves with a potentially dying pop star on their hands, their only agenda had been to get rid of me as quickly as possible. They took my money but not my cards, which was sensible. They were clearly not so fooked up that they couldn't see that if I were found dead the following morning then hanging on to my credit cards would be a bad idea.

'The bin men might have saved my life. I don't know if that big smoke would have killed me, but unconscious in the dustbins of a sink estate is not a good place to be anyways, so I'll always be grateful. My office still sends one of them a Christmas card.'

Ten Downing Street

Peter had never been in the Cabinet room. The great ring of chairs around the huge shiny table, so often photographed occupied by earnest ministers, were empty now save for four. His, the Home Secretary's, the Chancellor of the Exchequer's and, at the centre of it all, the Prime Minister's.

There was a phrase Samantha often used in the warm afterglow of their lovemaking . . . *'It doesn't get any better than this.'*

Peter always thought it rather an effective sentence, somewhat tainted now, of course, in the light of his discovery that she was either a frigid, father-obsessed emotional timebomb or else a sex-mad, father-obsessed emotional timebomb. But nonetheless it was still a good phrase and as Peter sat facing a smiling Prime Minister he knew that, Aids scares and worryingly intense and unbalanced lovers aside, it certainly did not get much better than this.

Then the PM spoke. 'Peter, I've asked you here today because I want you to do something very tough for me. Very tough indeed. I want you to drop your Private Member's Bill.'

The coffee cup froze in Peter Paget's hand. The smile fell from his lips with an almost audible thud. Such disappointment was unbearable. Had he been brought into these elevated surroundings merely to be lobbied once more to fall upon his sword?

The Prime Minister smiled. 'No, we want you to bring your proposals into the fold, Peter. We want to put your bill into the next Queen's Speech.'

Peter had been wrong a moment before. This had just got a very great deal better. 'You . . . You mean make it policy?'

'Yes, I do. What we're proposing is the biggest, bravest, boldest shift in the social management of this country since the introduction of the Welfare State. If it works, this administration will be seen as one of the true greats, and it's down to you, Peter. You are our weapon, you have the credibility, the insight, the experience and, if I'm honest, the wounds of battle to swing the country behind us. I'd like to invite you to join the Cabinet, Peter. I'm creating a new post, Minister for Drugs, and I want you to fill it.'

The Paget household, Dalston

Peter Paget's daughters had fought their way back from the local newsagent, a journey that required a police escort to get them up their own garden path.

'Dad, it's crazy, it's berserk. There're *eight* pages on you in the *Telegraph*.'

'There's fifteen in the *Independent* and twelve in the *Guardian*. Both leaders are claiming they thought of the whole idea first.'

'Which is *so* not true. They were going for de-criminalizing pot or whatever, as if that would do anything.'

'It was *you*, Dad. You did this. You've electrified the sodding country!'

It was true. The announcement of Peter Paget's new position and the speech he made that same evening in the house had caused a genuine sensation. A *world-wide* sensation. He was not only on the cover of every British newspaper, but many of the papers around the world had given him serious coverage too. What was more, so far at least, most of the coverage had been on the whole favourable. Not every editorial on the planet was backing wholesale legalization, but nobody was denying that this was a debate that was far too late in coming.

'They're calling you Churchillian, Daddy.'

'Well, it was one hell of a speech . . .' Cathy was devouring the front-page quotes. ' "Life of the nation" . . . "defence of the very values by which we live" . . . I must say, though, I thought the bit about it being May 1940 in the war against drugs was perhaps a teeny bit OTT. It did sort of invite the comparison with the Great Man.'

'Of course it did,' Peter replied happily. 'I'm no fool.'

After the girls had disappeared to their respective rooms to begin the daily task of emailing and texting their friends, Angela and Peter Paget found themselves alone together, or as alone as any two people can be when their garden is full of journalists. They had scarcely had a private moment since the maelstrom of Peter's needle prick had engulfed their lives.

'It does seem incredible that you've come so far so quickly, Peter.'

'Well, it's all down to that ridiculous accident, I suppose. Absurd, really, as if that makes any difference.'

'It's not all down to that. People were beginning to think differently anyway. It's the power of the argument. You're right. That's the point, and they can all see that.'

'Well, I hope so. I certainly didn't expect to gain a seat in Cabinet on the issue.'

'Congratulations, Peter. It's been a long time coming.'

'All the sweeter, I suppose, to get it through campaigning for something that truly matters rather than for oiling and toadying about the place.'

'Peter. Are you having an affair with Samantha?'

It was so sudden, so unexpected.

'I . . .'

He had known Angela for twenty years. She was too sensitive, too clever, to ask such a question unless she knew.

'I . . . I've had sex with her.'

She stared at him for a moment and then turned away. Turned away in what seemed, to Peter at least, like revulsion.

'Oh dear. Oh dear, Peter. That's a bit painful, I must say.'

'I'm sorry, Angela . . .'

Angela's body twitched in a manner that suggested she was not currently interested in apologies. 'How long has this been . . . Oh God, I can't believe I'm about to frame that pathetic sentence. It's ridiculous.'

Silence.

'Well, come on, then. Let's get it over with. How long has it been going on?'

'Not long. It's over . . . I mean, it has to be over. It was just a silly thing. Sex—'

'Do you love her?'

'No!' That at least he knew was true. 'No. It was sex, that's all . . . a couple of times.'

'A couple? A politician's couple or an actual couple?'

233

'Four. Four times.' He plucked the figure from the air. He did not know how many times. Twenty? Thirty?

'Do you want to know where? When? I'll tell you.'

'I'm going to ask you again, Peter. Do you love her?'

'No.'

'Did you ever?'

Good question. 'I was . . . fond of her. She's been very—'

'Yes, I know how fucking supportive she's been. You've told me often enough.'

'It was madness, Angela. I should have been stronger, but I wasn't . . . We spent so much time together, we were working so hard—'

'Does she love you?' Angela Paget had a lot of good questions.

'I doubt it. Well, she's fond of me as well, but no, not love. She knows I'm married, I'm unavailable—'

'Don't be too bloody sure of that!'

'Angela, please.'

'Look, Peter, this is tough. Very, very tough. I don't know how I'm going to deal with it, but I know that this can't be about me at the moment. You may be about to be pronounced HIV positive, for Christ's sake! Besides, everything you've worked for, everything we both believe in is finally beginning to happen. Why did you have to ruin it all?'

'Angela, none of that matters. I love you . . .'

And he meant it. The sudden realization that he might be about to lose her had brought him hurtling back into the heart of his marriage.

'It *does* matter, Peter! It matters a lot right now, and what matters most of all is Cathy and Suzie.'

'Of course.'

'So what I need to know now and, believe me, Peter, everything depends on your answers being honest, is the nature of this relationship. What it was, what it is and what you intend it to be. You say that it's not a love affair, that you had sex four times?'

'I'm thinking, looking back, this is awful. Five. Perhaps five.' In a way he sort of believed it. Did the detail matter? Not if the substance was honest, surely. He did not love Samantha . . . He had never loved her . . . and if perhaps he had thought in some insane moment of otherness that he did love her . . . if he had even said as much to her . . . on numerous occasions . . . well, he knew now, standing before the wife whom he was in danger of losing, that it had all been an illusion. Nothing more. Illusion.

'You see, Peter. Right now I'd like to leave you.'

'Angela!'

'But I shan't. There's too much at stake in our lives, too much that honestly matters. A diversion now, a stupid scandal, would be just the kind of pathetic thing that people in this country would seize upon to avoid actually having to think about anything, and you are making them think, Peter. Besides, you're too famous. Three months ago if I'd left you we probably wouldn't have made the papers. The girls would have at least been able to watch their home break up in private. But now, my God, everyone on the planet would know their business. I can't do that to the girls, or to myself, quite frankly—'

'But, Angela, you mustn't leave me anyway.'

'Afterwards, who knows? I expect things'll get easier. I'll hate you less . . . But that's why it's so important that you're honest with me, Peter. Is it over?'

'Yes.'

'Would it have been over if I hadn't discovered it?'

'Yes! Yes, absolutely.'

'Does she know it's over?' The tiniest pause was enough. 'So it isn't over yet, then. When will it be?'

'It's over now, Angela. It was before you found me out, I swear it. I've been agonizing about what a fool

235

I've been and how to let Samantha know that we've been stupid and we mustn't—'

'So you don't think she'll feel the same as you? You don't think that it'll be easy to get out of this? Admit it, Peter, she loves you.'

'She's fond of me.'

'Peter. This is going to be very messy. If she loves you, she'll fight.'

'She doesn't love me! She only thinks she does.'

'Peter. You are in shit, we are in shit. These things can *never* be ended easily. But end it you must, and if I am to stand by you, you must swear to me now, from the bottom of your heart, that you will do it immediately.'

National Exhibition Centre, Birmingham

The two Brummie teenagers were very, very excited.

'I can't believe 'ow good these seats are! Only forty-eight rows from the front. That's mental, that is.'

'Well, Sonia queued all night the day before they went on sale, didn't she?'

'Don't, it just makes me want to croi just even thinking 'bout her. All them foreign women an' 'er sleeping on the floor, it's disgusting.'

'Did her mum tell you she'd written to the Thai royal family? No reploi yet, but I think it's supposed to work sometimes.'

'It's just so weird. I mean, it's like surreal or something . . . Thinking of her, in jail in Thailand! I mean, I can just close moi oies and see her, 'ere with us, 'aving a laugh, 'ear her voice . . . it's loik . . . she went off for a week's 'oliday. We all said, "See ya, babes," and she just evaporated.'

'That bastard at the Rum Slinger, 'im what give 'er all them Es. He said she'd be all roit.'

'Yeah, but come on, Sal, would yow 'ave done it?'

'Don't be sodding stupid.'

'Exactly. Only Sonia would be that mad. That's why she didn't tell us what she were up to. We'd 'ave stopped 'er. Sonia was always mad, weren't she?'

'It was so nice of 'er mum to give us her Tommy tickets, though.'

'Well, she would have taken yow anyway.'

'Rubbish, she'd have taken yow.'

For a moment both of Sonia's friends thought that they would burst into tears.

'Actually, she probably would have taken some wanker of a bloke she'd met that day, wouldn't she?'

'Yeah, that's Sonia . . . 'ang on, I think it's starting. This is sow cool!'

Tony, Tommy's tour manager, was not often charmed by the women who sought access to Tommy, but Gemma was different. Quite apart from anything else, her brother had cerebral palsy, which was how she and he had been able to get past all the Exhibition Centre security and manoeuvre their way right up to the door of Tommy's hospitality lig. Gemma knew that nothing unmans the vast bulk of a security guard better than a sweet girl with a disabled brother, and she had worked her passage well. Now she had only to get past Tony and she would be in.

'Please, he'd just like to meet Tommy, that's all. Just to thank him for such an amazing show and all the things he's done for Comic Relief. Comic Relief have given some big grants to initiatives in the disabled community here in the Midlands.'

Tony knew that Tommy actually took his charity work seriously when he was straight enough to think about it, and since the after-show party was hardly rocking he decided to let Gemma and her brother in. 'I'll take you to him, but please don't stay long. He's too polite to disengage and so he gets trapped.'

'We won't. Promise.'

They made their way through the crowd of liggers and fans, local DJs who'd supported the shows, record-shop bosses, a few Midlands celebrities, and local footballers and athletes.

When Tony brought Gemma over Tommy was sitting behind his minders idly thinking about a song lyric . . . *I'm too fashionable to pay for my drinks . . . I want to be seen, but not with you . . . If nobody's photographing me, do I exist?*

'This is my brother, Gary.'

Gary's speech was quite severely impaired and the room was noisy. Tommy suggested that Gemma and Gary come to his dressing room. Gemma was aware enough of her good looks to see that Tommy's hospitality was only partly driven by sympathy for Gary. Nonetheless, Tommy made a considerable effort to talk to him, discovering that he was studying civil engineering at Birmingham University but that the facilities for the disabled were by no means everything they could be.

The three of them talked for about fifteen minutes, after which Gemma smiled at Tony, who was hovering at the doorway, and said that she and Gary must go.

'No way,' Tommy protested. 'Let's go back through to the party. Have another drink.'

Gemma smiled. 'Pretty amazing getting pressed to hang out with you, Tommy, but we don't want to overstay our welcome and the late-night buses are crap.'

'Bollocks to that. Have another drink, we'll get you a car later.'

'Well, that's just stupidly nice of you, but in fact Gary has an exam at nine in the morning.'

This was true, but Gary pointed out that Gemma did

not. He was a good brother and reminded Gemma that, while he had to go, she could stay. It had become clear during the conversation that Gemma was at least as big a fan of Tommy's as Gary was. In the end, despite Gemma's protests, it was decided that Gary would take Tommy's kind invitation of a car home and that Gemma would stay for a drink and the car would return for her later.

'Or not,' said Tommy, who was nothing if not forward.

Gemma's blush was the prettiest thing that Tommy had seen in as long as he could remember. The ridiculous bender that had followed his Brits adventures, the hectic rehearsals, the weeks on the road had all passed in a blur of beer-soaked, speed-driven, coked-up, acid-tasting nastiness, and now suddenly he was sitting in his dressing room with a real person. A nice person. Prettily dressed, but not trying to get laid. Admiring of Tommy, but not gushing or boring about it. Blushing sweetly at his naughty innuendos. What a change she made.

That old cliché 'a breath of fresh air' fitted her perfectly. Tommy knew that he just had to shag her.

The Hyatt Regency, Birmingham

The Home Secretary was on fine tub-thumping form.

'My friends. My comrades. Great issues require great men and great women to face them. This party has produced many such people but none greater, I suggest, than Peter and Angela Paget, whom you see beside me here tonight!!'

The conference simply went berserk. A mile or two up the road at the NEC, Tommy Hanson himself had scarcely received a bigger reaction. Nonetheless, the Home Secretary thundered on above the tumult.

He was not being left out of the loop for anyone.

'Her Majesty's Minister for Drugs! His wife and their two lovely daughters. A British family! A Labour Party family. A family who have together faced the worst that our ruptured and fragmented society can throw at them and yet have remained a shining example to us all. Together they embody all that we believe in when we employ that much misunderstood and misapplied term "family values". It takes a man armed strong in honesty to pursue the course that Peter has taken, from being a lone voice in the wilderness to being the leader of a national crusade. Peter Paget *is* armed strong in honesty! His stake in the drugs war is his family, his beautiful daughters, his lovely wife! And there can be no higher a stake than that.'

Sitting behind their parents, Cathy and Suzie Paget squirmed. They had agreed to accompany their parents to this conference, but they had not expected such star billing. They thought that the Home Secretary was a bit of a tosser. What was more, they knew that this had been their father's opinion until he had been invited to join him in the Cabinet.

'Friends, comrades, representatives from the worlds of business and the media. I give you the Right Honourable Peter Paget, MP, Minister for Drugs!'

The cheering was thunderous. The whole ballroom shook with it. The entire audience rose to its feet in one great mass of cheering, waving humanity. And at the back, standing at the very back, amongst the people for whom no chair could be found, amongst the waiters and runners and the other parliamentary assistants, was Samantha, not waving, not cheering. Tears in her eyes.

'Ah yes. Yes, indeed-ee-do,' said a soft voice behind her. 'The perfect family man . . . not.'

The voice had spoken almost into her ear. There was no other way that Samantha could have heard it above the furore, so when she turned round her nose almost touched that of the speaker. A woman. A journalist, in fact.

'Hello, Samantha. My name's Paula.'

'I know who you are. You're the one who's always so mean to Peter. What did you just say? What did you mean?'

'Just that it must be very hard for you, all this, Samantha. Now that things have gone so well for him. To see him scuttle back to his wife like this.'

'I have no idea what you're talking about.'

Paula smiled. 'You don't have to lie to me, Samantha. I *know*, you see. Did he tell you he loved you? Of course he did. Lots of times, I expect . . . Look at him now. Whose shoulder is his arm round? Not yours, my darling, not yours.'

Paula knew it was a risk to adopt such a direct approach with so little real information and no proof. But try as she might, she had been unable to get any further in her pursuit of Peter Paget's private life. But when she had seen Samantha's face just then, seen the pain that rippled across it as the Home Secretary eulogized Paget's perfect family life, she knew that the proof lay with the girl and that the time was right to strike. Paula knew a besotted, jealous, agonized young woman when she saw one. 'He'll never leave her, you know. He's used you, that's all.'

'I . . . I really don't know what you're talking about. Please go away. I want to listen to the speech.'

'Fine, not a problem, I'll go, but I'll just leave you my card . . . If ever you want a sympathetic ear . . .' Paula produced her card. 'Like I say, stay in touch, and if ever you want to start screwing him instead of his screwing you, I'm your girl.' And with that Paula melted away into the crowd.

Samantha hardly saw Paula leave. Her eyes were too wet with tears. It did not draw attention to her, though, as so many people in that hall had tears in their eyes. Peter was giving the performance of his life.

'Comrades. The Home Secretary mentioned my family. He mentioned the fact that like many of you here today I have teenaged children. Two girls. But right now I should like to tell you the stories of three very different girls, three of the many stories I've encountered since first I began my campaign. Picture young Jessie, a teenaged runaway, gone to London because of abuse at home in Scotland. I met her at a drop-in centre at King's Cross. A bright girl, beautiful, articulate and addicted to heroin. Addicted because the evil predator who took her in gave it to this innocent and vulnerable seventeen-year-old prior to pressing her into a life of prostitution. What a brilliant plan! Foolproof! Sanctioned by Parliament, no less! Jessie has no choice but to co-operate with her abuser, for he is her only source of heroin. She has no choice but to walk the streets because it is the only way she can hope to earn enough to pay the exorbitant prices that this illegal substance commands. For Jessie it is a case of either whore or steal! And for a small, frail, pretty teenager it is obvious where she is going to end up. In the backs of strangers' cars, ladies and gentlemen. Yes. Many times a night. Courtesy of Her Majesty's Government! The law is her pimp. Make no mistake. We here today are directly responsible for her plight. For we make the laws that create her abuser!'

When the applause had died down, Paget continued.

'Recently, burdened somewhat by my own private fears, the fears that have resulted from my accident with the addict's needle, I returned to the King's Cross drop-in centre. I was determined to see young Jessie again. I had some idea of explaining to her that we were now both victims of the drugs war and that perhaps we might draw strength from each other's plight. I hoped that somehow or other I could provide a catalyst for her to seek help or perhaps return to Scotland and face her problems at home. Ladies and gentlemen, I am here to tell you that Jessie had disappeared. The people at the centre had not seen her for some time and nor had any of the other habituées to the centre who knew her. Where is she now? Nobody knows. She's gone. Lost. Either dead or out there somewhere in the cruel night existing at the mercy of the underworld. Seventeen years old, ladies and gentlemen. Seventeen years old and lost to us!'

Peter Paget turned and looked at his daughters. It was not a cheap trick for the cameras. Like all who listened to his speech, he could not help comparing the story he was telling to the good fortune that he himself enjoyed. Cathy and Suzie smiled at their father, no longer squirming and self-conscious but proud, proud to be part of something so important, so fundamental.

'Let me tell you about another girl,' Peter continued. 'Sonia, a young woman from this very city of Birmingham. I know where she is. Oh yes, so do all of you who read the papers. She is currently rotting in a Thai jail! Eighteen years old, her life effectively over, and why? Because she was stupid? Yes, of course. Because she was criminal? That I don't argue with. Sonia did a wicked and foolish thing, she agreed to smuggle drugs in exchange for a thousand pounds and a week in Bangkok. But Sonia was also bored. She was naturally adventurous, she was also extremely young and impressionable. She lived in a culture where she and all her friends took drugs every weekend, where the law was and remains entirely in disrepute. A joke, something to be ignored. She fell in with rich and cunning men, men grown fat on the profits of our stupid laws. They flattered her, gave her drugs, seduced her into their service. Promised her one thousand pounds from an operation that they knew would net them many tens of thousands! I should like to remind you here today that whilst we know where Sonia is, we don't know where the men who entrapped her are. They, as always, have escaped. They, and all their comrades in crime. We rarely see them, we never catch them, their power grows daily. They are invisible while the results of their wickedness – Jessie, Sonia – are all too visible! I have written personally to the King of Thailand and have hopes of obtaining mercy for Sonia, but she is only one, and her like will never be truly free until we remove the laws that promote their abuse.

'Let me now mention the story of Natalie, a girl from Salford, another heroin addict. I don't know her – she's just one of many thousands of similar addicts who live outside the law. Her story was brought to the attention of the world simply because her boyfriend Jason, who robbed and burgled *every single day* to feed their mutual addictions, happened to steal from the home of a celebrity's aunt. He was caught trying to pawn the pop singer Tommy Hanson's Brit Awards, and when he led the police to the hovel he shared with Natalie, it was discovered that these two addicts had a baby, Ricky. A baby who was dying of neglect and whom the police arrived too late to save. The social services had been aware of Ricky and had attempted to help Jason and Natalie with him, but as the parents' lives drifted further and further into direct conflict with authority they disappeared from view, taking their baby with them. Just another story. Just another statistic. Without the tenuous connection with celebrity, Natalie, Jason and Ricky's story would never have been heard. On the subject of celebrity, I'd like to bring your attention to the life of one other young woman. Emily Hilton-Smith – you've all heard of her – she was a wild child, an "it" girl. She's here today, having come at my invitation.' The eyes of the gathering and the lenses of the cameras focused on Emily, who was attending the meeting with

244

her mentor from Narcotics Anonymous. Her glamorous clothes and perfectly smooth bronzed legs had already been the focus of much attention.

'Emily wrote to me,' Peter continued, 'in support of my campaign. She explained that although she no longer took drugs and hoped never to do so again, she had been in their thrall for ten years. Ten years, ladies and gentlemen, and large quantities. Jessie, the King's Cross heroin addict I was telling you about, told me that she had her first hit of the drug only months before we met. Sonia took Es only at weekends. I don't know how long Natalie was addicted, but I doubt it was as long as ten years. And yet while Jessie, Sonia and Natalie's lives are ruined, Emily sits here with us today, a picture of glowing health and beauty! And why is that, ladies and gentlemen. I'll tell you why. Because she could *afford her drugs*, and when she needed help she was a part of a society that was able to give it to her. She was protected by her family and friends. While her addiction was certainly supplied by criminals, she didn't need to steal or whore to pay for it. She was able to avoid sinking into the squalor that engulfed Jessie and Natalie! Ladies and gentlemen, I abhor the effects of many drugs and wish sincerely that people were not tempted to take them, but I say to you here tonight that in the vast majority of cases it is *not* drugs that kill people! Look at Keith Richards, Eric Clapton, Emily Hilton-Smith, Tommy Hanson! It is the *law* that kills people, because the law turns addicts into criminals.

'How pathetic is our society, ladies and gentlemen! How utterly debased our culture! How petty our priorities and our resolve when year after year we allow the streets to be flooded by the likes of Jessie, the prisons filled with Sonias and the hospitals and cemeteries filled with baby Rickys. And yet we have not the courage or the intelligence to pull the rug from beneath the feet of the entire rotten network that creates these tragedies!

'This party has never been afraid to take tough decisions and we have never taken a tougher one than that which we are joined here together to endorse. Tough! But also easy, easy in that we have no choice! Just as in the past right-thinking men and women had no choice but to proceed towards universal suffrage, universal literacy, universal health care and universal welfare benefit, today we have no choice but to move towards universal sanity and face down the demon of worldwide organized crime! We must have the courage to acknowledge that which is self-evident! We can deny it no longer. You don't like it. I don't like it. As the father of teenaged girls I would rather it was any other way! But the fact is that the only option that offers even the remotest chance of success in the battle against drugs is to bring them under government control. Our control. Let us take these dangerous substances out of the hands of the criminals and place them firmly in the hands of the Home Office and the Exchequer! Let us be the first but certainly not the last nation to legalize drugs! Not to decriminalize a few, or even all – that way leads to further madness, a confused, half-baked policy which the criminals will exploit – but to *legalize* all of them and legalize them now!'

That which had been unthinkable merely months before had now become government policy and would, considering the size of the government's majority, not to mention the sympathetic ears on the opposition benches, shortly become law.

It was all much more difficult than Tommy had imagined. Gemma had not wanted to be pulled, and it had taken all of Tommy's wiles even to coax her back to his hotel, let alone up to his bedroom.

246

Nonetheless, he had managed it. The impossibility of Tommy's sitting exposed in a hotel bar had given him the excuse he needed to suggest that they seek sanctuary in private. The bar was particularly crowded that night because of the Labour Regional Conference dinner taking place at the hotel. Tommy was of course a magnet for politicians looking for photo opportunities and he had been invited to join the Home Secretary and Peter Paget, his old friend from *Parky* and the Brits, for a private drink. Under normal circumstances Tommy might have been interested. Like everybody else in the country he had heard of the Paget Bill and now that he understood it he supported it.

But Tommy was not a politician, he was a rock star, and when it came to a choice between ligging with suits or cracking onto a beautiful girl, there was no choice. However, even though Gemma had agreed to accompany Tommy to his room, she was suspicious, very suspicious.

'Look, I'm not going to just sleep with you, Tommy. Believe it or not, some girls don't.'

'What's wrong with just sleeping with someone, then? It's great.'

'Tommy, I don't know you.'

''Course you know me. I'm Tommy Hanson. Everybody knows me. In't that where this started? 'Cos you know I'm Tommy?'

'Well, yes, of course. I know you as a star and I think you're great. Gary was right, I'm easily as big a fan of yours as he is, and I don't mind admitting I was always going to use his condition to try and get to see you. We once met Neil Kinnock by the same method. That was brilliant too.'

'Eh, he didn't try and pull you, did he?'

'Tommy, not everyone is a sex maniac like you. He was amazing, though, so funny, and he talked to us for over an hour about European policy on travel for the disabled.'

'Sounds fookin' dull if you ask me.'

'Not if you're my brother, Tommy. Anyway, he was truly kind, and he cracked all these jokes as well, and—'

'Why are we talking about Neil Kinnock?'

'I . . . don't know.'

'You were saying that you're my biggest fan, which is why, apparently, you won't sleep with me.'

'Tommy, it's not that I don't fancy you. Obviously. I love your stuff and it's pretty obvious that you're a bit gorgeous.'

Again that heart-melting blush. The nervous shift of shapely legs, the skirt, just above the knee. So proper. So tantalizing. So nice not to see it all at once. These days Tommy felt girls wandered round nearly naked. You saw the lot before you'd even had time to be intrigued. Whatever happened to subtlety?

'Of course I fancy you,' Gemma repeated, 'and I'm completely amazed that you seem to fancy me, being as how I'm not exactly a supermodel, although from what I've read in the papers you fancy all girls . . .'

'To a degree, I do.'

'But I don't *know* you at all, and I've never in my life slept with a man I didn't know. How could you? You'd feel such a slapper.'

'Nowt wrong wi' slappers, love.'

'I'm sure that there isn't, but I don't want to feel like one.'

'All right, then, so you don't know me well enough. What do you want to know about me?'

'It doesn't work like that: date of birth, brief résumé of schools and early love affairs, sex.'

'Why not?'

'Because it doesn't.'

'Why not?'

'Tommy, stop saying, "Why not?" You're not a three-year-old. Or perhaps you are.'

'Well, what else do you want to know? I'll tell you anything you want to know.'

'Do I have to promise to sleep with you?'

'No, but you have to admit that you want to.'

'All right, I admit that I want to sleep with you, and I promise you that I'm not going to.'

'We'll see.'

She was so fresh. So different. Tommy was enchanted. Once more he found himself staring at the cute knees, the couple of inches of leg that the skirt revealed above them. It was as if an angel had got a job as a secretary and then dropped in on his gig.

'Come on, then, first question.'

'All right. Have you ever had a gay experience?'

'Blimey, what makes you ask that?'

'I don't know, I just thought I would. Have you?'

Tommy laughed. 'How about I'll tell you if you take off an item of clothing?'

'Strip questions?'

'Why not?'

'Because I'd rather die.'

Gemma put down her Diet Coke and got up. 'I think we're both getting very silly now and that I should be going home.'

He was losing her. The skirt was being smoothed down, the coat picked up.

'I've only had one gay thing in my life, but I admit it were pretty full on. I mean, we slept together more'n once . . .' He was gratified to see that the pale-pink blush was suddenly beetroot coloured. She picked up her drink once more, seemingly in order to hide behind it.

'It were with one of the judges on *Pop Hero.*'

Gemma nearly choked on an ice cube. 'Wow! That *is* big goss.'

249

'Yeah, in't it? It were the smoothie, you know, the record-producer guy that everybody hated. But that weren't why I won, though,' Tommy added defensively. 'I won 'cos I was the best. The gay thing only started near the end.'

'Except that he was a judge and he clearly fancied you.'

'Well, what's wrong with that? You're supposed to fancy your pop heroes, aren't you? That's the whole point.'

'So did you do it because you thought it would help your chances, or are you bisexual?'

'Dunno. Well, if I'm honest, and for some stupid fookin' reason I've decided to be with you, I were seduced. That's the best word for it. He seduced me wi' his wiles. I don't think I'm bi, I mean, I've never noticed myself fancying men before or since. On the other hand, I did it, didn't I? I mean, there weren't no bum-shaggin' or nowt like that. No way. I couldn't 'a handled that. But there were an awful lot o' slappin around an' blowjobs an' all the other business.'

'So you liked it?'

'Yeah, I suppose, sort of. The first time, anyway. I think I were flattered and I admit he had some superb drugs to go with it. Sextasy, he called it, the very best pill I ever had sex on. He always 'ad the best of everything. I loved that. I were still only seventeen an' he was so fookin' cool, an' elegant an' powerful an', yeah, all right, I were very aware that 'is vote and support were going to make me the biggest thing in the country that week. Like I say, I were flattered. I loved the sextasy pills an' the vintage champagne an' the fancy food an' all the goss 'e had on all my rock heroes. It was like a different world an' when one night he stuck his tongue in me mouth I thought what the hell. I reckoned it were like John Lennon going on that holiday wi'

Brian Epstein. Didn't John say he tossed 'im off? Experimenting, really.'

'And you did win *Pop Hero*.'

'Yeah, that's true. Maybe it were just because I were a great wanker.'

Gemma looked away coyly, refusing to meet Tommy's stare. She was wearing a sweet little pale-pink cashmere cardigan over her white blouse. She began to unbutton it.

Perhaps because she was hot, although it was not particularly warm in Tommy's hotel suite. She did not explain herself or look at Tommy at all, she just undid the buttons slowly, one by one. When she arrived at the last one she raised her head and looked Tommy in the eye before undoing it and finally taking the garment off. Her lacy bra showed vividly beneath the white of her blouse as she pushed her shoulders back in order to take the cardigan off.

'So. You won a garment. I wasn't going to play your rule but, wow, I think you deserve it for that. Can I ask another question?'

'You certainly can.' Tommy simply could not remember anything arousing him quite the way Gemma's combination of tortured innocence and obvious desire were doing.

'Why do you act so stupidly most of the time, Tommy?'

'What?'

'You're a brilliant performer and a damn good songwriter, you have such talent and charm. You're rich and you're beautiful.' She was blushing again but also proud and defiant. 'You are. You're a very, very, very beautiful man, and what's more now I've met you I can see that you're a real person, a lovely person, a complex person. So tell me, please, why is it that everything I read about what you say and do makes you sound like a complete idiot? At best a rather

251

immature jack the lad and at worst an insensitive bullying moron. Why, Tommy?'

Tommy just sat there. He didn't know what to say. And then suddenly he was crying. He wept and he wept, just as he'd done on the day when he ran out of the Soho AA meeting, and he didn't know why.

The drugs, probably. The bitter residue of previous highs, the paranoid tightrope of the current evening's ingestion. The gut soup of booze and dressing-room catering that left him feeling permanently slightly nauseous. The exhaustion. So many things to make you cry. And now this. This nice, pretty, clever girl poleaxing him with her clear-eyed honesty. So perfectly putting her finger on the Tommy Hanson dilemma. Why was he such a complete arsehole?

He didn't need to be. He didn't mean to be. But nonetheless he knew that he was. A complete arsehole. He had long suspected it, but now Gemma, the first trustworthy witness he had met for a very long time, had confirmed it. He looked at her through his tears. He was no longer trying to get her into bed, he really wanted to try to make her understand.

'I don't know, Gemma. I don't know. Drugs, o' course, too many of them . . . But, then, I think maybe it's the power thing . . . You know, I'm just *so fookin' famous*. I never expected it, I don't even like it most of the time, but I'm addicted to it. I hate it but I'd die if I lost it . . .'

'Why do you hate it, Tommy? It's everybody's dream.'

'Yeah, and I ain't complaining, honest, really I'm not. It's just like, well, for instance, when everybody's paid to be nice to you, who do you trust?'

'Well, I suppose you trust whoever you feel like trusting. You have to judge people by what you see in their character. It's up to you, Tommy. Everybody risks something when they give their trust. Not just superstars.'

'Well, yeah, sure, but once you've decided to trust someone . . . Can you trust them? It's like Princess Di were always getting betrayed, weren't she? I really empathize with her.'

'But I think that perhaps Diana was naturally vulnerable. You aren't, Tommy. You're strong.'

'I'm not. It's like The Who said, in't it? Who are you? It's like you think, well, hang on, at least I can trust me old mates, they were with me before any of this . . . But then you go back and everyone's so strange. They say, "Warra you doing back 'ere, then?" People act like you must be thick to want to get sat in the shithole pub you used to drink in, or else that you're patronizing them an' slumming it. Honest, even my best mates from the old days say things like, "Ooh, now you're a millionaire why in't you drinking champagne wi' Kate Moss 'stead of coming back 'ere, then?" It makes you feel dead uncomfortable. An' confused. Honest, Gemma, I'm that confused sometimes I don't know me arse from me elbow.'

And once more Tommy began to cry. Gemma murmured words of sympathy. He was kneeling on the floor beside her now, his head upon her lap. She stroked his hair. 'It's like I've got everything, but it ain't what I expect it t'be, and I've forgotten what it was I thought it would be anyway. So I don't know what it was that I used to want, and I don't know what I want now. All I know is that I don't like what I've got.'

'Well, if you don't like it, give it away.'

'That's the point, Gemma, I can't. 'Cos although I may not like what I've got, I'll still fight like a fookin' maniac to hang onto it.'

Gemma smiled. 'Well then, you're a hopeless case, Tommy Hanson.'

'D'you know that old song? By Peter Sarstedt? "Where do you go to, my lovely, when you're alone in your bed?"'

'Yes, I know it.'

'That's me, that is. I'm the lovely. Except I ain't very fookin' lovely.'

Gently Gemma lifted Tommy's head from her lap and cupped his face in her hands. 'You are lovely, Tommy, and you don't have to be alone in your bed tonight.'

A few rooms up the corridor from Tommy's suite, Peter Paget was experiencing what was thus far the most excruciating moment of his life. He and Angela had emerged from the lift with the intention of heading for their room. The girls were still downstairs bopping to the party disco which, despite the disdain they'd shown for it, had still drawn them. They were of course celebrities now, up there with the Prime Minister's kids and the young Princes, and they were discovering that fame was an intoxicating thing.

Their parents, however, had decided to retire early. The back-slapping and constant cheering had been fun for a while but the question mark about Peter's health still hung over them both and the fact that every single one of the people at the conference knew it too had become wearing. It was all the manly hugs and hand-shakes and painfully sincere pecks on cheeks. Everyone seemed to be saying, 'We know you may be dead soon, but you're our hero.' A few days hence all would be well, they hoped, but for the time being, Peter's triumph notwithstanding, the Pagets still felt slightly like freaks. And so they slipped away.

And now, as the lift door closed behind them and escape was impossible, they realized that Samantha was waiting for them.

'Peter, I'd like a word with you, please.'

'Um . . . really, Samantha, tonight? Can't it wait?'

'No, it can't.'

Angela Paget grimaced. 'I'm going to bed, Peter. Give me the key.'

'Angela . . . !'

'I think you should stay, Mrs Paget. You should hear this.'

'Do you, Samantha? Well, I don't. Anything you have to say about any private arrangements you and my husband have enjoyed can remain private as far as I am concerned.'

'So you've told her, then?'

'Give me the key, Peter. If you're going to be late get a copy from reception.' Angela Paget took the key and started to walk away.

'Give him up, Angela. He loves me.'

Peter grabbed Samantha's arm. 'Samantha! Please! Are you out of your mind?'

'Will you give him up, Mrs Paget?'

Angela did not reply. She turned the corner of the corridor and could be heard letting herself into her room. Samantha and Peter were left staring at each other. Now it was Samantha's turn to grab Peter.

'Come to my room tonight, Peter. Sleep with me.'

'For God's sake—'

'If we do this now, if we make a clean statement of our love, you'll survive it, I know you will. Come to me now. Let me put you inside me.'

Her face was a mask of tears, her eyes swollen, but they flashed nonetheless. She looked mad.

Peter's mind pounded with a single thought: *End this now. Get out of it now.*

But how? This was not a girl who was minded to let go. She would do anything to stay in his life. She would maintain a direct and intimate connection with him for better or for worse. Because she loved him and Peter knew that love is very dangerous.

Peter looked into her desperate, tear-stained face and knew that her agony was all his fault. If only he could let her down gently. If only he could explain to her that he *had* loved her, yes, a mad, wrong-headed love but love nonetheless. His passion had been real and from the heart and he did not want to fight her, he did not want to hurt her. If only he could take her aside and beg her to disengage slowly and as friends, agree to part as people who had shared something beautiful but impossible. Something impossibly beautiful.

If only he could say, 'I loved you, Samantha, and I will never forget that love, but from now on it can be no more than a treasured memory.'

But he couldn't say that and the reason was that he knew that he must disengage utterly and immediately. *Now*.

With a woman of Samantha's passion he knew that any half-measures would be no disengagement at all. He had decided that the only path he could possibly navigate through the horrors that lay ahead was denial. Complete and absolute denial.

Peter had decided some time before to pretend to himself and to everyone else that the affair had never happened, and although he had intended to discuss the plan with Angela, Samantha had now pre-empted the situation and he knew that he must begin immediately. Quite apart from anything else, Peter knew that such were the workings of modern journalism that one day Samantha might come to him wired for sound. He had therefore resolved from the moment he had walked out of the lift and seen her standing there to claim in every word and every circumstance that Samantha's talk of an affair was complete fantasy.

'Samantha, I deny absolutely that we have had any relationship beyond that which is appropriate between an MP and his parliamentary assistant. Regretfully, in the light of your fantastical and paranoid accusations, I must terminate your employment forthwith. If you wish to communicate with me further, please do so via my lawyer. Good night.'

She looked like she had been shot.

Peter allowed one small digression from his firm resolve. 'I'm sorry. So very sorry,' he whispered. Then he turned on his heel and walked away.

Although he was upset for Samantha, he was a practical man and his mind was working furiously. Had he left anything incriminating behind him, in her flat, perhaps? On her clothes? Like with President Clinton, was there some splash of semen somewhere that would come back to haunt him? He was sure that he had not. If she had anything of his in her possession she could easily have taken it from the office in order to use against him. They had only ever once been in the company of others, that time on her birthday. He would deny that it had happened, claim a conspiracy against him. DNA? How many times had his paranoid mind asked himself if she might have taken a swab after making love with him, if she might be in a position to triumphantly produce his semen in a court of law? But that was impossible. Even if she had done something so extraordinary as that he was not obliged to co-operate with such a strategy. He was a Minister of the Crown, he could not be forced to hand out semen willy-nilly. There was, after all, no paternity case involved.

Peter felt that he could tough it out. He knew that he could tough it out and he also knew that this was the only strategy.

As he turned the corridor and headed towards the bedroom door that Angela Paget had left slightly ajar, he heard Samantha begin to sob.

He awoke to a gentle whisper in his ear. 'Tommy . . . Tommy.'

Soft mouth, sweet breath, subtle but distinctly feminine choice of scent. He remembered now. He was in bed with an angel. He could feel the lively, perky nipples he had earlier guzzled with such affection brush against his shoulder as she leant across him, her lower lip murmuring delicately against his earlobe as she breathed her message of sensual, erotic love.

'I want more. I want you to take me again, Tommy. I want you inside me now.'

That small soft hand upon him once again. Impossible to deny. He could feel himself involuntarily springing to life. He would not need to be asked twice. He turned in the bed to face her, feeling for her mouth in the darkness with his lips. Her head was high on the pillow, which she had propped up against the bedstead, the sheet at her waist. Perhaps she intended to climb on top this time. Now her breasts were against his chest as she embraced him and worked her mouth upon his, sucking his tongue against her back teeth.

Then there was a flash of light. Tommy knew what it was, of course. He had spent the last four years constantly in their glow. But he could not believe it. He simply could not believe it.

A second later another flash illuminated the room and the truth was undeniable. He had turned towards it, as she had done, instinctively drawn towards the light. And in that moment of brightness, the little tripod beyond the foot of the bed with the tiny digital camera atop it was clear as day.

Then darkness again, rendered thicker and blacker by the disappearing flash, its imprint still throbbing on his retinas. Tommy scarcely knew where he was. Gemma was less confused. He felt her leave the bed, heard her walk around it. Then she was at the door. She opened it. In the light from the hotel corridor he saw her standing naked with another woman. Gemma handed the camera and tripod to the other woman, then she crossed the room to where her handbag still lay on the floor next to the chair on which she had sat and before which Tommy had knelt. She gathered up the bag and returned to the door. There she produced a small minidisc recording device and handed that also to the woman who was waiting. Then, as the other woman departed along the corridor, Gemma began quickly to gather up her clothes.

'Sorry, Tommy,' she said. 'But you've been done over.'

Tommy could only stare.

'If it's any comfort I think you're a lovely bloke. Completely fucked-up, of course, but lovely. Terrific sex as well, well not terrific exactly, but you can't help thinking, "Wow, this is Tommy Hanson," which is exciting in itself, I don't mind admitting.'

He still couldn't believe it. It had to be a wind-up. 'But . . . your brother.'

'Ah yes. Never fails, not my brother, of course, just someone who needs the money. He really is a student, by the way, so you've helped him out there.'

She was buttoning up the blouse now, not bothering with her tights, which she simply stuffed into her bag. 'Well, as I say, Tommy, I'm sorry. Don't think I feel good about this sort of thing because I don't, although I'm pretty proud of how well it's come off. My editor wanted to send a Pamela Anderson lookalike, but I swore blind I knew what you'd like. Bit of reality, bit of the real thing, I thought, that's what he needs. Bit of feminine gentility. And it worked.'

Tommy roared. That is the only way to describe it. He roared.

'YOU FUCKING SCUMMY FUCKED-UP TOERAG BITCH!'

His hurt, his shame and his fury were so complete that he was almost incapable of speech. The expletives simply poured forth. Then he hurled the telephone at Gemma, but because it was wired to the wall it only got to the end of the bed before being pulled up short.

'Bye bye, Tommy.' Gemma closed the door behind her. The room was dark once more. The woman who had briefly played the part of Gemma was gone.

* * *

Gemma's was not the only exclusive being planned in Birmingham that night. As she scuttled out of the hotel to join her colleague in the waiting car, the chill of the night raising goosebumps on her bare legs, she passed another colleague walking in. Paula had been returning to her own, less expensive hotel when she got the call from Samantha Spencer. She had not expected it so soon, nor that Samantha would want to meet her immediately, that night.

'I've been having an affair with him for nearly four months.' These were the first words that Samantha spoke as Paula approached her in the long-since-closed coffee shop of the hotel. No greeting, no formalities. It was as if the girl was fearful that if she didn't confess immediately her firm resolve would disappear. Sensing this possibility, Paula also dispensed with formalities. Reaching into her handbag and clicking on her tape recorder, she almost pushed Samantha into a chair. 'Did he ever promise to leave his wife?'

'He never promised but he said that sex with her had been boring for years. He said that I blew his mind.'

'Did you spend whole nights together or just grab moments?'

'Sometimes whole nights, at my flat. MPs have lots of excuses to be away from home.'

'How often would you do it in a night?'

'Excuse me?'

'Samantha, when we go public with this we're going to get questioned on detail. Was he insatiable?'

'Well, yes, at first. Sometimes we'd do it for hours.'

'Would you say five times?'

'Well . . . perhaps, I don't know.'

Paula was almost bursting with the thrill of it. 'His wife doesn't satisfy him but my bonking Minister thrills me five times a night.' Minister of Drugs? Minister of . . . ?

'Did you ever do it on the carpet?'

'Lots of times.'

Yes! Result . . . Minister of RUGS . . . 'He begged me to satiate him on the SHAG pile.' Paula could not believe her luck.

'What colour is your carpet? Not leopardskin or anything, by any chance?'

Samantha's eyes were far away. She was almost smiling, although she was clearly also on the verge of breaking down. 'Well, one night I remember, one very special night, the carpet was pretty much any colour we wanted it to be . . . That was the ecstasy, I expect.'

Paula froze. Had she heard right? Was this a wind-up? It had to be. It simply could not be true. 'What did you say, Samantha?'

'I was just thinking about the night I introduced Peter to ecstasy. We took it with Viagra and made love for three hours.'

Paula was a tough and experienced journalist but she was now in uncharted emotional territory. Nothing, literally nothing this exciting or important had ever happened to her.

'Would you be prepared to swear to this, Samantha?'

'Yes, I would. He says he's never taken drugs except for a few joints when he was a student, but he's done more than that with me.'

'Beyond your word, do you have any proof?'

'No, I don't think so . . . Oh yes, yes, there was one night, just once, my birthday, we had friends round . . . We all took cocaine. Peter loved it, but he wouldn't make love to me afterwards. He insisted on rehearsing his speeches at me while I lay there in my best lingerie.'

This was of course in itself a fabulous story, enough to ridicule and demean any man, but Paula knew that this story went much further. It went to the heart of the government and the nation.

'Do you think your friends would be prepared to corroborate your story that Peter Paget took cocaine?'

'When they know how he's abused my love. Yes. Of course.'

'Mr Hanson. The police have been called.'

'Good, fookin' call 'em.'

Thus far the hotel security guard had refrained from using his pass key to enter Tommy's room, but when he heard the next crash he finally did so.

The television set had flown out of the window in classic rock-star style.

'Don't worry, man, it didn't work anyway.' This being because Tommy had smashed its screen with the kettle. In fact this had caused the initial crash, which had awoken the people sleeping in the nearby rooms. After this first effort at destruction those slumbering further afield had been sequentially disturbed as Tommy's fury grew ever wilder. Whatever there was to destroy, Tommy destroyed. The mirrors in the bathroom, both basins and the toilet bowl, this with the help of a Corby trouser press, with which Tommy also destroyed both glass coffee tables and the other toilet in the lobby of the suite. Tommy smashed vases against wardrobes and standard lamps against walls. The stereo and video system went through another window.

All this fury had taken place in a matter of only a few minutes, and when the Security Chief entered Tommy's suite it was only a quarter of an hour since Gemma's departure.

'Mr Hanson, will I have to have you physically restrained?'

'Fook off.' Tommy pulled on his boots, jeans and a T-shirt and, grabbing his big coat and beanie hat, he walked past the hotel staff and out into the corridor. 'Send the fookin' bill to my fookin' people. I'm goin' for a drink.'

With that he put on his shades, even though it was the middle of the night, and headed for the lift. The Security team decided to let him go. The incident would certainly be a matter for the police, but it was no part of their brief to start fighting with guests who had taken leave of their senses. Their job was to restore order so as to disturb as few of the other guests as possible. In this case, clearly the best way to achieve this was by allowing Tommy to leave the hotel.

Fallowfield Community Centre, Manchester

'How angry was I? Never in my life have I felt so completely shite. To be tricked like that, abused. I mean honestly, absolutely devastated. That's the only word for it: totally devastated. I were feelin' more sorry for meself than I had ever done an', believe me, I've 'ad me mawkish moments. I'd trusted that bird, see? Honest, when we was at it, an' it were great, I actually thought I were in love wi' 'er . . . Stupid, eh? I'd only known her five minutes . . . I think it were the sweet little pink cardigan, and the blushes and those cute knees and the disabled brother an' all . . . No, it were what she *said*. I listened to her and I trusted her. Fook me. 'Ad I been kippered or what? I felt sick with it, I really did, physically sick. Hadn't I told her *I can't fookin' trust anyone*, and hadn't she fookin' proved it? I was screaming and shouting at the night. Honest, when I got out o' that hotel I nearly puked I felt so rotten wi' it. So I got in the car park an' had three lines 'o speed, which made everything worse, and then took a cab up town.

'So I'm wandering round with my beanie hat pulled down low and my big coat on and I'm still feeling so angry with the world and meself that I just had to do something. It was like I could only feel better if I made matters worse. I wanted to show that I could have more contempt for meself even than that spy woman had had. Like I could only get my pride back if I could kick meself harder than she had. I don't know, I felt so demeaned that I didn't want even to respect meself.

'Well, I were wanderin' round the streets, shoutin' an' ragin', an' I sees this sort of hippy café place, you know, all fookin' brown rice an' all you can eat for fifty pee, an' at the back there's a sign sayin' tattoo parlour. Well, obviously the whole place was clearly a front for the purposes of dealin' drugs an' I was quite happy to 'ave some o' that, but besides that, I were that filled wi' self-loathin' I think to myself, "Right, I'll get a fookin' tattoo."

'Not a word of a lie. That was me new plan, I was so angry with meself for being tricked an' for givin' my trust away that I decided to have "Twat" written on me 'ead. Funny what years of drugs do to you, eh?'

Late-night tattoo and piercing parlour, Birmingham

' "Twat"?'

'Yeah.'

'You want me to shave your head and tattoo "Twat" on it?'

'Yeah.'

'Don't you think that'll make you look a bit of a twat?'

'That's the idea. I'm filled wi' fookin' self-loathing, me.'

'Full of beer and shit drugs by the look of you. It'll look completely crap.'

'Have you any idea who I am?'

'Yeah, you're the twat who wants "Twat" written on his head. I don't do disfigurement. Fuck off, Tommy.'

'Here, it says "Tattooist" in your window, not fookin' art critic.'

'Look, mate, honest, forget it. You'll hate yourself for the rest of your life.'

'Exactly!'

'Why make it worse?'

'Because I don't fookin' care, me. Besides, my hair will grow back over it. I 'ent that stupid.'

'What if you go bald in later life?'

'I hope I die before I go bald.'

'It don't work like that. You go bald, live another forty years, then die.'

'I'll have a weave.'

'Look, mate. Forget it. I run a respectable business here – well, apart from a bit of drug-dealing, obviously – and I am not writing "Twat" on anybody's head. First of all, I'm not that cruel, and second, you'd probably try and sue me in the morning because you're obviously out of your head. Then I'd have to find the barman that sold you the booze and the dealer that dealt your drugs and sue them for giving you the wherewithal to get in the state you were when you got to me, and then the barman would have to sue Scottish and Northern Breweries and the dealer would have to sue the peasantry of Afghanistan or some hippy chemist in Wales, and it's Sunday tomorrow and quite frankly I can't handle the aggravation.'

'Look, I'm not going to sue you. I want to make a statement. I've been demeaned and cheated and abused and I need to purge myself through self-abuse.'

'Stick a Stanley knife in your arm.'

'Too painful. I ain't into pain.'

'All right. How about I write "Exploited"?'

Tommy thought for a moment. 'That's brilliant, that. Like when Prince had "Slave" tattooed on his face.'

'That wasn't a tattoo. That was just felt-tip pen. It washed off.'

'Well, anyway ... How about "Emotional commodity"?'

'Too many letters. They'll be too small. Come to think of it, "Exploited" is too long as well. How about "Had", 'cos later on if you were feeling a bit better about yourself you could change it to "Bad" or, at a pinch, "Lad".'

'Nah.'

'Well, if you liked Prince's "Slave", how about "Victim"? That'd be perfect, that, it'd go from the back of one ear to the back of the other, wrapped round your rear cranium. I could do it in German Gothic if you like.'

'Fookin' perfect.'

Padstow holiday cottages, Cornwall

The Leman family had been on holiday for two weeks when early one evening Craig Thompson met Commander Leman at the last bus stop before the holiday village in which the family had been staying. During those two weeks the Lemans had shown themselves about the place quite a bit, chatting at the post office and the local shop, always enthusiastic regulars at the ice-cream stall on the beach. Commander Leman, it seemed, had a very distinct holiday style, or at least he did for this holiday. He had let his beard grow and was enjoying the opportunity to wear sunglasses, an affectation he would never allow himself or his officers when in uniform, believing that a policeman should look the public in the eye. He also had taken to wearing the same sunhat every day, a wide-brimmed straw panama pulled low over his forehead. This he combined with a light windshielded jacket, the collar always turned up against the inevitable chill of an English summer. Sadly, of late he had developed a

266

sore throat, and his voice had become no more than a whisper. All in all, Commander Leman on holiday had become a difficult man to miss.

Craig Thompson had driven all the way from London on hot and crowded roads, but the journey had been no more or less arduous a way of spending the time than every other waking moment that he had endured since his daughter had killed herself. He had no life now, just a kind of existence, and the way in which he paced out the empty days that remained to him was a matter of no interest at all.

He pulled into the bus stop and got out, leaving the keys in the ignition. Without a word, Commander Leman slipped into the front seat and drove off.

Craig Thompson had also grown a beard. He wore a windshielder the same colour as that of Barry Leman, and a straw panama hat. It also seemed that he had taken up a pipe, which was something else he shared with Leman. After about ten minutes, during which Craig Thompson struggled to light his pipe, a process with which he was clearly unfamiliar, Christine Leman walked up to the bus stop.

'Come on, darling,' she said. 'Let's walk the last half-mile. We'll be just nicely in time for supper at the Angler's.'

The Eeezy Club, Birmingham

'You'm Tommy 'anson, roit?' The man was shouting at the top of his voice in order to be heard over the ear-shuddering *duf-duf* of the beat, his beery, faggy, spit-filled breath landing heavily in Tommy's face. Tommy had been in the club for half an hour and had consumed three pints of snakebite in the dark and thunderously noisy anonymity. Despite the heat he continued to wear his big coat and he had his beanie jammed down over his head. The gang of lads who had sidled up beside him were the first to recognize him.

'Yeah, I'm Tommy Hanson!' Tommy screamed back.

'Buy us a drink then, mite. Go on.'

Fallowfield Community Hall, Manchester

'It's the gobbing I can't stand. Lads recognize you in clubs and stick their faces in yours and just fookin' spray you. It's always lads what comes up first. I'm lookin' at the girls, but it's always some big cocky lad that gets in my face. That's the worst of it. It's not like everybody in a club is going to be an arsehole, the problem is whatever arseholes there are about the place are going to come up to me. Don't get me wrong, a fan's all right, that's fine, nobody minds an auto-graph, even a little chat. But in a club or a boozer, with a belly full of ale, it in't a fan coming up, it's some bloke what reckons he's a *rival*, some bloke what reckons *I* reckon mesel' and he's there to make it clear that I in't so special. Like I give a fook. They just colonize you, these blokes. It starts with, "All right, Tommy," and next thing he reckons he's got full rights of occupation on your fookin' space an' your evening. That's why people 'ave minders, not 'cos they think they're gonna get stabbed but just to stop arseholes comin' up an' shoutin' an' spittin' about fook all in your face for half an hour 'cos they reckon they're as good as you an' why shouldn't they.

'Like I say, if it were some nice bird, or even a bloke with a brain an' a bit o' conversation comin' up, I wouldn't mind, but out on the town it's always the club arsehole, the big, nasty, chippy bastard that reckons he's boss. I fookin' hate 'em. An' there I was with six o' the bastards on me 'ands. Six big pissed-up Brummie dick'eads full o' beer an' KFC. They appropriate you as their property, even to the point of warnin' off other interested parties . . . It's like, "Don't yow worreh, Tommy, we'll keep yow safe from the arseholes . . ." Supremely confident in their pig-ignorant arrogance that they in't the biggest arseholes themselves. They're shoutin' and laughin' an' sayin' stuff to me an' o' course I can't hear a fookin' word 'cos the music is makin' everybody's ears bleed. Not that I could 'ave understood them anyways what with them being so pissed up and their Black Country accents thick as a brick sandwich. Funny that about the Midlands, fook me, can they rock or what? I mean, they done the lot, didn't they? Led Zep, Purple, Sabbath, Slade, loads. It's true to say that no part o' the country has contributed such consistently awesome, humun-gous power throbbers to the mighty pantheon that is British rock music as the Brum/Wolverhampton axis, but you 'ear 'em talk an' they all sound like fookin' hod carriers! That were part o' the charm o' that whole MTV thing Ozzy Osbourne done wi' his missus. It were the accent that made it funny.

'Anyway, what I'm sayin' is I know a bunch o' cocky, nasty, leery bastards when I'm stuck in the middle of 'em, an' I wanted out. Quite apart from anythin' else I weren't in no mood to talk to anyone. I mean, after what 'ad 'appened wi' Gemma, if that was her fookin' name, I didn't think I ever wanted to talk to anyone ever again. Yet there I was. Chief mascot o' the arsehole gang, principal talkin' point, conversation piece and general humorous diversion for a bunch o' shaven-headed, tattooed apes.

'Right, I thinks, I'm off out o' this sharpish. If I'm gonna feel sick wi' self-pity I'd rather do it on me own or wi' a bird. All them big red beery faces leaning inta me, hands on me shoulders, noses in me ear, was making me feel dead uneasy. So I shouts that I was off. Now I couldn't hear what they was saying and they couldn't hear me, but they knew I'd said I was leavin' an' I knew exactly what their reaction would be. It's always the same, no matter how much time you give to the sort o' person who sticks his face in yours when you're tryin' to 'ave a nice pint or chat wi' a mate. When y'try an' move on that's when 'e gets all chippy an' hurt an' says, "What? So that means fook off, does it? I see, goodbye, done wi' you, then. Is that it?" or summat similar. Which is why so many celebs don't talk to anyone but other celebs. Honest, that's the truth, an' then everyone calls 'em arrogant. Like I say, the problem is, out late, on the piss, it is always, invariably, definitely, for certain, the person you would least like to talk to who gets in your face.

'So I know what these lads are thinkin' an' I'm thinkin' . . . Move quick, get out, fook off. So I'm over to one o' the bouncers and lettin' him see my face and then o' course it's all lovely lovely Tommy. I'm straight inta the VIP bit, the manager's over wi' the champagne an' there's three or four lingerie models already hoverin'.

'But that's no better, is it? Believe me, the VIP area in clubs is a con. Just because you're a VIP don't stop you bein' borin'. An' of course now I've got two local footie stars, the club DJ an' the manager shoutin' an' spittin' in me face an' all I actually want is t' be on my own an' contemplate just how totally sorry I am for myself, how beaten up I feel, how abused, how used, how angry. How I must be the most put upon and misunderstood bastard in Britain.

'"I'm off," I says.

'"Can we get you a car?" they says.

'"No. I'll walk."

Big mistake.

The Bull Ring Centre, Birmingham

'Or roit, then, Tommeh?'

'Yeah. You?'

'I'm foin. Why d'yow piss off, then?'

' 'Cos I were sick o' the music.'

'Ow. We thought yow was sick of us.'

'Nah, just wanted to fook off, that's all.'

'Gi's some moneh then, eh, Tommeh? Ow much yow got, Tommeh?'

'Fook off.'

'An' your coat. Top coat, that, Tommeh. Gi's that too.'

'Fook off.'

The Hyatt Regency, Birmingham

Neither Peter nor Angela Paget had felt like sleeping, and as the dawn came up she lay on the bed listlessly flicking through a magazine while he sat on the couch nursing a minibar brandy.

'D'you think she'll cause a scandal?'

'Probably.'

'And you'll lie?'

'Yes, I will. I've thought about it a great deal. I know now that Samantha won't let me simply walk away. She isn't entirely balanced and has conceived some fantastical notions about me as a father figure. Whatever I might say to try and let her down gently would never be enough. She'd try to ruin me just the same, just as she did to the professor I told you about. Therefore, I'll have to fight her, and I intend to do that by denying everything and claiming to be the victim of a deluded and besotted girl being manipulated by a corrupt media.'

'Jesus, Peter. The point is that you did screw her.'

271

'No, Angela,' Peter said very firmly. 'I did *not*. That is the point I am making. I *did not* have improper relations with that woman.'

Angela looked down at her magazine for a moment, trying to collect her emotions. Did Peter realize he was virtually quoting Clinton?

'Supposing she has proof?'

'She has no proof, because as I have just said, *it never happened*.'

'Peter, you don't have to play this fucking game with me. Do you want me to lie too?'

'Yes.'

Fallowfield Community Hall, Manchester

'D'you know what? I've never been beaten up before. Not properly. I mean I were in fights at school sometimes an' all that, but somehow I've avoided what most lads have to go through at some point, which is being in a proper fight. Or in this case a proper massacre, which I can assure you is a whole lot worse. I'd been wandering up the road that runs around the Bull Ring Centre, or at least what were the Bull Ring Centre till they started knocking it down, thank God. I'd been looking for a little West Indian café or drinking club. There's loads of them in Brum. Y'know the sort o' place, where they do them weird curries that in't Indian at all, wi' them big thick tough bananas that in't bananas either. Plantains? Whatever, I'm not sure. I were thinking that maybe some rum and a bit o' yam an' lamb curry would be nice. I s'pose in my persecuted mood I reckoned that black people would be the best company. You know, proper people, people what had suffered the kind of abuse an' prejudice I'd suffered. I think I had some idea o' sittin' round 'avin' a big fat spliff wi' some real down-home Rastas who thought I were great and gassin' on about the pain o' being an original and what cows women were.

'What I actually got was dragged into a Marks and Sparks delivery dock an' mugged good and proper. It were the lads from the club. They slammed me up against the steel roller door a couple o' times, callin' me a fookin' arrogant cont, an' then I'm down on the ground an' the boots are goin' in. I'm curled up in a ball pleadin' an' spittin' blood and they're standin' round me in a ring, kickin' an' kickin' an' telling me that if I reckoned mesel' then this ought to sort me out.

'Funny that, I've often noticed how even violent bullying bastards 'ave a sort of vague sense o' decorum. I don't know, a kind of need to justify their actions. I mean, you'd think being an unhinged maniac was explanation in itself, wouldn't you? But you see, those blokes what were kickin' me wanted to be the *victims*. I'm on the ground in the piss spitting out bits o' teeth an' they're standin' round kicking the shit out o' me, sayin' that it's my fault. Apparently I'd dissed them personally by having number-one hits and them 'aving to work down Tesco's. What's more, on top o' that and to compound my crime, I wouldn't even spend the entire night wi' 'em payin' for their beer and letting 'em spray spit in my face. What kind of bastard was I? Well, now I were payin' the price.

'I've had better nights, I must say, what with one thing and another. It really is a strange and terrible experience being kicked unconscious, I can tell you. Suddenly I just blacked out. That was it. Gone. One boot too many. I'm convinced that one day that boot will kill me. You know, like wi' Stuart Sutcliffe? The original fifth Beatle? John Lennon's mate. Got beaten up in the 'pool then died of a brain haemorrhage a year or two later, an' they reckon that was what did it. Mind you, I've been up Harley Street an' had a brain scan an' apparently everything's fine.

'I don't know what time it was when they did me over. I know it was already half-light so it must have been after fiveish, an' I reckon it must have been five thirty or so when I came round. They'd nicked me coat and me 'at, me watch and me phone. Thank Christ they'd left me a T-shirt, jeans and boots. At first I couldn't even lift me face off the pavement because it's stuck to it with congealed blood. I finally manage to gently prise it away and I staggered off into pre-dawn Birmingham.

'There was nothing for it, of course, but to go back to the hotel, eat a bit of humble pie and ask if I can get me bag with me spare kecks in it. I also had a couple of back-up credit cards and a second phone. I go through phones like bags o' crisps, me, so I always 'ave a few about the place. I only use 'em to ring out, I never answer one, so Tony just buys ten a week, programmes all the production numbers into it and puts one in every bag and pocket I've got.

'I know Birmingham pretty well and was able to get back to the Hyatt in about half an hour. I reckoned the hotel would probably let me have another room if I grovelled hard enough and did photos with all the chambermaids. Of course they would. I'm a celebrity. In fact, I'm *the* celebrity, and when you're top of the A-list you get what you want. It were a Sunday morning so there was no one about and I was beginning to start thinking about a nice bath and a bit o' brekkie. It wasn't that I felt better or anything, no way, I still felt like the most exploited, used, sad, lonely bastard on earth, and I were proud of me new tattoo, "Victim", which said it all. Victim of everybody. Everybody wanted a bit of me and I got nowt in return. I was the ultimate anti-hero in a shitty little world. In fact, I were beginning to think about a song . . . Victim/Anti-hero . . . not bad. Have to avoid "zero". Everybody does that. "Nero", obviously . . . "anti-hero. Modern Nero . . .

playing guitar while England burns." Fookin' brilliant. I wondered whether the hotel would let me have a piano in me new room if I promised not to push it out of the window.

'Some fookin' hope. A room wi' a piano? I couldn't get past the doorman, could I? At first they didn't even believe it *was* me, but once I'd convinced them, I soon found out that they hated me. I hadn't realized just quite how badly I'd fooked up their night. I'd woken half the guests up, totally trashed a room, they'd had about a million complaints, and apparently the fookin' Home Secretary 'imself had been 'aving a go, 'cos him and his missus 'ad been disturbed. The front desk had been inundated and they just hated me. Now suddenly I turn up again. All I've got on is a T-shirt and jeans. Me face is half covered in blood, I've got a fat lip and a black eye, me head's completely shaven, with tattoos on it. What I looked like was a completely screwed-up, burnt-out, drugged-up, sad load o' trouble, which was, o' course, what I was.

'Like I say, maybe if I'd grovelled, but the minute the doorman and the head of night security started givin' me attitude I got all chippy again, sayin', "Gi' us a fookin' room. I'm Tommy Hanson."

'Well, I may be Britain's biggest pop star, but they were one of Britain's biggest hotels an' the big hotels get all the celebs through. If you trash your room an' you fook them off, it don't matter who you are, 'cos you don't pay any more than all the businessmen whose sleep you're ruining.

' "Fook you!" I shouts. Sort o' provin' their point, and that's it, I'm back out there, alone in the night.

'Right, I thinks, get back to the gig. The boys! That's who I need. They load out at night, can't have finished yet. Even if they don't recognize me I know names, heads of security, chief rigger, I'll soon convince them. Fook me, what a story it'll be when they see me. I

275

expect they get sat in an early opener when they've finished de-rigging. I'll get stuck in with them and we'll have a laugh.

'The gig! My boys, my people, my posse, my crew. That's where I need to be. As Liam famously remarked when probably no less fooked up than I was, "I want all my people right here right now."

'So I ran through the streets of Birmingham, following signs to the NEC. I'd hoped to find a bicycle to nick. That would 'ave been funny, if the lads saw me turning up on that . . . But as it happened they didn't see me turn up on anything because the bastards were just too efficient, and as I ran sweating and gasping towards the vast scenery docks of the arena, that same arena where the night before I'd been king, the last of me juggernauts thunders out and past me. The last of my awesome, twenty-wheeled rock 'n' roll armoured strike force guns its gears and thunders off towards London, where I'm supposed to be doing ten nights at Wembley Arena starting Thursday. The last of *my* trucks. Mine. Well, mine for the period of rental anyway. Every nut, every bolt, every headlight and nodding dog mine and everything in 'em, what's more, including the people.

' "Stop, you bastards! I own you!" I shouted, but they didn't and that were that. I was stuck, well and truly. Birmingham, eight o'clock on a wet Sunday morning. I've got no money, no phone and I don't know any of the numbers to call even if I had one. I've got no clothes to speak of, no cards or ID of any kind. I'm bald and I'm covered in blood. The only thing I possessed was a mandy that I found in my pocket so I dropped that, but it didn't help. I had one last try at retrievin' the situation by turning up at a police station.

' "I've been beaten up," I said, and they said, "What do you want us to do about it?" I said, "I want you to catch the bastards," an' they said, "How would you suggest we do that, sir?"

'I mean, fookin' hell, what's the world coming to? I'm not a copper, am I? So I tells 'em it don't matter anyway, and that I'm Tommy Hanson and I needed to find out the phone number of my road manager or one o' me PAs. Well, the copper just looks at me, an obvious casualty. Bald, bleeding, penniless. Tommy Hanson? No chance.

' "Fook off," he says. An' I did.'

Millbank, SW1

Detective Sergeant Archer of the Drug Squad approached the parked car in which Commander Leman waited and got into the passenger seat.

'Thank you for coming, Sergeant Archer.'

'That's all right, Commander. I thought I might hear from you sooner or later.'

'I want you to know that I intend to drop all investigations into corruption within the Drug Squad.'

'Yes, I imagined you might, and I learn from your website that you're giving up on the Paget campaign as well. Sounds like a sensible move to me.'

'I do these things on the understanding that I have your absolute assurance that no further threats will be made against my daughter or anyone who is acquainted with my family.'

'Ah . . . I suppose you're talking about the sad case of that girl who got date-raped, right in the middle of your manor. Very nasty. Killed herself, didn't she? No need for that, eh? Kids've got no spirit these days.'

'Are you going to lay off my daughter?'

'Well, all I can say is this, Commander. I can only imagine that whoever raped that little girl, a little girl who just happens to be best friends with your little girl . . . Anna, isn't it? Well, whoever did that was probably trying to get at *you*, weren't they? You've certainly drawn that conclusion, haven't you, Commander? Although of course I couldn't possibly say.'

'Now listen—'

'And why would anyone want to get to you? Well, it has to be about your investigations, doesn't it? And your meddling in drug policy like the cunt you are. Can't be anything else, really. So I would *imagine* that if you promised to shut your pious little mouth and keep your nose out of what ain't your business, then whoever it was who did that terrible thing would have no further reason to do it, would they? Of course, I'm only speculating, you understand.'

'Jo Jo Thompson was repeatedly violated in the most disgusting manner.'

'Oh well, them's the breaks, eh?'

'Her suicide has traumatized not only her family but mine also, particularly my daughter. She believes that she can only come to terms with this tragedy and get on with her life if she can establish what she calls "closure".'

'Excuse me, Commander, but you seem to be confusing me with someone who gives a fuck.'

'I've seen the photographs—'

'Bet you loved 'em too. Cute girl, I understand. Lovely bod.'

'I've seen the photographs and I know that the animals who raped the girl, the hired thugs, will be impossible to trace, so no chance of closure there—'

'Not unless their names were tattooed on their arses.'

'But the men who put them up to it . . . Ah, now them I do know.'

DS Archer did not have long to speculate on where Leman was taking him. He sensed movement behind him and, turning his head round, found himself facing a bereaved mother. A bereaved mother whose face was a mask of contorted pain and rage.

A mother who was holding a gun.

Commander Leman spoke to her gently, but his voice and his eyes were as cold as death. 'Do it as I told you, Sylvie. Both hands on the handle, squeeze the trigger gently.'

'What the—' Archer had no time to comment further. Those were his last two words on earth. Sylvie Thompson put the silenced muzzle of the gun between his eyes and shot a hole through his head.

'Well done.' Commander Leman took the gun from the woman and together they left the car.

'I joined the police force because I believe in upholding justice,' Leman said as they walked away from the stolen vehicle. 'I still do.'

Fallowfield Community Hall, Manchester

'By about ten I were getting desperate. I'd wandered for hours. I was tired and cold and thirsty. I'd also begun to realize that I had a big problem. Nobody believed I was who I said I was. Not cops, not a bloke at a cab rank I tried to persuade to drive me to London. I even did a verse or two of "Heaven" for him under a dripping bus shelter, but he just laughed. I were wet an' filthy an' lookin' less an' less like a multi-millionaire wi' every minute that passed.

'Think about it. For four years I'd had my people. Every second of every day I'd had people to do everything. Get everything. Arrange everything and make everything that I'd fooked up all right. Now I was on my own. I knew that I wouldn't be missed till Monday, because when I'd gone off wi' Gemma after the gig the previous night I'd told Tone to wait till I called him. Yeah, at the time I was getting all gushy and romantic, remember, and had been indulging in fantasies o' spending the whole of Sunday wi' that bird, shaggin' an' eatin' in our room. The hotel wouldn't chase my office to pay for the trashed room till the next week, so as far as my people were concerned I was 'aving hotel Sunday brunch wi' a lovely bird and was not to be disturbed. That was one o' my rules, when Tommy's 'aving it large, keep your distance till called. To be honest, I were terrified. The first chance I reckoned I'd have to make contact with anyone who'd know my voice an' who I could convince would be the following morning. I knew the name of my management company, so the minute offices opened I could beg twenty pence, get the number from directory enquiries and call the office reverse charges. It wouldn't be the first time that's happened and I knew they'd accept it. Then they could send a big fook-off limo full o' food an' booze and I'd be off back to London. But that was Monday morning, nine a.m. Fook, I think my office opened at ten, in fact, rock 'n' roll time . . . Ten a.m. It was only Sunday morning. I had twenty-three hours to get through without money or influence. Without a fookin' coat! And there was literally nothing I could do about it.'

Dean Street, Soho

'The art of not being noticed is confidence,' Commander Leman explained to Sylvie Thompson as they walked together along Dean Street. 'We'll be entering the third doorway ahead of us on the left. Just follow me in, quietly and confidently. Don't hesitate, don't look around, go in as if it were your own front doorway.'

What few stragglers there were on that late-night street paid no attention to the two people who entered the open doorway with its red light and its little illuminated bell with the word 'Model' written above it. If they'd thought about it they might have imagined that the bearded man had picked up a rather unprovocatively dressed streetwalker and was returning with her to her room.

Commander Leman's investigations had given him a fairly intimate knowledge of Detective Sergeant Sharp's habits and so he was aware that the sergeant tended to round off his evening's work with a visit to the particular 'model' who had put the sign above the bell. An illegal Ukrainian girl.

Sharp was a person of regular habits and always arrived for his tryst at around four a.m. Leman had timed his and Sylvie's arrival for ten past. If Sharp was not there, then vengeance would have to wait for another day. If he were, then Leman's family and the Thompsons might hope to move further towards some vague hope of closure.

Once inside the building, they mounted the dirty stairs, passing a number of doorways until arriving at the one Leman was seeking. A sign on the door indicated that the room was occupied. Leman handed Sylvie Thompson a mask and donned one himself.

'Don't worry when I speak. The girl he's with speaks no English,' Leman whispered in Sylvie's ear.

She had begun to shake. Leman could see that her courage was waning. 'Anyone who can organize what was done to Jo Jo,' he said gently, 'simply in order to warn off a third party, is too dangerous to live.'

Sylvie Thompson nodded. 'I know,' she whispered.

'Do you want to do it or was once enough?'

'I don't want to do it again.'

'Good. I understand. Do you want to see him die?'

'Yes. If it was really him, I do.'

Without another word Leman opened the door. Inside the room Detective Sergeant Sharp was having sex with the Ukrainian prostitute, whom he had tied to the bed using thin wire. The girl was paying a high price for her police 'protection'.

'Detective Sergeant Sharp,' Leman said, without a hint of emotion in his voice.

Sharp spun round.

'Be very careful how you answer my question, because I'll ask it only once. What's more, I already know the answer, so if you lie to me I'll kill you instantly.' Leman levelled his silenced gun at Sharp.

'Did you organize the Rohypnol-induced abduction and rape that resulted in this photograph?' Leman waved a picture at Sharp. He knew that Sharp would recognize his voice – the voice of a man who kept his word. Sharp would not risk a lie. He'd tell the truth, if only to buy time.

'Yes, but . . .'

'But' was the last word Detective Sergeant Sharp said before Leman shot him between the eyes. The dead man fell from the bed to the floor.

Fallowfield Community Hall, Manchester

'Well, here's where it begins, then. Here's where my life starts.

'How many people can put their finger on the exact point at which their life changed for ever? St Paul, obviously. Epiphany. He wrote the groundrules, didn't he? I know all about it, I were a choirboy. He saw the light on the road to Damascus. Just came to him, bang, somewhere along the dusty road. He thought to himself, "Hang on, I'm a fook-up, me. I have got it *so* wrong it in't funny. I'd best get things sorted before it all goes very pear-shaped." Like I say. Epiphany. Well, I saw the light in Birmingham city centre in the doorway of a locked-up Burger King on a rainy Sunday morning.

I'd been just walking and walking. No better plan than to kill time till the following morning. Try to get warm, try not to get beaten up, common thoughts for a vagrant, I imagine.

'I'd managed to wash the blood off my face, anyway. That were essential if I wasn't going to cop another beating sharpish. Yeah, true. The funny thing about being a victim is that it's a virulent condition. The more you are one the more you become one. What I'm trying to say is that abuse breeds abuse and pain breeds pain. It's like wi' money. The more you got, the more you get. Well, the same's true wi' poverty and deprivation. Particularly deprivation. I saw this documentary once, it were called "The Wet House", about the irredeemable winos at the very bottom o' the heap, people for whom recovery was not an option, people with literally rotting limbs, and semi-shut-down bodies whose only fully functioning part of their system was their ability to swallow alcohol. Well, do you want to know what the greatest danger these people faced was? These bits of disabled and incapable human wreckage? *Other people*, that's what. Pissed-up yobs setting 'em on fire for a laugh. True, that's what they faced. The more utterly debased you are the more chance there is of some drunk bastard casually killin' you as he passes by. I don't know why, maybe he's tryin' to kill his fears. The fears of what he thinks he might become. Or maybe people are just complete and utter conts. Like I say, I don't know. But I do know that all that caked blood on me face and shirt, the swollen eye and busted lip were drawing a lot of very angry and aggressive looks from the gangs of late-night straggling lads coming down off their speed and Es, and I knew that unless I became less conspicuous very quickly, one gang o' blokes or other were going to take it into their 'eads to finish me off while they waited for the bus.

.

283

'Cleaning up in't easy when you're homeless. Most o' the public bogs have been locked up to stop people using them as shooting galleries an' sole-trader knocking-shops. Brilliant, that, eh? You can imagine the council meeting ... "Now then, Mr Mayor, people are jacking up an' givin' blowjobs in the municipal facilities. What are we to do about it?" "Well, in't it obvious? Lock the fookin' bogs." No. All it means is you can't get a wash or have a piss any more unless you own property. An interesting by-product of which is that every fookin' shop doorway now reeks o' piss. Even the bloody station bog wanted twenty pee, which I didn't have, an' the twenty-four-hour fast-food joints got wise to people trying to pinch a piss without buying a burger years ago.

'In the end I washed in a puddle. It was a nice clean-looking one on that big new piazza sort o' place outside the Symphony Hall. All lovely flagstones and sculptures. Most inspiring. So anyway, I cleaned up as best I could, which was not very well, an' o' course made me colder, but it had to be done and then I wandered off towards my epiphany, which were the last thing I expected. Well, let's face it. Epiphanies are by definition the last thing you'd expect. Well, you can't plan for 'em, can you?

'So what did I see?

'The light, of course, like I say. Same as St Paul. He saw God, didn't he? Or maybe it were Jesus, but they're the same thing anyway, aren't they? Them an' the Holy Ghost, whatever that's about. He saw God, an' God is love, right? Of course he is. Well, then, that's what I saw. I saw God. Because God is love. If you believe nothing else in life you 'ave to believe that. Don't you?

'I swear to you I thought it were just a coat. A big coat in a doorway. I'm thinking. Result! Oh yes. That is *for me*. See how quick it all changes in life? Your priorities. A man who's well and fed can have all sorts of dreams and desires, but a man who's hungry and cold just wants a meal and a coat. The previous night I wanted so much out o' life I couldn't begin to say it all. I wanted to be understood, appreciated, meet real people who weren't fooked-up like me. I wanted more and better drugs, bigger and more profitable gigs, I wanted to get off drugs, I wanted to do a small anonymous acoustic tour of pubs. I wanted a bigger swimming pool at my place in LA, and I wanted it completely full o' naked women. I wanted a simple peasant life with one beautiful girl to cook me Tuscan stew an' home-made gnocchi. To quote the mighty Queen, I wanted it all and I wanted it now.

'Following morning, all I wanted were that coat. Same quote applies, though, because on that wet Sunday that coat was it all. So I reached into that doorway and grabbed the coat.

'Fook me, there were a bird in it! A bird wi' a knife. I'm tellin' you now, I am staring down the blade of a ten-inch bayonet. It ain't more'n another inch from my nose an' behind that there's a pale thin arm and above it a snarling mouth and two flashing jet black eyes. Honest, I thought I were goin' to die right there an' then.'

Birmingham city centre

'Fuck off, shithead. I'll fucking kill ye if ye fuckin' touch me or ma fuckin' coat ever again, ya fucking cunt!'

'Sorry!'

'Ah said, fuck off! Did ye hear me, cunt! Fuck off or I'll stick it in your eye!'

Fallowfield Community Hall, Manchester

'Why didn't I run? I don't know. I can't answer that. I hadn't had my epiphany yet. I know that, how could I have? All I could see was a snarl and a knife . . . All right, maybe I'd already clocked those flashing eyes, but honest, all I could really see were the knife. So why didn't I run? Maybe I wasn't capable. Or maybe something deep in me macho psyche meant that I don't run away from birds. Well, whatever, I didn't.'

Birmingham city centre

'I'm sorry! I didn't know, I thought it were just a coat . . . Honest, I'm cold, that's all. I thought someone had chucked it out. Please . . . I'm new to all this. The street an' all . . . It's my first day. Sorry. I'll fook off, shall I?'

'What do ye mean, first day on the streets? It isn't a job, ye know. Fuck off home, idiot, and get your ma tae make your breakfast.'

'I can't.'

'Hen. You've had a rough night, I can see that, but you are not homeless. Fuck off.'

'How do you know I'm not homeless?'

'Because ye don't look homeless. Ye look like you've been mugged.'

'I have.'

'Well, just because you've been robbed does not give ye the right tae steal ma coat.'

'I've told you, I didn't mean to steal your coat. I didn't know you were under it. I'm cold, that's all.'

'Where did ye spend last night?'

'In a hotel.'

'Oh, I *see*.'

'What d'you mean, oh, I *see*.'

'I know why wee boys like you spend nights in hotels, hun. Was it him that beat ye up?'

'I in't a fookin' rent boy, if that's what you think.'

'OK, so you're not. D'ye have a home at all? I mean an old one?'

'I've got lots of homes. But I live in London and I've lost all my money and my ID.'

'So phone your ma and reverse the charges.'

'I can't remember her number.'

'Phone somebody else.'

'I can't remember anybody's number.'

'Well, phone directory enquiries, give 'em your ma's name and address and they'll put you through.'

'I don't know my mum's address. I've just bought her a new house and I don't know where it is apart from it's in Jersey. I've been there, but my people arranged a helicopter.'

She smiled. 'It makes it easier, doesn't it?'

'What does?'

'Living in another world. Ah mean tae the one ye actually occupy.'

'What do you mean?'

'Where did ye get those nice boots an' trousers?'

'They're mine.'

'Mebbe now. Did ye steal 'em off your trick?'

'I've told you, I in't a fookin' bumboy.'

'So who paid for this hotel you wuz in, then?'

'My people, or at least they will when they get the bill. I got chucked out.'

'Why's that?'

'I trashed the room.'

'You are a rent boy, aren't ye, darlin'?'

'No.'

'Ye shagged some yuppie in a nice hotel last night, nicked his trousers and then security chased ye off.'

'No.'

'OK, what are ye?'

'I'm a rock star.'

'That's nice.'

'I'm Tommy Hanson.'

'Good for you. If you're gonna live in someone else's world make it a biggie, eh? Ah mean, ye could a' been some one-hit wonder, or an ex-member o' Boyzone. But you're Tommy Hanson. Actually, you look a bit like him too, if ye weren't bald. Ye could use that, ye know. Specialist whoring is very profitable if you can get intae a decent house.'

'I've told you, I'm not a prostitute. I'm Tommy Hanson.'

'And like I say, good on ye. I love Tommy Hanson, or Ah did once, before he went all Radio Two. Great songs, great looks, bit of a wanker, Ah imagine, but Ah quite like that in a man.'

Fallowfield Community Hall, Manchester

'I think I could possibly have convinced her o' who I was if I'd really tried, if I'd taken her step by step through the events of the previous eighteen hours. Maybe, maybe not, who knows. Anyway, I decided not to. She'd come to the conclusion that I was a street hustler, a rent boy an' a damaged fantasist who wanted t'be a rock star, and I just thought, fook it, why bother tryin' t'convince her? I *hate* Tommy Hanson, anyway, I think he's a twat an' a victim. It's even written on me 'ead. Why not have a day off from the bastard?

'So instead I asks if I can sit in her doorway with her for a while since I'd been on me feet for hours, an' she moves over an' I sit down next to her on the dirty tiles. I'd found that I still had a softpack o' Marlboro Lights squashed in me back pocket and on the streets you're always welcome if you've got a pack of fags.

'So we're smokin' fags an' talkin' an' I'm askin' her

about where she comes from, being as how she's a long way from home, what wi' her obviously being Scottish an' all, an' I'm tellin' her how I love all them mountains they have up there an' one day I'm gonna climb 'em, an' she says she feels the same. She says she reckons she's goin' t'wash herself in one o' the little lakes they have at the top, which sounds fookin' horrible t'me, besides which I don't think you get lakes at the top o' mountains.

'Anyway, after a while she starts t'tell me about her life an' about her stepfather comin' into her room, an' how for years she reckoned it were all her fault because her mum never protected her, an' as we're talkin' . . . I'm thinkin', see . . . an' secretly . . . deep inside . . . I'm coming to a decision.

'Because in that first hour or so I was in Jessie's company, that's her name, by the way, Jessie, I decided I was going to save her. That's right, I was going to save her. And then she could save me.

'Epiphany, y'see. You don't fook wi' it when it 'appens. It taps you on the shoulder and says, "Hallo, all change please, different agenda, let's be 'avin' you now! Stand by your beds!"

'I think actually it must have all started with Gemma the night before. I mean it sounds pathetic, but I had really trusted that bird and she done me over big time. I were talkin' to her about how I had no friends an' couldn't make any and then bang! I wake up wi' a camera in my face and she proves my whole fookin' point, don't she? Then, the very next morning, I bump into Jessie.

'There I was, fookin' blunderin' about the place, wallowin' in self-pity, hatin' everythin', trustin' nobody, comin' t'the depressin' conclusion that absolutely nothin' in my fooked-up world is real, including myself, an' suddenly I meet a bird who's so real it en't funny. This bird's got nothing, right? Nowt.

Absolutely fook all. But for all that, for all the fact that she's half skin an' bone, it's totally clear to me that there is more actual substance to her than everything else currently happenin' in my life put together times ten. Real? This girl is so real she's actually got a *bayonet*. What's more, a bayonet which she seems to be prepared to use.

'How fookin' real is *that*?

'So I'm sittin' there, watchin' her smoke me fags an' listenin' to her talk, an' like I say, I realize that my new mission in life has leapt fully formed inta me brain. I am goin' to save this girl. I am goin' to transform her life fookin' big time.

'What can I say? You probably think I'm being pathetic. Maybe I am. Maybe we see only what we want to see an' chuck out the rest. Maybe we're all carryin' pedestals round wi' us, lookin' for someone to put on 'em. Maybe after gettin' stitched up by Gemma what I wanted to see was a lost girl that I could love and who would love me. Maybe all I wanted was somebody I could trust.

'But, you see, I think *that*'s the point. Trust. The thing that first started me on the course I'm now on and intend to remain on until it's finished. This girl *did not know who I was*. She didn't know and she didn't care. That were an amazin' feelin' for me. Call me an overindulged whining little cont if you like, but I can't tell you how relaxin' I found it.

'What's more, she was beautiful. Oh, I *see*, you're all thinkin' so *that*'s what this is all about. Tommy got all romantic about sufferin' an' wanted to shag her.

'Well no, as it happens. That weren't what it was about at all. I'm just sayin' that she was beautiful, all right? Because it's true. For all the fact that she was dirty an' pale an' her skin weren't in the best of nick an' I could see from the bones at her neck an' the way her tits hung that she were very underweight, for all that and more, she was beautiful. Big, big dark eyes, delicate features, cute little legs curled up under her coat, an' . . . an' . . . well *I* don't fookin' know, do I? All I know is that as I sat there in that doorway talkin' to her, I found her beautiful. And I will never forget those big dark eyes set in that pale face as long as I live.'

KFC, the Bull Ring, Birmingham

'You really done the turkey . . . in a brothel?'
  'That's right. Ah did it.'
  'That's . . . well, that's just fookin' incredible.'
  'Aye, Ah know.'
  'So what happened after you escaped?'
  'Well, like Ah told ye, Ah blagged these clothes offa the Oxfam man an' headed off tae start ma new life. Ah was out o' whore's clothes for the first time since Ah'd met François an' Ah felt so uplifted and lightheaded Ah think Ah could ha' flown away if Ah'd wanted. Tae be straight an' free an' not being screwed by a stranger seemed tae me tae be about the highest possible summit o' human happiness.'
  'Well, I can fookin' understand that, quite frankly.'
  'Ah keep thinkin' about all the poor girls Ah left behind. Ah've thought about goin' tae the police, but the pathetic thing is, Ah've no idea where Goldie's place is. Ah just ran and ran from it. Ah could no retrace ma steps if Ah tried.'
  'So what now, then?' Tommy asked.
  'Ah have tae be very clear about that. Getting out from under isnae easy. Everything ye need tae climb up from the pit is up there above ye where you're trying tae get. Can't get a job without ID, can't get ID without an address, can't get an address without ID. It's catch twenty-two. There's a ladder all right, but it's on

the next floor up. There's a safety net for sure but we're under-fuckin'-neath it.'

'So what are you going t'do?'

'Well, Ah have a little list, see. It's no written down because Ah don't have a pen. Ah can't remember the last time Ah wrote anything down. Ah don't know if Ah can still write! It's in my head, see, and number one, at the very top, is stay straight. One thing Ah know is that being offa drugs won't necessarily get a person back tae the planet they came from, but being on them will stop ye for sure. So ye have tae stay straight.'

'Well, you've proved you can do that, haven't you? I mean, it can't get any worse than cold turkey, can it? Not the way you did it.'

'Ah can see ye weren't lyin' about the number o' nights ye've spent on the streets. It gets cold, believe me, even now in May. Cold and very lonely. Ah can't tell ye what a comfort it would a' been last night huddled in that doorway tae hit masel' up, oh Jesus, it would a' passed them long, lonely terrifying hours, for sure. But I mustnae. If I'm tae get off the streets Ah have tae stay straight.'

'What's next on the list?'

Tommy looked at the clock above the counter. One thirty. In twenty hours or so Jessie could write 'Get whisked away to paradise by famous rock star' on her list and chuck the rest away.

Fallowfield Community Hall, Manchester

'I hadn't changed my mind, see. No way. My sense o' purpose was gatherin' wi' every moment I spent wi' Jessie. I'm not sayin' it were love at first sight or anythin', because quite frankly I don't know what that means, but it were definitely a commitment, that's for sure. An emotional commitment, an' if you want t'laugh at that then go ahead. Believe me, I've heard all the arguments about why this is all just my fantasy, that in effect I've made this girl up. Made her what I want her to be. Created a damsel in distress who I can save to assuage me own feelin's o' fookin' inadequacy. I've got a therapist. He's told me what a wanker I'm being. I pay a hundred quid an hour to get dissed by a bloke wi' all the romance an' passion o' Steps' greatest hits. How stupid is that?

'I *know* that I've invented this fookin' bird in me 'ead. I know that it's all a reflection of me own need to compensate for me feelings of self-loathing. I also know that I fookin' love 'er an' I always will. Whatever 'appens.'

KFC, the Bull Ring, Birmingham

'OK, so point one is to stay straight. I'll buy that. What's point two?'

'The next priority is definitely tae get off the streets. Ye cannae make any improvement in your life until you're off the street. Ye'll learn that very quickly, Tommy. It's *My Fair Lady*, isn't it? The ultimate dream. "All I want is a room somewhere, far away from the cold night air." If ye can get off the streets ye can sign on, ye can get a job, ye can keep away from pimps.'

'Right, so you need a room somewhere.'

But where? Tommy was thinking. Mustique? The Seychelles? Florida? He would offer her a world of choice.

Tomorrow. Tomorrow morning, when he could get to his people.

'Ah've already spied out a couple o' drop-in centres and got ma name down for an interview for a halfway house hostel. Ah managed that Friday, straight after Ah left the Oxfam shop. They didnae like the look o' ma arms, but Ah assured them that Ah was clean an' my plan was tae get indoors somewhere an' then work ma arse off tae save. Ah'll have no problem getting work, crap work but work. Ah scrub up well an' Ah know how tae catch the eye o' a McDonald's recruitment manager. Not that Ah'll ever do more than flutter ma eyelashes, Ah can assure ye, Tom. A subsection o' point one on ma list, the one about gettin' straight, is tae never ever whore again.'

'Good plan.'

'Then once Ah've got a job Ah'll be able to rent masel' that room an' Ah'll work days an' evenings an' weekends and sleep on ma own in ma own room in between times. That's all point two. Get in a hostel, get work, get a room, get more work an' every second Ah'm no' workin' an' savin' up ma money, sleep – alone. Quite frankly, Ah can think o' nothing better than point two . . . except for point three.'

'What could possibly be better than living in one room on your own and working yourself to death?'

'Are ye taking the piss?'

'Sorry.'

'When Ah was a wee girl at home Ah had ma own room until one day ma daddy fucked off an' ma step-father moved in, an' he reckoned that room was his too. After Ah run away Ah had doorways an' Ah can tell ye Ah made sure that Ah was never on ma own in them, because getting raped in the entrance tae Marks an' Sparks is no' ma idea of a great night. Then after François gotta hold o' me Ah spent ma nights on pavements and inside o' kerb crawlers' cars. Since then Ah've shared a ten-bunk dormitory in a brothel wi' a bunch o' birds from the Balkans who don't speak English. So don't and Ah mean *don't* fuckin' laugh at me when Ah tells ye that ma dream is the same as Eliza fuckin' Doolittle's, OK? Particularly when Ah'm buyin' the fuckin' coffee.'

'Yeah. OK, fair enough. Like I said, sorry.'

'Apology accepted. Ya twat.'

Tommy smiled at Jessie. The puppy-dog eyes still held their power, even under the bruises. Jessie smiled back.

'So what's point three, then?' Tommy asked.

'A holiday! That's point three. A holiday . . .' Jessie's smile broadened at the very thought of it.

'Wi' sunshine . . . *Sunshine!* Oh ma Goad, how Ah *long* tae feel the sunshine. Not just a little bit, but endless, endless sunshine, all-day sunshine, sunshine everywhere, dappling the ground, rippling in your clothes, getting caught up in your hair . . . like havin' a bath in it . . .'

Such was the intensity of Jessie's fantasy that it almost seemed to Tommy as if the sun was inside her already, shining through those dark, haunted eyes, glowing beneath the pale skin at her neck.

'An' a beach! A long, long, long lonely beach o' glistening white sand, sand so white it hurts your eyes. Sand so fine ye cannae feel the grains . . . sand like talcum powder . . . wi' an ocean o' turquoise blue lapping upon it. A warm ocean, but cooler than the sand, so getting in it just makes your skin feel alive . . . an' no one, an' Ah mean *no one*, botherin' me at all. Not one single solitary person tae have any single solitary thing tae do wi' me lessen Ah tells them it's OK, that it's what Ah want. That's ma point three, Tommy Boy. Ah'll work an' work until Ah can afford it, an' then Ah'll send a solicitor's letter tae ma ma, demanding ma birth certificate or some other proof o' ma existence so Ah can get me a passport, just like a real fuckin' proper human person, and Ah'll fly away for three weeks or whatever Ah can afford, no less than two, tha's for sure. Ah'm not goin' anywhere jus' for a week. An' when Ah return Ah'll be returning tae a world of which Ah'm a member. An then Ah'll begin tae consider point four, which will be tae get trained up somehow or other, maybe study, get a proper job an' a house an' find some way or other o' bringin' justice tae the bastard that ma ma brought into our lives an' let intae ma room an' who completely an' utterly fucked up ma entire life.'

'You're going to report him to the police?'

'If Ah feel Ah can punish him that way then Ah will, but unless there's others who'll come forward an' back me up then it's his word against mine an' Ah'm an ex-whore an' junkie, don't forget.'

'So what will you do?'

'Somethin', Ah don't know. Ma fantasy is tae stick knitting needles in his eyes, but Ah won't, he's taken five years o' ma life already, Ah shan't go tae prison for him. Ma current idea is tae stand outside his house every morning and then follow him tae work shouting that he fucks little girls while they're tryin' tae sleep.'

Not necessary, thought Tommy. Because he would personally be putting the biggest, best, most humungously expensive, fuck-off, scorched-earth, attrition, predator, bastard legal team in the country at Jessie's disposal on the very following morning. Every lawyer in Scotland would be immediately bought off their current cases and pressed into the sole service of bringing that molesting little shit to justice.

Tomorrow morning. Everything would be all right in the morning.

They sat in the KFC for as long as they could. It was so warm and bright. Jessie had taken off her big coat. She still wore the tight little top in which she had run away. Once more Tommy noted the delicacy of her shoulders, the small, elegant bones about her neck, the slim white damaged arms, the curve of her breast, and he thought again that Jessie was beautiful.

How she'd have laughed if she'd read his mind and known the truth, that he, Tommy Hanson, who had famously slept with half the supermodels at London Fashion Week, should find her beautiful. Of course, being able to read his thoughts would not have been enough. Even if she'd read them she'd never have believed them.

Fallowfield Community Hall, Manchester

'Jessie was just so . . . I don't know, different. She was honest an' funny an' she didn't give a fook about anythin' except bein' left alone. It were . . . what can I say? . . . Look, I know I thought I'd been in love only the night before with that lying slag Gemma, but I don't care. A man can get it absolutely wrong and absolutely right in the space of a day, can't he? I've done that loads o' times. I'm telling you. Jessie was . . . *riveting*. I could not take my eyes off her, an' the more I looked at her an' listened to her, the more beautiful she got. Even the old track marks on her arms were beautiful to me, not least because I intended to ensure that those tracks would be the last ever made on Jessie's lovely skin and also because I knew that once the plastic surgeon I was going to pay for had done his work that soft alabaster surface would be perfect again.

'But that too was going to 'ave to wait until the Monday. Everything was going to be all right in the morning.'

The Bull Ring, Birmingham

'Oh my Goad!' Jessie remarked suddenly in mockingly dramatic tones. 'There's you on the front o' that paper, Tom Boy! What have you been up to, you naughty naughty thing!'

Sure enough, there it was, left behind by another

diner who had had his fill of sport and scandal. Yet another Tommy Hanson front-page exclusive. And what an exclusive it was.

'*I Slept with Pop Hero Judge to Win . . . Tortured Tommy weeps as he confesses gay affair with record boss.*'

'Fookin' 'ell.' Tommy snatched up the paper on the front of which was a photograph of a rather surprised-looking Tommy wrapped around an intrepid investigative journalist.

He had never imagined that Gemma would have been able to move so fast, but these days of course to email a photograph is the work of an instant and for such an incredible exclusive all presses had been held. The editor, who had put the paper to bed the previous evening, had been woken in the small hours and knew immediately that he had to remake the front page. The banner headlines about the Home Secretary's call to arms on drugs policy would have to be pushed back to page eight or nine, as would the associated news that the paper's own doctors had confirmed Robert Nunn the junkie's continuing clean bill of health. The Tommy Hanson exclusive needed the first eight pages at least, and it needed them now. The editor knew only too well that if he let the story lie for a week Tommy's publicists would quickly do their muddying work, spinning countless other contradictory and misleading Tommy exclusives into rival newspapers, dropping veiled hints about stitch-ups and conspiracies until nobody would know what to believe.

Tommy put the paper down. He always tried not to read the things that were written about him. They only depressed him, and this one looked particularly depressing. Besides, why would he be interested? That newspaper was reporting on the last night of his old life. He was a different person now. That Tommy was yesterday's news. Not to Jessie, of course, who devoured the article hungrily just as eight million other people had done that morning.

'My Goad! He slept with that *Pop Hero* judge! Ah can remember watching the whole thing, Ah even voted for Tommy. Turns out now Ah needn't a' bothered, eh? He was going to win anyway.'

Tommy could not allow this lie. 'That is not true. He won on merit.'

'Who'd 'a' thought he wuz a poof?'

'He is *not* a poof, it was a weird one-off, that's all.'

'Oh yes, and of course you'd know, wouldn't ye? Bein' as how you *are* Tommy. Sorry, Ah was forgetting . . . But fuck, this is an incredible story. The bitch actually slept with him to get it. She's no better than Ah've been. Actually she's quite amusing about it. Listen to this: *"And if anyone thinks I've been a tad immoral in my investigative techniques, let me ask you this, girls. Wouldn't you mix a bit of pleasure with business if you had the chance to get your leg over Tommy Hanson?"'*

'So she says I was good, then?'

'No, she does not say *you* were good, Tom Boy. She says nothing could ever live up to what you'd expect from shagging Tommy Hanson and Tommy Hanson certainly didn't.'

'Bitch.'

'Ah'd still have him, I must say.'

'You would?'

'Yeah, of course. He's gorgeous, best-lookin' bloke around. But what a *wanker*. Ah mean, Ah thought he were a wanker before, but you just *have* to read this, it's *pathetic*. You'll give up any dreams o' wanting tae be the arsehole. Listen to this . . . *"He wept and wept as he confessed to me his feelings of doubt and self-loathing. He feels that for all his wealth and fame he is lost and that his unhappiness seems to increase alongside his success . . ."'*

Jessie laughed and laughed. Tommy tried hard not to mind.

'What a *prat*! Jesus Christ. We'd swap a bit o' our shite lives for his, wouldn't we? Unhappiness and all. We should gi' him a ring an' tell him, eh, Tommy, spend a night on the fuckin' street an' see how unhappy your success makes ye then.'

'Come on, be fair. I mean, just because you're not at the bottom of the pile doesn't mean you don't have a right to be unhappy.'

'As far as Ah'm concerned it fuckin' does. Honest, you have to read this, Ah mean Ah know ye admire the guy, obviously ye do tae want tae be him so much, but what a whining, whingeing, self-indulgent, self-pitying little *prick*. Ah can't believe Ah used tae like him.'

Tommy was finding it increasingly difficult to feign indifference. In fact momentarily his face flashed with anger. But then he smiled. This was the post-epiphany Tommy. Love had mellowed him. 'Yeah, you're right, what an idiot. All that money, all that fame, and he can't even find a way to be happy. Stupid, eh?'

'Well, Ah'm sure you're right and that rich people can be depressed, but he's just so self-obsessed about it.'

'Isn't he.'

'All this poor little me bit.'

'What a cunt.'

'Oh no! "*Ah cannae trust ma old friends, Ah cannae trust ma new ones.*" '

'Arsehole.'

'Well, give your fuckin' money away then, ya silly twat.'

'Well, some of it, certainly.'

The Hyatt Regency, Birmingham

Peter Paget finally picked up the phone. It had taken

him more than twenty minutes to gather sufficient resolve. It was noon on the Sunday after the Labour Party gala dinner and amongst the mass of congratulatory emails, faxes and phonecalls Peter had received there were two that were life-changing. The first had been a call from Dr Wellbourne to congratulate Peter on the results of his final blood tests. He was completely in the clear. The second call was the reason that Peter was now agonizing about calling the Prime Minister. It had been from Paula Wooldridge, who took great delight in enquiring whether Peter would like to make any comment on the story her paper intended to run the following morning.

Samantha had turned on him more quickly and with greater venom than he could have imagined. Peter had thought that it would be a sexual affair that he would find himself denying. He had not reckoned with the accusations of drug-taking. How could he have been so stupid?

'Yes. It's Paget here, Minister for Drugs. I know that the Prime Minister is at Chequers. Could you possibly put me through . . . Yes, it's very urgent.'

The wait seemed interminable. The Prime Minister had had to be summoned from the garden.

'Prime Minister, I have bad news. I'm afraid we're under attack. Your favourite newspaper and mine has a piece which they seem intent on running. They've cooked up a sex scandal. My ex-parliamentary assistant is claiming that we had an affair. No, Prime Minister, there is no truth in it whatsoever. I have never so much as laid a hand on her. The simple facts are that she developed something of a crush on me and made advances which I rejected. Hell hath no fury and all that . . .'

Across the room Angela Paget struggled to maintain her composure. Her eyes were red; she had not slept at all that night.

'Yes, Prime Minister, of course I've told them that the girl is a fantasist and that if they publish they'll be sued to within an inch of their lives, but I think they're going to pursue me none the less. There is another factor ... The girl is claiming that we took drugs together. Cocaine and ecstasy. I suppose their theory is the old Goebbels adage: When you tell a lie, make sure it's a big one.'

Once more, across the room, Angela Paget gulped. Peter tried to ignore her until finally he put the phone down. 'I have to go to Chequers immediately. They're ordering a car.'

'Peter ...' Angela hesitated for a moment. 'This thing about your taking drugs with her. That bit really *is* a lie, isn't it?'

'What do you think?'

'I have no sodding idea what to think any more!'

'Of course it's a lie! For heaven's sake, don't you see what's going on! This is a press conspiracy. They want to destroy my bill and the only way they can do that is to destroy me. Sex wouldn't be enough, not with the head of steam I've built up. People like me too much, they need something special, and I have to admit that this is a pretty good shot. If they can smear me with drug-taking, then every single thing I've said is utterly compromised.'

'So you never took drugs with her?'

'I have just fucking told you! No!'

'Then they are being total bastards and you have to beat them. *We* have to beat them.'

'Thank you, Angela.' He began to cross the room towards her, but she stopped him with a gesture.

'No, Peter. Not yet. We'll fight this together as a family, but that doesn't make me feel like you are part of the family. Not yet, I'm afraid. But what you've achieved so far is too important to let them destroy it. You have singlehandedly brought the drugs debate into the twenty-first century. Nobody must be allowed to stop that . . . Not even your ex-lover.'

Angela went into the bathroom to cry.

The Bull Ring, Birmingham

They had been begging together for some hours, but early Sunday evening in a provincial city centre does not offer the richest of pickings.

'I always thought them beggars in doorways made fookin' thousands.'

'Then you're an even bigger twat than I thought, Tommy.'

'Yeah, but that's what everybody says, in't it, that they make loads?'

'Not anyone who's ever tried it.'

It was getting cold. Particularly for Tommy, who had no coat. They had found some cardboard boxes, which when flattened out provided a little insulation from the chill of the floor of the shop doorway in which they sat.

'So will ye sit wi' me the night, then, Tommy Boy?' Jessie asked.

'You want me to stay?'

'Sure, ye can share ma coat an' blanket an' we'll keep each other warm.'

'I thought you liked to be alone.'

'On a beach, maybe, or in a room o' ma own. But not on the streets, not at night.'

'I'd love to stop here with you.'

'Good. An' tomorrow mebbe we can both try tae get intae a hostel or somethin'.'

'Yes. Tomorrow everything will be all right.'

Across the street a big car had drawn up beside a telephone box. Tommy watched idly as two men got out of the car and one of them entered the phonebox.

He was putting something on the windows. Tommy did not know what.

Jessie had not noticed the men. She was inspecting their meagre takings. 'Three quid,' she said. 'Shall we gi' it a bit longer or go and get some chips?'

'Let's stick it out, eh? Another pound and we can have a sausage.'

Fallowfield Community Hall, Manchester

Tommy's voice was no longer steady. 'If only I'd said yeah, let's go an' get some chips. But I didn't, and instead of getting up and moving on, we just sat there . . . Who knows, if we'd walked away there and then maybe we'd have been all right, or maybe they would've noticed us anyway. I don't know. All I know is, we sat there and it happened. The bloke across the road comes out of the phonebox and he's about to get back into the car with his mate when he glances across at us. Just a glance, but that were enough. I reckon him and Jessie recognized each other at exactly the same time. "Oh no," she says. That was all, and I looked at her and she's like paralysed, that's the best way I can put it, fookin' paralysed with fear. The next thing is the bloke across the street is walking towards us, real fast, almost running with his mate following. I think Jessie tried to get up, but she couldn't, her legs was all wrapped up in her coat.'

The Bull Ring, Birmingham

'Hello, Jessie. I think you owe us for a broken skylight, don't you?'

'Fuck off! Please! Leave me alone, you bastards! I'm out now, I'm clean.'

The first of the men reached down and, grabbing Jessie by the shoulders, hauled her to her feet as if she were a bag of shopping.

Tommy jumped up too. 'Hey, get your fookin' hands—'

The other man wore a knuckleduster. He knocked Tommy down with a single blow. As he lost consciousness for the second time in twenty hours, Tommy saw Jessie being carried across the street towards the men's car.

Fallowfield Community Hall, Manchester

'When I came round they were gone and I had my mission in life set out for me.' Tommy stared at his shoes, biting his lip, clearly trying to master his emotions.

'It felt like nothing I've ever felt before, nothing. Like I'd had my stomach cut out o' me, like the whole world had been painted black. Eight hours I'd spent wi' Jessie, eight hours during which time I'd begun to discover that I might actually still have a heart or a soul or whatever you want t'call it. That I might not be the totally irredeemable arse'ole that I'd thought I was. That there were more important people in the world than me. Oh, *fook* it. Can you hear me? I'm *still* talkin' 'bout myself, *still* seeing everythin' as a reflection of how I feel! Seein' the worst fookin' tragedy I'd ever personally been close to in terms of my own pathetic little ego. I'm a *cont*. A bastard, that's all. I don't deserve even to have *met* Jessie, a bird who could do cold turkey *on her own* aged seventeen or whatever in a brothel! I've spent hundreds of thousands of fookin' pounds on fookin' recovery, me – Betty Ford, the Priory, they should fit a revolving door for conts like me! I've done the whole bastard LA thing, rollerbladin' round past Geri an' Robbie, carryin' me poxy bottle o' water an' doin' interviews about bein' clean. I devoted every second o' my life to *me* an' my problems, an' then one day I meet someone who's for real, wi' real problems, the reallest person I ever knew, an' then I lose her. An' what am I like? I'm goin' "Oh, look everybody, this is how it changed *me*." Honest to God, what *am* I fookin' like? An' here's me, *still* goin' on about me by goin' on about how much I hate meself for goin' on about *me*! I mean, *fookin'* 'ell.'

Once more Tommy struggled with his emotions. 'So she's gone, right? An' everything's turned black. It's like I'm looking through a tunnel which has all blurry dark edges. I'm sitting there just shouting at the gathering night. "*Jessie! Jessie!*" An' I'm cryin' an' acting like a total fookwit for about five minutes, kicking the door o' the shop an' lookin' at the place where she'd been sitting like she's going to reappear. An' suddenly this copper's standin' there, this big Brummie copper's asking what the fook I think I'm playin' at, an' I tells him that the girl I love 'as just been fookin' kidnapped! So he asks me who she was. What was her surname? Who kidnapped her? *What* were the reg' o' the car? An' I realize that I don't know any of those things, so the copper says in that case there's not a lot he can do about it, is there, but if I keep on shoutin' an' kickin' doors he's goin' to nick me.

'So after he fooks off I'm sat there like shakin' but thinkin' to meself that the trail is never going to be warmer than at that very moment. Every minute that passed was gonna take Jessie further and further away from me. I couldn't wait for the morning. I couldn't wait for my money and my people and my whole fookin' fookwit support structure. I had to do it now. But what? Who were those bastards? Well, the bastards what grabbed her the first time, had to be, but who were *they*? Where had they taken her? Even Jessie hadn't known where the house was, else she were goin' to try and save the other girls. So I'm sat there an' I'm thinkin' an' I'm thinkin' . . . Like there must be a clue. If I relive every moment from when I first noticed the blokes to when they punched me out, there must be somethin'. I picked up Jessie's coat an' put it on, it were all I had left of her, an' I walks across the road to where the car had been parked. I don't know what I'm thinkin' . . . somethin' really fookin' thick like maybe there's tyre marks that I could get photographed an' have tracked or else perhaps one of 'em dropped a fag packet with a mobile number written on it or an address that might lead me to her. But of course there was nothin'. An' I'm thinkin' an' thinkin', an' for fook's sake the answer were staring me in the face. The telephone box! What had they been doin' in the telephone box? Makin' a phonecall, had t'be. If I could find out who they'd phoned . . . the last call that were made from that box . . . So I jumps into the box like a shot, thinkin' if some other fooker gets in there an' starts makin' loads o' calls I'm fooked. An' then it hits me. The bastard *never made a phone call*. That's right! He were just sort o' messin' about, weren't he? Hang on, 'e were puttin' *somethin' on the window*!! Of course! He's a fooking whoremaster, he's advertising! The whole phonebox is covered in all them prossie stickers. "New Asian girl – Young" . . . "Petite, young Aussie, willing" . . . "Like it 'anging from the chandelier wi' a bunch o' roses stuck up your arse? I'm your girl" . . . You know the stickers. Weird, some of 'em . . . And bang on top of all the others, brand new, not half picked off an' covered in biro scribble, there was a bunch o' nicely printed little stickers sayin' "Sexual Services. Many girls. All new. All young. Asian. Russian. Bosnian. All willing." An' there were a phone number t'call.'

Chequers

Peter had always wanted to visit Chequers, the Prime Minister's country retreat. To visit the place where Lloyd George had planned the convoy system in 1916, where Churchill had pondered the battle against Nazi Germany, where Attlee had taken respite from his titanic struggle to bring the welfare state into being. Now that Peter had been elevated to Cabinet status, he had been looking forward to many evenings dining amongst the myriad souvenirs of administrations past, basking in the history that had been made and the history that he was playing such a central part in making. But such had been the speed of Peter's ascension to the very highest ranks of public life that there had thus far been no time for such niceties, and this was Peter's first trip. The circumstances were not remotely what he had hoped.

Charlie Ansboro, the Prime Minister's Press Secretary, a man known within the Labour Party as the Wild Pig, stared Peter straight in the eye. 'Minister. Tell me now and tell me absolutely straight. Is there any truth in what they're about to throw at you? What they're about to throw at us?'

They had barely sat down. Peter had not even been offered a drink. There had been no niceties, the Prime Minister had not yet joined them, and he would not do so until the Wild Pig called for him. Peter was either about to be cast out or to remain in, it was a matter of spin control, and the decision lay with the Press Secretary. If Charlie Ansboro decided that the government and the party would be better off dumping Peter, then the process would begin immediately and Peter would not see the PM at all.

'I do not lie to the Prime Minister, Charlie. As I told him earlier, there is no truth in these allegations whatsoever,' Peter replied, answering the Pig's stare with an unblinking one of his own.

All the way from the Birmingham hotel to Chequers Peter had been agonizing over his strategy, going over every moment of his affair with Samantha. An affair which, thank God, he had conducted with the greatest care and secrecy. There was only one occasion when any other person had been in direct contact with Peter and Samantha during their relationship, and that had been the birthday dinner party. The occasion on which he had taken cocaine for the first and only time in his life. Apart from that the whole thing was a matter of his word against Samantha's. If he had been spotted going into Samantha's flat, so what? She had been his parliamentary assistant. As a backbencher he shared office space with countless other MPs. Was it any wonder that on some evenings they had made use of Samantha's place in which to work, and if anyone said why hadn't he used his own home, he would enquire whether they had ever tried living with two noisy teenaged daughters.

But there was that birthday dinner party. Samantha's best friends would be bound to testify against him. Pondering this on the drive to Chequers, Peter had conceived a plan. He intended to produce witnesses of his own.

Charlie Ansboro leant forward in his chair. 'Peter, I've known for months that you've been fucking her.'

Peter Paget did not flinch. 'You've known more than me, then, mate.'

The two chairs in which they sat were uncomfortably close together, close enough for Ansboro to reach across and grip Peter's knee. He gripped it hard, a most intimidating gesture. 'You've been fucking her rigid, you bloody fool, and if you think I'm going to let your poxy little sex life bring down this government then you're a bigger arsehole than even I took you to be. Tell me I'm a liar if you dare, you fucking – stupid – bastard.'

'Take your hand off me right now.'

Charlie did not move his hand, in fact he increased his grip, and his stare became even more intense. He seemed almost to hiss through his clenched tobacco-stained teeth. 'Tell me I'm a liar or I'll hang you from Big Ben by your bollocks.'

'Get your hand off me right now.'

Still Charlie's hand did not move. His eyes were a picture of madness. This was a man possessed. Possessed with keeping the Prime Minister in power.

Peter shocked even himself with what happened next. He punched Charlie Ansboro in the mouth. His clenched fist shot out and smashed into Ansboro's clenched teeth.

Charlie let go of Peter's knee. He was shocked but did not seem angry. He even managed to smile. 'Well done, Paget,' he said. 'You're the first one who's ever done that.' He nursed a lip already growing fat from the blow. 'And the very second you're of no further use to us you'll pay for it. OK?'

Peter's stare remained steady. 'As I told you, Charlie, there is no truth in any of the allegations that Ms Spencer is making against me.'

Ansboro rang a small bell, and a butler appeared.

'Tell his nibs he can come through now, will you, mate?'

The Prime Minister entered and did not offer Peter his hand. Greeting him with the merest nod he turned straight to his Press Secretary.

'Well, Charlie?'

'Paget's sticking to his story as hard as the press are sticking to theirs.'

'Of course I am, Prime Minister, for the simple reason that—'

'And what's our story?' The Prime Minister was continuing to ignore Peter.

'I say we're in too deep to turn back. Drop Paget now and you're admitting that he's an adulterous, drug-taking hypocrite, in which case the bill's dead anyway, and in my opinion the government fatally wounded as well.'

Peter could hardly believe he was being so callously sidelined. 'Excuse me, Prime Minister, but—'

'Peter, please, I'm talking to Charlie.'

'We'll just have to tough it out,' Ansboro continued. 'Can they prove their allegations?'

'Paget obviously doesn't think so or he wouldn't be going for straight denial.'

Again Peter butted in. 'I'm going for straight denial, *Charlie*, because the allegations are false and—'

Now it was the Prime Minister's turn to butt in. 'Peter, Charlie told me about your knocking off your PA the day I proposed you for Cabinet.'

'Well, Charlie was *wrong*, Prime Minister. Charlie-Wild Pig-fucking Ansboro was *wrong*. I have not been knocking off my parliamentary assistant, and I have not taken any drugs, OK? I am a man with an important job to do and a lot of people don't want me to do it. That's all that this is about. And while I'm speaking plainly I might as well tell you that your Press Secretary is the most despised man in the party bar none, and the fact that people suspect you value his counsel above that of your ministers is the single greatest threat to your government's authority. This man is a shit, Prime Minister, and if you have summoned me from the bosom of my family in order that this unelected, unaccountable, foul-mouthed toady can call me a liar, then in future I will thank you not to waste my time. Now, it's getting late and it is Sunday. You deserve some rest and so do I. What this arse needs is another smack in the mouth to go with the one I just gave him.'

The Prime Minister's eyes widened with surprise.

'I therefore have only two questions to ask you: am I still the Minister for Drugs, and are you still expecting me to steer our legalization through Parliament after the next Queen's Speech?'

Charlie Ansboro was about to speak.

'Shut up, Charlie,' said the Prime Minister. 'Yes, Peter. On both counts.'

'Thank you, Prime Minister. Then if there's nothing further I'll bid you good night.'

As Peter crunched across the gravel towards his car every particle of his body felt alive. He had started as he meant to go on. He was going to be strong and he was going to win. He would maintain the new truth upon which he had decided completely and absolutely because it *was* the truth, a higher truth, a greater truth . . . at least, in as much as the *actual* truth would mean the end of his bill and hence the further perpetration of murder and crime that its failure would allow.

Peter was going to fight. He would fight because he was right, and he would win for the same reason.

Fallowfield Community Hall, Manchester

'I still had the three quid that me an' Jessie had begged, so I was able to make the phone call an' get the addresses of the brothels advertised on the sticker. There were three of 'em and I was promised the best I'd ever had.

'So that were it. I had to get over there an' spring Jessie sharpish, but not in an Oxfam shop coat, a bald tattooed 'ead, a face all bruised up and three quid in me pocket minus a phonecall. Well, I couldn't do much about the bruised face, but I knew enough about brothels to know that there was no way I was getting into one lookin' like a tramp.

'I don't know if you've ever mugged someone at all,

but let me tell you, if you're not born to it, it's fookin' 'orrible. I were waitin' round in this quiet street tryin' t'judge up blokes' size an' weight as they went by. I let two who were perfect go by 'cos I bottled it before I picked one. He were about my size but weedy-lookin'. Well, I weren't goin' to pick Lennox Lewis, was I, even if I did still have Jessie's bayonet?'

A quiet street, Birmingham

'Gi' us your fookin' shirt an' jacket.'
  'Don't hurt me!'
  'I'm not goin' t'fookin' hurt you. Just gi's what I said.'
  'Please don't hurt me!'
  'Look, I've told you I'm not goin' t'fookin' hurt you.'
  'You're not?'
  'No! How many more fookin' times.'
  'Oh, well, in that case fuck off.'
  'What?'
  'I'm not giving you my jacket. Fuck off. Help! Help!'
  'Look gi's what I say, now! Or I'll stick this in ya!'
  'You said you weren't going to hurt me!'
  'I've changed me mind.'
  'Are you sure?'
  'Of course I'm fookin' sure! I'm desperate!'
  'Please don't hurt me!'
  'For fook's sake! Listen! These are the rules, OK? If you give me what I say, I won't hurt you. If you don't, I'll stab you. Now is that fookin' clear!'

Fallowfield Community Hall, Manchester

'I swear I never want to 'ave t' roll someone again as long as I live. I mean we were fookin' jibberin' at each other, both absolutely cackin' it. It were like a sketch

on the telly. Anyway, I got his shirt an' jacket in the
end, and his wallet. I bunged him me coat an' ran like
fook. Actually, as I ran away I felt dead good, 'cos I'd
done it for her, see. I'd committed an unselfish act.'

A brothel, Birmingham

'Why'd you break the window in the roof, Jessie? There
was like all glass everywhere. Any of the girls could 'a
got themselves cut. I mean that was just fuckin' out of
order, you know what I mean?'

Jessie did not answer. She was back. *She was back.*
Right at the very source and centre of her torment.

'I ought ta cut you up good, Jessie. Beat the livin' shit
outa you. You know what I mean?'

Jessie did indeed know what he meant. Having the
living shit beaten out of her was something that she did
not need to have described to her.

'But you see,' Goldie continued, 'lotta the punters
have missed you, Jessie. Oh yeah, did you know that?
You got quite a following, quite a fanclub. Most of
these Balkan babes we got on offer is olive-skinned,
OK? Which is nice, tasty, melts my fucking Magnum, I
can tell you, but on the other hand some geezers like
'em pale. They like skin all whitey-white, like yours,
pale as *death*, if you know what I mean. Fact is, Jessie,
I've met punters that liked 'em *dead*, oh yeah, snuff
muff. It happens, baby, don't think it don't. Necro-
howsyourfather. Sick, I call it. But that ain't my
business. Babes like you what look so good are
precious and, like I say, there's payin' public asking
me, Goldie, where's the Scottish babe? I don't want no
Balkan bitch, I want Jessie. Yeah, you should be proud.
Only five minutes ago some geezer rings up, describes
you exactly, had you three times when he was last in
town, he says; wants another taste. In't it lucky we

314

found you, Jessie? I'm sure you'd hate to disappoint your public.'

The void opening up in front of Jessie was cavernous. An immense black hole engulfing her totally. There was no precipice to teeter on; she had already fallen into a grave as big as the world.

When one of Goldie's boys offered her the needle she hardly bothered to resist.

The Paget household, Dalston

The four of them sat around the table together. It was past midnight and Peter had returned from his trip to Chequers an hour before. Since then, Charlie Ansboro had been on the phone to confirm that the journalist Paula Wooldridge was sticking to her story and that her editor intended to publish in the morning. Ansboro reported that Wooldridge was aggressive and confident and claimed she had two witnesses of good character and professional standing to support Samantha's cocaine allegations.

In the face of this crisis Peter and Angela Paget had decided to wake their daughters and explain to them the maelstrom that would engulf the family with the morning's papers. When he had finished explaining the situation there was a silence as the remaining three women in his life stared into their coffee cups.

'Well, girls,' Peter said, turning to his daughters, 'it's kind of you not to ask me the one question that you must be burning to ask. However, I'll answer it anyway. No, I did not have sexual relations with this woman and nor did I take drugs with her.'

Suzie, the younger of the Paget girls, got up and kissed her father. Cathy was a little slower in her response. Her eyes flicked across to her mother; she seemed to be asking for confirmation.

Angela Paget rose to the occasion. She knew her duty. 'Your father is the victim of a press campaign against him, girls. This woman has clearly been put up to it.'

'What are you going to do?' Cathy asked.

'We're going to sue them,' Peter replied.

'Will we win?'

'It depends,' Peter said quietly. 'The core of their case is the fabrication that I attended a birthday dinner with the girl Spencer and her two friends. All three are prepared to swear that they saw me take cocaine that night. The two friends also corroborate Spencer's story that I subsequently spent the night with her.'

'Quoting your own speeches, apparently,' said Suzie, who had already clicked onto the internet and found early reports of the coming scandal.

'Yes, all right, Suzie,' her mother admonished. 'We're not interested in the detail of these disgusting stories.'

'So where were you on the night in question, Dad?' Cathy enquired, and Peter could only admire such intellectual focus for one so young.

'Ah well, you see, that's where they've been clever, because, you see, I *was* with Ms Spencer and they know it and, what's more, at her flat. We were working on papers together and needed space.'

Momentarily Angela Paget's eyes fell. Cathy noticed this but said nothing.

'So if I tell the truth about that night,' Peter went on quickly, 'that I was at her flat, then it's three words against one and I think they'd be able to make the story stick. It would certainly be hard for me to get a clear libel judgement when I'm outnumbered so heavily . . .'

'So you're going to have to lie, aren't you, Dad? That's obvious.'

'Yes, I'm going to have to lie. I'm going to have to tell a small lie in order to establish a greater truth.'

'Your innocence?'

'I don't care about myself overmuch, Cathy,' Peter said sincerely. 'Or us, in fact. I'm quite sure that our love as a family can survive a press smear campaign. No, the great truth I'm going to lie to defend is that thirty years of drug policy have failed the public utterly and it's time to move on. That's the truth they're trying to smother.'

'So you have to have been somewhere other than at Samantha Spencer's flat on the night they say you took the cocaine,' Cathy observed matter of factly.

'Yes, Cathy, that's true.'

'For which you need witnesses. Witnesses you can trust absolutely.'

'Yes.'

'Well, we'd better get our diaries out, then.' Cathy had brought matters to a head far faster than Peter had intended, but she had read his intentions perfectly. This was indeed where he had been leading.

'If you're prepared to do this thing, yes,' Paget said, almost in a whisper.

'Lie for you.'

'Yes.'

'In court?'

'It may come to that.'

Angela Paget had turned almost white with the horror of what Peter was proposing. 'You don't have to do this if you don't want to, darling,' she said.

'Of course she doesn't.'

'Dad, Mum, we're a family. We're all each other has got and I've never been more proud of Dad than during this campaign. Can you get away with just me or do you need Suzie too?'

'I think one of you should be enough.'

'You don't need Mum?'

'No. I think the story is better if it's not too obvious. Your mother was at home.'

'Christ, Dad, you'd better hope I wasn't out with other people that night.'

Cathy went off to her bedroom and brought back her Young Socialist Student Diary.

Meanwhile, Angela Paget went to bed, instructing her younger daughter to do likewise.

'You're lucky,' said Cathy, studying her diary. 'The previous night I was at drama class and the following night I was at Debating Society, but on the night in question I am free to have been with you. What do you think? A movie? Nice and anonymous. Nobody could swear that we *hadn't* been there. I bought the tickets with cash while my famous dad discreetly studied a popcorn machine. We spent the next two hours together during which you were so utterly riveted by ... What were the big movies five months ago? ... What would you like to have seen? *Toy Story 3*? *Jurassic 6*? *Mission Impossible 3*? Or shall we be patriotic and support a small-budget Brit pic hailed by the critics and ignored by the public?'

'Cathy, you do realize how serious this is, don't you? This may easily go to court. You will have to perjure yourself.'

'Dad, how many times do I have to tell you? A: I don't believe in God; b: I don't think much of the state, and c: most importantly, c, a person should answer to their own conscience, not some arbitrary set of rules imposed from above. Of course it's wrong to lie, but I know that this silly cow is lying too, and I intend to fight fire with fire. What was it Polonius said? "Above all to thine own self be true," and that's what I intend to be.'

Cathy Paget took up a ballpoint pen and wrote 'Movies with Dad' onto the blank date in her diary.

'Fortunately *Mission Impossible 3*'s out on DVD,' she said. 'Watch it as soon as possible. It's not bad, actually, and Cruise is gorgeous, despite being a rather reactionary male stereotype. You don't want some clever brief saying, "So who was in this movie you're supposed to have seen?", do you?'

Not for the first time Peter Paget looked at his young daughter with what was something approaching awe.

Padstow holiday cottages, Cornwall

At around the time that Peter and Cathy Paget finally retired to their beds, Commander Leman was driving out of London, arriving at the family holiday home at ten in the morning. There he exchanged places once more in the Thompson family car with Jo Jo's father. Craig Thompson had dined highly visibly and until very late with Christine and Anna Leman at the Angler's Arms on the previous evening and, having slept fitfully on the couch, had been on a lengthy walk on the promenade with them from early that morning. In fact, they had dropped in at the newsagent's before six, less than two hours after DS Sharp's death four hundred miles away in London.

Craig Thompson drove off and Barry Leman, having listened on Radio Four to the breaking news of two terrible murders of Drug Squad officers in London, sat down at his computer to compose a message for his personal website.

'I knew both Detective Sergeant Archer and Detective Sergeant Sharp,' he wrote. 'Both were fine officers, shock troops in our so-called war on drugs. These two men and countless other dedicated police-men and women stand every day in the front line facing an enemy that is better armed, better funded and better motivated than they are. An enemy which knows that it is winning, an enemy which knows why it is fighting. The fact that these criminals, these gangsters, these low-life animals who grow fat in the sewers of our society feel that they can gun down Drug

Squad officers in such an open and casual manner shows to just what levels their confidence has soared. I had recently decided because of threats to my family to bow out of the drug debate. But now I feel I must return to it. While neither Sharp nor Archer was married, they had families too, we all have families, and for the sake of every family in Britain, and in the memory of the two decent officers who died last night, let us take away the motive for this and a thousand other crimes of violence which occur every day on our streets. Let us legalize drugs now.'

A brothel, Birmingham

Tommy approached the door making full use of his legendary swagger. The man he had robbed had had good taste in clothes and over a hundred pounds in his pocket. There had also been some credit cards with a signature on them that Tommy felt he could copy with ease.

'All right, babes,' he said through the intercom at the heavy, barred front door. 'Gentleman about town in need of a little extracurricular R and R, which I believe this establishment is in a position to supply.'

All Tommy's life he had known that weakness invites abuse. Confidence, on the other hand, can carry much before it.

The door opened.

'Evening, darling,' Tommy said to the madam, and even with the bruises he was able to win a welcoming smile from her. Some people just have charm. Tommy knew that he was such a blessed individual. 'Lovely to be back, best shop in town, this, beautifully run, clean, tasteful and your young ladies are just that – *young* ladies.'

'You've visited us before, sir?'

'Oh yes, but I don't remember you, my love, and I'm quite sure I would. Must have been your day off, or else perhaps you were upstairs showing some of these young girls how a real beauty handles a punter.'

This was laying it on thick, but the plump and painted madam preened herself nonetheless.

'So now, my darling,' Tommy went on to say, 'I phoned ahead to make sure that the girl whose charms I appreciated so fully on my last visit was still employed at this establishment. I mean, it wouldn't surprise me if she'd gone and got proposed to by some well-heeled punter and was now out of the game altogether.'

Tommy described Jessie to the madam as he had done previously on the phone. 'Beautiful girl, Scottish, small-boned but nice big boobs. Large dark wild eyes. Cute legs, good calves, bit short for some but I've never been as into tall birds as some blokes. Raven-haired, but with lots of copper in there . . .'

'Jessie,' said the madam.

'Yes, that's it. Nice name, too,' Tommy remarked, struggling to appear casual, desperate not to show the thrill that had shot through him like a bolt of lightning at the mention of her name. 'Yes, that's the girl. That's who I want.'

'Well, she's with a gentleman right now, sir, but I'm sure she won't be long.'

Just as sharp as the thrill of hearing her name was the pain that this revelation caused to Tommy. They hadn't been slow in putting her back into harness. Somewhere in that house, literally a few metres and a few sheets of plasterboard away, Jessie, the girl who had changed his life, was being used as a sexual slave. Tommy swallowed hard to contain and control his rising emotions. Desperate not to succumb to the desire to grab the painted crone by the throat and choke her until she told him the room that Jessie occupied so

321

that he might liberate her that instant, Tommy was painfully aware of the two thugs who lounged against the opposite wall. He knew that there would be more downstairs in the basement. Violent men and armed. He would have to wait.

The madam had noted Tommy's fallen face. 'Don't worry, dear, we can't keep girls for your exclusive use, can we? They have to earn a living, just like anybody else. You can wait, or else we've got some absolute peaches on offer this evening, some of them only just arrived from overseas.'

Tommy allowed himself to be shown into the 'lounge', where half a dozen girls sat about in various stages of undress.

'Perhaps you'd like to take one upstairs, sir, and when young Jessie's finished we could send her up to join you?' the madam suggested.

'No thanks, darling,' Tommy replied casually. 'Never been a threesome man meself, never know where to put anything. I'll just 'ave a beer and wait.'

Shortly thereafter a man whom Tommy would gladly have killed came into the room, took his coat from the madam and shuffled out, avoiding anybody's eye.

'Jessie will just be a few minutes,' the madam assured Tommy. 'She's just making herself nice. This is a very clean house. In the meantime it's seventy-five pounds for half an hour. If you stay longer we charge you on the way out.'

Tommy paid by stolen credit card, which the establishment was happy to accept, and was shown upstairs and into a small cubicle containing a bed, a washbasin, the sort of shower unit to be found in cheap holiday chalets, a box of tissues, a packet of condoms, and Jessie.

She was sitting on the bed wearing white ankle socks, pink shorts and a white Nike sports bra. The pupils of her eyes were like pinpricks.

'Jessie?'

'Hello, handsome,' Jessie slurred. 'Is it full sex yez after?'

'Jessie, it's me . . . Tommy . . . the boy who tried to steal your coat this morning.' He could see that Jessie was as high as a kite. The pupils suggested a big hit of heroin, but God only knew what else she had in her.

'Oh, yeah,' Jessie said. 'Hello . . . Ah remember . . . Is it full sex yez after?'

'No!'

'It's the same price as oral, no refunds, all takes much the same time.'

'Jessie, I've come to get you out.'

'I'm never gettin' out, pal. Now do you want sex or no'?'

Jessie was not really there at all. Just her body and her name; the rest was gone. The eyes had lost their sparkle, the voice came from a different person, a different soul.

'Jessie, please . . .'

But Tommy knew enough about drugs to be able to see that Jessie was doped up good, no longer a person of free will. Besides which, it was pointless to ask Jessie to run. She couldn't do that even if she wanted to. She was the bonded property of the house. He sat down on the bed and tried to think. What had he been hoping would happen? A convenient window that he and Jessie might leap through? A balcony to jump from, hand in hand? Tommy realized that in his haste to find Jessie he had not really considered what he might do when he did.

'Come on, baby,' said Jessie. 'Don't ye want me?' Even in her raddled state Jessie knew that her livelihood depended on customer satisfaction.

Tommy looked at her. He knew that he did want her, one day, one glorious day, floating on a cloud, lost in love somewhere. For now, though, all he wanted was a plan. They sat together for a further twenty minutes, Jessie lost in her dreams, Tommy's mind working furiously. Eventually, when a suitable time had passed, he got up and went to the door.

'Goodbye, Tommy,' Jessie said.

Fallowfield Community Hall, Manchester

'That were the last thing Jessie ever said to me. Because I fooked up her rescue like the stupid bastard that I am. If only I'd just left it there and then. If only I'd said, "See you tomorrow, Jess," and fooked off out of it. If only I could've had the courage t'leave her in that house for one night, leave her to half a dozen more blokes. What difference would it have made after all she'd been through? If I'd done that, then the next morning I could've gone back with the fookin' SAS! The fookin' Wehrmacht! I could've got every security bloke, every lawyer, every off-duty copper, every mercenary soldier, every gun for hire in the British Isles an' banged on that fookin' door an' said Oi! Hand over the birds! Not just Jessie, but all of them. Every one of 'em could 'a been in a safe house or a hospital or whatever by lunchtime with a civil rights team workin' on their cases, wi' me an Jessie on a private jet to the most humungously luxurious detox clinic on the planet! That's what could 'ave 'appened if I was not such a *stupid, stupid cont*!'

A brothel, Birmingham

Tommy swaggered down the stairs, a look of studied but casual arrogance on his face. 'Lovely girl. Lovely, lovely girl, that Jessie.'

'Glad you enjoyed her,' the madam replied. 'Do call again soon.'

'Well, do you know what, love? I'm that taken with the dishes on offer here I was thinkin' of seein' if I could arrange a little carry-out. Y'know what I'm sayin'? That Jessie's a top shag, but to be quite honest I don't reckon much to 'avin' to gi' 'er one in that little room, not that it in't lovely an' all that, but you know what I'm sayin'? It in't exactly romantic, right? I'm in that cubicle getting one leg caught under the basin and one bangin' against the wall an' I'm thinkin' 'ang on, I've got a top hotel suite up at the Halcyon wi' a fookin' jacuzzi bath an' I could be bangin' in that. So what I'm sayin' is, What do you charge to rent 'em out, eh? What will it cost me to take Jessie back to my hotel for a few hours?'

'I'm afraid we don't do home or hotel visits, sir. This is a brothel. What you want is an escort agency.'

'Ah, but you see Jessie works for you and it's her I want.'

'I've told you, it's not a service we provide.'

Just then Goldie appeared at the doorway. Tommy knew him from the stories that Jessie had told him in KFC.

'Two grand,' Goldie said, 'till seven a.m., then one of the boys'll pick her up.'

Tommy did not want to appear suspiciously eager. 'Two fookin' grand? Fook off! She can't turn more'n seven fifty in a night. I'll gi' you eight hundred.'

'Two grand, mate. Take it or fuck off.'

Tommy shrugged. 'All right, I don't care. I wipe me arse wi' two grand.'

'Then you're a very stupid bastard,' Goldie replied. 'Two grand's the price and not any two grand you've wiped your arse with.'

Casually Tommy produced his stolen credit cards and handed over a gold Amex. Gold? Did they have a spending limit? If they did it had to be more than two thousand, didn't it? Everything depended on the card being good for the money.

The seconds ticked by after the madam had swiped the card. Tommy tried to appear unconcerned, but every atom of his being was focused on that little telephone credit card machine. Goldie seemed almost as focused on Tommy.

'The line's busy,' the madam remarked.

Just then Jessie came into the room. No further clients having been sent up to her, she knew automatically that her job was to come down and sit in the lounge until another punter was attracted to her. Tommy smiled at her, the smile that an owner might give to a favourite dog. Inside, his nerves were quaking, but he was determined to play the part of the casual, rich dilettante for all it was worth.

'Card refused,' the madam said.

Tommy's world collapsed.

'Fook. No way! That's outrageous.'

'Not really, considering the card's been reported stolen.'

'Fook.'

The thugs who lounged casually by the walls stirred a little at this.

'Well, well,' said Goldie. 'Who's a naughty boy, then? Trying to buy birds with a nicked credit card.'

'No, you don't understand!' Tommy bleated.

'I understand very well, mate, and now it's for you to understand that you have ten seconds in which to fuck off.'

Tommy continued to gape, his mind racing, the penny dropping swiftly that his best and only move was to leave immediately. Leave her there. Leave Jessie sitting waiting for her next client.

Fallowfield Community Hall, Manchester

'I would have gone too, I think. At that point I would 'a left, but then the bastard did it, didn't he? That shit turns to Jessie an' says, "Come on, girl, you've got a living to earn here, get your tits out." Well, he done it just to 'ave a go at me, obviously. All bullies 'ave a cunning. They know how to really twist the knife, an' this bloke was just 'aving a laugh at my expense. He knew I wanted her and couldn't afford her. Punters are fallin' in love with prossies all the time, any pimp knows that, an' this cont wanted to make me squirm. So just as I'm about to leave he makes Jessie get 'er tits out. An' she did. She just takes off her sports bra and sits there in her socks and shorts wi' her tits hangin' down in front of her, her eyes a thousand miles away.

'Well, that were it. I just ran forward and grabbed her by the hand. I turns and starts to pull her to the door. Of course I didn't get two steps. I hardly got one. I don't think Jessie even raised her arse off the chair she were sittin' on. I saw the butt of a gun comin' towards me an' that was it. Nothing more.

'Not for a week, as it 'appens. That's how long it took for me to wake up from the coma they left me in. An' do you know what? When I did come round, the first thing that happens is I get arrested for the muggin' I done.'

The editor's office, a national newspaper

Sometimes, not often but sometimes, there can be just too much news. This was just such an occasion. The editor and his team had now remade Monday's front page four times.

The first version had concerned Tommy Hanson; a rival paper's Sunday-morning scoop had put all Fleet

327

Street on alert, and every single paper from red top to broadsheet carried follow-up stories commenting on the extraordinary mix of drugs, homosexuality and vote-rigging that currently swirled around Britain's biggest star, a star who seemed, not surprisingly, to have gone completely to ground.

Then, around midnight, the page had had to be made for a second time as news came in of the murder of not one but two senior Drug Squad officers. The first had been found shot in a stolen car in central London, the other in a prostitute's room in Soho. Yardie gangs were suspected of both shootings, and Scotland Yard was already hailing two new police martyrs in the war against drugs. The drugs debate had never raged so spectacularly, and never had the chances of Paget's bill getting through looked better.

Then had come the third piece of news. Peter Paget, the nation's new hero, had been finally cleared of all infection following his terrifying needle prick accident. That news surely had to share the front page with the story of the murdered Drug Squad officers, along with a front-page editorial supporting the Paget Bill.

But then had come the fourth bit of news and quite suddenly all bets were off. Every editor in London had become simultaneously aware that they had all been scooped in a quite comprehensive fashion. Paula Wooldridge, the disgraced columnist who had maintained all along that Paget was a dangerous hypocrite, had somehow produced a gorgeous young woman who was prepared to swear that she had taken drugs with him – Peter Paget, the Minister for Drugs! The family man! The man who had insisted from the beginning that he himself never touched drugs. This was truly momentous news, because if it were true then surely it was evidence that those who sought to legalize drugs were doing so in order to make their own addictions easier to maintain.

While remaking the front page for the fourth time, the editor discreetly removed his editorial supporting the Paget Bill. If Paula Wooldridge had got her facts right, positions would have to shift.

The Paget household, Dalston

Once more Peter Paget stood with his family on their now familiar front doorstep. This time his daughter Cathy stood beside him.

'As I have already made clear to the Prime Minister, the outrageous allegations that have been published about me are a wicked fabrication. Not only did I not attend a dinner party with Ms Spencer and her two friends in which cocaine was taken, but I was nowhere near Islington that night, having taken my daughter to the pictures.'

Cathy butted in holding up her diary. '*Mission Impossible 3*,' she said. 'Not bad, not great, I gave it two and a half stars at the time out of a possible five . . .'

Cathy had indeed stuck two and a half silver stars into her diary. A brilliant little detail which she knew instinctively would play well.

'Although to be quite frank one and a half of those stars is for Tom Cruise, who is, let us face it, a *babe*, and Nicole was mad to let him go.'

'Yes, well, as I was saying, my daughter and I were here in Dalston on the night in question, and we have both made statements to the police confirming that. As far as they are concerned, there are no grounds for an investigation. Therefore all that remains is the transparent attempt to blacken my name and destroy my work. I intend to answer these slurs in court.

'I should like to add that I wish Ms Spencer no ill will. She is a vulnerable and emotionally damaged girl whom I have always tried to support. She lost her father as a young child and I have long been aware that this tragedy was a seminal incident in her life. During the time I worked with Ms Spencer she developed a strong affection for me, I believe coming to see me in some ways as a father replacement figure. I'm deeply saddened that Ms Spencer's obvious psychological disturbance has led to these accusations and only hope that she comes to her senses before any further damage is done.'

Behind Peter, Angela Paget clenched her fists so hard her nails began to pierce the skin on the palms of her hands.

'I believe,' Peter continued, 'that Ms Spencer is the highly vulnerable victim of a vicious and predatory group within the media who are determined to destroy my drug legalization bill and with it the current government. This is clearly what lies behind the preposterous claims that I am a drug user. That the nation's attention should be diverted from the main issue by such trivia on the very morning after we learn that two Drug Squad officers have been murdered, two more heroes sacrificed in this ludicrous war on crime, is a tragedy indeed. The journalist responsible for this and her editor should be ashamed.'

The assembled press could hold back no longer. They didn't mind prepared statements, but this looked like it might go on a bit.

'Do you feel these allegations have damaged you at all?'

'Are the attacks political?'

'Do you intend to sue?'

Peter raised his voice above the clamour. 'I do not believe that Ms Spencer's motives are political, but those of the newspaper that is exploiting her clearly are. That is why I most definitely do intend to sue. Indeed, the proprietors are already in receipt of my lawyer's letter. Thank you. That will be all.'

Peter Paget turned and attempted to usher his family back into the house, but Cathy Paget was having none of it. She had expected Winston Churchill to appear on the doorstep and instead had got John Major. Her father's performance had been dignified, certainly, but where was the fire? Where was the passion of his parliamentary début?

'I want to say something!' she said.

'Darling . . .' her mother murmured.

'No, Mum, this is our house, our doorstep and this whole thing is just pathetic!'

'How do you mean, pathetic, Cathy?' the journalists enquired.

'Because it is. Obviously it is and you all know it. Look, first let's get one thing straight. This whole stupid scandal thing is bollocks, all right? If my dad says he didn't shag some nutty bird who worked for him then he didn't. I know him. He may be a pain in the bum, but he's not a shagger and he's not a liar. I'm telling you that straight. Plus, the drugs thing is just a joke, right, a complete sodding joke. My dad wouldn't know an E from an aspirin! He still calls skunk "pot", for Christ's sake, he's a classic boring dad, he's a square, *he brews his own beer*, guys. Think about it. How sad is that? My dad may be a bit embarrassing, but he is just so *not* a drug-taker and I've known him for sixteen years.'

Cathy was on the front step now, standing beside her bemused father while the assembled media lapped it up.

'But the point is, supposing all this stuff *was* true! Supposing he had been knocking this loser off and he *had* tried a toot of Bolivian marching powder to celebrate her birthday? And as I say that's about as likely as Paula Wooldridge who trumped this rubbish up constructing a decent sentence . . .'

Big laughs, of course, from all but the representatives of Paula's paper.

'But supposing it was true. *So what?* My dad has

made his arguments and people have listened to them. They've seen the sense in what he's saying. Finally the world's waking up to the drug madness we've created. Now you come to our doorstep and say that maybe Dad lied about his sex life and also about not taking drugs! Like I say, so what! Who cares! Who doesn't lie? You guys? Your readers? Don't make me laugh. You lot've all taken drugs, that's for sure, probably last night! Half of you will have cheated on your partners. Does that make you any less able to judge an issue? Are you people honestly so pathetically weak intellectually that you only respect my dad's arguments as long as you can respect him? That's insane! The media's gone mad! If Kennedy's womanizing had come out in the middle of the Cuban Missile Crisis, World War Three might have started while you lot asked him about his knob!'

This was truly a bravura performance. The press did not normally like being ticked off, but something about this pretty sixteen-year-old's open style was making them laugh.

'Well, let me give you a bit of news to add to all the crap you're going to write. My dad hasn't taken drugs since the odd spliff at uni, I'm sure of that. But I have! I've taken E twice so far . . .'

'Darling!' Angela Paget was astonished.

'And what's more, I've been pissed up on alcopops and I preferred E. So did my mates. What are you going to do about it? Come down our school and arrest us all? Put us on the front page? Shock horror, "Britain's monged generation!" Maybe it would be better to accept the inevitable and concentrate on making sure the stuff we take isn't cut with smack and speed.'

'Yeah!' shouted Suzie, who did not wish to be left totally out of the limelight. 'And me and my boyfriend smoked a joint!'

'You did not, Suzie,' Cathy snapped. 'I checked it out. It was dried parsley.'

'No way, it was a proper spliff!'

'It was *parsley*, Suzie.'

'Suzie! Go inside.' This was Peter Paget attempting to regain some control of the press conference.

'I think we should all go in,' said his wife through gritted teeth.

But the press were reluctant to allow such an entertaining and newsworthy event to come to an end. 'Anything to add, Cathy?' they shouted.

'Who's your parsley-dealer, Suzie?' a young man from the *Sun* enquired.

'Piss off!' Suzie Paget snapped back. 'It was grass and we got totally monged on it.'

'That's it!' Peter Paget shouted. 'Thank you, ladies and gentlemen.'

'Sorry, Mum, but I had to say something,' Cathy said as the family retreated, before turning round for one final sally.

'Whatever my dad has done, and he hasn't done anything, it's got nothing, absolutely *nothing*, to do with his bill. Just you lot remember that.'

It was probably the first time in the history of modern journalism that a full-scale doorstepping had ended with the journalists giving their prey a round of applause.

The telephone was already ringing when the family got back inside.

'It's Charlie Ansboro,' Angela said. 'He's with the PM.'

Ten Downing Street

'Paget. Fucking brilliant,' Ansboro said. 'I mean, seriously fucking unbelievable. Not you, obviously. Bog standard, over-formal, looked defensive, adequate but a bit crap, frankly. But those girls of yours! Fuck me, they're awesome. What is it? Cathy? Incredible, quite a looker, too, which always fucking helps. Well, they both are. Here's the boss.' He pressed the conference-call button on the phone so that the PM could speak to Paget.

'Peter, they played the whole thing live on Sky and BBC News 24. It was superb, honest, funny, it made the whole thing look so inconsequential. Amazing what a bit of honesty will do. We really should try it more often ourselves.'

'Bollocks,' Charlie Ansboro interjected. 'Honesty plays well from sixteen-year-old cuties. It just looks like naivety from old cunts like us.'

'Shut up, Charlie, I'm talking to Peter,' the PM snapped.

'Is young Cathy a party member? Young Socialist? Good God, do we still have them? Sounds positively Stalinist. Anyway, keep her upfront, mate, she's gold, solid gold. The public love her even more than they love you.'

The Paget household, Dalston

Peter and Angela lay in bed together. Not touching.

'You know, Peter, Cathy was so good today. So right in what she was saying, that who you are and what you do doesn't matter at all if what you're saying makes sense. If only we hadn't lied. If only we'd just admitted it. This bloody affair of yours. Now we'll never be out from under this lie as long as we live. We'll never have . . . What do the Americans call it? When you can finally walk away from something?'

'Closure,' Peter replied.

'That's it. Closure. We'll never have it.'

Something in Peter Paget stirred. 'You know what, Angela? Fuck closure. Who gives a damn about closure? I made a mistake, a terrible mistake, and you're my wife and you have to carry the burden of it with me. That's all that's happened. I had an affair and made us vulnerable and now we're fighting back. That's all, we're fighting back. And we're going to win. Good night.'

'Good night.'

A flat, West Hampstead

Kurt had just finished watching the news, which of course had led with Cathy Paget's two-fisted performance, when the doorbell began to ring. He made the mistake of answering it only once.

'Kurt, you're supporting Samantha Spencer in her story about Peter Paget, is that right?'

'Yes, that's so, but I don't wish to discuss it with you now.'

'Kurt, if Paget took cocaine who supplied it?'

'What?'

'We know that it could easily have been you, Kurt, because we've been asking around your local and you take quite a lot of drugs, don't you? Do you deal, Kurt? Could you sell us some now?'

Kurt shut the door, but the journalist outside continued his interrogation through the letterbox. 'You work for the Affiliated Union of Rail and Sea Workers, don't you, Kurt? Junior legal officer? Isn't it the case that the AURSW has recently disaffiliated from the Labour Party, Kurt? Did you not recently attend a chapel meeting in which you accused the Prime Minister of being a Tory stooge? Is your support for Samantha Spencer politically motivated, Kurt?'

When Kurt phoned his friend Laura, he discovered that she was being subjected to similar harassment.

'They're saying I'm some sort of communist junkie

drug-dealer! Just because my chambers is always fighting the government over something, they're implying I'm backing Sammy just to get at them. It's amazing.'

The spin had gone firmly against Samantha Spencer and her friends. The popularity of Peter and his cause, the honest good humour of his daughter's arguments, the obvious personal agenda of the journalist Paula Wooldridge, had kept the public firmly behind the Minister for Drugs. With the exception of Paula's own newspaper, the media were currently proceeding under the assumption that Spencer and her friends had formed a conspiracy to destroy Paget.

The following morning photographs of both Samantha and Laura topless on their respective holidays appeared in all the papers.

Birmingham Central Hospital

Only one figure was sufficiently newsworthy to intrude briefly on the media feeding frenzy engulfing the Paget family and Samantha Spencer and her associates as they moved towards the libel action brought by Peter Paget against his accusers. That figure was Tommy Hanson.

Tommy was unconscious, in the coma in which Goldie and his henchman had left him a couple of streets away from the brothel in which Jessie was imprisoned. For a week the identity of the unconscious man had remained a mystery. The man in the coma was clearly not the man whose clothes he had been wearing. He was a thief who had mugged a passerby, taken his clothes and credit cards and paid for a prostitute on the strength of them before falling foul of some gang of toughs or other. Now, as the unconscious man's bruises and his swollen face began to heal, the nurses began to notice an increasing resemblance to the country's most famous pop star, who had also been famously reported missing on the day after the unconscious man had been admitted to hospital.

That *Tommy*, the press reported. Muggings, prostitutes? What would he get up to next?

Parkinson, *BBC TV Centre*

'My next guest is never out of the news and seemingly never out of trouble. Only three months ago he was a guest on the first programme of this series, having been arrested for crowd-surfing down Oxford Street. Now he faces charges of a much more serious nature. It seems that Tommy Hanson held a man at knifepoint, stole his clothes and his money and used the latter to visit a brothel. He is currently remanded on bail and he's with us tonight. Ladies and gentlemen, Tommy Hanson.'

The applause that greeted Tommy was as warm as ever. The public still loved their Tom, and why wouldn't they? Anybody who could surprise and entertain them as consistently as Tommy did was fine by them. Besides, as always Tommy played it beautifully. No cocky swagger this time, instead naughty-boy body language and please-forgive-me eyes. He stood at the top of the stairs for a full minute while the applause, which had been warm to begin with, grew and grew. Tommy worked the crowd with nothing more than his eyes, eyes that said it all ... I'm sorry, but I'm mad, me, what can I tell you? It's tough being a tortured boy genius, but I promise I'll try to be good.

After a few brief words of greeting, Michael Parkinson got straight to the point. 'Tommy. What the hell did you think you were doing?'

'Parky, I screwed up big time, but I've come on here to tell the world why I done it. First an' foremost, I 'ave t'say a public sorry to the bloke I pointed the knife at . . .'

'And I believe he has already accepted your apology.'

'For sure, Parky, for sure. We're mates because I told him why I done it an' got his little kids in to see S Club.'

'And why did you do it, Tommy?'

'Eh, straight to the point, Parky. I like that, that's why you're the king.'

'Well, I do my best.'

'And fair play to you.'

'So why did you do it, Tommy?'

'Love, Parky. I done it for love.'

'You mugged a man for love?'

'Yes, I did. Let me tell you 'ow it 'appened.'

'Please do.'

'I'd been stitched up by this journo, see, the one who done all that crap about me winning *Pop Hero* 'cos I give a couple o' hand jobs t'the judge, which I in't denying but that's not why I won, right. Plus, I'm not gay even though there's nowt wrong wi' bein' gay. I just in't, that's all. Least I in't till I've 'ad three tabs o' sextasy, that's for sure.'

'In vino veritas, Tommy. In vino veritas.'

'Eh?'

'It means that wine or in this case drugs often reveals the truth about a man.'

'Yeah? Well, I've 'ad more drugs than they've got at Boots, an' the only thing they reveal is the tosser in the man, which is what I'm saying, 'cos that's exactly what I done to that *Pop Hero* judge.'

Tommy took a sip of water while Parky and the audience applauded his good-humoured honesty.

'All right, so you'd been stitched up,' Parky reminded Tommy. 'What next?'

'Well, I chucked a total mental and stormed out into the night, didn't I? Just buggered off inta a Brummie

338

Saturday night and ended up getting the crap kicked out o' me. Honest, it were like *Trading Places* or whatever. I wake up, nobody can recognize me, I've got no phone, no money, me office an' all that is closed, me manager wouldn't 'ave 'eard the phone anyway 'cos Sundays he's always got 'is 'ead stuck between the pendulous breasts of a busty model . . . So that's it, I ain't Tommy Hanson superstar any more, I'm Tommy Anonymous street kid, an' that's what I'm gonna be till the following morning . . .'

'Amazing.'

'Yes, Parky, amazing an' horrible. Really, truly horrible. If anybody out there wants any proof that kids don't beg on the streets for fun, just give it an hour or two. It were absolutely terrible, Parky. Cold, filthy, terrifying.'

'Is that why you mugged someone, because you were cold?'

'No way, Parky, no way. Listen, mugging that bloke took every ounce o' courage I 'ad. I were more scared than 'im, I swear. It takes something very special to push a bloke to do somethin' like that and in my case it were love.'

'You met someone, on the streets?'

'Yes, I did, a girl called Jessie, the loveliest girl I ever saw or ever will see . . .'

'What happened? How did you meet?'

'I were trying to nick her coat.'

'You tried to mug her too?'

'No! I just thought it were an empty coat in the doorway. But it weren't, it were Jessie, an' when them big dark eyes looked up at me in that Marks an' Sparks doorway I knew I was gone, an' I was, an' I still am. But let me tell you, Parky, that girl had the toughest life you can imagine. She were abused at home so she ran away, right? Came to London, starving, homeless, got picked up by a pimp, who introduced her to smack and that were that. Just seventeen an' a junkie prossie. Y'see this is why that Peter Paget bloke's so right. The whole criminal drug subculture is a trap, man, it's a trap for the weak and defenceless. Once Jessie were hooked there was nowhere for her to go but to the people that abused her . . .'

'You support Peter Paget?'

'Yeah, I do. If he'd 'a been around a few years ago Jessie would never have ended up like she did.'

'And where did she end up?'

'In a brothel in Brum, right, but get this. She actually managed to kick smack on her own while she were workin' as a whore and then she ran away. That's when I met her, Parky, while I were a street kid for a day. I met her an' she shared her food and her coat wi' me.'

'And you fell in love with her?'

'Yeah, I reckon I did. At least I swore t'God I were goin' to 'elp her find a new life. The day we spent together sittin' in a KFC an' then in doorways was the most important of my life. It were the day I discovered that there are more important things in the world than Tommy Hanson . . . almost everything, in fact.'

'But you lost her.'

Tears welled up in Tommy's eyes. 'Yes, I did. Her pimps found her an' took her back, and I followed her to where they took her. But I were a street kid, remember. There was no way they'd 'a' let me through the door o' that house they put her in . . .'

'And that's when you stole another man's clothes?'

'I had to, Parky. The girl I loved 'ad been stolen away.'

'And you went into the brothel?'

'Yes, I did, but they'd already give her a needleful o' scag, and she were just totally monged out, selling her body, so I tried to grab her and run and they beat me up bad and that were the end of that . . .'

'You were in a coma for a week.'

340

'That's right, and when I come out, after the judge released me on bail, I got all my people, right? I'm on the phone t'my management team sayin' I want all my people right here right now. So I've got like an army o' people, two coachloads, one muscle the other brains, an' I'm in front in a white stretch 'cos when I save her I want it t'be like a cowboy on a white horse, an' we drove through Birmingham an' I went back to that house to get my Jessie an' also all the other girls which I knew was what Jessie would want ... But when we got there it were empty, Parky. Because o' the beating I'd took an' the fact that the last credit card transaction 'ad been from there, the police went an' had a look at the place an' it all broke up because the blokes what run establishments like that one know how to keep their exits covered. They just moved on, takin' Jessie with them. I've lost 'er, Parky. She's gone, evaporated, disappeared into the air. Except I know she's out there somewhere an' I intend to find her. I will, Parky, I've given up me career, I've kicked the booze an' drugs, this time for real. I'll take whatever the law wants to throw at me for mugging that bloke and I'll find Jessie if it takes me as long as I live.'

Some of the women in the audience were moved to tears at Tommy's anguish. Even Parky dabbed at an eye.

'Good luck, Tommy, and when you find her come and see us again, all right?'

A brothel, Birmingham

Perhaps the person who was moved most of all was the madam of Goldie's premier brothel, which while having changed location remained essentially the same institution as it had been before. The madam, whose name was Nina, was passing the dull hours during

341

which the sad, haunted-looking clients came and went, by watching *Parkinson*. And with growing astonishment she recognized the distraught superstar on the screen as the bruised and cocky jack the lad who had tried to buy one of her girls on a stolen credit card and had been beaten senseless for his pains. Nina could scarcely believe the truth as it sank into her slightly stoned and brandy-raddled brain. Goldie and his boys had nearly killed *Tommy Hanson*! There was a girl working upstairs with whom Tommy Hanson was *in love*. As Nina struggled to get her mind around the scale of her discovery she heard footsteps. One of Goldie's boys was approaching. How fortunate she had been that he had had to go to the lavatory at the exact time when Tommy had been describing Jessie's story. It was just possible that the penny might have dropped for him as it had done for her. How fortunate also that the girls who sat about waiting for clients spoke no English and were too out of it to bother much with Nina's nine-inch portable TV anyway.

Nobody knew the truth but Nina. Quickly she turned the television to another channel, thrilling plans already forming in her mind.

Cambridge Technical College

The moment Peter Paget mentioned to Charlie Ansboro that he was not the first victim of Samantha Spencer's obsession with older men the Prime Minister's Press Secretary had seen that it was the knock-out punch that would bury the scandal for good. He spun the story carefully, placing just a hint of it with a trusted ex-colleague who was currently working for *The Times*. The journalist had traced the disgraced ex-Professor of Politics and Modern History's story in exactly the same manner as Peter Paget had done, reviewing back issues of the *Cambridge Evening News*. Perhaps not surprisingly, ex-Professor Crozier had been cautious of the press at first but after a little persuasion had poured out his story eagerly.

'She ruined me, there's no doubt about that,' he said. 'I have no idea whether Peter Paget had sex with Samantha Spencer or not, but I did and I have never for one moment denied it. I am not proud of the incident. I was thirty-seven and in a position of authority, but she was an intelligent nineteen-year-old, and what I did was not a crime. We made love only twice, but she claimed I had harassed her. She claimed numerous private tutorials had taken place during which I coerced her into sex. This was a complete lie. I have always followed a policy of never taking private tutorials, and she had no supporting evidence whatsoever. Nonetheless, in the atmosphere of the time everything she said was believed and everything I said was dismissed.'

The man from the newspaper murmured sympathetically while being inwardly thrilled.

'As I say, I was ruined, and I now teach as a lecturer at a technical college,' the ex-Professor continued. 'The stigma of harassment has hung over me to this day. Now I see that this damaged girl is at her tricks again. What's more, her victim on this occasion is a very important man, a man who may just be in the process of changing society for the good. Those are the stakes. My disgrace is unimportant, except, of course, to me and my loved ones. But if Samantha Spencer succeeds, through some wounded sexual pride or some misplaced sense of filial betrayal, in bringing down Peter Paget, she may very well succeed in bringing down an entire generation with her, a generation that will be forced like previous generations into the hands of criminals . . .'

The Editor's office, a national newspaper

Paula Wooldridge was almost too upset to speak. Milton, on the other hand, was beside himself with glee. The awful weeks during which Paula had been the toast of the newspaper, bestriding its narrow confines like a colossus, were over. The sensational effort to bring down Peter Paget, which had begun so stunningly promisingly, had collapsed in ignominy. The paper was discredited, the financial cost would be huge, and Milton as a loyal employee was absolutely delighted.

'It's still three to two,' Paula protested, but even she did not sound convinced.

'Yes!' her editor yelled. 'Three to two . . . and let's just look at those five witnesses, shall we, you fucking idiot! On our side we have two cynical commies, both habitual drug-takers, one a dealer—'

'Oh, come on. Dealer? Who hasn't sold a wrap of charlie to a mate?'

'Brilliant! And perhaps you'd like to make that point to a libel jury, Paula.'

'Sammy's friends are entirely ordinary, respectable, professional—'

'I don't care what they *are*, you bloody fool! I care what they look like, and the rest of the media have made that decision for us. They look like a couple of sharp-operating, coke-snorting, posh snob bastards, and everybody hates them. Then, queen of the bunch, you have your darling Sammy, an embittered, emotionally retarded, tit-flashing slapper of an ex-employee—'

'Tit-flashing slapper!'

'Yes, tit-flashing slapper! They've dug up so many topless shots of that bird I'm sick of the sight of them.'

'These days lots of girls go topless when they're on holiday.'

'And of course they all flash them about at student parties, don't they, Paula?' This was Milton, who had been privately delighted when a rival paper had unearthed shots of Samantha at a May Week Ball obliging some fellow student's camera by popping one of her breasts out from the front of her strapless evening gown. 'Five of her Cambridge boyfriends have come forward so far, Paula. They all have the same story: nasty little cockteaser, egged them on, then watched them squirm.'

'On top of which, the broadsheets are getting in on the act. Did you see yesterday's *Times*?'

Paula had done but she pretended otherwise.

'They've got this fucking old Professor of Politics who reckons your precious Sammy has been in the business of destroying her seniors before . . .'

The editor hurled the newspaper down, the front page of which carried yet another sexy photograph of Samantha Spencer, although in deference to the serious journalistic traditions of that newspaper it was not a topless shot. Milton had brought along his own copy of the rival paper and quoted the headline eagerly. 'Paget not first victim of unbalanced graduate.' He smirked.

Professor Crozier's intervention had been a bombshell, and Samantha Spencer's entire psychologically disturbed history suddenly became public knowledge. Medical reports were leaked, anonymous therapists spoke out.

'So that's your three witnesses!' The editor shouted directly into Paula's face, flecks of his spittle falling on her glasses. 'Two druggy lefties and a fucking father-fixated bunny-boiler. They, on the other hand, as you so rightly point out, have only two witnesses, witnesses who just happen to be the two most popular people in the fucking country! Paget, a man who took on his own party and the entire parliamentary establishment to alert society to the dangers it is facing.

A man who risked contracting Aids in order to protect teenaged girls from a drug addict's needle, a man whose lovely wife stands behind him . . . Plus . . . *plus* Cathy Paget, media star *numero uno*! The one who first caught the attention of the world by demolishing . . . who was it? Remind me again? Oh yes, of course, it was *you*, wasn't it, Paula? You, the embittered nasty old hack who just happens to be the person who produces this ludicrous drugs and sex conspiracy against her father now. Cathy Paget, giant killer, the little girl who taught the press a thing or two about honest dealing, out of the mouths of babes and fucking sucklings!'

'You know she's been offered a record deal,' Milton added, 'and they want her to join the *Newsnight* team to give a youth perspective.' Milton could not conceal his glee in imparting this thrilling information, information which, had Paula not heard it already, would have been a knife to her heart.

The editor hardly even heard what Milton had said. 'So, *Paula*, we have the most trusted and popular politician in the country plus the most trusted and popular *fucking person* in the country saying that they were at the pictures together watching a Tom Cruise movie on the night when *your* bunch of sad acts claim he was sitting in Islington snorting cocaine and shagging birds not much older than his daughter. Tell me, Paula, bearing in mind the British public's natural love of a conspiracy theory, given their almost pathological suspicion of the press, given the fact that you've spent the last five months attacking Paget, given that, as Cathy Paget so succinctly pointed out, her dad does not look like a fucking cokehead! Who do you think the jury are going to believe?'

'All I know is that I trust Samantha Spencer.'

'Do you? Well, I'm delighted to hear it—'

'And I believe that when the libel jury gets the

chance to hear the detail of her story they may well trust her too . . .'

Paula's editor was suddenly more surprised than angry. 'Excuse me! You don't actually think we're going to let this *go* to fucking court, do you?'

Paula was horrified. 'You mean . . . you're going to settle?'

'Of course we're going to fucking settle! Haven't you been listening to me? If we go to court we'll get *killed*. A halfway competent brief with Cathy Paget in the dock will run rings round us! It's damage control now. We're going to offer half a million plus an abject apology—'

'Apology! But . . . but that means . . . I'll be disgraced. You're throwing me to the wolves.'

'Well, the apology's not going to look particularly sincere if we still see fit to employ such a monumental and immoral fantasist as yourself, is it?'

'You mean . . .'

'Yes, that's it, Paula. You're fired. Now fuck off.'

'Yes, fuck right off out of it,' Milton added, somewhat redundantly.

Pop Goes the Weekend, *BBC TV Centre*

Cathy Paget was the star guest on *Pop Goes the Weekend*, the BBC's flagship Saturday-morning pop show. Chloe was the show's new presenter, having been recently promoted from a similar show on cable. After she had been seen in the Met Bar with Tommy Hanson and front paged exiting from his Notting Hill home the following morning, the BBC Children's Department saw her as an obvious choice.

Cathy Paget was appearing in the phone-in part of the show, a section called 'Press Gang', in which the young audience was invited to interrogate a celebrity.

'OK, let's go to the phones again,' said Chloe in an excited manner, fuelled not exclusively by strong coffee. 'We have Tawny from Bradford.'

'Hullo, Chloe, I'd like to ask Cathy is she worried that her father's bill will make more kids take drugs?'

'Top question, Tawns, mental. Go, Cath.'

Cathy smiled prettily, looking as if she had been on television all her life. She was six years younger than Chloe, but she made the professional presenter look like an over-excited fraud. Cathy Paget was no fraud, she was genuinely warm, sexy, authoritative and utterly convincing. A true natural in everything she did.

'Well, I suppose it's possible, Tawny, but alcohol is legal and also highly addictive, and not everyone who drinks it is an alcoholic, are they? I suppose the point is that even if, say, twice as many kids became drug-takers as currently take them, and I doubt that would happen, then better for it to be out in the open and properly regulated and protected than run by gangsters.'

'Top answer, Cath, mental,' Chloe assured her. 'Let's go to Billy from Fife.'

'I want to ask Cathy what her dad will do with the half-million pounds he got because the papers lied about him.'

'As I think most people know, he's giving it to charity, to drug rehabilitation charities, in fact, but let me tell you this. Me and my sister Suzie have told him he's got to keep ten grand of it for a cracking, top-notch, totally humungous holiday! Well, why not? Four hundred and ninety thou to charity and a nice ten K for us to have a laugh together as a family. Because you know what, Billy? These last months have been quite stressful for us, what with Dad's campaign and then him getting that needle jab, plus all these media smears. I reckon we've earnt a holiday courtesy of the press!'

The whole studio cheered. Even the camera crews and harassed floor managers joined in. Without even trying, Cathy had got it just right again. Charity, yes, but let's not be boring about it, eh? She was a breath of fresh air.

'Top question, top answer, Cath babes,' Chloe gushed. This was a girl with nervous energy to spare. What was more, her energy seemed to increase every time she found a moment to pop to the ladies.

'Now, Cathy, as you know, we get loads and loads of emails, and we've never had a bigger response than you've got. It's true, babes, and how good is that? And the big question everybody wants to know the answer to is: *Why aren't you Prime Minister*?!'

The entire studio erupted once more into cheering.

'Well, Chloe,' Cathy said, once the noise had died down. 'I definitely want to go into politics like my dad, and like him I want to do it because I believe in things. I know that a lot of things need changing and if you want to make a difference it's no good sitting around on your bum complaining about them. You have to get involved and do your bit. So I'll definitely have a go at getting into politics, after uni, of course, because it's really important to get an education before anything else. And then? Well, we'll see what happens. I'm only sixteen, so who knows? You have to dream, don't you?'

'Big up to that, babes. Big up to that.'

Fallowfield Community Hall, Manchester

'So after I done *Parky*, I come up here, which is why I'm attendin' a self-help group in Fallowfield, Lancashire. An' why am I doin' that, you may well ask? Well, the self-help thing is because this time I really am going to stay clean. I owe that to Jessie. I'm goin' to go to all me NA and AA meetings an' get through all me points an' get to the fookin' serenity bit if it kills me. It's no good searchin' for a bird to save if you're pissed up an' totally monged, is it? You'll never find 'er that way, will you? And as for me bein' here in Fallowfield, well, as it 'appens, right now, personally, I prefer it to London's glamorous fookin' West End anyway, an' also I'm 'avin' a week up here lookin' for Jessie. Got a lead, see. I get leads all the time, ever since *Parky*. People keep ringin' me up sayin' they saw a skinny bird wi' big eyes an' nice tits beggin' here or solicitin' there. There's plenty of girls like Jessie in the world, believe me, an' young lads in trouble too, an' that's something else I'm going to do. I'm goin' to set up fookin' centres to help all them young people. Cool places wi' decent cheap food and guitars and computers or whatever, an' get this, I in't even going to put me name on 'em. How surprising is that? Tommy Hanson, the ego what landed, not puttin' his name on something. I'm goin' to do it through the Prince's Trust. I've already had a meetin'. I know everybody's laughing at me, drug-fooked Tommy falls for a bird he's known for a day then fookin' makes a twat of himself on telly over her an' suddenly he reckons he's Mother T'-fookin'-resa, but I don't give a fook, me. I'm going to make summat o' what I've got. I'm goin' to 'elp other people and what's more I'm goin' to find Jessie. I'm going to look in every doorway and dosshouse, every knockin' shop, every drop-in centre, every fookin' morgue if I have to. But I will *fookin' find her!*'

Tommy's mobile rang. It was not strictly speaking good etiquette to have one's mobile switched on in such a meeting, but Tommy didn't care. He was determined never to be incommunicado again. At least until he found her. Then perhaps he'd turn off all the phones . . . if she wanted him to.

A motorway service station, M6

The phonecall had been from Tommy's tour manager. He had news. Nina, the madam from Goldie's brothel, had called Tommy's management office telling them that she knew where the girl was. The office had immediately put her on to Tony, who did all of Tommy's fixing, and he had arranged a meeting according to the woman's instructions.

It was lunchtime in a busy service station. Tony had been there since eleven holding the specific table Nina had asked for against all comers. Using a second driver, Tommy had joined him at twelve twenty-five, heavily disguised, of course.

'Funny how I always used to love service stations when we were on the road,' Tommy remarked. 'It were a good laugh then, weren't it?'

'Can't say they ever did a lot for me, Tom,' Tony said wearily. 'But it were your tour. You were in charge.'

At twelve thirty on the dot a woman approached them, heavily made up with absurdly pouting collagen lips, and a look of permanent surprise imparted by one eye tuck too many. The woman put her coffee on the table and sat down. She did not introduce herself. 'As I told you on the phone, I know where the girl is.' She slid a photograph across the table. It was a Polaroid shot of Jessie, who was holding a copy of that morning's newspaper.

'I can bring her to you,' the woman continued, 'but it's dangerous. The people who're keeping her are very violent. I want a million euros, half now, half later.'

'Yeah, we know, you already told us,' Tommy said. 'Tone, give it her.'

Tony was very unhappy. 'Tom, this is blackmail. Blackmail plus slavery. We should take this woman straight to the police.'

351

Nina pushed her coffee cup away from her and got up. 'If you do that you'll never see Jessie again. Don't forget, her owner is part of an international operation. He could send her overseas any day now. We move our girls about all the time. Punters like a bit of something new.'

Tommy stared into his tea, trying to master his emotions. His every waking moment was plagued with thoughts of what was happening to Jessie. His dreams were worse. 'Pay her the money, Tony.'

'And what's to stop this woman just going off overseas herself?'

Nina had the answer to that. 'The other five hundred grand, of course. You think I'm going to walk away from that? Now listen to me, you do not have any time to lose, all right? Like I say, these people are very dangerous, and Jessie is no more than a sack of flour or a side of beef to them. A commodity. Who knows what plans they have for her? By next week she could be in Holland being forced to suck donkeys' dicks for underground videos. Or worse. I've seen rape films, even snuff ones.'

'Give her the money, Tony.'

Tony put a small steel flight case onto the table.

The woman took the bag and got up. 'You have the instructions for the exchange,' she said, her big, pointy, puffed-up mouth making her look like some sort of fish. 'You'll have the girl back tomorrow.'

Samantha's flat, Islington

It was eleven o'clock in the morning on the eleventh day of the month. Samantha read her poem aloud to herself. Eleven lines of predictable rhymes in which she spoke of her shame in ever imagining that anyone could ever take the place of her father. This fundamental mistake was, Samantha felt, what had brought all the troubles down upon her head. The public shaming of her, her mother, her friends. The media had created an image of her as some sort of man-eating monster who spun webs of lies around innocent, noble figures, destroying their careers while frolicking naked about the place at pretty much any opportunity.

It was all so unfair. Samantha had never imagined the press could be so cruel and misleading. If ever there was a girl whose breasts were less likely to appear in the newspapers it was Samantha, and yet now the entire country was almost sick of the sight of them, if Britain's newspaper readers could ever be said to be sick of naked breasts.

'Sorry, Daddy,' she said as she put the poem into a saucepan and set it alight. 'There was only ever one decent man in this world, I know that now,' she said to the picture of her father that she conjured up out of the flames and smoke.

Then Samantha counted out the sleeping pills into lines of eleven. There were thirty-five in all, so she discarded two of them, and at eleven minutes past eleven she began methodically to eat the first line.

She did it very, very slowly, because in truth she did not actually want to die. For this reason she decided that it would be fitting for her to eat one pill every eleven minutes, and so she had fallen asleep long before completing the first line. When she awoke she felt sick but in a way rather better.

She had tried, honorably, to kill herself, and she had failed. Her father clearly did not want her to die. What he wanted was for her to fight back. What he wanted was closure.

A brothel, Birmingham

Nina had thought long and hard about how best to spirit Jessie from Goldie's establishment. She had agonized over whether it would be best to try to get her out of the front door while the girl sat awaiting a new client or to wait until the morning lull when the girls slept and try to sneak her down the stairs while the establishment was at comparative rest. Eventually she decided on the latter and had crept up to the girls' dormitory, almost identical to the one from which Jessie had escaped only a few weeks before.

'Jessie . . . *Jessie*!' she hissed, shaking the girl from her drug-induced slumber. 'Come with me. I'm going to get you out of here.'

At first Jessie refused to move. She did not understand what was going on and the heroin in her system had made her lethargic. Eventually Nina got Jessie partially to her senses and together they crept down the stairs, past the rooms in which the girls performed their labours and into the viewing foyer. Here there would normally be a couple of Goldie's men lounging about the place, but it was a Monday morning, the slowest time of the week, and Nina reckoned that they would be downstairs in the kitchen going about their usual activities, making coffee or freebasing crack to sell. The room was empty and Nina led Jessie towards the front door.

It was locked.

This was a considerable shock to Nina, who held the keys and had checked that it was open only a few minutes before. The mystery was soon solved when the terrifying face of Goldie appeared from behind one of the couches.

'Peek-a-boo. I see you,' he said, grinning through his gold teeth.

'Hello, Goldie,' Nina stuttered. 'I was just—'

'You were just what, babes?'

'A client. We had a call ... He wanted Jessie. I thought I heard him at the door.'

Goldie went to the door and looked through the little hatch. 'Nobody out there, Nina.'

Nina had no answer.

'You were stealing my property, weren't you, Nina? That's what you was doing. You gotta understand that a man does not survive long in my line of business without being naturally suspicious, see? So when my madam says to me she needs a morning off an' a car to borrow on a specific date, I'm suspicious ...'

Two of Goldie's men joined them from the next room. 'So I had Bernie and Jah here follow you just to see what was up an' lo an' behold you has some sort of meeting in a service station, of all things! Hardly the sort of place a glamorous girl like you would choose to spend her morning off. Give us your keys, will you, darling? You won't be needing your set any more.'

Nina handed them over and Goldie walked around her and Jessie and slipped the bolts back on the front door. 'We never close, eh? Although someone else is going to have to greet the clients till I can get a new door bitch.'

'Please, Goldie,' Nina spluttered.

Goldie was enjoying his little moment of drama. He sat down at a table and produced a big bag of rocks of crack cocaine. He felt that he had earned a celebration and began to prepare a pipe. 'And what do Bernie and Jah see happen at this weird little Road Chef rendezvous? Why, only a fuckin' bag drop. Only a fuckin' dump!'

Jah now produced the flight case that Tony had given to Nina.

'Broke into your flat this morning, Nina,' Jah said. 'Hidden in a kitchen binliner. Not bad, too big for the cistern, after all.'

'Got fucking scrambled egg and yoghurt on me strides,' Bernie interjected.

'Now what we need to know, Nina, is who the *fuck* is paying you *half a million fucking euros* for this little slagbag, who is quite frankly three parts shagged out already.'

Jessie was not listening to the conversation. Her consciousness was drifting about the place on a drug-fuelled cloud. However, one firm thought was beginning to coalesce in her head, pushed to the surface on crystals of amphetamine.

The thought was that Goldie had unlocked the door.

'You see, I just presumed,' Goldie was saying, putting his arm around Nina's shoulder, 'that you was trying to get into my trade, flogging birds to other cunts like me, so frankly I was just going to kill you straight off. But then when we found all this money I started to wonder. Now I got to tell you that little Jessie here is cute, I'll give you that, and she's still got a bit of youth and strength about her, useful bit of goods, no doubt. I'd pay three, maybe five thousand for her ... The Albanians might give you five hundred and a herd of fucking sheep. But half a million euros, three hundred and fifty thousand quid? Like I say, Nina, who the *fuck* wants Jessie that much?'

'I'll tell you if you promise to split the—'

Nina's suggestion ended in a dull, agonized exhalation of air as Goldie buried his fist in her stomach.

'You'll tell me anyway, darling ... Pick her up.'

Bernie and Jah picked up the groaning woman and slammed her against the wall, holding her there while Goldie shoved his face into hers.

'So, let's have the question again, shall we?'

Jessie still wasn't listening; she was trying to focus. Focus on a series of observations. Beyond the table Goldie and his men were busy with Nina. On the table was Goldie's bag of rocks of crack and the set of keys that he had taken from Nina. Jessie was standing near the table, and behind her was the front door.

And nobody was looking at her.

Goldie, Bernie and Jah were staring at Nina and Nina, a hand choking her neck, was pleading with Goldie.

Jessie slipped off her stiletto-heeled shoes and took two silent steps towards the table. Still she went unnoticed. Now she reached forward and gathered up the bag of drugs and the keys, terrified that the keys would tinkle as she lifted them.

Nina was choking loudly as Goldie tightened his grip upon her throat. 'Who were you selling her to, bitch?'

Jessie walked backwards to the door as Goldie continued gleefully.

'Do you know what? I think I know. Yeah, see, I don't read the papers much, but Jah here does and he saw something in them the other day about a pop star. Tommy Hanson, no less, looking for a bird, a bird he'd met in Birmingham . . .'

Jessie opened the door. The latch was well oiled and efficient. Goldie needed to be able to trust his locks; in his business doors needed to shut quickly and cleanly. The hinges were in equally good repair and the door swung open noiselessly. Jessie stepped through it and shut it behind her. Then, from the outside, she inserted the Chubb key into the deadlock and turned it.

Only then did the thugs inside notice that Jessie was no longer in the room.

But even as they realized this, once more Jessie was running from one of Goldie's houses. It would take Goldie over a minute to descend into the kitchen, get his own keys from his coat and return to the front door. Even then he would not be able to open it, for Jessie had had either the good sense or simple good fortune to leave the Chubb key in the outside lock. Goldie would not get his key in. He would need tweezers and a nailfile to work out the key that Jessie had left.

She was free.

The House of Commons, Westminster

It was, as Peter Paget and the Prime Minister had both predicted, one of the most radical and reforming monarch's speeches in the history of the British Parliament. George VI, Queen Elizabeth's father, had announced the nationalization of health and medicine; Edward VII, her great-grandfather, had delivered the great Liberal reforming budget that introduced old-age pensions, but nothing had ever quite electrified the country and indeed the entire world as the speech prepared by Peter Paget, Minister for Drugs, for Elizabeth II to deliver.

'My government,' she said, 'will introduce legislation to legalize, license and control all recreational drugs.'

Peter Paget had achieved that thing denied to most men and women: he had fulfilled his destiny.

Simpson's Restaurant

After the State Opening of Parliament, Peter hosted a splendid lunch for family, colleagues and friends at Simpson's on the Strand. When the Paget family entered the restaurant every diner in the room rose to applaud them. There was a genuine sense of celebration in the air. The general consensus was that Britain had finally broken the terrifying deadlock which the drugs war had imposed upon society for so long. Once more the British were world leaders, and, whatever the future held, at least something new was finally being tried. Of course there were many doubts, the greatest fear being that young people would simply descend into a life-long drug-induced stupor, but in reality people asked themselves, How likely is that? The nation was not continually drunk, and the use of tobacco, one of the most highly addictive drugs of all, was on the decrease. The popular presumption was that if a man of such obvious intelligence and integrity as Peter Paget, a man who could produce such an extraordinary daughter as Cathy Paget, felt that all would be well, then surely all would be well. Besides, as was said over and over again on that happy day, really, who cared how many drug addicts there were as long as they were not breaking into one's home and mugging one's granny for a fiver?

At the end of the meal Peter Paget rose to make a speech.

'Today, as you all know, is a very special day for Britain and in particular for me. I have been truly fortunate in having been able to be the guiding hand in what is clearly a world-historical piece of legislation. Many kind voices have been joined in my praise and I cannot deny that it is sweet indeed to suddenly find oneself loved and admired after so many years of feeling that one's voice would never be heard. But today as we sit here, family, friends and colleagues, I should like to state unequivocally that I do not deserve one iota of the praise and good wishes that have been heaped upon me. For whatever the country owes me, I owe tenfold to my wife, Angela, and so it is in Angela's debt not mine that the country now finds itself.'

There was of course much cheering at this, although Cathy Paget noted that her mother did not smile or look up.

'And what I should like to say right here and now is

that I am nothing, nothing whatsoever without Angela. She is my life and my love and the enabler of all my happiness. I adore her and I thank her from the bottom of my heart for her kindness and patience in the face of my imbecility and my far too common weaknesses. I love you, Angela, and I'll love you for ever.'

There was a brief silence. Peter had clearly finished and stood looking at his wife. Angela eventually returned his look with an attempt at a smile, but she seemed strangely unmoved by such a glowing tribute. The assembled company were a little perplexed. Nobody knew what to say. As was now becoming common in the Paget family, Cathy saved the day. She had noted her mother's apparent unhappiness and she did not understand it. More urgently, however, she had noticed that an embarrassed silence had fallen on what had until then been a very jolly lunch. What was more, the embarrassment was spreading to other tables. Damage control was required, a bit of family spin.

Cathy got to her feet. 'Dad never did know how to end a speech,' she said, and then, raising her glass, 'To Angela and Peter Paget, my mother and father.'

The toast was enthusiastically drunk and the embarrassment passed.

Samantha's flat, Islington

'For God's sake, there must be something! Some small thing proving he's been here,' Laura said, her head emerging from beneath Samantha's bed.

'He doesn't deny he's been here,' Kurt pointed out rather testily from a stepladder from which he was inspecting the top of a cupboard. 'He admits he was here many times, working with Sammy. That's how he's got away with it.'

'Look!' Samantha said. 'He shagged me in this flat

360

loads and loads of times. We live in a DNA world. He must have left some trace.'

'What? Cum on the sheets? Sammy, you're the cleanest woman I ever knew, you wash your sheets every other day.'

'I know, I know. That's why I haven't found anything till now, but we've never really *looked*, I mean really torn the place apart . . . I don't know what I'm hoping to find, but we have to search every single millimetre of this flat until we find *something* – a note, a condom, a hotel check-in receipt signed by the bastard. *Something* that links him sexually with me!'

And so they searched. Samantha shed tears over every diary entry that she had written about her love for Peter Paget but found nothing in his hand beyond a few discarded parliamentary notes, with not so much as a love heart or SWALK scrawled in the margin.

'It's quite obvious that he deliberately left no traces from the very start,' Kurt observed.

They examined every bill and receipt. They looked under carpets, between floorboards and between the neatly piled pairs of spotlessly clean knickers in Samantha's underwear drawers.

'The bastard bought me these,' Samantha said, holding up the lingerie which had been his first present to her. 'But I can't prove it. I'll throw them out, I think.'

'I'll have them,' Laura said.

Then Kurt pulled the black plastic binliner out of the swingbin in the kitchen.

'You can't be going to search that,' Samantha protested. 'That's only the last couple of days' rubbish. Paget hasn't been here for ages.'

'You may have only just thrown something away that was left from his time . . . I don't know, a match book with the number of your preferred sex shop on it, a pair of his underpants you've been using as a rag . . . We said we'd search everything.'

'You're right, we must,' Samantha replied, although she was beginning to lose enthusiasm for what was looking like a thankless task. Then she happened to glance into the empty swingbin. Into that unpleasant place normally concealed by the binliner, which in most kitchens means a soiled tissue or two and a squashed carrot made all moist by the rank liquid residue from leaking binliners.

But Samantha's swingbin was not like that. Samantha emptied her bag long before it burst and leaked. There were never any soiled tissues lurking beneath the bags in Samantha's bin. It was pristine.

Except not quite. There at the bottom Samantha saw two tiny bits of rubbish. Two screwed-up bits of paper rolled into tiny balls, each not much bigger than a pea. One was the pale yellow of a credit-card till receipt, the other was shiny white – the shiny white of a Switch payment slip.

The Cabinet Room, Ten Downing Street

The Cabinet were busy discussing how to distribute the predicted cash bonanza that drug legalization would surely bring. Even if tens of billions of pounds were put aside for hospital services on the unproven prediction that addiction would rise dramatically, there would still be countless billions left over.

'The police will be dripping with surplus,' the Home Secretary grinned. 'We won't have to vote them any more for decades. Same goes for Customs and Excise.'

'If we make as much out of it as we do from cigarettes,' the Health Minister gloated, 'I shall have twenty new hospitals this time next year.'

'New schools!' added Education.

'A new generation of fighter aircraft and a decent medium-range missile,' said Defence.

'An aid budget we don't have to be ashamed of,' Overseas Development added.

'Tax cuts. Tax cuts. *Tax cuts!*' thundered the Chancellor of the Exchequer. 'There's no point improving people's lives if the bloody Tories get straight back in and reap the benefits.'

It was at this point that Charlie Ansboro marched in unannounced, strode straight up to the Prime Minister and without a word put a photograph in front of him.

'What's this, Charlie?' the PM enquired, furious at such a perfunctory interruption.

'Ask – that – *cunt* – sitting – there,' Ansboro replied with studied nastiness, pointing his finger at Peter Paget.

The Prime Minister pushed the photograph across to where Peter was sitting. One glance and Peter knew exactly what the photograph was of. He recognized the tiny mole on the rim of the belly-button. He had kissed that small dot many times. The photograph was of his ex-lover's stomach.

With a sparkling jewel in its navel.

Peter Paget could not reply. Speech had deserted him.

'Well?' the Prime Minister enquired once more. 'What is this?'

'I'll tell you what it is,' Ansboro said. 'It's Samantha Spencer's belly-button plus a jewel, a jewel for which Paula Wooldridge of the *Daily Bastard* now has the Mastercard receipt, a receipt signed by PETER LYING FUCKING BASTARD PAGET!'

Never before had the Cabinet room been the scene of such puerile drama. This majestic apartment of state, the very room from which Neville Chamberlain had announced that Britain was at war with Nazi Germany, was now rocked by horrified protest as one minister after another stared at the photograph.

'You promised, Peter,' the Prime Minister said, his

voice shaking with fury, 'that you had not had sexual relations with this woman.'

Peter spoke for the first time since Charlie Ansboro had entered the room.

'Yes, I did,' he said, and his voice almost croaked with the effort to keep it steady.

'Then perhaps you would like to explain to us all what business a man who is *not* having sex with a woman has giving her a belly-button jewel!'

The eyes of the entire Cabinet were fixed on him.

'I was . . . fond of Samantha, I admit I gave her the occasional gift . . . I intended this jewel for her ear . . .'

'One ear?' the Prime Minister enquired.

A little of Peter's strength was returning. *Tough it out. Deny everything.*

'Single earrings are fashionable.'

'The receipt,' Charlie Ansboro shouted, banging his fist upon the table, 'says *belly-button ring*! For Christ's sake, you stupid bastard, why didn't you just buy her a vibrating dildo and make it *really* obvious?'

Peter Paget breathed deeply. *Deny. Deny. Deny.*

They were not going to beat him. *Make day night and night day, but deny everything.*

'I did *not* have sexual relations with Ms Spencer,' he said firmly, 'and the fact that I bought her a small and entirely innocently meant piece of body jewellery does not change that.'

Starnstead Prison

'Ma name's Jessie and Ah'm a heroin addict.'

She was healthier now, still a gamine, but her face and figure were fuller. The colour had returned to her cheeks and although she had cut her hair quite short, the deep rich red that flashed from within the black was bright once more. For the first few months that

Jessie had been in prison she had continued to take heroin regularly. It was easily available and to her surprise it had been of a rather higher quality than that which she had been used to at the hands of her pimps. It was supplied to her by way of a powerful fixer on her block, who had taken a liking to her. Jessie was not a lesbian but the sexual barter with which she fed her drug habit inside prison was considerably less arduous than that with which she had supplied it outside, and she succumbed to her lover/protector's advances with the abstracted indifference of one who has long since lost any sense of the sanctity of their own body. Jessie shared her protector's bunk and together they took their drugs until eventually they decided to try to kick the habit together. It was clear to them both that if by the time they were released from prison they were still junkies, Jessie at least would not survive. Therefore, having undergone a methadone programme that had simply left them addicted to methadone, they had formed their own private prison branch of Narcotics Anonymous.

'As Ah ran out o' Goldie's house makin' ma second escape from that hellhole in as many months Ah was formulating a radically different plan to the one Ah'd made on ma first bid for freedom. Ah had a long list that first time. Ah can remember going through it one morning with some weirdo who'd tried to nick ma coat. He was a strange one that. Funny how I remember him, though, probably because his thing was pretending tae be Tommy Hanson. I suppose that was how he got through his shitty little rentboy life. Fuck, I settled for just pretending tae be a human being.'

One of the listening group stirred somewhat at this. It reminded her of something, something she'd heard or read.

'Ma new plan was very simple. Sell Goldie's bag o' crack and fuck off tae a new town. That was it, the whole plan. Ah reckoned Ah had at least a grand's worth but Ah decided Ah'd take seven fifty. And havin' run for a while Ah literally went up t'the first derelict-lookin' person Ah found an' says where can I sell some crack? Who's a big fuck-off dealer? Well, the fella sends me off down this street full o' right tough-lookin' bastards an' Ah goes up t'the toughest lookin' o' the lot an' says, Ah have a few rocks o' crack t'sell. Fuck me, but the fella was a cop. Can you believe it? Ah've no had a lot o' luck in my life, have Ah? An' there's me tryin' tae sell crack cocaine tae a copper. Although as it happens, mebbe it was the luckiest break Ah've had in a while because he nicked me, o' course, an' dealing a grand's worth o' crack has got t'be custodial, hasn't it? So that's how Ah ended up here, clean for the longest period since first Ah had a taste. An determined tae stay clean for ever more.'

The Paget household, Dalston

The tabloid newspaper with its banner single-word headline lay on the bed. 'Gotcha!' Underneath was a huge picture of Samantha's stomach with its jewel and Paget's credit-card signature superimposed across it. Not since the heady days of Tommy Hanson's engagement to posh-totty Emily had a belly-button so caught the attention of the nation.

Angela Paget's long-held and painfully suppressed anger now bubbled over. 'You bought her a fucking jewel for her navel, you bastard! A couple of shags, you said it was . . .'

'It was . . .'

'Don't lie to me, Peter! Just *stop lying!* You bought her body jewellery! When was the last time you bought anything romantic for me! Admit it, you loved that girl and she loved you and when you dumped her she decided to destroy you!'

'Angela, it wasn't like that!'

And it really hadn't been. He hadn't loved her. He *knew* that, and yet . . . he could no longer quite remember how it had been.

'That poor girl obviously trusted you, Peter! Just like I trusted you.'

'Angela, please!'

'Peter, I *know* you, and I know that you wouldn't buy such a gift for anyone you didn't care for. This was no reckless one-off bang! You were having a full-scale affair! Admit it! And let me tell you, Peter, I'm only standing by you through this because of two things: the future of your bill, which is bigger and more important than you, and the fact that you've dragged our daughters into this. But I promise you this, when your bill is law and the papers have left us alone, then . . . well, then I just don't know what I'll do.'

Downstairs Cathy tried not to listen to the row. She hated the way the pressure of these disgusting allegations and insinuations was affecting her mother. She wished her mum would be tougher, that she would stop looking so careworn, stop being such a pain. This was no time for scenes, this was a time for clear thinking and a united front. Her father was under attack. A nasty, puerile and premeditated attack. Her mother should be standing by him, not undermining him.

Cathy certainly intended to stand by him.

So he bought the girl a crappy bit of jewellery. So what? He said that he had not had an affair and that, in Cathy's opinion, should be good enough for his family, particularly his wife.

Suzie Paget peeped through the curtains at the assembled journalists. The Pagets had promised yet another family news conference to explain away this latest embarrassing development. Well, Cathy at least

367

was ready. She knew that she had won the day on that doorstep twice before and she intended to do so again.

Peter and Angela Paget descended the stairs in silence and together the family went out to face the press for the last time.

As soon as the front door started to open the questions began, or rather the *question*. For the only question that the press wanted answered was why had Peter Paget given so intimate a gift to a woman with whom he had claimed to have had an entirely proper professional relationship, which he had ended when the *girl* had begun to become overfamiliar?

'Well . . .' Peter began weakly, squirming with embarrassment.

'Because he's a silly old git!' Cathy Paget announced before her father could get any further.

Once more all eyes turned to Cathy.

'Because,' she continued, 'like lots of middle-aged men who work too hard and worry about their bald patches, he was just being a sad, silly old git!'

The press were thrilled. They always expected good copy from Cathy Paget, and once more this inspired and talented sixteen-year-old was delivering.

'Hello-o? Excuse me. Anybody home?' Cathy continued. 'You've seen the pictures! Samantha Spencer is gorgeous! God, her knockers have been in just about every publication under the sun! And they are *fit*. What's more, by her own admission she was in love with Dad! How would a situation like that affect some of you blokes standing here right now? You'd be flattered, wouldn't you? You'd get a little thrill, am I right? Of course I am. A few of you might even try to get a shag. Oh yes, you would! But *not my dad*. My dad loves his family and he loves his work and there is *no way* he would ever put that at risk.'

Cathy put her arm through her father's before continuing.

'So what does he do, eh? Faced with this giggling little pricktease? This little ray of office sunshine who unbeknownst to him is actually a deeply disturbed psycho? He's flattered, he's a little bit thrilled and one stupid morning, burdened with the usual measure of middle-aged male sexual frustration, he buys her a saucy gift. He can't *touch* her, can he? He doesn't *want* to touch her . . . Well, of course he *does* want to touch her, like any of you men here today would, he's *desperate* to touch her, but the point is he *isn't going to do it* . . . So instead he flirts a little bit, he lets her tell him his ties are boring or whatever, he shares his KitKat with her and in a moment of madness he even gets her a special birthday present. Yes, like the silly old git he is, he buys her an entirely inappropriate gift. A jewel to hang on the belly-button ring that she has no doubt been making a point of flashing at him for months. Blimey, the way she seems to flash her tits at every opportunity I'm surprised he didn't buy her a nipple ring! And why shouldn't he buy her a gift? It makes him feel young, romantic, it's a laugh, he needs a bit of fun after spending day after day trying to convince a bunch of brain-dead MPs that seeing as how they're surrounded by trees they'd better start noticing the wood! But that's *it*. End of story. He doesn't kiss her, he doesn't pat her arse, he buys her a little gift and it feels good.'

The media mob were smiling, laughing. Some even applauded Cathy yet again. The girl's honesty was so refreshing.

'Now leap forward a few months to when my dad is the bravest, most celebrated politician in the country. To when this sad woman decides to accuse him of an affair because he's told her to back off. Is he going to mention that gift at this point? Is he going to say, "I didn't shag her, but I did buy her a belly-button jewel"? No. He is *so* not going to do that.

Because if he does, then somebody like Paula No Life Sodding Wooldridge – yes, I can see you skulking there, Paula, in *our* garden – someone like Paula Wooldridge is going to twist that gift into something dirty, which is *exactly* what she's done, because when she was scrabbling about in Samantha Spencer's dustbins she found a Mastercard slip. Well, congratulations, Paula. I hope you're proud of yourself. It's not exactly the Watergate tapes, but hey, you aren't exactly Bob Woodward, are you?'

It was another joyous bravura performance and once more it charmed a besotted press corps completely. Gorgeous teenaged ingénues who wrote their own copy were few and far between. Instinctively other journalists moved away from Paula Wooldridge, who was as usual looking isolated, alone.

But then Paula smiled. A big broad smile. 'What a lovely speech, Cathy,' she said. 'So your daddy is a man of courage and integrity?'

'Yes, he is. Not that I would expect you to be able to recognize such qualities.'

'Oh, I'm pretty good at recognizing certain qualities, Cathy. How about yourself, by the way? How's your integrity?'

'I sleep well at nights.'

'Do you? Do you really? Tell me, then, that evening you went to see *Mission Impossible 3* with your father. The night the much vilified Samantha Spencer claims your father was taking cocaine in Islington with her and her friends prior to spending the night in her bed. What were you *actually* doing, Cathy?'

'Watching *Mission Impossible 3* with my father.'

'Really? Were you? You see, I've checked the time of the screening and it started at seven forty-five.'

'That sounds about right.'

'Then perhaps you can explain to me how the Minister of Drugs was able, while watching a film in

Dalston, to buy four bottles of Moët and Chandon champagne in Islington at *precisely* that time. At an off-licence which happens to be just one hundred metres from Samantha Spencer's flat, that same flat where she has always claimed he spent the evening and the night.' Paula produced the second of the receipts that Samantha had found at the bottom of her swingbin. Or at least a blown-up copy of it. It was a National Westminster Bank Switch card till slip, which carried the date, the location and Peter Paget's signature for all to see.

'I . . . well . . .' For the first time almost since she had learned to talk, Cathy Paget was lost for words.

'I can't show you the original of this receipt, Cathy, because it is currently in the hands of the police, to whom both you and your father lied while they were investigating the taking of Grade-A drugs.'

The sensation was absolute. The questions came in one great roar.

'Is it true?' 'Did you lie?' 'Did he put you up to it?'

'Oh Peter,' Angela Paget murmured almost to herself '*Four* bottles of champagne?'

Cathy Paget was strong, she was clever, very clever, and witty, too. But she was only sixteen, and she had believed in her father utterly. Now . . . now . . . As the cameras closed in on her she burst into tears.

Angela Paget led her family back into the house.

The House of Commons

The Shadow Home Secretary could scarcely conceal his glee. 'Madam Speaker, for many months now I have been forced to sit with growing dismay while this house began to resemble nothing so much as an asylum over which the lunatics had taken.'

This rather convoluted image met with some slightly

confused muttering, but the house knew what he was getting at.

'Last week's State Opening represented what in my opinion was an all-time low for British democracy. Like many of my colleagues, I sat dismayed and dumbfounded at the sight of Her Majesty being forced to align herself with criminals, pushers and junkies while announcing what must now go down as the most ill-conceived and -considered piece of legislation in history – the insane, irresponsible and utterly unworkable plan to legalize and make readily available some of the most insidious poisons known to man. And where is the architect of this madness? Where is the loathsome Peter Paget? Is he here today?'

The government front bench could only sit in stony silence. Everybody knew where Peter Paget was.

'No, the Right Honourable Member for Dalston North West is *not* here today. Her Majesty's *Minister for Drugs* is nowhere to be seen, and why? Why? The whole world knows why. Every news organization on the planet is speaking of nothing else but the excruciating embarrassment that this government has allowed Britain to be dragged into. For, as I speak, the Minister for Drugs is being interviewed by the police! Interviewed in connection with his *own* drug-taking! His cavorting with known dealers and cocaine-fuelled sexpots! He is being interviewed about the fact that he, a Minister of the Crown, *lied* to the police in the course of what was potentially a criminal investigation. And what is even more astonishing and disgusting is that he corrupted his own sixteen-year-old daughter into lying also, into making false entries in her student diary no less!'

The Shadow Home Secretary's voice rang round a chamber in which no other member felt minded to comment. Peter Paget had let them all down comprehensively. They felt like complete fools. That appalling man and his smug, irritating daughter had bamboozled them and the nation into a sort of collective madness, a madness from which they had been saved in the nick of time by the tireless efforts of an investigative journalist.

For who could support the Paget bill now? With its architect exposed as a criminal liar and cocaine user? The whole business had been based on the people's trust that Paget knew what he was talking about. Now the common assumption was that even his famous needle prick accident and subsequent miraculous recovery had been a put-up job. Paget had betrayed the nation.

Finally the Prime Minister rose to speak.

'In reply to my Right Honourable Friend the Shadow Home Secretary, of course we must await the outcome of the police's investigation, but in the light of what is already known, Peter Paget is clearly an unfit person to be a Minister of the Crown or indeed a member of this house. I have therefore relieved him of all Cabinet duties as of this morning.'

'And what of his foul theories!' the Shadow Home Secretary shouted.

The Prime Minister had read that morning's polls; he had seen summaries of the mood of the radio phone-ins and morning chat shows. He knew that the public saw Paget and his bill as one and the same thing. They had come quickly to despise the former and hence had no stomach for the latter. He bowed to the inevitable.

'I wish also to make it clear to this house that for the time being the bill on which Peter Paget had been working will be withdrawn from our legislative programme pending a full review.'

The Paget household, Dalston

The scale of the disaster that had fallen upon Cathy Paget's life was almost too huge for her to understand.

Almost, but not quite. She was far too intelligent and astute an individual not to realize the implications of her own personal disgrace.

In a matter of minutes she had been transformed from the nation's favourite teenager, the brightest spark in the land, quite literally the girl most likely to succeed, to Public Enemy Number Two. A wicked, immoral, lying little minx who happily blackened other women's names in support of her father's corrupt ambitions and sexual adventuring.

She was branded for ever and she knew it.

'I'll never go into politics now, Mum,' she said in a voice that no longer sang. 'Or run the BBC or write important novels and plays. I'll never do anything at all. All my life, for ever and ever, I shall be first and foremost the girl who lied through her teeth to the nation, the girl who rewrote her diary. No one will ever trust me again.'

'It'll pass, darling. These things always do.'

'No, they don't, not when they're this big. What about Profumo? Archer? Aitken? Aitken's *daughter*, for Christ's sake. None of them will *ever* get out from under the shame of what they did! People will never forget. And I'm one of them now. I lied publicly and to the police! Christ, I might even be charged yet! I'm defined by my crime and I always will be. I can't go back to school, they're already giving me hell by text and email. They were so jealous before and now it's all coming out. Suzie can't go back either so her life's fucked too, how could it not be? She's my sister, she was on that doorstep, next to me, the girl now clearly recognized as a disgusting, lying bitch. If I apply for college or try to get a job it will always be Cathy Paget, the smart-alec, smug, deceitful, scheming little cow who's applying, trying to sneak her way back into society.'

Cathy closed the suitcase she had been packing. Suzie appeared at the door. She had also packed a case.

'But all that doesn't matter, as it happens, not now. It will soon, but not now. Nothing really matters except that Dad completely and utterly lied to us and I'll hate him for ever. You lied to us too, Mum.'

'I know, darling, and all I can say is that he told me he'd had sex with the girl and that was all. He swore it was a moment or two of madness, nothing more, and I believed him. I trusted him too, Cathy, when he said there was no romance, that the drug accusations were rubbish. I believed him . . . And then suddenly the newspapers are hurling receipts for champagne and body jewellery at me . . . doorstepping us. . .' Angela Paget broke down in tears and then all three of them began crying. Together they gathered up their cases and went downstairs.

Peter Paget was sitting alone in the living room, staring into space. His family passed by the open door behind him in silence.

'Goodbye, my darlings. Goodbye,' he said.

They did not reply.

Outside Starnstead Prison

Tommy sat in the back of the long stretch limo. In his hands he held a letter he had received from a member of the Starnstead Prison Narcotics Anonymous Group. The letter had given him certain information for which Tommy had gladly paid generously. Now he could only wait and hope.

The door of the prison opened and a number of women emerged. One of them was Jessie, more beautiful to Tommy than he remembered her. A little fuller of face, certainly, but the same elfin bones. And those eyes, dark, flashing, angry eyes set in milk-white skin.

Tommy's heart felt as if it would burst. He had found her.

Most of the other women who were leaving the prison had loved ones to meet them and they soon dispersed in excited little family groups, but Jessie was alone. She had no one. As she turned and walked away up the street Tommy instructed Tony to drive up alongside her.

Tommy wound down the window and spoke to her. 'Hello, Jessie.'

'Fuck off.' She spoke without looking round.

'It's me, Jessie.'

'Ah said fuck off, mate, all right? Ah'm not for hire any more.' Still she did not look.

'Jessie, please . . . I want to give you something.'

Jessie swung round in fury, blazing eyes, snarling mouth. 'Listen, you dirty little cunt! Ah *said*—'

Tommy spoke quickly. 'I want to give you Point Three! Point Three of the Great Plan! The holiday . . . The sunshine . . . I want to give you the *sunshine*. All-day sunshine, sunshine everywhere! Dappling the ground, rippling in your clothes, getting caught up in your hair . . . like havin' a *bath* in it . . .'

Tony had stopped the car. For what seemed like an age Jessie stared at Tommy through the open window. 'Have we met before?'

'Yes. Once. I've been looking for you ever since.'

'Who are you?'

'Like I told you last time, I'm Tommy Hanson.'

The Old Bailey

Peter Paget was convicted on witness evidence of using a Grade A drug. Laura, Kurt and Samantha testified against him in exchange for immunity from prosecution regarding the fact that they had taken the drugs also.

'Peter Paget,' the judge's voice was charged with withering contempt, 'your crime is far far worse than that of any unfortunate teenaged drug-taker who has appeared before me. You held a position of unique trust and responsibility, you were privileged to have been elevated to amongst the highest in the land. Of all people in this country you had a duty to set an example to others and yet instead you chose to indulge your loathsome appetites for sex and drugs to the full, preying on young innocent girls and using your powerful position to force sex and drugs upon them. What is more, once the evidence of your immoral and criminal tastes emerged, you sought to mislead the entire nation in whose service you were employed. You lied to Parliament, you lied to the police, you lied to your family and you lied to the people. Can ever a sorrier catalogue of mendacity have been brought before a court? I doubt it. I sincerely doubt it. Peter Paget, it is my solemn duty to sentence you to four years in prison with a recommendation that you serve at least two. Take him down.'

Bangkok Women's Prison

Sonia rocked back and forth in her seat. She spoke only one word during her interview and that was *kharuna*, Thai for 'please'. This she repeated many times. She was dirty and unkempt and appeared to have little awareness of herself or her surroundings.

She had recognized her mother, though, and had wept.

'I'm so sorry to have to inform you both,' the Consulate representative explained, 'but his Royal Highness has declined to exercise clemency in Sonia's case. He had as you know been giving serious consideration to Peter Paget's request for an early release for Sonia, but in the light of revelations concerning Paget's own drug-taking the King is no longer in any mood to do Britain favours. Attitudes in Asia have hardened considerably towards Western double standards and special pleading.'

Sonia's mother had known. From the moment she had read in the papers of Peter Paget's disgrace she had known what must follow. Nonetheless the blow was almost too much to bear.

'All I can say,' the official continued, 'is that in the light of Sonia's deteriorating mental condition we will continue to pursue the appeals process on medical grounds.'

'*Kharuna*,' said Sonia.

An island far away

The beach was long and empty, just as she had imagined it, with glistening white sand so bright in the sun it hurt the eyes. Sand like talcum powder, with a warm turquoise ocean lapping against it. And there she sat, day after day after day, all alone, basking in the sun. With nobody bothering her at all.

Wormwood Scrubs

Peter Paget sat in his cell on his bunkbed. The letter he had been reading had fallen from his hands and now lay on the floor between his feet. Angela Paget always wrote in longhand, with a fountain pen, and now Peter's tears smudged the ink as they fell onto the paper below.

'Cathy wants us to go abroad, perhaps to France, although such was the size of your celebrity that we're scarcely less notorious there. I don't know, perhaps we'll go overseas. I know that we can't stay in London. Nobody really wants to know us here any more, not even our friends. At best we're an embarrassment and at worst, well, we've all been shouted at in the street, and spat at too. Suzie has gone very quiet; she hates her name and refuses to use it, and says that she'll change it by deed poll the moment she's old enough. I'm afraid to say that both of them have begun to take drugs. I know this because they're quite open about it. There's a terrible fatalism about the girls now, as if nothing really matters. Perhaps it doesn't. They mainly smoke marijuana. You probably saw that Cathy was sold some by an undercover journalist and was back on the front pages briefly. She almost seemed to revel in it. It's obviously a way of getting at you.

Now I must come to my own position, Peter. I'm divorcing you. You have destroyed all of our lives, we'll never get them back and I don't think any of us will ever forgive you. I can't bring myself to love you any more or even feel pity for you. I feel nothing beyond a sort of dull weary anger. If only you'd told the truth I would have stood by you, I'm sure I would. But you didn't, you lied and then you kept lying, and it's all finished now.

Peter wrung his hands and sobbed.

In the bunk above one of his cellmates stirred. 'If you don't shut the fuck up I'll personally fucking break your fingers, Paget.'

An island far away

Jessie sat watching the ocean, running the sand through her fingers and toes and listening to music on her brand-new, state-of-the-art Sony Discman. Jogproof, light as a feather. Beautifully rounded and smooth to touch.

A little further up the beach sat Tommy. He did not try to speak to her. In fact, he didn't bother her at all. He was quite content.

They both had their music, and books to read. Their own private thoughts.

Perhaps one day she would share hers with him.

Tommy was happy to wait.

THE END

DEAD FAMOUS
Ben Elton

'ONE OF THE BEST WHODUNNITS I HAVE EVER READ...A FUNNY, GRIPPING, HUGELY ENTERTAINING THRILLER. BUT ALSO A PERSUASIVE, DYSPEPTIC ACCOUNT OF THE WAY WE LIVE NOW, WITH OUR INSANE, INANE CULT OF THE CELEBRITY'
Sunday Telegraph

One house, ten contestants, thirty cameras, forty microphones, one murder . . . and no evidence.

Dead Famous is a killer read from Ben Elton – Reality TV as you've never seen it before.

'THE PERFECT MODERN-DAY WHODUNNIT. A CRACKING READ FULL OF HILARIOUS INSIGHTS INTO THE *BIG BROTHER* PHENOMENON'
Mirror

'A BOOK WITH PACE AND WIT, REAL TENSION, A DARK BACKGROUND THEME AND A BIG ON-SCREEN CLIMAX'
Independent

'WRY, FAST AND FIENDISHLY CLEVER'
The Times

0 552 99945 8

BLACK SWAN

INCONCEIVABLE
Ben Elton

'EXTREMELY FUNNY, CLEVER, WELL-WRITTEN, SHARP
AND UNEXPECTEDLY MOVING . . . THIS BRILLIANT,
CHAOTIC SATIRE MERITS REREADING SEVERAL TIMES'
Nicholas Coleridge, *Mail on Sunday*

Lucy desperately wants a baby. Sam wants to write a hit
movie. The problem is that both efforts seem to be
unfruitful. And given that the average IVF cycle has about
a one in five chance of going into full production, Lucy's
chances of getting what she wants are considerably better
than Sam's.

What Sam and Lucy are about to go through is absolutely
inconceivable. The question is, can their love survive?

Inconceivable confirms Ben Elton as one of Britain's most
significant, entertaining and provocative writers.

'THIS IS ELTON AT HIS BEST – MATURE, HUMANE,
AND STILL A LAUGH A MINUTE. AT LEAST'
Daily Telegraph

'A VERY FUNNY BOOK ABOUT A SENSITIVE SUBJECT
. . . BEN ELTON THE WRITER MIGHT BE EVEN FUNNIER
THAN BEN ELTON THE COMIC'
Daily Mail

'A TENDER, BEAUTIFULLY BALANCED ROMANTIC
COMEDY'
Spectator

'MOVING AND THOROUGHLY ENTERTAINING'
Daily Express

Now filmed as *Maybe Baby*.

0 552 14698 6

BLACK SWAN

POPCORN
Ben Elton

'ONE OF THE MOST BRILLLIANTLY SUSTAINED AND
FOCUSED PIECES OF SATIRE I'VE EVER READ'
Douglas Adams

'KILLER PROSE . . . A VICIOUSLY FUNNY SATIRE THAT
ALSO WORKS AS A TONGUE-IN-CHEEK THRILLER'
Sunday Times

Bruce shoots movies. Wayne and Scout shoot to kill. In a
single night they find out the hard way what's real and
what's not, who's the hero and who's the villain. The USA
watches slack-jawed as Bruce and Wayne together resolve
some serious questions. Does Bruce use erection cream?
Does art imitate life or does life simply imitate bad art?
And most of all, does sugar-pie really love his honeybun?

'AN ABSOLUTE COUP OF BLACK COMEDY'
Daily Telegraph

'FIERCE, GARISH AND FRIGHTENINGLY FUNNY'
The Spectator

'SERIOUS, MORALLY COMPLEX, STRUCTURALLY RICH
AND BITTERLY FUNNY'
Independent on Sunday

WINNER OF THE MACALLAN ® CRIME WRITERS'
ASSOCIATION GOLD DAGGER AWARD

0 552 77184 8

BLACK SWAN

THIS OTHER EDEN
Ben Elton

SMALL, WELL APPOINTED FUTURE. SEMI DETACHED.

If the end of the world is nigh, then surely it's only sensible to make alternative arrangements. Certainly the Earth has its good points, but what most people need is something smaller and more manageable. Of course there are those who say that's planetary treason, but who cares what the weirdos and terrorists think? Not Nathan. All he cares is that his movie gets made and that there's somebody left to see it.

In marketing terms the end of the world will be very big. Anyone trying to save it should remember that.

0 552 77183 X

BLAST FROM THE PAST
Ben Elton

It's 2.15 a.m., you're in bed alone and the phone wakes you. As you wake, in the tiny moment between sleep and consciousness, you know already that something is wrong. Only someone bad would ring at such an hour. Or someone good with bad news, which would probably be worse. You lie in the darkness and wait for the answer machine to kick in. And then you hear the one voice in the world you least expect . . . your very own Blast from the Past.

'ONLY BEN ELTON COULD COMBINE UNCOMFORTABLE QUESTIONS ABOUT GENDER POLITICS WITH A GRIPPING, PAGE-TURNING NARRATIVE AND JOKES THAT MAKE YOU LAUGH OUT LOUD'
Tony Parsons

0 552 99833 8

BLACK SWAN